TRACKLESS SEAS

Novels by James L. Johnson

Code Name Sebastian
The Nine Lives of Alphonse
A Handful of Dominoes
A Piece of the Moon Is Missing
The Last Train from Canton
The Death of Kings
The Tender Summer

TRACKLESS SEAS

A *CODE NAME SEBASTIAN* ADVENTURE

by
James L. Johnson

Crossway Books • Westchester, Illinois
A Division of Good News Publishers

JAMES L. JOHNSON is the author of 16 books, Director of his own Johnson & Johnson Literary Agency and Associate Executive Director at World Relief, Carol Stream, Illinois.

Trackless Seas. Copyright © 1987 by James L. Johnson. Published by Crossway Books, a division of Good News Publishers, Westchester, Illinois 60153.

All rights reserved. No part of this publication may be reproduced, stored in a retrieval system or transmitted in any form by any means, electronic, mechanical, photocopy, recording or otherwise, without prior permission of the publisher, except as provided by USA copyright law.

Cover Illustration by Paul D. Turnbaugh

First printing, 1987

Printed in the United States of America

Library of Congress Catalog Card Number 86-72063

ISBN 0-89107-400-7

Author's Acknowledgment

Special thanks to Mr. W.B. "Berry" Berryman, Sydney, for his invaluable assistance in showing me the "town" and pointing out the parts of that beautiful city that fit into this book. And also for his help in steering me to a sailing charter company who gave me excellent service and a very fine crew to provide invaluable sailing research.

In dedication to

All the Sebastian fans who kept him, his Lady Churchill and the author alive through the years by all the support and encouragement. May the journey have been a pleasant and rewarding one.

"O we can wait no longer,
We too take ship, O soul,
Joyous we too launch out on trackless seas,
Fearless for unknown shores."

—Whitman

Prologue

NOVEMBER 25

THE PRESIDENT OF THE UNITED STATES
WASHINGTON, D.C.

PRIORITY: FOR YOUR EYES ONLY

CODE CLASSIFICATION: JUMPING JACK

HIGH PRIORITY INFO ALICE TRACKING STATION PINE GAP, AUSTRALIA. HAVE MONITORED RUSSIAN LAUNCH SUPERSATELLITE CODE OPAL AT 1300 HOURS GMT TODAY THE 25TH. CONFIG SUGGESTS HEAVY KILLER CLASS WITH LASER DEFENSE CAPABILITY AND NUKE WARHEAD DELIVERY. EVIDENCE REENTRY ROCKET PODS SUGGEST POSSIBLE OFFENSIVE POWER ENDANGERING U.S. AND OTHER WESTERN POPULATION TARGETS. SUGGEST OUR SATELLITE ALAMO REORBIT TO TARGET FOR PHOTO RECON CONFIRM OUR CONCLUSIONS. WILL CONTINUE TRACKING OPAL AND TRANSMIT FINDINGS.

GENERAL MASON AUBREY, USAF
CODE NAME: RED FOX

TO: GENERAL MASON AUBREY, USAF
TRACKING STATION PINE GAP, AUSTRALIA

CODE CLASSIFICATION: RED FOX

U.S. SATELLITE ALAMO DELAYED IN REORBIT FOR OBSERV. RUSSIAN KILLER SAT. OPAL FIVE DAYS TECHNICAL PROBLEMS. EXPECT RESOLVED NOVEMBER 30. NASSAU AND HOUSTON TRACKING CONFIRM YOUR FINDINGS. MUST WAIT ALAMO RECON FINAL DETERMINATION. ADVISED NATO OF ALERT. NORAD STANDING BY FOR STRIKE ALERT. PRESENT WESTERN SATELLITE CAPABILITY NOT ADEQUATE TO NEUTRALIZE OPAL IF WARLIKE OR OFFENSIVE INTENT. APPRECIATE YOUR COMMUNICATION NEW FINDINGS. STAND BY FOR ALAMO UPDATE FIVE DAYS.

THE PRESIDENT OF THE U.S.A.
CODE NAME: JUMPING JACK

One

Nobody said anything meaningful for a long time.

In the living room the three of them sat in close proximity to each other, looking like blackbirds on a clothesline huddling together for protection. Sebastian sat in a wicker chair facing them, unable to grasp the purpose of their visit through the smoke of the small talk.

He glanced out the window of his eighth-floor apartment overlooking Oak Street waiting for them to get through the polite overtures and to the point. He could see the last breath of fall as the stubborn gold-brown leaves that had been desperately clinging finally tumbled to the earth to complete their vows of death. Beyond that, Lake Michigan had taken on a pristine blue, as if it were pulling a protective coat of lacquer over itself against the coming cold. It was November 24. The holiday season was just beginning in Chicago. Whatever that meant to him now.

He sensed a pause in the banal talk and the curtain slowly went up. Act I. "Mr. Sebastian," the heaviest of the three men said, the voice somewhat meditative like a doctor's explaining the extent of a spreading carcinoma, "the reason we've come here to visit is to determine the legitimacy of the nature of your clandestine activities internationally over the past years. To address the question more specifically, the denomination does not see any of this befitting the vows you took when we ordained you to the ministry fifteen years ago. May I add that this is not a trial, Mr. Sebastian, only a hearing to determine what action we should take."

His name was Dr. Martin Backstrom, chairman of the Credentials Committee for the Faith Community Church of America (FCCA). He was heavier than the other two men and had a round pumpkin face and large, brown eyes behind double-strength gold-rimmed glasses. He sat in the soft-cushioned, brown colonial chair and looked as if he had accidentally fallen into a tub of mud and couldn't get up.

Sebastian did not respond immediately, feeling the room take on a stillness as if the detonator of a bomb had loudly clicked, portending imminent explosion. For one thing, his mind could not compute the exact tone of Backstrom's voice nor the implication of the statement. Then again, he wondered how these men knew anything about his "clandestine activities" overseas. He had kept a low profile in all of them. Still, the CIA had a line on him all the time, and though never hostile to his influence in their affairs, they were not always pleased that he did end-runs on them either. They probably had dropped a few points of inquiry on Backstrom in the past since Sebastian had to put down his denomination to substantiate his clergy status on those endless CIA reports.

"More to the point, Mr. Sebastian, by what or whose authority do you do these things?" the man named Alnutt spoke up. He sat on the sofa closest to Backstrom, a thin man, almost skeletal, wearing a gray suit that emphasized the washed-out gray of his face and eyes. He was completely bald. His voice was more accusatory than Backstrom's, as if he had nursed this moment for a long time, as a prosecuting attorney would anticipate the courtroom. His pointed nose seemed to grow longer with the question, and he chopped the words out as if he were reading them one by one from a computer screen.

"God Himself, Mr. Alnutt," Sebastian responded, feeling the beginning of an inquisition.

"Consorting with international gangsters is surely not of God," the third man, named Winston, added in a voice that deliberately begged the question. He sat a foot or so away from Alnutt on the couch, dressed in a navy blue academic suit complete with a vest that strained against his broad chest. He had a scholar's eyes, flinty green and narrowed, as if from staring at the fine print of theological books all his life. He had big ears standing out from his head, like satellite dishes monitoring every signal in his theological/academic world.

"Mr. Sebastian," Backstrom picked up again, anxious to keep the conversation from sliding into exchanges of innuendo, "I trust you realize that we are here not to question whatever God wants you to do. We are here, as I said—and I remind my brethren of this—because of some questions we have about your ministerial activities that do not fit the ordination articles charged to you. In other words, we are concerned for any clergyman engaging in activities that do not fit pastoral or mission ministries."

"And they certainly are not redemptive," Alnutt insisted with a sniff.

"Charles," Backstrom warned him in a mediating but firm voice.

Sebastian had no ready answer for that. The eyes of all three men fixed on him, waiting. He felt stunned now that it had become clear what they were after, and yet he was not totally surprised either. He had to admit that what he had been doing for ten years, since he had left the pulpit to take on bizarre roles internationally that led him into Super Power chess games, was not exactly within the "pale of ministry" as these men defined it. He had not engineered those scenarios himself. He went mostly in response to a personal friend who needed help. God did the rest.

"I understand, Mr. Backstrom," he said, not seeking to provoke them with argument. "But I have simply gone where God has led me, to do justice and mercy on behalf of people who have no priest, pastor, or anyone else who comes anywhere near being a representative of God. I see no contradiction to my ordination in that."

"You have become a partner of violence," Alnutt countered, his dull gray eyes widening in the challenge. "You have aided and abetted that violence, as we see it."

"On what judgment do you make that statement, Mr. Alnutt?"

"A man from the CIA called on us some time back," Alnutt replied. "He explained some of your activities and then pointed out that no private citizen, clergyman included, is authorized to engage in highly sensitive espionage operations. He was most concerned for the image of our denomination."

"Do you cultivate such affiliations?" Backstrom asked, placing each of his index fingers on his temples, as if to ease a pain in his head.

"No." Sebastian wondered what the CIA was up to in making any kind of statement of concern of that nature to these men.

"Are you aware of the taint you bring on your spiritual calling by allowing yourself to be linked with this sordid espionage world?" Alnutt pursued, leaning forward a bit as if to give his words some extra weight.

"I deal with people, Mr. Alnutt . . . the people who are in it, not the violence that goes with it."

"The CIA turned over to us a newspaper account out of Hong Kong referring to 'the saint of international espionage,'" Winston said, incredulous. "How do you react to that?"

"With some amusement, in a way. Some innocent people get caught up in the crossfires, as I do, Mr. Winston. Afterward they talk. I happen to be in it, so they talk about me. Journalists look for the unique and unusual. I myself have not sought to be a 'saint' and certainly not a 'saint of international espionage.'"

There was a pause. Backstrom cleared his throat and looked down at his neatly typed papers in his pudgy hands, as if the script for all this was written there. A frown knitted a stitch between his eyes.

"Mr. Sebastian," he began again, slowly, thoughtfully, as if picking his way through a bramble bush, "mankind hangs on the brink of a total spiritual calamity. Works are fine, Mr. Sebastian, as you remind us here. But what we declare of Christ—that is what fulfills His commission as an ambassador for Him. Unless there is a clear witness to redemption by you in your contacts with men and women, no matter where you find them, your ordination credentials stand in jeopardy. We simply want to make that clear."

"Of course, if you wish to renew your vows," Winston said, giving a spasm of an ingratiating smile, "after proper declaration of your repentance and turning away from this fruitless clandestine business, the denomination council might be willing to reconsider . . ."

A flush of heat burned in Sebastian's chest then. The words rushed up into his throat. He took a deep breath to get control, not willing to charge the air with more invective. He waited. They waited, watching him. Winston's smile was still there, frozen on by false politeness. Alnutt's eyes had grown larger, looking like a frog's. Only Backstrom retained the face he had come in with, as readable as wet pavement.

"I have not considered repenting of anything I have done up to now." Sebastian spoke quietly, but he let the edge remain in his voice. "I simply believe you cannot confine Christ to church buildings, cathedrals, and television studios in a sit-com American scenario. Most of this world never gets into those buildings or tunes in. I simply go where people are dying and do what I can in His name. I do as the Scriptures adjure in the Gospel of John, chapter one, verse 14 . . . that only when our Lord came to earth and became flesh did mankind see the glory of the Father full of grace and truth. . . ."

He waited for any challenge. There was none. Then he added,

"There was a theologian in Germany who once said, 'The Christian must plunge himself into the life of a godless world without attempting to gloss over its ungodliness with a veneer of religion. . . . He must live a worldly life and so participate in the suffering of God. To be a Christian does not mean to be religious in a particular way, to cultivate some form of asceticism . . . but to be a man.' That's where I stand, gentlemen . . . and I can do no other."

"You are using Dietrich Bonhoeffer as your example?" Winston chided after a short pause. "The man who translated those very nice words into a plot to kill Adolf Hitler and finally was hanged for his crime? That is your example?"

"The words form my credo, Mr. Winston," Sebastian replied. "How Bonhoeffer translated them in that terrible hour of suffering in Germany is his before God. The method is not necessarily mine."

There was a long silence. The verdict had been passed, and Sebastian knew it. The baby Big Ben on the mantel tolled 4 o'clock in muffled chimes as if declaring the hour of mourning.

"Well, Mr. Sebastian," Backstrom finally said to tie it off, stuffing his papers into his attaché case with deliberate movements, "if that is your case, then so be it. The Committee on Credentials meets in December, early, to weigh your words as of this day. I have to say in light of your testimony here that I doubt your ordination will be sustained. But that will be determined in time. I trust, as we all do, that God will use you as He sees fit wherever He leads you . . . if indeed He is, in fact, doing that. I think now that we shall take our leave. Thank you for your time."

The shades came down over Alnutt's eyes as if the computer screen had gone blank and there were no more messages for him to relate. Winston's satellite-dish ears seemed to retract into the clumps of his graying hair, having heard all that he needed.

Then they stood, extending hands in token gestures of fellowship, and were gone without further word, satisfied that they had restored order to God's universe.

Sebastian did a lot of walking along the lakefront during the next two days. The indictment had left him shaky, uneasy, unsure. To be defrocked would be a humiliation. It was even worse as a penalty for not measuring up to "ministry" in what he had been doing for these past years. But their condemning judgment had left him wondering if they were not, after all, correct.

He mulled it into the valleys of the night empty of sleep. On the third day, the 27th, he decided it was time.

He pulled out the metal box from the top left desk drawer, took the key ring from his pocket, and opened the box. He removed the passport case. In the back he found the special section that carried the code classifications and numbers. He picked up the phone, touched the three digits that would put him through to the security section of the CIA in the Chicago Federal Building.

The phone rang three times, as the card stated it would. Then came a pause, then a click as the computer engaged and a woman's voice came on, sounding precise as if she were teaching English as a second language to new immigrants. "This is a security check . . . repeat . . . security check. Please give your code classification number. Now."

He read it off the card in front of him.

"Thank you . . . You may send your message . . . Please provide the accurate call number, code classification of your party, as well as the security station. Now."

"I want Barbara Churchill at the Israeli Secret Police, Special Securities Section, Tel Aviv. Code name Spartacus . . . repeat . . . Spartacus." Then he gave the number.

"Thank you," the canned voice responded. "You may dictate your message. Now."

He sighed against all the picky protocol in this business. The "Company" knew him well enough, even if it were not an entirely warm friendship. Still, he obeyed and spoke the message, feeling uneasy as if someone were actually listening to him, even though he knew the voice was recorded.

BARBARA CHURCHILL—

THE SUMMER IS PAST. WINTER IS COMING. GETTING COLDER. SO AM I. LOVE YOU. WANT TO MARRY YOU. NOW. LIVE ON A HOUSEBOAT OFF MALIBU, SAN JUAN, CYPRUS, YOU NAME IT. SOMEPLACE WHERE WE WILL NEVER BE COLD AGAIN. AM TIRED OF BATCHING IT, THINKING OF YOU ALL THE TIME BUT NEVER SEEING YOU. YOU AND I HAVE DONE OUR BIT IN THE COLD WAR. LET'S SERVE GOD IN A MORE PASTORAL SETTING. URGENT REPLY.

He signed off with his "Code Name Sebastian" signature and waited.

The bored voice came on again: "Thank you . . . Your reply request has been noted. We will notify you when it comes through." There was a click, as cold as a gun hammer snapping down on an empty chamber, then the dial tone.

"Thank you," Sebastian groused as he hung up the phone. "Don't call us, we'll call you."

He sat down in the swivel chair at the desk and turned to look out the window toward the lake. He felt no satisfaction in sending the message. Was he rebounding from the sting of Backstrom, Alnutt, and Winston? Was he in fact bowing to their condemnation of him and seeking a way out, a way back to "normal" ministry as befitting his ordination? If so, it was not right to impose his tension about that on Barbara.

Still, the torpidity he felt had been with him long before the confrontation with them. He felt burned out, lonely, and desperately in need of a life with the woman he loved. Backstrom and Company had only intensified that feeling and confirmed what he had been sensing for some time.

But he felt awkward about it. To retreat from the field now would substantiate their charges of his dereliction as a minister in what he had tried to do during the last ten years. It would make a mockery of God as well and question the Incarnation in terms he had tried to explain to them, bluntly but out of strong conviction.

He thought of canceling the message to Barbara. But the overwhelming need for her negated that. It *was* time for both of them. Maybe he should have called Tel Aviv directly. It would be easier to explain it to her on the phone. But protocol demanded that he go through the CIA channels. They had arranged the classification communications to keep track of him, had insisted on it. He was not a CIA man, just a "free agent." But he had muddled into their territory too many times in the past for them to allow him to operate outside their umbrella totally. He tried to comfort himself that the message would be in Tel Aviv in a few hours. Provided, of course, whoever monitored it in the Pentagon did not ponder too long over what he was saying to Barbara. No one in the network sent proposals of marriage over highly classified communications channels. Maybe he should have booked a flight instead and walked in on her?

No, that was not her style either. He would have to wait. He glanced at the picture of her on the desk, a color slide enlarged to fit an 8 x 10 frame. He had taken the picture in Hong Kong a year ago up on Victoria Peak overlooking the harbor. The puffiness and fatigue still showed around her eyes from the beating she had taken in the "Operation Rosebud" scam. Still, the smile chased away most of the shadows, as it always did; her blond hair tumbling around her face in a cascade of liquid gold brought a luminous quality to her face. Her eyes were dulled some due to the strain of "Rosebud," but the shafts of light that came whenever she smiled were there. There were soft tints in the blue like the sun breaking through the clouds to dance on an azure sea.

She was British born, the only daughter of missionary parents who had combined their skills in agricultural development among the Israelis with a quiet spiritual Christian lifestyle that had won them many Jewish friends. She had gone through Cambridge and taught archaeology at the Hebrew University between her assignments for the Israeli Secret Police and Interpol. When her parents died, she was only twenty-five and in her first year of teaching at the university. After that she took on more and more of the espionage and detective business.

A plane crash in the Negev had brought her into Sebastian's life as they had to combine their wits and prayers to lead eight survivors out of the most hellish desert in the world. Hellish, at least, to Sebastian. He had emerged from that experience to a dimension of Christian manhood he had never known. After that, he had given himself to God to go anywhere to help people caught in the struggles for life they could not handle alone. She had insisted he do it. Oddly enough, every adventure after that had the CIA or the KGB or the British MI-5 in it somewhere; so he accepted that world as God's choosing for him.

At the same time, the plane crash and the subsequent struggle for survival in the desert had welded both of them in a bond of mutual respect; and in the years that followed, when they found themselves bumping into each other in the twisting corridors of the Cold War maze, the relationship between them took on deeper meaning.

It had locked finally during their month together in Hong Kong during the R & R following "Rosebud." She had been ordered to stay over for medical care, recovering from the drug torture inflicted on her while she had been held prisoner for three weeks on that old rust-bucket of a ship.

But in that month of recuperation they had come to know the love that had been denied them during the years since the Negev. They drove the mountain roads on the island in Hong Kong, lingered for hours over dinner in Chinese restaurants or the hotels; sometimes they just rode the Star Ferry back and forth from the island to Kowloon, enjoying being together on the water, unmindful of the rush of crowds that pressed on and off the ship.

Many times he had wanted to ask her to marry him. But he knew her commitment to the Israeli Secret Police and Interpol was strong, and he was afraid of rejection. And he was afraid that in asking her, the beautiful oneness they had would be lost.

The month disappeared like vapor, and it was time for her to leave for Tel Aviv. At Kai Tak airport he tried to say what he felt and what he was sure she already knew. But the airport was crowded and the tyranny of time elbowed out his best intentions. He felt increasingly tense as her departure time drew near. And uneasy. She worked a dangerous trail, even as he did. He could not tolerate the thought of her leaving him again and ending up dead somewhere on her next assignment . . . and without him.

She seemed subdued as well, feeling the turmoil they were both trying to ignore in the parting. When her flight was announced, she looked at him with a certain fear in her blue eyes, as if it were the last time. He pulled her close to him, kissed her lightly, and held on to her. She slowly put her arms around his neck and looked into his eyes. He felt her soft, warm breath on his face. He saw the contrasts of the warm lights in her deep blue eyes, along with a mist of uncertainty about what was right or wrong in what they were doing.

Then she put her cheek next to his and said softly into his ear, "Bye." He caught the choke in her voice as she tightened her arms around his neck, squeezing lightly. "You are my love forever. Will you remember that?"

"We are running out of forever," he warned, pulling her closer.

She touched her soft lips to his right earlobe and then pulled away, easing gently out of the circle of his arms. She gave him a smile, her head tilting a little to the right in that familiar way, kissed him lightly on the lips, then stepped back, took his hands gently in her own, squeezed them, and turned and walked to the gate. He watched her, all the sirens of alarm going off at once in him, watching her familiar athletic stride moving her body in that easy cadence. She paused at the gateway, turned, and glanced back at him, giving him a lingering intent look, storing up the memory of his face. With a quick, flashing smile of benediction, she disappeared inside.

He had never felt so depressed in his life as then.

Now he turned from gazing at the picture and looked at the typewriter on the side table. He had to continue writing his summary of the Hong Kong venture for the record, as he had all the others. This was one CIA requirement he acceded to but hated doing, and he was taking his time, much to the exasperation of Washington. Barbara's presence remained strong in the room, distracting him. Her face haunted him in his dreams, forcing a preoccupation he could not shake. He needed to get on the move again.

But Messrs. Backstrom, Alnutt, and Winston had shaken him, forcing him to hesitate. Nevertheless, despite them, he knew that his adventures across the world would have to finish sooner or later. The timing was not good now, but would it ever be? He had nothing in mind as to where he should go anyway. There was no moving of the Spirit on him like before, when God had sent him on journeys that had ended up in bizarre scenarios. Maybe God was telling him it was time. He decided then that if Barbara responded positively to his message, he would accept it as a sign from God that it was indeed time. And if she didn't? If she said no? What then? Could he be content to sit it out here in Chicago, defrocked and with no ministry?

He thought of the Negev, Cuba, Berlin, the Arctic, Hong Kong . . . twisted trails littered with pain and death. He thought he had left people who had come closer to God because of him . . . But Backstrom had forced him to double back, to rethink, and in doing that he felt fear that he might have failed, as they had said, his "true ministry."

His only hope for knowing which way to go was in Barbara. She had enough miles herself in running through the ring of fire for the Israelis and Interpol. They could run an orphanage together, or a halfway house for drug addicts, even without the official clergy sign hanging over him. It would be "legitimate ministry" at least. But would she go for it?

He rubbed his hand across his face, feeling the lines there. He glanced at his own picture next to hers, the one she had taken of him sitting on the hotel porch rail at Repulse Bay beyond the Hong Kong city limits. He still had those Lincolnesque features, the aquiline nose and cheekbones, the wide mouth and full lower lip, the shock of black hair that was thinning now. His gangly six-foot-three frame filled out the white tennis shirt a bit too tightly, reminding him that he was 190-plus pounds in that picture, thanks to all the Chinese food. The greenish-blue eyes receded into slightly sunken sockets, giving him another touch of resemblance to Old Abe himself.

Usually his eyes were neutral, ever since his wife, Carol, had died in an auto crash fifteen years ago when he was still trying to make the pastorate in Wisconsin. It was as if they could not compute his inner emotions after that. But in that picture on the desk his eyes mirrored the unguarded love he had for Barbara, a mixture of longing and lights of laughter she always brought out in him.

Finally, feeling the constriction of the apartment, he stood, got his jacket from the closet, and went out for a walk. The late November chill hit him with a slap.

It felt like an omen of his demise.

Two

He decided not to wait any longer.

He had held off two more days with no word from Israel. He chose then to break protocol and put a call through to Tel Aviv. He got her security section all right, but no one was there to talk to him. Finally a Colonel Kahn came on the line, responding only because Sebastian had come through on Barbara's classification number.

"Miss Churchill is not in, Mr. Sebastian," Kahn said politely but with finality.

"Just tell me where she is," Sebastian shouted back over the poor connection.

"I am sorry, sir, but we are not permitted to give out that information," Kahn replied, sounding as if he were talking from a coal mine ten miles underground.

Sebastian sighed, thanked him, and hung up. He had only one other possibility—Inspector Jacques Henri at Interpol in Paris. Henri anchored Barbara's log when she was under assignment to them. When the Hong Kong flap was over, Henri had visited Barbara there and met Sebastian. Sebastian had come to enjoy the short, mustached, fiftyish Frenchman who looked a lot like Charlie Chaplin, bowler hat and all. Henri had told Sebastian to get "in touch" if he needed anything.

This was one of those times. He put the call through, waited five minutes for the connection and the classification number to clear. Then a voice came on the other end, heavy with a French accent and carrying a bit of light banter that was Jacques Henri. Sebastian identified himself and Henri gave a short laugh of delight. "Ah! *Bonjour, mon ami,* Sebastian!" he chortled. "It is a pleasure to speak to you again. I trust this call does not mean trouble, no?"

"Inspector Henri," Sebastian said, not quite sure how to ask it, "do you happen to know if Barbara Churchill is on assignment with you at this time?"

There was a pause, a sound of voices in the background. Finally Henri came on again. "Yes, *Monsieur* Sebastian," he said guardedly, "she is on a—what you say—kind of assignment-holiday. . . ."

"Which is it, Jacques, assignment or holiday?"

Henri gave a short, embarrassed laugh. "It is like that, *monsieur,* just like that."

"Could you tell me where?"

Another pause. "*Monsieur* Sebastian, you know how delicate such information is, yes? Highly forbidden to tell you on a direct line . . . Is it so critical?"

Sebastian hesitated. How could he phrase it? Henri would think him a fool if he told him he wanted to marry Barbara. So he said, "A matter of life and death, Henri."

There was another pause, then Henri exclaimed, "Is it you, *monsieur,* or *Mademoiselle* Churchill who is critical?"

"Both of us, Jacques . . . I don't want to muck up what she's doing on the assignment-holiday. I just need to know where she is."

He heard Henri talking again to someone in the background, and Sebastian was sorry that he was creating tension for the Frenchman over so silly a thing as a proposal of marriage.

"*Monsieur* Sebastian," Henri came on again, sounding as if he were still not sure he should continue, "she is in Sydney. . . ."

"Australia?"

"Correct. . . ."

"Where in Sydney, Jacques?"

"Sorry, *mon ami,* I absolutely cannot tell you that."

"All right . . . how long has she been there?"

"*Monsieur—*"

"Jacques, she's on holiday, right? So how many days has she been gone?"

A pause, then a sigh from Jacques. "Six days now, *monsieur. . . .*"

"One more very important thing, Jacques . . . bear with me," Sebastian bore down, hoping to keep Henri on. "Is she with anyone on holiday there?"

"Pardon, *monsieur?*"

Sebastian knew it was out of line to ask. "Is she with anyone there?"

"Too delicate information, *monsieur. . . .*"

"Jacques," Sebastian dared to push the barriers now, "it is very important that I know . . . for both of us."

There was a hissing sound on the line, mocking the exchange. "Well, *monsieur,* it is dangerous to give you all this even on a classified line . . . but . . . well, *monsieur,* yes, she is seeing a man there. . . ."

Sebastian let out his breath slowly and unevenly. "What man, Jacques?"

"*Monsieur,* not that kind of man," Henri responded with a short laugh. He knew there was something of an attachment between Sebastian and Barbara, as he had undoubtedly seen in Hong Kong.

Sebastian felt the burn of embarrassment creep along the hairline on his neck. "Well, Jacques—" Suddenly the line became cluttered with crackles, pops, and wheezes. "Hello, Jacques? Are you still on?" Again the snapping and hissing and buzzing. He knew then that Jacques had put the scrambler on the line, indicating he had to get off the conversation for security's sake.

Sebastian slowly hung up the phone. Goblins of suspicion planted seeds of doubt in his mind. Another man? Why not? Her job brought her into contact with men all the time during the course of her assignments. But she was on holiday! She had promised him in Hong Kong that if she ever had any free time to relax she would call him to join her. Still, she was on an Interpol assignment too. She couldn't or didn't want to involve him.

But the "other man" bothered him. He felt the menacing constriction of jealousy laying hold on him. He took a deep breath, knowing he was acting like a jilted lover and that it should be beyond him to act like that. Anyway, he had more faith in her than that. He glanced at the baby Big Ben, computing the time in Australia. He paced the floor, pondering, then picked up the phone and dialed Agnes at the travel bureau.

The cheerful voice came on and Sebastian said, "Agnes, get me a flight to Sydney right away. . . ."

"As in Australia?" the fifty-year-old efficient and likable lady asked.

"As in . . . yes . . . now. I have my passport and will get my visa downtown tomorrow. Agnes, pull out all the stops. I need to get there immediately."

"Has it ever been any different with you these years, Mr. Sebastian?" Agnes moaned in a good-natured tone of voice.

"Keeps you from getting bored, Agnes," he quipped and hung up.

He stood at the desk a long time sniffing at the acrid smells that still remained in the room from his encounter with Backstrom, Alnutt, and Winston. How big was Sydney? Four million anyway. She could be anywhere there. He got out his atlas and studied the statistics. A lot of beaches, a lot of city.

He felt some uncertainty about going. What would she say to him if he did find her there? What would he say to her? Some things you had to leave alone in the tricky business of espionage. Would he say, "I had to find out what man you are seeing in Sydney"? He laughed, and it sounded almost sardonically harsh. Why? Well, it was stupid and juvenile for him to chase her now. Yet something inside him continued to push the walls of credulity. He had to see her. He couldn't stay in the apartment another day. He had to settle it between them. Anyway, he wanted her answer directly, looking into those deep blue eyes; not by phone or by telex. That was it.

He had no contacts in Sydney. And he could not go to the police or the national security people. That might blow her cover if she were trying to work incognito. He flipped aimlessly through the pages of his book, hoping the name of someone would jump out who was even remotely connected. He paused and looked at a card in the folds of one page.

HARRY JAMISON
FEATURES
THE MORNING HERALD—SYDNEY

He remembered then that it was Jamison who had gotten to him in Hong Kong while he was working another news assignment. Word had leaked out that Sebastian had something to do with "Rosebud," and Jamison had cornered him in the Happy Valley Hotel begging for some kind of story. "You're unclassified, Mr. Sebastian," Jamison had pleaded. "You can say what you want . . . How about it?" Sebastian was sure now that it was Jamison who was responsible for the Hong Kong *Times* bit about Sebastian being the "saint of international espionage." Peter Chang, the wacky cab driver who had been with him during the hot times there, probably talked to Jamison about the flap. Chang had no restriction on talking about it either.

But Sebastian had played innocent with Jamison, promising

him instead that one day, if he lived, he would give Jamison a story about himself.

So now if it meant giving some of it to Jamison in exchange for help in contacting Barbara in Sydney, it was worth it. He packed, went to bed, woke up in three hours, and could not get back to sleep. Finally he got up, put on his jacket, and went out for a walk on the lakefront, feeling the constriction of uncertainty and some depression about that uncertainty.

Who was the other man?

Harry Jamison was in his early forties with thinning reddish hair, a hank of which flopped over his right eye, forcing him to slap at it continually as if it were a pesky fly crawling across his eyebrow. He had small, studious blue-crystal eyes that went with a man who did a lot of research on facts and people. Glints of inner amusement showed up in those eyes as well as if he had a bag full of jokes he wanted to unload on anyone willing to listen. He was about five foot nine and built square and solid, like the cab of a semi-truck. His full reddish mustache curled upward at the corners of his wide mouth, especially when he smiled, which lent a double bonus of humor to anyone who appreciated that in him. Sebastian did.

Jamison pushed the battered four-year-old Honda Accord with spurts of acceleration all the way from the Sydney airport to the city, as if he were carefully punctuating every sentence of his conversation. At times his voice sounded like that of a tour guide; he had obviously picked up a lot of people before who were new to Australia. And like all good Aussies, he pointed out buildings and old monuments with considerable pride.

"All those brownstone buildings are a mark of Sydney," he said to Sebastian. "Urban renewal won't allow destruction of the Old Sydney. Got a lot of ethnics here . . . Refugees, mostly . . . Most of 'em drive cabs."

Sebastian sat beside him, half-awake, not having slept well on the fourteen-hour flight from Chicago. But he dutifully nodded as Jamison went on pointing out the sights.

"I put you in the Old Sydney Hotel on The Rocks," Jamison went on. "Right on the harbor, that . . . You can see the Harbour Bridge from your window and walk the Circular Quay around the harbor if you like . . . The new opera house is on the Quay . . .

Could have put you in the Sheraton or the Regency . . . But you'd want something of the real Sydney, I reckon. . . ."

"The Rocks?" Sebastian asked, mystified.

"Right on, mate . . . Place where Sydney began really . . . Where old Captain James Cook hit ground way back in 1788 or so . . . Lots of nice shops there . . . and the hotel is quiet . . . Nice decor, all of that . . . We're on George Street now, Sebastian, maybe ten minutes from your hotel. . . ."

Sebastian noticed that the city streets were clean, the old buildings preserved or refurbished, the new ones kept in good taste, modern but not garish. It was a busy place but controlled, as if people didn't want to take industry too seriously.

"Now then, it's spring here in Sydney," Jamison went on, giving the Accord a spurt of acceleration, "even if it's December 2. Lots of beaches here . . . Bondi is not too far . . . popular . . . not crowded usually . . . Now you be wantin' something from me, Mr. Sebastian?"

Sebastian straightened up in his seat. "I need a calendar of social events, Jamison, each day of the week coming up. And I'd like a calendar of what went on this past week if you can get that."

Jamison grunted a half-laugh. "That's bloody good, ya know?" he quipped. "No vacationer I know wants last week's social calendar. You've got a flap on then, have you, Mr. Sebastian?"

"Jamison," Sebastian said with a yawn, "I'm here on holiday. I simply want to know what kind of social activities go on in this city, that's it."

"Of course, of course," Jamison responded, a tone of humor still in his voice. "I can get you all of that, I suppose. Provided you promise me to get me in on anything big you might be bobbin' into, right?"

"You'll get your story, Jamison, when I get what I came for," Sebastian chided him.

"A promise now? Fair dinkum?"

"What?"

"Fair dinkum . . . That means the gospel truth to us Aussies. . . ."

"Fair dinkum then, Jamison."

"All right, you sleep it off, and I'll run you a list of bashes off the calendar . . . Do I get to follow you around?"

"No . . . You've got my phone number at the hotel, I have yours. . . ."

"Right. Old Oriental Hotel there, see? Oldest building on George Street here on The Rocks. We're in Old Sydney now, Mr. Sebastian . . . Colorful place . . . Ah, here is the hotel then. . . ."

The Old Sydney sat on top of a gradual grade in the street, a building of traditional brownstone, unassuming in its structure. Jamison pulled up in front of the glass doors. A red-uniformed bellman came out and opened Sebastian's door. Sebastian got out and looked toward the Harbour Bridge with its huge spans and girders prodding the sky. There was an odor of fish and chips in the air, or something akin to it, giving him the feeling of friendship and neighborliness.

He walked into the hotel lobby behind the bellman. The interior of the hotel was cool and spacious and done up in maroons and beige. He glanced up and noted that there were railings around the upper levels and doors to rooms there as well. There was a quietness to the place not like the rushes at the Sheraton or the Regency.

"Good choice, Jamison," he said, and Jamison grinned in appreciation.

"You'll like the room too, Mr. Sebastian," Jamison said, anxious to please. "I'll be off then . . . Have a deadline, ya know? Give you a call in twelve hours . . . If you want to get me, it's any time . . . Have a good rest, Mr. Sebastian!"

The room met his expectations. It had a view of the harbor and the bridge which Jamison had promised. A king-sized bed, a desk, a big window with beige drapes against the maroon walls, shower and bath . . . all of it. He was on the eighth, a level that fit his purposes, high enough to be away from street noise, low enough to get down to first in a hurry if he had to. Not that he thought he had to here.

He thought of Barb Churchill as he unpacked. The city was her kind. A mixture of the old and the new, a lot of harbor area and beaches. He wondered even now where she might be, what she was doing. He glanced at his watch. It was 3 in the afternoon Australia time. He had lost a day coming over the date line. He pictured her on one of those beaches somewhere here, enjoying the sun. With whom? Always that jabbing thought that had kept him awake on the flight over.

He undressed, showered, and climbed into bed. This was the loneliest time. A new hotel room in some far-off city . . . alone. He heard a woman's light laughter passing by his door, a man's responding chatter. No man should ever have to be alone in a hotel in an exotic city anywhere in the world, Sebastian thought. He had been saying that for ten years now, since he had begun globe-hopping, but never had he felt the pressure of it quite like now.

He let the much-needed sleep creep through his brain as the soft hum of the air conditioner lulled him further into surrender. Hollow, echoing voices took up a beat in his brain. Alnutt challenged, ". . . certainly not redemptive . . . certainly not redemptive . . ." But overriding that was Barbara's soft voice in his ear, ". . . you are my love forever . . . forever . . . forever . . ."

Three

He felt the jab in his brain.

Years of becoming accustomed to aberrations of any kind in sleep snapped him to, and he lifted his head off the pillow, forcing his eyes open.

The alarm on the radio continued its raucous squawk. He fumbled for the button, mumbling thickly, "Whatever happened to chimes?"

He rolled over and looked around the room, at the sun coming in through the crack in the drapes, his clothes hanging over the back of a blue-cushioned chair. He glanced at his watch with the dial showing U.S. and Australian time. It was 7:30 A.M. Had he slept sixteen hours?

The sound of the phone scraped his still foggy brain with demanding screams. He reached over and picked up the receiver.

"Good morning, Mr. Sebastian!" Jamison's voice came on with a chirp. "Trust you had a good one, sir! Time for breakfast down here on the mezzanine. What say?"

Sebastian yawned. "What is the correct time here, Jamison?" he asked, still not believing his own watch.

"Seven-thirty in the morning, Wednesday, December 3, Mr. Sebastian. Beautiful day, sir! The eggs and sausages are the best anywhere in the world. I go on duty at 9, so we've got some time to go over your social calendar as you asked. . . ."

Sebastian ran his fingers through his tumbled hair, forcing his sluggish mind to compute. "Sure, sure," he finally said, his tongue thick with sleep. "Give me a half hour, Jamison. . . ."

"Right on, mate!"

Sebastian hung up and sat on the edge of the bed, resting his head in his hands. "Rise up, O man of God, and put thine armour on," he mumbled. It was a litany for him through the years since he was such a poor starter after waking up. "'It is by Thy mercies we are not consumed . . . Thy promises are new every morning . . . Great is Thy faithfulness.'"

He reached over to the radio built into the side table, flipped the dial until he found some classical music, and then staggered to the shower with the sound of Wagner following him.

Forty-five minutes later he met Jamison on the mezzanine, the breakfast and dining area for the hotel. Sebastian felt a bit more human, but his mind and body told him he was out of sync as to time.

They both helped themselves to the breakfast buffet. It was quiet, with very few people up yet. The two of them sat down at a table with a white tablecloth and silver.

"Give me the day again, Jamison, do you mind?" Sebastian asked.

"Wednesday, December 3, Mr. Sebastian," Jamison said cheerfully. "You are one day behind because of the date line. Try the eggs."

Sebastian tried the coffee first. It was black and hot, snapping his brain to attention. He went to the eggs while Jamison began reading the coming week's social calendar from a printed tearsheet.

"Let's see, the yacht club regatta in the harbor today at noon . . . Launching of our biggest oil tanker at the yards at 3 . . . Frank Sinatra at the Regency tonight . . . One of your chaps, Mr. Sebastian, yes? Concert at the Botanical Gardens tonight as well . . . Kind of tough competition with your Sinatra in town . . . That's in front of the Governor General's house which lends a bit of class and it's just off the Quay a few minutes away . . . Early Christmas pageant at The Rocks tomorrow beginning at 10 A.M. . . . Anything strike you, Mr. Sebastian?"

"Keep going, Jamison," Sebastian said, gulping more coffee.

"Well, now . . . tomorrow again . . . there's a reception at the Sheraton Wentworth on Pitt Street in honor of the retirement of Dr. David Julian . . . at 2 o'clock in the James Cook Room, fifth floor . . . Should be quite a bash with about seventy or eighty top government wogs there. . . ."

"Who's Julian?" Sebastian asked offhandedly, gulping more of his coffee around his eggs and bacon.

"Quite an interesting chap, really." Jamison responded as if the invitation to hold forth was a challenge to his journalistic sense of recall. "He's eighty now . . . Just turned . . . Been the biggest man in communications satellite and tracking systems. Everything we've got in satellite tracking at Alice Springs, outside Sydney, is due to him in one way or the other . . . You know Australia has the most sophisticated satellite and space tracking, even better than your NORAD or Nassau. . . ."

"Oh, I wouldn't think of arguing the point," Sebastian replied lightly, the coffee and the food beginning to bring him back from the "grave" of sixteen hours of sleep.

"Right," Jamison returned with a short laugh. "Anyway, Julian's been in astronomy and physics mostly, but is a keen electronics man on top of it . . . guidance systems and all that. He's considered the father of ComSat, the communications satellite technology which you American cousins have used. . . ."

"Hmmm," Sebastian grunted, not sure yet that any of this had credence.

"Sad thing for old Julian is the loss of his daughter two years ago . . . Just up and disappeared . . . Never did find her. Was a genius herself. Just twenty-seven. Elisa Julian. Lovely lass. Learned a lot from her daddy on space stuff but was a step ahead of Pop on computer guidance systems for space vehicles . . . Was working on lasers for satellites for peaceful purposes when she vanished. . . ."

"She die or what?"

"Don't know really . . . I was on that story for a full year or more trying to track her down . . . I guess it's a cold trail. The old man thinks to this day that your CIA did her in before she could get to the Russians with her satellite knowledge. She was anti-American anyway . . . Hated you Yanks for your nuke arms buildup."

"Maybe the Russians got to her first," Sebastian offered, sensing the issue was going from remote to a real possibility now.

"Maybe," Jamison acknowledged, his lips puckering in doubt. "But David Julian is convinced it was CIA, and he's down on your chaps for good. Your government brass have been trying to proposition him into working for them, but no go. Julian is a stubborn anti-alignment character, and he can smell out an agent from either side a good mile away, so I've heard anyway. . . ."

"So what about his wife?"

"Died a year ago . . . brokenhearted over the loss of Elisa . . . and that left the old man even more antipolitical, antiwar, all of it. . . ."

"So what's he going to do in his retirement?" Sebastian pursued, sounding as if he were simply making breakfast conversation and trying to keep Jamison from thinking that he was interested in any of it.

"Plans to sail around Cape Horn and home to his birthplace in

Plymouth, England," Jamison went on, more animated now in unloading all of his research on someone who would listen. "He said it's the one thing he always wanted to do. . . ."

"Alone?"

"Well, maybe he'll have to." Jamison paused while the waitress filled their cups. "Thank you," he said to her, then leaned his elbows on the table. "He's had classifieds running in the papers asking for three crewmen to join him and offering five thousand Australian to each on arrival in Plymouth."

"And?"

"No one has come forward yet. You see, Julian is a different breed of sailing man than most. He's the kind who will run full-sail in a force eight blow and never mind the hull or mast for the fear of broaching. Still, he won the tough International Yacht Race, held every year December 25, 630 miles from Sydney to Tasmania. Won it two years in a row in fact. Anybody who can even make it the last miles across Bass Strait into Tasmania is some kind of sailor. It's the toughest stretch of water anywhere. But the crew Julian had with him won't ride with him again. Anyone who does can figure on a blow-the-man down kind of sailing. So you see, five thousand quid payable at the other end around the Horn doesn't whip up much appetite even for the veterans. And besides that . . ." Jamison's eyes twinkled with amusement as he swiped at the twig of hair over his right eye. ". . . the boat he built for it, a forty-five footer, he's called *The Pequod* of all things . . . You know of course—"

"Yes, Captain Ahab's doomed ship in Melville's novel *Moby Dick*," Sebastian finished for him.

"Right on, mate! And you're right! A death ship she was. Sailing people have a thing about omens like that, fiction or not. The death of *The Pequod* with all hands lost doesn't go over with the sailing blokes Julian would like to have for his crew."

"Sounds as if the man has a macabre sense of humor," Sebastian commented, sipping on his coffee, his mind running ahead, wondering if this event could be on Barbara Churchill's calendar.

"That he has, that he has . . . Takes great amusement from it all. Maybe it's a buffer to the pain the poor man feels in the loss of his family, ya know?"

"Hard to believe no one would take him up on his offer," Sebastian said. "Ought to be plenty of young sailing bucks around here who'd risk it, *Pequod* or no *Pequod*."

"You ever sailed the Horn, Mr. Sebastian?"

"No . . ."

"All right then . . . let me tell you, it's the toughest sailing challenge in the world, even worse than Bass Strait across to Tasmania . . . Those who made it say they can't describe the seas there . . . like hell boiling all over the place . . . crosswinds, cross-seas, force ten winds . . . waves up to thirty feet high. . . ."

"Some have sailed it alone, Jamison, if I recall. . . ."

"Not at eighty, Mr. Sebastian . . . Old Julian still has good eyes, but his stamina won't hold up the three thousand miles from Sydney to the Cape, around it and another six thousand to Plymouth. . . ."

"So what will he do then?"

"Oh, the blighter will probably try it himself anyway . . . He has one sure deckhand in his adopted son, Ryan Bosco . . . He's a late seventeen and built to handle rigging . . . adopted by Julian five years ago. Bosco was an orphan kid making a few coins to stay alive by playing a banjo with a dancing monkey act down at the railway station on the Quay . . . But in between he got to hanging around the Sailing Center down at the Spit watching the boats. Julian was running a thirty-five-foot cruiser then . . . invited the kid aboard for a ride . . . Ryan took to the sails in a hurry. Julian liked him, so did his wife. So after a few months of sailing together, they adopted him. . . ." Jamison paused, sipping at his coffee, his eyes now steady on Sebastian, a glint in his eyes that said he had spun a good yarn and that Sebastian was interested. "How about it, Mr. Sebastian?"

"Meaning what?" Sebastian asked innocently, looking over the rim of his cup at Jamison. "I'm not that much of a sailor, and I don't know the first thing about satellites . . . What else you got there in your calendar?"

Jamison laughed as if he knew he had Sebastian hooked on David Julian. "I'd love to cover that reception, ya know?" he added. "But I got an assignment up in Manley on Thursday. The old man is kind of a legend in Australia. Would make a good feature. A bit odd, but geniuses are supposed to be, right?"

"The calendar, Jamison, if you have the time," Sebastian prodded him, anxious to get him off Julian lest he suspect Sebastian would go to that reception.

"OK . . . well," and he went back to the calendar. "A football match between Sydney and Melbourne tomorrow at 4 . . . Also tomorrow Women for the Protection of the Outback at the Regency at 2. . . ."

"What's that about?" Sebastian asked, feigning interest, trying to convince Jamison that the Julian information was not important to him.

Jamison smiled as if he knew. "Well, Mr. Sebastian, you wouldn't want to get in that meeting of a hundred and fifty or so Aussie women fighting to keep thousands of acres of Australian outback free from land speculators, would you now?" He laughed heartily at that. "Mind you, I bless 'em just the same. . . ."

"Sounds interesting," Sebastian replied with a poker face. "May try it. . . ."

Jamison laughed again, glancing at Sebastian as if to say he knew very well where Sebastian was going on Thursday. "Well, then," he went on, looking at his calendar, "you want to go over last week's big events?"

"Just let me have the printout," Sebastian said. Jamison handed him the tearsheet.

"Well, got to run, Mr. Sebastian," he said, checking his watch. He moved to get up and then changed his mind. "Mr. Sebastian, I know you said you are on holiday. But I'm a journalist with the nose of a news hound. I know you have a way of cranking up things wherever you go, judging from what I learned in Hong Kong and checking a bit . . . I know too that sometimes your Barbara Churchill shows up where you do. I'm only asking that if she does and anything of a flap blows up, you'll let me have the inside dope on it."

"I told you, Jamison, that you'll get your story when I finish my time here," Sebastian reminded him. Then, on second thought, he added, "Why don't you sign on with Julian, Jamison? That would make a cracking good story for you, wouldn't it?"

"Thought about it a few times, sir," Jamison replied. Then he shrugged. "I'm not all that good at sailing. And old Julian is picky about that. But I'd give anything to have a go at it, yes sir, Mr. Sebastian." He sighed then as if he knew that was beyond him. He reached for the tab, made a move to go, then paused again. "One thing more, sir . . . I'm having a bit of a prang making a fit between you, a religious man, a clergyman at that, with all the tacky, bloody hell—excuse me—that goes with the Cold War stuff and all that. Do you mind, sir?"

Sebastian looked into his cup, sipped the last of the coffee, and put the cup back down. "Well, Jamison," and he remembered Backstrom, Alnutt, and Winston again, "our Lord came into this 'tacky, bloody hell' of a world, as you call it, as a baby almost two thousand years ago. He didn't fit either. I like to think I'm in good company, especially considering what He left behind because of coming."

Jamison's small blue eyes remained steadily on Sebastian's for a minute while he computed that, as if not believing it or not being able to absorb it. Then he nodded, smiled, and stood. "Fair dinkum, Mr. Sebastian?"

"Fair dinkum, Mr. Jamison."

"Good. Mind if I use that—what you said then—when I get your story?"

"Be my guest, Jamison."

He nodded. "By the way, there's a nice navy chapel up on Watson's Bay, about forty-five minutes from here by cab . . . Looks over the harbor, facing the sea. Quiet place. Or there's the Garrison Church around the corner from here, up Argyle through the Argyle Cut and to Mills Street . . . I mean, in case you might be needin' some time. . . ."

Sebastian smiled. "Thanks, Jamison . . . That's kind of you."

"And if you need a car—"

"No, thanks. I'll go by cab. It's a habit of mine."

Jamison nodded. "Call me if you need me, sir. I'll check on you late Thursday to see how you're doing. Have a good day!"

Sebastian waved to him as he took the stairs down to the lobby. Jamison knew Sebastian was going to that reception at the Sheraton. Sebastian sensed the journalist had a quick eye and an acute sense of human behavior. What every journalist needed, of course, but Jamison's was even sharper than most.

Anyway, Sebastian liked the man. He had a disarming way about him, even when he pushed for information. That, again, was the mark of an exceptionally well-trained or perhaps instinctive reporter. There was no doubt that with Jamison in his corner, Sebastian could count on finding Barbara.

The thought made him feel less tense. Now he was content to let the day unwind and enjoy what he could until Thursday. First, he'd head for the library, check the Australia *Who's Who* and any past news stories to get a better feel for Dr. David Julian. He had a hunch Barbara had been on that trail before him. No man with

Julian's background would simply retire for a sail around the world to good old England.

Still, why not? At any rate, Sebastian figured he'd know or get a hint on Thursday if Barbara showed up at the Sheraton. If she did, then something was indeed in the making around Julian. He only hoped it wasn't going to be anything like the hair-raising flap in Hong Kong. And even if there was something going with Julian, would she let Sebastian join her?

She'd have a hard time keeping him out of it. He had come too far now and had made up his mind that he was not leaving Australia, nor was she, until she had answered his big question. As irrelevant as it might seem to her.

Four

He spent three hours in the library downtown and read everything he could find on David Julian. Most impressive, even as Jamison had told him. Satellite wisdom in particular. He also found clippings on the missing daughter, Elisa, quite a few of the stories written by Jamison. The picture of her was a combination of childlike innocence offset by a certain snapping in her large eyes and the tough, sharp angle of her jaw that jutted out pugnaciously. Two combs pulled her dark-colored hair in back of her ears. There was a stark quality of beauty hidden behind the granite of anger.

The last few articles by Jamison and another reporter indicated that the Australian Security Organization had concluded that she was dead. Julian was quoted, however, as saying, "She will be considered among the missing persons until proved otherwise." Julian also gave some tough remarks indicting the CIA for "meddling with Elisa's life . . . If she is dead, the Americans are likely to blame."

Sebastian found a picture of Julian himself in one of the editions. The photo did not bring him out clearly, but Sebastian saw a man with almost white, short, bristling hair looking like bramble, bushy white eyebrows, a narrow craggy face, and large intent eyes behind steel-rimmed glasses. His nose was pointed. The thin mouth had lines of humor at the corners, although the caption under the photo indicated he was delivering a vituperative comment on "the clumsiness of the Australian Security people in carrying out the search for my missing daughter." The face had strength and daring in it—a lot of fight and a capacity for vehemence. The photo was dated a year ago, but even at seventy-nine he did not show many lines of age in his face. Sebastian wondered if the man still carried that facade of vigor and youth now. Mourning the loss of a daughter and a wife in so short a time inevitably drained anyone. And with that loss, age caught up quickly with its menacing work of debilitation of body and mind.

About noon Sebastian left the library and took a cab back to his hotel. Instead of entering it, since the mellow sun was turning the bright blue water of the harbor into a bright playful blue, Sebastian decided to walk the Circular Quay and kill some time pleasantly. He moved on down the concrete pier crowded with people who seemed to be heading toward the boat regatta around the bend. He passed the ferry docks and watched the hydraplane pull out, probably the one Jamison would take tomorrow for Manley. There was a festive flurry in the air as he strolled on by the railroad station. A young man was standing in the broad cement courtyard in front of the station facing the harbor. He was playing a guitar while a huge St. Bernard did a shuffling dance on his hind legs. The crowd applauded in appreciation and threw coins into the open guitar case. Sebastian thought of Ryan Bosco, the adopted son of Julian, who once had made his living playing the banjo here, as Jamison had told him. Sebastian moved on by the row of shops that offered all kinds of food—hot dogs, burgers, fish—and gold replicas of koala bears and kangaroos. Hanging over the Quay was a cacophony of music and the laughter and gaiety of a holiday crowd.

Then he turned to the left and moved under a canopy leading toward the Opera House. He glanced across the harbor and saw the huge Gold Shield Building and Qantas next to it, seeming to elbow each other out of the way to get a better look at the harbor. The Harbour Bridge was straight ahead, curving a half-loop over the water, a gigantic humpbacked structure that looked even bigger and more awesome from this angle. Sailboats in their bonnets of white canvas danced playfully beneath it, like children frolicking under the watchful eye of Grandpa.

Halfway down the walk Sebastian paused to watch an accordion player. Next to him, a short, bearded man stood, offering postcards for sale. Sebastian moved toward him and the man, wearing dark glasses, shoved a card out to him.

"Here ya go, mate," he said.

Sebastian glanced at it. It was a color photo of the Harbour Bridge. "Not now," he responded, and smiled at the man.

"I think you should take a second look," he said. "You might change your mind."

Sebastian looked again at the card. The man had turned it over, and Sebastian saw block letters written in black ink across the back.

/ 41 /

SEBASTIAN—BENTLEY AT THE STAIRS LEADING TO THE OPERA HOUSE—YOUR SIDE.

Sebastian looked at the man wearing the dark glasses. He wanted to ask who Bentley was. The man just stood there waiting, shuffling his postcards in his hands. Finally Sebastian dug out a few Australian coins and handed them over, taking the card and putting it into his shirt pocket, print side in. The bearded man, in his late thirties maybe, nodded and turned away, waving his cards to other passersby.

Sebastian walked on toward the Opera House, wondering how he had been identified so soon. Whoever Bentley was knew him well enough and had been ahead of him. For how long? Long enough to post his man there, selling cards in order to get the message to him. It unnerved him, even yet, how quickly the wheels of espionage and law enforcement worked to close the space around him. But could this perhaps mean that Bentley had news for him about Barbara? Or, again, was he being set up by unfriendly forces? But who would that be?

He walked on across the blacktop to the Opera House, peering through his sunglasses, looking for someone who would be standing near the stairs leading up to the broad deck by the building. People walked up and down those stairs, but Sebastian saw no one lounging nearby. He waited, looked around, and then climbed the steps. He stopped, looked around, and then walked back down the stairs again.

"Mr. Sebastian?" a voice called to him. "Do you like the view of the Harbour Bridge?" Sebastian turned his head to the right and saw the man. He was heavyset, a bit rotund, wearing white slacks and a casual maroon tennis shirt. Salt-and-pepper hair hung down over his collar.

"Bentley?" Sebastian called to him.

The man flashed a smile that looked like shark's teeth in the sun. "At your service, sir. I understand you wanted a guide around the Quay?" He pronounced it "qhy" as Australians usually did, even as Jamison had.

"I could use one, yes," Sebastian responded, knowing the man was throwing up smoke in case anyone was watching or listening.

Sebastian took the man's extended pudgy right hand in a quick shake. The skin felt dry and smooth. He was about Sebastian's height, wider in the shoulders than what he had seemed earlier. He was maybe going on fifty.

"Shall we walk on then?" he asked, extending a bag of popcorn with his left hand. Sebastian accepted the bag, playing this out as he knew he should, took a few kernels, and handed the bag back. They walked on through the Queen Elizabeth Gate, leading to the main concourse of the Quay, going by the Botanical Gardens on the right, the harbor on the left.

"Now, you see that ugly thing out there?" Bentley asked as he paused to view the harbor. Sebastian looked at the brown lump that sat like a wart on the shimmering, sun-kissed blue water of the harbor. "We call it Pinch Gut. An old fort from way back. Kept convicts in there, the ones the Brits sent over to be the work gang to build our glorious colony. Over to the right up there, you see that lighthouse on the peak? That is Watson's Bay Naval Station. Just beyond is a place called The Gap where people jump off now and then when they find life too hard to carry. Strange, that . . . The naval chapel is right next to it . . . People go in, see the chaplain, talk it out with him, then either walk out the side door to the right to The Gap, or out the front and into the arms of life again. Depends on how good the chaplain is, wouldn't you say, reverend?"

Sebastian glanced at him. Bentley was checking him over to make sure. "We are deputies of God, Bentley, not God Himself," Sebastian said shortly, anxious to get on with this.

"But of course," Bentley replied, smiling his shark's-tooth grin and popping more white lumps of popcorn into his mouth. "Now, then, Mr. Sebastian," he continued, seemingly satisfied, tossing some popcorn to seagulls waddling on the cement nearby, "I have a message from your friend Jacques Henri of the Paris office. You know him?"

"Of course."

"Yes, well, he sent me a message . . . Excuse me, I am what you Americans call a 'stringer' for Interpol. I hole up at the Australian Security Office." He took a card out of the popcorn bag, gave a quick glance around him at the people passing by, and handed the card to Sebastian.

Sebastian glanced at the card and returned it. It seemed genuine. "Go on, Bentley."

"Yes . . . well, *Monsieur* Henri sent word about Barbara Churchill . . . That name familiar?"

"You know where she is?"

Bentley lifted his hand to ward off the question. "No, no . . . I am sorry. I am not privy to Interpol's special projects here. I am only a courier, Mr. Sebastian. And now and then some undercover perhaps. Jacques Henri wants you to know that *Madamoiselle* Churchill is not really herself . . . not like you knew her before . . . You must be prepared for the change in her. . . ."

"Like what?" Sebastian prodded, feeling a quickening of his heart, an answering tightness in his throat. "She been hurt?"

Bentley chewed on more popcorn, frowning at Pinch Gut out in the harbor. "The drugs forced on her in Hong Kong . . . you know about that?"

"Yes, yes. . . ."

"Well, she has withdrawn well under methadone. But as is often the case, such large doses as she was given can alter personality somewhat . . . change attitudes, sometimes to former friends and relationships . . . She is still highly competent in her work, still quick in her mind . . . But she is, well, tougher, and perhaps more businesslike . . . He said you would know what he meant. But you must be patient, *Monsieur* Henri says . . . Allow her time to work it out, to heal properly—"

"Did Henri give you any clue as to where she is?" Sebastian demanded, feeling the alarm rising in him.

"It is not in Inspector Henri's style to reveal such things specifically, Mr. Sebastian. He apparently knows you are a persistent man when it comes to finding *Madamoiselle* Churchill. He simply wants you to be prepared when you do find her—shall I say if?"

"How did you know who I was, Bentley?" Sebastian asked, a bit irritated at the neutral way the man laid this out.

Bentley smiled again, a kind of spasm in his thin lips. "Mr. Sebastian, we have all the photos and logs on you from the past. Henri had a man on you when you left Chicago, since he knew you would come to Sydney. We got your flight number here and were at the airport when you arrived. I have been on your trail since Mr. Jamison picked you up. We know what we are doing here, you see. . . ."

"Henri must be concerned that I either find Barbara Churchill or that I don't . . . Which is it?"

"Do not ask me to determine motives from the head office, Mr. Sebastian. But I must say I have reasons to believe you will find her. I watched you in the library all morning. You seem to be preoccupied with Dr. Julian. . . ."

Sebastian glanced at him quickly as the shift in subject almost got by him. "How do you know that?"

Bentley laughed, sounding like a bark. "Oh, yes . . . Well, I watched what you checked out from the reference librarian. I passed behind you a couple of times and saw that you were reading the newspaper reports about Julian and his missing daughter . . . You were intent on every word. Sad case . . . Julian . . . his daughter . . . then his wife. . . ." Bentley sounded as if he were reading the obituary on them rather than commiserating.

"Yes, well, so I gather," Sebastian said, still not sure of Bentley's intent. "Is that all you have to tell me?"

Bentley crumpled the empty bag in his large right hand and tossed it into a wire trash barrel by the rail. "Only watch every step here, Mr. Sebastian." The tone of his voice was serious. "Remember that Julian is a high-priced item in terms of his scientific knowledge of satellites, as you may well know by now. That draws a crowd around him, people who want to buy his brain . . . or perhaps destroy it. Your Miss Churchill is—shall we say—in the line of fire. At any rate, how serious that is, is known only to her and Inspector Henri. I would be careful how much you complicate things for her. . . ."

"Did Henri tell you to tell me all this?"

Bentley stared out into the harbor. "It is what I learned in my time here," he answered, his voice taking on an edge. "Whatever your feelings for Miss Churchill, she could be in a dangerous situation with Julian. And she is not well. Inspector Henri counsels it best to stay removed. . . ."

"And if I don't?"

Bentley turned from gazing out into the harbor and looked at Sebastian. A frown dug two small furrows over the bridge of his nose; his jaw had gone a bit harder, jutting out.

"We all pay our bills in the end, Mr. Sebastian," he said crisply. "I am telling you under orders that, as you Yanks put it, you are hedging your bets if you do . . . But it is imperative you understand all that I am saying to you."

"Very well," Sebastian said, anxious now to be away from Bentley's tolling of the funeral bell. "I think I had better head back to the hotel."

"Well, then . . ." Bentley rose to Sebastian's dismissal and gave that file-tooth grin, his voice coming back to the friendly bantering of a park-bench conversation. "I shall be glad to walk you back to the Opera House." He removed his sunglasses to rub his eyes and squinted at Sebastian. "Shall we?" His eyes were a neutral gray. He put on his glasses again and extended his right hand in the direction of the Opera House.

Sebastian followed him, unable to sort out his emotions about the encounter. As they walked, Bentley rambled on in a tourist guide's tone of voice about the Governor General's house "just beyond the Gardens" and orated on "you'd think we would have shed the mother country by now" kind of commentaries. When they arrived back at the stairs of the Opera House, he put out his hand to Sebastian, who took it briefly.

"You know the wisdom of Solomon better than most, reverend," he said, giving an ingratiating smile. "I trust you will use it." He reached inside his back pocket, took out his wallet, slipped out a card and extended it. Sebastian took it and read it: SHERATON WENTWORTH HOTEL. "I think you might enjoy listening to Dr. Julian, Mr. Sebastian. He will be there tomorrow at 2. Place will be crawling with security, but you might catch something of the sap of the man." He turned then and walked up the stairs in that peculiar elephantine gait.

Sebastian watched him until he disappeared inside the Opera House, looking like another curious tourist. He looked back at the card. Why would Bentley steer him there? Just for Julian? Maybe. Or did he think that Barbara might be there?

Unable to sort out the motives of the man, Sebastian turned and walked on toward the Quay. The sun was bright on the harbor water, turning it darker. The yacht regatta had begun as the crowds lined the Quay railing cheering them on. There was conviviality in the air, but he did not savor it as he walked. His mind was elsewhere. As he headed up Argyle to George Street to the hotel, he felt mixed emotions about seeing Barbara: anticipation certainly, and a sense of concern that he get to her to find out for himself what was happening to her. At the same time, he felt uneasy about approaching her . . . She was not expecting him. He could complicate things for her by showing up. And he was unsure about how changed she was—did that include him?

Well, he wasn't even sure she'd be at the Sheraton. But Bentley seemed to act as if he knew she would be. He decided to take it as intended; his main concern was to talk to her again. That was his whole reason for coming here. He let it stand at that, pushing aside the gnawing gremlins of Bentley's warnings.

He took a cab to 338 Pitt Street—the Sheraton Wentworth—at 2:30 the next afternoon. He deliberately delayed his arrival, wanting the guests to have finished with the refreshments and be inside the main reception area. He had no idea of the layout of the James Cook Room, but he assumed it to be like that of any other hotel conference room.

The cab turned into the circular drive to the front of the stately building and the waiting doormen clad in maroon and gold. One of them opened the cab door and welcomed Sebastian. He nodded, paid the driver, and walked on through the huge glass doors to the hallway and the foyer. Sebastian was aware of the hotel's luxury, the maroon walls and golden trim, the guests dressed to the limit. Huge crystal chandeliers hung like flaming ice from the ceiling.

He checked the schedule board and noted: DR. DAVID JULIAN—JAMES COOK, FIFTH. Sebastian entered the elevator, trying to ignore the quickening of his pulse and the tightness in his throat. *Will she be there*? The elevator doors opened with a soft whisper, almost like a romantic invitation. He was facing the James Cook Room straight across the hall.

Slowly Sebastian crossed over to it, feeling as if he were picking up his first date in high school. He entered the outer reception room area and noticed the long refreshment table at the wall to his left. There were still some wilted sandwiches on a silver platter and a quarter of a bowl of red punch. He noticed through the two open doors ahead of him that the main reception room was crowded.

"May I help you, sir?"

He glanced quickly to his right where an attractive brunette sat behind a small table with a few name tags. Sebastian realized that he probably could not get in without one of those tags, undoubtedly prepared from an invitation list.

"I'm sorry," he said, searching for a way to get by this one, "I don't have an invitation . . . But I would very much like to listen to Dr. Julian . . . if I may?"

As he said it, a heavyset man in a blue suit came through the double doors and stopped. He had a pocket intercom phone in his right hand. Security. With steady, intent brown eyes, he stood there sizing up Sebastian.

"I'm sorry, sir," the brunette said, "but no one can go in without a name tag. Your name?"

"Sebastian . . ." No point to that. He glanced at the security man, who seemed to be getting more interested.

"Yes . . . here we are, Mr. Sebastian." She smiled up at him and handed him the name tag. "Compliments of Mr. Jamison of *The Morning Herald. . . .*"

"Oh . . ." Sebastian replied and smiled, trying not to look surprised. He took the tag, thanked her, pinned it to the left lapel of his brown suit. Jamison. Sebastian figured the long-nosed news hound knew he would attend this event today. And Jamison would be looking for a reward later, some kind of news summary of this whole thing strictly through Sebastian's eyes.

Sebastian helped himself to some punch. The man at the door watched him pour a cup and take a sip before he finally turned his back, apparently satisfied that Sebastian was legitimate.

Sebastian sipped the punch, glancing into the main reception room, listening to the applause now and then. A muffled voice came over the PA. More applause. When it ceased, another voice came on, stronger, booming over the power system. Sebastian couldn't quite make out the words, so he put his cup down and moved through the double doors. The security man glanced at him from where he stood against the wall to the left. Sebastian slid over to the wall on the right, next to a row of news photographers whose cameras began to buzz and click.

He stood with his arms folded, his glance sweeping the room. He could not see her among the hundred or so people. On the dais up front was a long table draped in deep velvet with a podium in the center. The man standing behind it had to be Julian. He was taller than Sebastian had imagined after viewing him in the newspaper photos, perhaps a little more than six feet. His hair had gone longer and maybe whiter. But the shoulders were broad under the conservative blue suit, and his hands gripping the podium were tanned and strong-looking with knobby knuckles. His face had become more lined, weather-beaten to the texture of brown leather. But his dark eyes behind the steel-rimmed glasses were alive, widening at times with his remarks as if for emphasis. Shafts of humor were there, or anger—which? His body moved with the words, leaning into them with intensity. Julian was an old tree walking, but Sebastian knew he never wanted that to fall on him.

Julian was reminiscing about his past, his education, his time teaching at the University of Sydney, the joy of creating new satellite systems for the benefit of all mankind. Then he added, "But for all of that, I treasure the memory of my sweet wife and darling daughter . . . both gone now." He paused, swallowed with difficulty, gave a ghostly smile, tossed his head, and added, "If you think I'm going to break down and blubber here on this day, ladies and gentlemen, you are mistaken." A relieved sigh went through the crowd. "No . . . I owe you all so much in making my journey so fulfilling . . . My father would be so proud of this day too. He once said, 'David, do something outstanding so I can say I knew ya!'"

The crowd stood and cheered at that and applauded loud and long. During the lull, Sebastian glanced to his left where the security man was now in the company of another one. No reason to believe that he was drawing that interest. So he looked around the room again as the photographers continued clicking and buzzing to get every angle of Julian. He stood behind the podium smiling almost sadly at the response, swiping at his white hair in a self-conscious way.

Then Sebastian saw her.

In the front row to the left, between two women. Her golden, wheat-colored hair was cut shorter, coming down only to her collar. It used to be long, down her back. The cut was a utilitarian one, the kind nurses often wore so that they didn't have to fuss with it around their patients. The change intrigued him; she had always liked her hair long. He caught just a slight profile of her nose as she turned to speak to the woman on her right. He saw the smile, a bit bashful as always and yet dazzling, her head tilted slightly to the right, which was her custom when she spoke to anyone, a kind of entreaty to be heard.

The crowd settled back in their chairs again. Sebastian continued to watch her. She wore a blue blazer with gold buttons and a white scarf with red polka dots at her neck. He had caught a glimpse of her white cotton skirt when she was standing. She looked thinner but still regal.

"So my good friends," Julian concluded, "I will remember this day with all of you . . . I hope you will." There was light laughter from the crowd. "And I do hope I have left something behind, dear me, that gives you reason to hope, or at least to laugh about, in the years ahead. Do no violence to my gravestone, that is all I ask."

The crowd stood and applauded. Julian remained there, bent in the shoulders, indicating humility or perhaps sadness. Then the emcee lifted his hands for quiet and the gifts were presented. A vice admiral from the navy presented a blue baseball command cap with all the "scrambled egg" frosting on the visor and ADMIRAL printed across the top. Then came a blue windbreaker with gold letters on the back spelling FAIR DINKUM. When Julian lifted that for all to see, the crowd cheered even louder.

But the big salute came from the portly man with the flushed face and sprigs of gray on the smooth pavement of his bald head. His name was Sir Michael Springston, director of the Australian Scientific and Humanitarian Society. Opening a small, black velvet-covered box, he held it in his hands, looking down at it as he spoke.

"Dr. David Julian, on behalf of your distinguished colleagues and the international community dedicated to scientific and humanitarian efforts, I am honored and privileged to present to you this medal for your outstanding service to mankind, which officially installs you as an honorary member of this most distinct and select company of men and women known for their unique contributions to science and humanity. May God give you the years to continue to serve with such dignity and accomplishment as has characterized your years to this hour for the benefit of people everywhere."

Then the room filled with noise again as the silver medallion was taken from the box and hung around Julian's neck on a ribbon of Australian colors, red, white and blue. The applause continued as Julian turned toward the podium. Then he lifted his hands for silence. Slowly the noise level dropped and they all took their seats again. The man was obviously loved, Sebastian mused.

"Your Lordship, thank you for this honor which I shall revere always, as long as I have breath," Julian responded, his voice cracking. He seemed a bit embarrassed by the award, or else he was so moved that he found it difficult to speak. Then he took a deep breath and added, "I only hope I can live up to it." He paused, looking a bit uncertain, staring down at the medallion dangling on his chest.

"When will you be starting your voyage, sir?" one of the newsmen called out.

Julian lifted his hoary head and looked toward the man. "I intend to go when I feel it is time," he said simply but dogmatically.

"Do you have a date in mind, sir?"

"Soon . . ."

"A week? Two weeks?"

"When I am ready . . ."

"Have you added any new crew members?" the reporter persisted.

"No. Just my son, Ryan . . . and maybe one other, but I am not sure yet."

"Will you still go if it's only the two of you?" another reporter called out. "I mean, sir, can just the two of you make it?"

Julian looked intently toward the new voice as if the question were an insult. "I can only say what George Macdonald said years ago: 'Said the wind to the moon, I will blow you out!'"

The roof came in on that one. Sebastian turned to watch Barbara. She seemed so distant, removed, behind the veil of the adulation for Julian. And Sebastian felt he was intruding. He sensed a lot of security men moving around on either side of him. Instinct developed through years of tuning in on that kind of activity made him wary. He was not on good ground.

He continued to watch her as she talked with animation to others around her. Finally he moved through the doors back to the punch bowl, feeling out of sync altogether. He poured himself some of the liquid and drained it in one gulp. The security men were moving through the outer area now, with their bleeper phones squawking. It seemed that Dr. David Julian was high-priced property indeed.

The crowd filed out, and Sebastian didn't know if he should go back or not. Why did he feel so diffident, uncertain, in greeting her? Maybe he didn't want to see the question in her eyes as to what he was doing here. And what would he say if she asked?

It took twenty minutes for the crowd to disperse. He returned inside and stood with his back against the same wall. Photographers still kept their cameras going on Julian. There were a few knots of people standing around.

Julian was in the aisle now, his broad back to Sebastian, Barbara facing him and looking up into his face as he talked. She smiled at him, the whiteness of her teeth like the flash of sun on mountain snow. Sebastian could see her eyes over Julian's left shoulder . . . the same deep blue eyes slightly slanted with the long natural lashes. He had once kiddingly called them "your lovely caterpillar eyes," and she had laughed and called it "a bit corny, but I love it." When she smiled, those dovelike eyes widened in the way he knew so well, as if she sensed deep pleasure in the act. Her face seemed to light up with it, giving off a luminosity that was madonnalike.

Only about twenty-five feet separated her and Julian from Sebastian. He felt increasing pressure building in him to get her attention. Then her eyes dropped from Julian's face and flicked over his shoulder to lock on Sebastian. Her eyes held his for only a few seconds. In that eclipsed time he saw her eyes reflect recognition and a trace of puzzlement and uncertainty. Then she was concentrating on Julian's face, who was talking to her and another woman. Sebastian noted some distraction in her then, perhaps consciously aware of him standing there. She did not look at him again.

Sebastian felt exposed, as if he had crashed the wrong party. With a growing sinking feeling, he found an envelope and card, one side carrying the official invitation to the reception, the other side blank. He wrote:

MEET ME AT ARGYLE CENTER, ARGYLE AND PLAYFAIR, BEHIND THE OLD SYDNEY HOTEL. TONIGHT AT SEVEN. URGENT. OR CALL ME AT THE OLD SYDNEY AFTER EIGHT. SEBASTIAN.

He pondered whether to add "I love you," but he felt an inner prod against it. If she was into something here, that would only complicate things for her. The less he pushed her, the more likely she would consent to see him. He turned to a waiter standing nearby and handed him the envelope and an Australian five-note. "To that blonde woman over there," he told the man, nodding toward her. "Very important . . ."

"Very good, sir," the waiter said and moved up the aisle between the folding chairs. He waited respectfully to enter the circle around Julian, and Sebastian was conscious of a security man watching the exchange.

The waiter finally gave up trying to get around Julian and simply pushed the envelope between two women, waving it at Barbara to get her attention. She reached over and took it without looking at Sebastian. She tucked it into her small, red purse and continued talking and smiling at those around her.

The curtain had dropped. Sebastian knew she wasn't going to acknowledge him here. He felt a bit of the fool in one way, as if he had pushed himself on her. What had he expected from her? That she would run into his arms? Still, why couldn't she have broken away even for a minute?

Something had to be in the wind here. She was either in tight on an assignment involving Julian and didn't want to risk widening her circle toward him; or else she had changed as Bentley had said. The lights in those eyes had gone out too fast when she had looked up at him.

He turned and walked out of the room to the elevators, feeling out of sorts. A walk would do him good. He began to make his way back to the hotel, up George Street, checking his back trail by crossing the street now and then and viewing people and activity through the shop window mirrors.

Nothing. His only hope was that she would make the effort to see him at Argyle Center.

At five to 7 he left the hotel and crossed the cobblestone courtyard of Argyle Center to the rear of Harry's Bar and the round tables and wooden benches. He sat at one and ordered a lime from the roving waitress. It was five after 7. She'd take her time, check it all out before approaching. The shopping crowd here was thinning out some. It was quiet, just the light tapping of high heels on the cobblestone. The sun was sliding off the opaque field of the western sky. But it still cast warm, soft saffron rays over the courtyard. The smell of cooking food, plus soft music mixed in with light laughter begged relaxation.

But he didn't relax. It was 7:20, and he was on his second lime. It tasted sour. At 7:30 he knew she was not coming. Or maybe she couldn't. Or maybe she had left a message for him at the hotel.

Finally he stood, crumpled the paper cup in his right hand, and tossed it into a trash bin. Some of the lime stuck to his hand, making him feel more gritty. Maybe she had "changed" toward him after all.

When he returned to the hotel lobby, he asked for any messages. There was one. His pulse quickened. But it was a yellow envelope. He knew it was a telex from overseas. He opened it and read:

> CREDENTIALS COMMITTEE HAS VOTED TO DENY YOUR ORDINATION AND DECLARE YOU NO LONGER IN THE MINISTRY WITH THIS DENOMINATION. OUR PRAYERS ARE WITH YOU.
>
> BACKSTROM

Sebastian slowly folded the message and put it into his shirt pocket. They had gotten the hotel and telex information from Agnes undoubtedly. So much for that. He tried to ignore the sag inside him as he walked to the elevators. The hammer blows kept coming, breaking up vital parts of his mind and soul. A plane home would be in order. He felt no constraint to stay anymore. He had come to ask her one question, the biggest of his life. He hadn't gotten within ten feet of her.

"Ludicrous," he said out loud in the elevator. He was still mumbling it when he entered his room. The phone was ringing, jabbing him, mocking him. He picked up the phone. "Yes?"

"Ah, Mr. Sebastian, sir!" Jamison's voice crowed on the other end. "Did you have a good day, sir?"

Sebastian didn't feel like talking to Jamison right then. But he owed the man something for arranging the invitation to Julian's reception. "Not one I'd remember long," he said, trying not to sound morose. "How was yours?"

"A bit of a bore, sir . . . government tripe and all that. Did you get to talk to Dr. Julian? And did you get to see your Miss Churchill?"

Sebastian sighed. "I did not get to talk to Julian . . . and I didn't get to talk to her either."

There was a pause as Jamison turned that over. "Oh, I'm sorry, sir. I heard it was quite a bash, lots of people." He paused, then added, "Well, you know, sir, your lady is probably staying with Julian. Any friend of his who comes to town stays there with him . . . He insists."

"Meaning what, Jamison?"

"Well, sir, you can always give him a ring . . . ask to join his crew or something like that. You'd at least maybe bump into her there, sir, you never know. . . ."

"Jamison, I don't even know where Julian lives," Sebastian replied. "And I doubt he'd consider me a fit candidate to sail with him anyway."

"You never sailed then, sir?"

"Oh . . . some, yes, a long time ago . . . but—"

"Well, sir, old Julian might lower the gate a bit now . . . We just got word his son, Ryan, did something to his knee playing tennis today . . . Don't know how bad yet . . . But it may be the good doctor will need another hand badly. . . ."

Sebastian weighed it. "Jamison, if you're trying to patch up a romance—"

Jamison broke in with a laugh. "No, sir, not me! But Julian lives at 110 Acacia Drive up on the north heads overlooking the harbor, if you are interested. . . ."

"Jamison, you said you wanted to sail with Julian as well," Sebastian said. "If Julian is dropping the gate, why don't you try it—"

"Ah, sir, I tried five times . . . All he did was give me that sailing quiz . . . fifty questions . . . You have to answer 50 percent even to get to see him . . . or be considered . . . I don't think I got 10 percent. Mind you, I'd try it again if I thought I'd have a chance . . . I'd give my liver to cover the good doctor on his last trip home to Plymouth . . . now that I hear he won that big award from the Humanitarian Society and all . . . But, well, Mr. Sebastian, some of us are born to stand and wait . . . I wish you the best, sir . . . But if I were you, sir, if you want to see your Miss Churchill, I'd try Julian's place . . . You never know . . . If I can do anything for you, let me know. . . ."

"Well, Jamison, even Julian doesn't know when he's going to sail," Sebastian said. "He may wait now until Ryan heals from whatever happened to his knee—"

"I don't think so . . . He provisioned the boat at Birkin Head a week ago. I don't think he'll let *Pequod* sit much longer with all that aboard. No, sir, Mr. Sebastian, it's my hunch the good doctor is ready to shove off . . . And all the boats are crowding the main harbor now getting ready to run the International Yacht Race to

Hobart Christmas Day . . . I don't think Julian would want to hang around trying to get through that traffic out to sea. . . ."

"I appreciate all of that, Jamison," Sebastian said, writing down the Acacia address on a white pad by the phone. "I'll give Julian a try . . . maybe. I rather imagine he'll send me a quiz too. . . ."

"Never know, sir . . . Worth giving it a whack anyway."

"Thanks for getting me into the Sheraton today, Jamison. That was kind of you."

"I had a hunch you'd try for it. I'm glad your lady is with him anyway. Give me a call if I can help on anything. Good night, sir."

"Good night, Jamison." Sebastian hung up the phone and stood staring at it a long time, then at the Acacia address. He wondered why Jamison could not get to see Julian about sailing with him, especially after all those news stories Jamison had done on Julian's daughter. But, of course, Julian was picky about the crew he selected.

Sebastian paced the floor, thinking. He sensed this would be his last chance to try to see her. He had a hunch she would be sailing with Julian. He had mentioned in his speech at the hotel that he had "possibly one other" crew member, besides his son, Ryan. Knowing Barbara—though not aware of how much she had sailed in the past—she'd get on that boat with Julian for whatever reason Interpol had given her.

He paused, staring at the phone again. If Jamison was right that Ryan was hobbled with a bad knee, forcing Julian to get somebody in a hurry, then why not himself? He had sailed when he was younger, too far back maybe, but he still remembered a good bit of it. And if Julian had provisioned the boat, as Jamison had said, then Julian had to find someone quickly.

Sebastian knew he was making some wild surmises, but it was his only hope now. Barbara, of course, could be a help or a hindrance, depending on how much she wanted him out of it. If that experience at the hotel indicated anything, she didn't want him in.

Finally he went to the phone. He took out the yellow telex from his shirt pocket, read it once more, then tucked it into his wallet. Something to remember in the long days ahead. Then he got the operator on the line and asked for Julian's number on Acacia Drive. A pause. "That number does not go directly to Dr. Julian, sir . . . it goes to security. You still want me to ring it?"

That could be sticky. Well, there were no long shots with God.

"Go ahead, operator," he said then. The phone rang three times. A male voice came on the line, crisp but polite: "Dr. David Julian's residence."

Sebastian took in a shaky sigh. It was go for it all now or return home.

Five

Captain First Rank Ilyus Aviloff was finishing up his personal diary entries in his cabin on the Soviet trawler *Minsk* when a knock sounded on his door. "Come," he said. The door opened and his communications officer, Captain Lieutenant Ovar Gorski, entered. Gorski walked stiffly to the small desk at which the captain sat and stopped a discreet four feet away. As the captain closed his diary, it snapped shut, automatically locking. He put it into his top drawer.

Then he faced Gorski, who stretched out his hand with the yellow code paper in it. Gorski was not more than twenty-four years of age and was very aware of protocol. The Naval Institute at Leningrad had instilled that in him very well. As for himself, Captain Aviloff preferred a much less rigid relationship with his officers. He had seen enough of war in the old days when officers and crew became as one in the commonality of blood and pain. And Aviloff was tired of all the pomp that went with the Annual May Day, boot-thumping, strutting puppets of the military parades, a poor charade for what it all portended of war. Besides, the heavy discipline and aloofness of command only made him more lonely.

"What is it, Gorski?" he asked, pushing aside official papers on his desk. He always asked his officers to express themselves first, to loosen them up. Gorski remained stiffly at attention, refusing the offer. He had blue eyes, a straight nose, and a thin mouth that he kept firmly in a straight line, making it look like a pen scratch on his face. It was as if Gorski was afraid to relax that line lest all his teeth fall out.

"Change of orders, comrade captain," the officer finally answered as Aviloff waited. The words came out almost garbled through his tight jaws.

Aviloff reached out and took the yellow paper from Gorski, sighed, opened it, and read:

PROCEED ACCORDING TO CODE DRAW STRING. AT 0400 HOURS DECEMBER 4. EXCHANGE GIFTS DECEMBER 17. CONFIRM. ADDITION PICK UP CLAY BIRD SW COAST AUSTRALIA. EXACT RENDEZVOUS POSITION FOLLOWS.

THE ADMIRALTY—KARKOV

Aviloff grunted. Of all the Russian trawlers moving through the South Pacific, they had to choose his. "Very well, Comrade Gorski," he said shortly. "Inform Captain Second Rank Popov to come to my quarters."

"Aye, sir."

Gorski turned and walked out as stiffly as he had entered. Like those May Day puppets, Aviloff mused. Children. All of them yet children. Never knew a war. Never knew suffering. Just the glory of *Rodina*—The Motherland. And the stiffness of uniforms and protocol. Aviloff knew then that he was getting old. There was a time when he was the same, a long time ago. In 1942 maybe. When he was an officer serving the Russian fleet in the Baltic trying to get British and American convoys through to Murmansk. He was a coding officer then on a corvette, proud of his uniform, proud of his heritage, a family of seagoing captains and admirals. Lenin and Stalin dominated his mind, burned his heart. Until the first torpedo hit the corvette; after that, the Party was the last thing in his mind. Life, only life, the fight to live and breathe, was all he cared about now. Gorski would learn about reality sooner or later.

Another knock and Popov opened the door and stood waiting. "Come in, Popov," Aviloff said. Popov was a tall, thin man in his early forties. His straight, dark hair had shafts of gray over his small, brown eyes, slightly slanted and showing he had Mongolian in him. His face was stoic, narrow, with pouting lips as if he pondered too much of life all the time. Sometimes Aviloff sensed a bit of sadness in that pout, although Popov was good at protecting himself from that with a veneer of neutrality maintaining his show of allegiance to naval protocol and the long, empty tunnel of Soviet life and service.

"Sit down, comrade," Aviloff said. Popov obeyed and slowly sat in the chair next to the desk. Aviloff rose and went to the wall safe, opened it, and withdrew the two sealed envelopes inside. He brought them back to the desk and dropped them on the metal top. "Sealed orders holding Draw String, Popov," Aviloff said. He sat down and pushed one of the duplicate envelopes toward Popov. It was necessary that two officers read the same orders so that there could be no contradiction or attempt to ignore them.

Popov looked at the envelope as if it were a summons, studying it. "Draw String?" he asked curiously as Aviloff slit open his envelope.

"Yes, comrade," Aviloff said, taking out the single sheet of instructions for himself. "Read it . . . Let us see what glorious adventure lies before us." Aviloff sensed the bite in his voice, but Popov did not seem to notice.

Popov finally picked up the second envelope, slit it open, and took out the sheet with the crisp, black letters on it, like letters chiseled on gravestones. They both read in silence the new course, the instructions as to the "exchange of gifts." Aviloff reached over and picked up the phone on the wall, pressed a red button.

"Comrade navigator," he said shortly, "what is your position and course?"

"We are one hundred and fifty miles northwest of the western coast of Australia, comrade captain," the voice came back crisply. "We are proceeding at one-one-zero degrees at twelve knots, sir. . . ."

Aviloff glanced at his watch. Four hours to change course. "You will leave word for the captain of the watch coming on at zero-four-hundred hours," he said into the phone. "New course and speed will be delivered to you by Comrade Popov."

"Aye, sir."

Aviloff hung up and turned toward Popov, who had a small frown growing between his eyes. He stroked his full lower lip with the edge of his right thumb, as if he were testing the fine edge of a blade, all the time staring at the message.

"Come on, Popov," Aviloff said, rising. "Let us see how it looks on the chart."

Aviloff walked over to the chart table ten feet away and began plotting the new course. Popov continued to sit in the chair, then finally folded the sheet of orders and put it back onto the desk. He would not be allowed to carry the message outside the captain's cabin. He got up slowly, looking uncertain, and joined Aviloff.

The captain turned on the light over the table, revealing the map of the Indian Ocean, Australia, and the islands of the South Pacific, up through the Solomons to Guam and then to Adak, Alaska. He studied the orders in his hand and used the calipers to plot the new course on the chart. The line of their intended assignment originated at Murmansk and went down through the Baltic, to the South Atlantic, around Africa and into the Indian Ocean, and on up to Guam. Once there, they were to monitor the naval maneuvers of the U.S. Sixth Fleet and SEATO forces. The *Minsk* was fully equipped to carry out highly sensitive radar and other electronic surveillance. She was one hundred and thirty feet long, driven by two high-powered diesel engines. Below the main deck were two other levels. Level Two was loaded with the typical fishing paraphernalia and supplies that provided the facade that all Russian trawlers utilized to look legitimate. Level Three, from bow to stern, was an electronics laboratory manned by forty specialized crewmen whose training was in electronics and tracking surveillance, along with code breaking. They had enough wizardry in their detection equipment to track any submarine two thousand feet down and one hundred miles distance in any direction.

But the new course line that Aviloff traced on the chart took them sixty degrees around to the south, skirting the western Australian coast and the Tasmanian Sea and out into the Southern Ocean toward Cape Horn.

"So," Aviloff said with a sigh, dropping the calipers back on the chart, studying the new line he had made. "Some good weather there . . . some bad . . . Such is our life, hey, Popov?"

"What exchange, comrade captain?" Popov asked, still studying the new course, the pout continuing to tug at his lips.

Aviloff shrugged. "We will be notified as we close to our contact point . . . about here," and he moved his caliper point to a spot down the line of the South Pacific into the extreme Southern Ocean. "On December 17 we make that contact . . . By then we will be notified of any course changes that will bring us into direct positioning with the target as well as its nomenclature . . . What we exchange is not ours to ask yet, Popov . . . But at least we know we must make a pickup of someone or something at that time. . . ."

Aviloff glanced at Popov. His second in command should know how it worked in these operations. But he seemed more preoccupied now. The two of them had been sailing together for more than a year on the *Minsk*. Popov was a good executive officer. As a boy, he had lived in the Urals. His father was high in the Party for years, especially during the Bulganin period. So Popov had enjoyed the best education, the best naval training, the best promotional possibilities. But Aviloff had noted the signs of weariness growing in Popov for some time now, the dragging uncertainties that often plagued himself as well. Aviloff was fairly convinced that Popov wanted to defect and could be planning to do so. The best time and place would be when the *Minsk* moved into waters off Guam, where the United States and SEATO naval forces would be carrying out their maneuvers within a week. A defecting Russian crewman from a trawler would be highly prized by the Americans, who wanted to prove the secret surveillance operations aboard Russian trawlers. Guam was Popov's best chance, the only logical place to make a jump. After that, the *Minsk* would not be close enough to American or other Western waters with circumstances equally advantageous for a defection.

Aviloff had been reminded of Popov's possible intentions by Captain Second Rank Ovar Romonovich, the arrogant political officer on board. His job was to present such incidents and remind the crew daily of their loyalty to *Rodina*. Romonovich had possessed the nasty style of creating suspicion about every crew member—even the captain himself. To him, everyone had a streak of treason. His hints about Popov's "introspective demeanor" as constituting growing disloyalty irritated Aviloff—even though Aviloff knew it to be somewhat true, but for good reasons.

Popov had showed signs of it more than a month ago at sea when he finally confided to Aviloff. He said then that he had left behind a dying wife in Moscow and that the naval commander in Leningrad had denied his request for shore leave to take care of her. A five-year-old son and a twelve-year-old daughter were also left to take care of themselves and his helpless wife. Popov might have taken that much easier except that his father had been punished for "disloyalty to the Party" a year ago because he had gotten mixed up in the Sakharov case. Sympathy for any dissident in Russia drew severe penalties, even prison. It was only a matter of time, Popov had confided, until his father would be banished to Siberia.

But now with the *Minsk* ordered south, the chances of Popov defecting in Guam were nil. Aviloff could see the disappointment in his face, though most of the time the officer was good at guarding his feelings. Pouting and frowning had been Popov's demeanor since he had joined Aviloff on the *Minsk*.

"This Draw String, comrade captain," Popov asked then, his

eyes frowning at the chart, following the line that would take him farther and farther away from his hopes, "is this not connected with the Code Name OPAL satellite project?"

"It is," Aviloff replied, turning from the chart to head back to his desk. "We have OPAL up in orbit, comrade . . . The biggest satellite ever with laser defense against any American missile attack from the ground. We have taken the Star Wars initiative from the West, comrade!"

Aviloff made it sound like a trumpet blast of victory to pick up Popov's spirits. Romonovich had a sharp eye for signs of depression or rebellion in any of the crew. Popov's moroseness was beginning to show even more.

Aviloff reached for the coffeepot sitting on the electric plate on the side table, brought out two cups from the cupboard beneath, and poured. He handed one cup to Popov.

Popov ignored the coffee and put his cup on the desk. "Comrade captain, why do we pursue Draw String," he asked, "if we have OPAL in position?" His voice carried the tone of a child asking a question about the stars.

Aviloff shrugged, sipping his coffee. "A part is missing perhaps in the finalizing of it. Somewhere out there in the Southern Ocean ahead of us is that part. On December 17 we will know who that is. If the weather does not delay us. How's that for posterity, Popov? You and I and the *Minsk* finally get to be a part of the force in changing the history of the world! Your coffee is getting cold, comrade!"

Popov did not appear to be enthusiastic about the amenities with Aviloff. But he dutifully picked up his cup and sipped it, frowning into it. "The message also said something about picking up a Clay Bird? Who or what is that, if I may ask, comrade captain?"

Aviloff shook his head. "That is the business of the political officer on board, Popov. Undoubtedly an agent working in Australia needs to find a way home. Or maybe he has something to do with OPAL and the exchange. You can be sure Comrade Romonovich will give it to us in his usual lengthy details."

Popov nodded, took another sip of his coffee, and stood. "You will excuse me, comrade captain?" he said. "I must check with the engineering officer . . . We still have a growing malfunction in the starboard engine."

Aviloff nodded and watched him amble to the door, his legs seeming to drag with the weight of his disappointment in the change of events. He paused at the door and turned to wait for the captain's permission to exit. There was such a forlorn look on his face, as if he were ready to buckle or break down and cry. "I will await your report, comrade," Aviloff said quietly. Popov nodded and slowly went out.

Aviloff continued to sit in his chair, staring into his coffee cup. He glanced at the picture of his wife and two sons on the desk to his left. How many nights had he and Soya whispered to each other about their dreams of one day being in the West? Five years of nights perhaps? *Rodina* had turned sour for both of them. So Aviloff knew what Popov was going through.

Ever since Soya had gotten that Bible from that crazy pastor in Gorky Park . . . the day he had stuck it in her grocery bag and moved off quickly. Since then something had altered within Aviloff, but he could not properly identify it, or even discern if it was really an alteration. He had scolded her for allowing herself to be so unobserving of the "bourgeois" people in Moscow, told her it would be found out sooner or later and that she better turn it in to the police. Once they found out she had kept it, what then? His command, and their sons' futures, would go up in smoke. But as much as she promised she would turn it in, she took to reading it out of curiosity. And as she read it, it seemed that the hard lines in her face softened, those lines etched in every Russian face, of never being certain of life or hope. The scars of worry under her eyes as she pondered the future of their two sons, both in naval commands, seemed to melt away.

Some nights in bed in the dim candlelight she read passages to him, whispering them, which was the habit of all Russians when they discussed anything that was contraband. No one in the military, as Aviloff was, could ever be sure that every room of his modest apartment was not bugged by the KGB. He listened to the words with detachment, finding no connection in them with his own life as a committed member of the Soviet military. But in moments he felt that the words had a certain lyrical sound to them, sometimes feeling like a spring wind, thawing the ice of his disciplined military self and the unquestioning loyalty to *Rodina*.

But there was nothing there to force any belief in him toward what was said. He sensed no command that would dilute his own

Marxist/Leninist philosophy about life and man. He gave Soya polite attention, but when she finished he warned her that the Book should be turned in. But then it was too late. Six months after she had come into possession of the Book, the GMU became more evident around them, always behind them wherever they went.

Still, it did not deter Soya's reading. There was terror in her eyes at times when she thought of what they could do to them, to him, to their sons. But that peculiar peace always came back to dissolve the fear.

But the GMU did their work relentlessly. Aviloff had commanded the nuclear submarine *Orion* out of Murmansk three years ago. He had been up for the flotilla command and a vice admiral's promotion. Instead, he was transferred to commanding a frigate on routine patrols in the Atlantic. Then came the move to the trawler *Minsk*. The message was quite clear: he was no longer considered for command in the future of the Russian navy. Trawler duty was the last step before oblivion. But his love for Soya and the boys prevented him from making any protests or deviating in any way from appearances of loyalty to *Rodina*.

Now he took out his diary again from his desk drawer and unlocked the clasp. He read over the passages he had written in the last six months at sea on the *Minsk*. He had written about how he missed Soya and their two sons. And how anxious he was to be home with them again. In one entry, one he thought he would never write, he said, "I miss the Book. . . ." Then he thought of Popov again. There was no hope for his first officer back in Russia. Popov thought only of a new life in the West.

But as for himself, Aviloff knew he had to go home. All he had was there. Yet, he could not fault Popov either. There was something in his friend that reflected too much of the emptiness, the cruelty of *Rodina*. Still, it could not be for him. He was fifty-six years of age. Too old to make sudden changes, even if he wanted to. All he could do was write his feelings in the log and hopefully, soon, share them with Soya back in Russia.

There was a knock on the door again. He locked the diary and shoved it into the drawer. "Come," he said. Popov stepped inside.

"Comrade captain, I am sorry to bother you, but we do have a problem in the starboard propeller shaft. Or it could be one of the propellers itself . . . out of line perhaps. We should lay over somewhere and repair it."

Aviloff looked at the Draw String orders on his desk. He had no time to spare in making the rendezvous. He had the exact course, longitude and latitude, for making the contact. His watch showed it to be close to 0100 hours in the morning. He would need all the speed he could get to make the rendezvous area as ordered.

"After the seventeenth, Popov, when our so-called exchange is made, we will heave-to at sea and take care of it." Popov nodded obediently, but he seemed a bit troubled by the decision. "What is the weather like out there, comrade?"

Popov shrugged. "Good, comrade captain. A full moon, calm sea, balmy breeze . . . Very good."

Aviloff sighed and stood up. "Well, then, comrade, let us drink a little of it while we have it, yes?" and he walked toward the door that led out to the aft quarter deck. Popov followed him obediently. They stepped out and stood to the rail, looking beyond the camouflaged three-inch gun and the cargo winch to the boiling wake of the ship that showed a brilliant fluorescence. The white froth churned out from the twin propellers to be captured by the silver wash of the moon until it disappeared, all too quickly, to settle with the mastery of the sea.

"In all my years of sailing, Popov," Aviloff said, watching the wake, "I have never left a trail I could ever pick up again or even remember. All the years of plowing the sea-lanes around the world, only a brief wake left behind that vanishes quickly never to be recalled again. No footprints in the sand, no fingermarks on stone, no evidence of our ever having been here. Even existing for this brief moment of time. Sometimes I think it is the greatest sadness a man can experience. The sea, Popov . . . leaving no history to retrace and wonder about. . . ." He turned to glance at Popov. Popov looked back; his eyes remained neutral in the bright moonlight. Whether he understood that his captain was trying to tell him he did not suffer alone in his private doubts, it did not show.

"I must see to the watch, comrade captain," he said.

Aviloff nodded, turning his eyes back to the boiling wake. "Good night, Popov."

He heard the door open behind him and Popov was gone. But Aviloff continued to stand at the rail, watching the wake as it swirled on out to emptiness. Maybe God kept track? Soya would say so. But he didn't know . . . and maybe he did not believe anyway.

President Jeremiah Fairfield met with five advisers in the Oval Office after the Cabinet meeting had adjourned. He took his time as he sat down behind the big desk, as was his custom when a crisis was brewing. He reached for a walnut from the wooden bowl near his left elbow, picked up a gleaming aluminum nutcracker, and squeezed. The crunch of the shell snapping was like a gunshot.

"Well, gentlemen," he began in a lazy tone of voice as if the nuts were all that mattered, "help yourself."

All of them demurred with a polite "No, thank you, Mr. President." Fairfield popped half of the shelled nut into his mouth and chewed slowly, his eyes studying the other half as though it had an amazing structure. He was nearly sixty years of age, carrying a six-foot-two frame that was all muscle from working out in the White House exercise room. "So," he went on, chewing the last of the walnut and leaning back in his chair to look at each of them, his hands locked behind his head, his soft gray-blue eyes widening some and taking on the sheen of marbles, "so do we or do we not have a Russian killer satellite upstairs with the capability of putting a gun to our heads?"

Each waited for someone else to respond. Finally Mark Townshend, head of the CIA, forty-three years old, wearing gold-rimmed glasses and sporting a short haircut he had carried over from his military officer days with the army, cleared his throat and said, "I have pictures that our photo recon satellite ALAMO got, Mr. President. . . ."

Townshend walked over to the desk and spread out five large black-and-white photos in front of Fairfield. The president adjusted his silver-rimmed glasses and peered at the photos, reaching for another walnut in the bowl.

"Monster, all right," he said simply.

"Almost two city blocks long, Mr. President," Bill Connors, Secretary of Defense, put in with his usual blunt manner. He was fifty-eight years old, recruited by Fairfield after his retirement from the presidency of General Engineering and Electronics. His company once designed more than half of the sophisticated armaments for the U.S. military. He was a retired Marine Corps general better known as "Wild Bill" in the Pentagon. Mild-mannered on the surface, he carried a drill instructor's ability to make a point that nobody missed or forgot.

"What are those things on the sides?"

"Rocket pods, Mr. President," Townshend said and reached over to use the blunt end of his fountain pen to tap the shape of them in the pictures.

"Reentry nuclear missile shelters, Mr. President," Connors added to be precise, his voice going to a gravel-sound indicating that he was steaming inside.

"So Pine Gap was right then," Fairfield replied, squeezing the nutcracker vice on the walnut shell in his hand. "So why were we all taken by surprise? How could we have sat in those summit meetings and not known that all the time the Russians were squawking about our SDI program they had a killer in the oven ready to go? How about that, Mark?"

Townshend backed away from the desk and sat down, adjusting his glasses nervously. "Our agent ROBIN HOOD could not get into the Murmansk complex itself, Mr. President," he answered after clearing his throat. "He knew something big was going on at the satellite construction site over the past two years . . . but his contacts would not talk or could not. The Russians were building a half mile or more underground anyway . . . Security was heavy."

The walnut shell popped in the jaws of the nutcracker, tearing the silence in the room.

"All right," Fairfield conceded, peeling the shell off the nut, "just how much of a threat is that thing up there?"

"It means we have no first-strike capability, Mr. President," Willard Banes, Secretary of State, put in with a dour note in his voice. Banes was a portly fifty-six, soft-spoken and diplomatic, as his role demanded. Banes knew how to bargain with the Russians and talk them down out of any escalation in arms buildup—at least on the surface. But he had not been able to counter Kamiloff's smooth talk and his public relations image as a man of peace. Now that the Russians had pulled off the big one, Banes was feeling particularly betrayed, his face taking on a pink hue that testified to a smoldering anger inside.

"So what about the retaliatory strikes we have in the bag?" Fairfield pursued, chewing slowly.

"That satellite is putting out heavy laser beams in the atmosphere, a sophisticated kind, scrambling our navigational systems in our missiles," Connors intoned again.

"How do you know that?" Vice President George Casey interjected, speaking for the first time. Casey sat somewhat apart from the others, as if all this was really not his area; his specialty was purely politics and government and a penchant for kissing babies. He was a tall, slim man wearing black horned-rims over smiling, innocent blue eyes. He was just turning fifty years of age and looked like a university professor. But his power to sway crowds had no peer. He was hoping to get the nod for president in the next election when Fairfield stepped down, a year away.

Connors glanced at him, his eyes dismissing the question as irrelevant coming from Casey, but he condescended for the president's sake. "We've been having blackouts in our launch drills the past two weeks, George. Power failures that nobody can trace. NORAD already reported inability to complete practice launch sequences to countdown. The atmosphere interference began just about the time that Russian satellite parked in orbit up there. . . ."

"Well, then, that also means they've cut not only our first strike but our retaliatory options," Casey replied in alarm, his blue eyes widening behind the horned-rims. "They can pull the shades down on the United States and on the whole Western Alliance, the entire Western world—"

"The point is, why don't they make their move?" Fairfield demanded. "That thing was reported up there on November 24 from Pine Gap in Australia . . . What are they waiting for?"

"Mr. President," Mark Townshend said, hesitating some as if he knew he were walking in a verbal minefield, "ROBIN HOOD, our special agent assigned to monitor Russian satellite programs in Murmansk, sent his last message four days ago that OPAL lacks complete guidance systems to launch those nuclear warheads to specific targets on earth."

"Can't the crew of that satellite launch from up there?" Fairfield asked.

Connors took over. "Mr. President, they don't have the sophisticated program guidance for reentry missiles from a satellite any more than we do in our space program. Like us, ground has to punch in the data properly to that satellite . . . All the crew does is hit the red button to fire on countdown."

"So why did they put up the satellite then?" Casey kept prodding as if his future life in politics was on the line.

"To get the jump on our UNIVERSE ONE, what else?" Connors retaliated impatiently. "They know we've got a big one of our own in the barn as part of our Strategic Defense Initiative. Anyway, they must be sure of completing ground guidance control before we can launch UNIVERSE. They want to hang that thing up there and dictate terms . . . maybe get us on our knees without firing a shot. They think we don't know they've got incomplete ground guidance control . . . It cost ROBIN HOOD his life to get that information over to us. . . ."

Fairfield studied Connors a long time, weighing the implications of the statement. He fondled the nutcracker in his right hand as if debating whether or not to try another walnut. "So why haven't they announced to the world that they have put OPAL up? Usually they are on the air two minutes after blast-off . . . Here we are, almost two weeks later. The *Post* and the *New York Times* have already hinted at a major Russian launch . . . Every tracking station around the world is buzzing about it. But nobody has any confirmation from Moscow. I've got Kamiloff coming here on December 18 for a goodwill mission to cement the work at the last two summits. Are you gentlemen making any assumptions that he's coming here to give us terms of surrender?"

They all caught the expression in Fairfield's voice, a tone of disbelief, some anger. No one said anything, each looking at the floor or their yellow legal pads in their laps.

"They'll hold the announcement of OPAL's launch until they are sure they have ground guidance operative, Mr. President," Willard Banes offered, sounding dogmatic, folding his arms across his chest in a pose of finality. "They want to be sure they can deliver those missiles from up there before laying it on us . . . If they announce the launch now and claim military dominance by virtue of reentry missiles and we call their bluff . . . well, they lose face . . . And more than that, we get the time to send something up there even if it's a paper tiger, which they won't know . . . And they're not sure how fast we can get UNIVERSE up and going either . . . They'll play it safe . . . Maybe an announcement of a new communications satellite, nothing more . . . I expect that will come soon."

"Maybe we should call Kamiloff," Casey said, his voice carrying tones of alarm.

Fairfield took off his glasses and rubbed his eyes with the heels of both hands. He sniffed loudly as if there were a bad odor in the room. Then he put on his glasses again. Two red spots the size of dimes began to show up on the skin under both eyes.

"Not yet, George . . . Anyway, what would I tell him? That he violated the peaceful use of outer space? We've been playing around with that a little ourselves, as you well know . . . No, let them think we don't know . . . See if we can buy some time for ourselves, if we have any. . . ."

"Well, excuse me, Mr. President," Casey insisted, "but if they can scramble our missile navigational guidance systems and neutralize our retaliatory ability, they've got us anyway."

"They don't know that yet, George," Connors said petulantly. "They're experimenting with those laser atmosphere scramblers. As long as we keep the lid on and don't let it out that we have a problem, they won't know. . . ."

"Someone is bound to leak it." Yancey Yarborough, National Security Adviser, spoke for the first time. He was fifty-nine years of age, had flour-white hair, a square jaw, and small, narrow eyes void of humor. He had sat through all of the exchange saying nothing, but he looked now as though he had been slapped in the face. "A major glitch like this in our missile capability won't stay buttoned up for long . . . The press is sniffing around already. Sooner or later, probably any time now, they're going to know the Russians have a big one up there . . . And they will dig until they find out that our nuclear striking power has been neutralized. . . ."

"So then," Fairfield said after a ponderous sigh, "the big issue now is, how much time will it take to get UNIVERSE ONE up there to neutralize OPAL?"

"It will take at least sixty days working around the clock, Mr. President," Connors replied, "and even then we don't know the power of their lasers against our offensive missiles. But their laser communication scramblers indicate they have enough—"

"Anyway sixty days is too long," Banes reminded them all impatiently, his cheeks more flushed now, his blue-gray eyes snapping in the heat of anger building in him. "The Russians have to be very close to completing their ground guidance system. They would not have launched OPAL otherwise."

"All right, then, we have to put everything on UNIVERSE ONE, gentlemen," Fairfield concluded, using a quick, swiping gesture to brush a piece of walnut shell off his desk. The "dimes" under his eyes were beginning to form into the size of quarters. "The only way to keep the Russians on their heels is to send something up there with the potential to neutralize OPAL or pose a retaliatory strike to their own country. So what will it take?"

"If we can get a counter-laser scrambler put together in a hurry, we can neutralize some of that laser jamming they're pouring down on us," Connors went on. "To launch UNIVERSE ONE we will need to be free of that interference. Once we have that, we still have to perfect our offensive laser power in UNIVERSE . . . We've only done a few tests on the ground. . . ."

"What's the problem then?" Fairfield kept pushing.

"In the software, Mr. President," Connors replied. "The last budget cut for satellite hardware put that on hold. To do the job, we have to program our guidance computers with the counter-guidance scrambler first to neutralize OPAL's laser power wave . . . And then we have to build another program to identify, track, and order the destruction of reentry nuclear missiles that OPAL will deliver. . . ."

"Thought we were well ahead on that," Fairfield said, his voice going testy. He was not interested in walnuts anymore.

"We lost our man heading guidance development to a nervous breakdown three weeks ago, Mr. President," Connors said. "Dr. Alan Parker . . . the best we had . . . We pushed him to the limit. . . ."

"Gentlemen, I need to know what is the key to getting it done in the shortest possible time . . . say, two weeks?"

Connors' face turned pale as he stared back at his commander-in-chief, whose eyes did not flinch. Townshend, sensing that Connors was cowed by that, offered, "The one man with the skill to program a counter-guidance scrambler and develop effective laser guidance defense capability for UNIVERSE ONE in a hurry is a man named Julian, Dr. David Julian . . . Sydney, Australia. . . ."

"He's aggressively nonalignment," Connors countered flatly. "Neither East nor West, American nor Russian, nor anyone in between. . . ."

"So when has that stopped us before?" Fairfield snapped. "Get him!"

"Bill is right, Mr. President," Townshend added. "His daughter was lost two years ago through what Julian claims was CIA meddling . . . She is or was a top electronics expert majoring in laser development for satellites . . . peaceful use in communications satellites mainly . . . twenty-nine years old . . . We think she has gone over to the Russians and given them the laser power they now have, but we can't prove that. She was radical and anti-American, anti-

West. Anyway, she disappeared, is now believed dead, but we have no verification of that. Julian thinks we did it to her, so he's in no mood to cooperate with us."

"If the man knows he's going to get dumped on by the Russians with a nuclear holocaust, he'll come around," Casey ventured again.

"He could care less," Townshend argued back. "We've tried cultivating him for two years now for our own satellite program. He's not buying. Anyway, we can't get near the man . . . Australian Security is heavy around him . . . And he can smell an agent a mile off . . . He blew the lid on a dozen of ours trying to get into his house as cooks, chambermaids, gardeners—"

"The Russians know about him?" Fairfield asked.

"No question about that, Mr. President."

"Which means," Yancey Yarborough put in, "they would be interested in keeping this Dr. Julian away from us . . . It would be a feather in their cap too, to get Julian for themselves, putting him out of our reach and gaining a top-notch satellite guidance man at the same time . . . For all we know, he's the man the Russians need to make OPAL work upstairs . . . So how do we get him over to us?"

"No way we know of right now, Yancey," Townshend said with a shrug.

"Maybe assassinate him before he gets to the Russians?" Casey asked, and he winced some as Fairfield shot a mean look at him.

"The Russians might try that to keep him from us," Townshend warned. "But you'd have a lot of people getting shot who have satellite communications in their heads."

"You're saying no way to get to him," Fairfield went on.

"I don't know right now, sir . . . I hear he's heading out to sea before long on a voyage back to Plymouth, England."

"Get somebody aboard with him," Fairfield demanded, the pink circles under his eyes spreading down his cheeks.

"We tried that a few times . . . The man is looking for additional crew . . . The few we tried to plant on him he smelled out. Americans don't go over at all with him . . . Australians don't do much better."

"Well, is there anyone around him now who might get to him?" Fairfield asked, sounding impatient.

"Well," Townshend went on, clearing his throat again in his

discomfort. "Interpol put one of their own on Julian a couple of weeks ago in Sydney . . . She's a friend of his through her father . . . She tried to pick up the trail of his daughter some time back . . . The old man appreciated it, so she's the only one who can get inside with him. . . ."

"Is that all we got?" Casey implored.

Townshend ignored him. "There is one other closing in, but I don't think he's going to make it . . . He's American . . . a clergyman," and Townshend hesitated, knowing how incredulous this was sounding, "a man named Sebastian . . . We have him on file . . . Been in the middle of some of our operations by accident . . . He and the Interpol agent, Churchill, have something romantic going . . . Our office reported him in Sydney a few days ago . . . We just got a call from our man there that this Sebastian went to a reception in honor of Julian's retirement . . . So the man is closing on either Julian or the woman. . . ."

"Who's anchoring the Interpol end?" Yarborough asked.

"Jacques Henri . . . Paris branch . . . good man. . . ."

Fairfield took his glasses off again as if they were a heavy veil and tossed them on the desk in front of him. "God help us," he said dismally, rubbing his eyes again. "The one man who can save the free world from going under the hammer and sickle is taking a cruise to England . . . and all the CIA can tell me is that two small fish, *maybe* two, are the only ones in the boat with him? And what is more incredible is that even if Julian knows the Russians are going to blackmail the free world with that thing up there, he won't lift a finger to stop it? I am suddenly too old for this job, gentlemen," he finished with a heavy note in his voice.

They all looked at him with alarm: Fairfield had never showed a point of vulnerability in all the time in office. Mark Townshend took to dabbing his sweaty forehead with a folded white handkerchief. The room had gone very still, only the loud ponderous ticking of the grandfather clock in the corner tapping out the editorial on the brevity of time.

"You want to let the Russian Embassy be aware that we know OPAL is up there, Mr. President?" Banes asked then, his voice almost hushed as if afraid to break the heavy silence.

"I don't think so, Willard," he said, staring down at his hands. "Let's keep them guessing as to what we know or don't know. If they announce the launch of a new communications satellite, we will know they are still in need of time. If they don't announce, it may be they are close enough to ground guidance to make the big news. Right, Mark?"

"I would think so, Mr. President . . . But they are unpredictable. . . ."

Fairfield grunted an affirmative to that. "All right, here's what we have to do in the meantime . . . Bill, I want a constant check on our missile capacity every hour on the hour . . . Notify NORAD and NATO command on highly classified code that we need to know the progress of this thing . . . Find somebody who can work on this scrambler . . . Check with this man at Interpol—"

"Jacques Henri," Townshend said.

"Yes, Henri . . . Mark, you follow up with that . . . Find out if this gal of his is on to anything, if she's on that boat . . . Find out if she's a heavy hitter . . . Check out this Sebastian fellow as well . . . I want to know from Henri if he thinks anything is coming through on Julian's daughter . . . I want any hunches he's got about what Julian's moves are right now . . . Tell him we've got a Condition Red that involves very sensitive satellite developments and that Julian is the key to it . . . All right?" Townshend nodded, jotting down the order on his legal pad.

"Now," Fairfield went on, still staring down at his clasped hands, squeezing them tightly together so that the tips of his fingers were turning red. "I am going to call a press conference for tomorrow morning at 10. Let's see how much the press knows about this . . . or any hunches. The *New York Times* is suspicious, yes . . . and these communication blackouts may have them bird-dogging even more. I imagine if other tracking stations have confirmed a major Russian launch, we'd better admit to that anyway . . . no more. And let's get our own UNIVERSE ONE up front . . . We are getting ready to launch . . . Let the Russians wonder about that. . . .

"But, Mark, the important thing is to get on top of Julian . . . Get the Prime Minister of Australia, Jonathan McCray, to track it down . . . No, maybe I better call him myself . . . We need to know when Julian is planning to launch out on his sail around the Horn . . . We can't lose track of him . . . Meanwhile, we will all meet in the Situation Room at 9 tomorrow morning. Jim Brandt will be in by then." Brandt was his Chief of Staff. "Bill, get General Hescott of the Joint Chiefs in with us . . . He might as well know what we have in front of us." He paused then and looked at each of them as if fixing their faces in his mind for future memory. "I just hope," he continued in a subdued tone of voice, "that this reverend in Sydney makes that boat and that he is a praying kind of reverend . . . But I hope he knows when to stop praying and start doing. On that, I'll say good-night if there are no other questions. . . ."

"Good night, Mr. President," they said in unison. They got up slowly and headed for the door.

"Mark?" Fairfield called out. Townshend turned back into the room. "What time is it in Sydney?"

Townshend glanced at his watch. "Well, Mr. President, it's almost 6 in the evening here. That puts them about 9 in the morning December 5."

"Fine, Mark, thanks." Fairfield turned and faced the grandfather clock. "I can't imagine what a clergyman is doing in all this," he added, speaking to the clock. "We need someone like Superman." He turned and looked at Townshend. "I advise you, Mark, to take your best girl out for dinner. Enjoy it while you can. . . ."

"Thank you, Mr. President," Townshend replied hesitantly, his face looking even more pale than in the meeting. "Good night then. . . ."

The door closed softly behind him. Jeremiah Fairfield turned from the clock and went back to his desk chair, sitting down heavily. Kennedy with his Bay of Pigs was a game of touch football compared to this. Lyndon Johnson's nightmare in Vietnam never had this weight on him. Nixon's Watergate was a flap in the wind, and Carter's Iran crisis was a bird song.

He sighed, feeling the constriction in his chest. He glanced at the color photos of his wife, Mildred, their married daughter, Susan, her two girls, both preschool, and her husband, Mel, then his son, Jack, teaching philosophy at Syracuse University.

It was time to have dinner with them all. So little time for togetherness now in the freedom they had known and taken for granted so long. A weight of sadness crept over him. Slowly, then, he slid out of his chair and down onto his knees, putting his forehead on the soft leather. It was the first time since boyhood, when his mother had stood over him, that he had prayed with such deliberation.

Now he found it wasn't at all hard to pray.

Six

Dr. David Julian's house was a large, two-story brownstone, overlooking the entry to Sydney Harbour. It reminded Sebastian of a medieval fortress with its two circular towers at either end of the roof and the tall, twin chimneys in between. It had to be one of the original buildings built on the site a hundred years ago or more. Sebastian could not see all the grounds, but he felt there must be a couple of acres at least. All was ablaze with flowers of every color, grass as green as chlorophyll and all carefully manicured. A high iron picket fence surrounded the place, much like Sebastian had seen at American Embassies around the world.

He paid the cab driver, got out, and walked to the main gate. Two security men confronted him there. "Identification, sir?" one of them asked.

Sebastian produced his driver's license. "I have an appointment with Dr. Julian at 10," he said.

The man nodded, walked to the phone box by the gate, and called. He returned and handed the identification to Sebastian. Then the man scanned Sebastian with a metal detector. He seemed to take a long time. "OK, sir, you may proceed up the drive to the door . . . You will be met there."

Sebastian walked up the circular drive to the door where he was met by a short, balding man in his mid-forties. He introduced himself as Frank Nagel, personal secretary to Dr. Julian. He ushered Sebastian inside and asked him to sit down at a desk. He handed Sebastian a single sheet of paper with fifty objective questions. "Underline the correct answer, Mr. Sebastian," Nagel said politely but indifferently. "Do not skip any, please . . . Also fill out the areas dealing with your occupation, age, nationality and so forth."

Sebastian turned to the quiz. A half hour later he had finished. He knew he had missed a lot of the questions, which included everything from types of sails, boats, and automatic steering, to how to handle a boat in various kinds of weather conditions. Sebastian gave the paper to Nagel, who took it to an office in back to grade it. He returned in five minutes and led Sebastian to Julian's study. Once inside, Nagel indicated the straight-backed leather chair in front of the large mahogany desk and then went out without a word.

Sebastian sat and looked around the room. It was at least twenty by twenty-five feet, decorated in dark mahogany with ivory accents. On the wall behind the desk were at least a dozen plaques of different sizes. The mantel on the large, brown stone fireplace had an assorted array of gold and silver trophies on it. The wall to Sebastian's right displayed a spread of framed photographs of sailing vessels, some blown up to tabloid size. The room carried all kinds of artifacts. From the beige rug to the dark leather cushioned couch and chairs, it described Julian as a man of accomplishment but with simple tastes.

Finally the door opened behind Sebastian and he stood, turning toward it. "Good morning, Mr. Sebastian," Julian said, walking with a quick step and his right hand extended. The smile was genuine enough, perhaps a bit turned on with the politeness that the occasion demanded. Sebastian took the bony hand in his. The grip was firm. Julian's eyes were dark blue-gray, almost the color of gun metal, showing a bit of a cloud and streaks of red, indicating that perhaps he did not sleep well. His face was as brown as his hands, showing cracks like clay baked too long in the heat. He was about as tall as Sebastian, six-three, lean and wiry in stature. The intensity Sebastian had noticed in him at the hotel was still with him, a coiled spring ready to pop . . . like a man who had been chasing the tattered ends of his life and is still unable to gather them all in. Yet, for a man of eighty years, he moved with the alacrity of a fifty-year-old, his full crop of white hair blown into tangles of frost grass. Barbara had entered the room right behind Julian, but Sebastian hardly dared to look at her.

Julian removed his hand from Sebastian's as he turned and said, "May I introduce Barbara Churchill? She will be accompanying my son and me on the voyage . . . Came along at the right time. We are like family . . . Go way back to Israel and her parents, in fact. . . ."

Julian walked to his desk. Sebastian reached out his hand to Barbara, finally looking into her eyes. There was some perplexity there, uncertainty again. Maybe even a little irritation. He was about to say, "We have met," but he caught that warning sign in her eyes. Apparently she had not told Julian about him, and obviously she wanted to keep it that way. For whatever reason. She was as lovely as ever, dressed in a light blue sailing sweater and white slacks, with a yellow scarf around her neck lighting up her golden hair and the pristine blue of her eyes. It was strange and painful for him simply to shake her hand, warm and soft but held aloof.

She said "Hello" in a neutral but proper voice and quickly removed her hand from his, almost in dismissal. She moved on to take the chair to the left of Julian's desk.

"Please sit down, Mr. Sebastian," Julian said, anxious to get on with it. He put on a pair of silver-rimmed reading glasses with the small lenses hanging over the tip of his nose as he read Sebastian's sailing quiz.

"You are not a strong sailing man, I take it, Mr. Sebastian?" he asked, pursing his thin lips either in disappointment or amusement.

"The terms are new to me now, sir," Sebastian offered. "But I sailed in the Mackinac Cup Race for two years . . . That was twelve years ago . . . From Chicago to the Straits of Mackinac up Lake Michigan . . . A four-day run given the right wind. . . ."

"Yes . . . I know of it," Julian said, not that impressed, still studying the form. "Did you skipper her?"

"No, sir . . . I decked mostly, took a time or two at the wheel. . . ."

"You win?"

"The first year we came in third out of thirty-six entries . . . Sprung a seam in the bilge and couldn't gain on it with the pumping . . . The next year we came in second."

"Hmmm . . . Racing a sloop is considerably different than sailing a ketch, as you may well know," Julian responded, his eyes looking at Sebastian over his glasses. "On the wall to your right are pictures of various types of sailing boats . . . Which one is a ketch?"

Sebastian glanced at the wall, his eyes running across and down the photos, his mind digging for recall. "That one to the far right . . . The larger one . . . two masts . . . mainmast for the main and genoa . . . It also carries a jib rig . . . The second mast aft of the dog house carries the mizzen. . . ."

Julian continued to study him like a professor listening to a recitation from a student. There was no way to tell if he was impressed with Sebastian's answer, or whether he was right or wrong.

"You get seasick easily?"

"Back then I never did, even in rough weather . . . and I don't think so now. . . ."

Sebastian flicked a glance at Barbara. She was intently examining the well-manicured fingernails on her left hand. The nails were a light pink that gave elegance to her long, tapered fingers. She kept herself as a spectator here, no more. That made him feel worse.

"Ocean sailing is quite different from Lake Michigan," Julian reminded him. "More unpredictable, more cranky. . . ." He paused, then added, "Well, you scored 55 percent correct here . . . just over the curve, Mr. Sebastian. Pass-fail as your American educators would call it." He looked up over his glasses to see Sebastian's reaction.

"Does that mean I qualify, sir?"

"Hmmm," Julian answered, frowning at the paper as if unsure. "What are you doing in Australia, may I ask?"

"Holiday, sir." Sebastian did not look at Barbara. She would know why he had come . . . probably. He sensed that she slowly lifted her head, and he felt her sidelong glance.

"I see here that you are a clergyman by profession."

"Correct, sir. . . ."

"What church do you hold to?"

"Interdenominational . . . but right now I do not command a pulpit."

"You are between parishes?"

"Something like that . . . more or less, sir."

Sebastian could tell the answer did not settle Julian's curiosity much. Sebastian glanced at Barbara. She was brushing lint off her slacks. She must surely be amused by that answer after all that she knew about him. "Between parishes" was not exactly what he was about.

"You know what it's like to sail around the Horn, Mr. Sebastian?" Julian went on, sounding more and more like a cross-examiner.

"I've heard it's rough. . . ."

"Good men, veteran sailors, have died trying . . . Are you prepared to do that?" There was a bit of challenge in his voice.

"If that is to be, I have no fear of it in God. . . ."

Julian's eyes continued to study him, computing the answer—or what else was he trying to find out?

"Mr. Sebastian," he said in a decisive, crisp tone, "I am not comfortable with a man of religion on my boat. I do not like or appreciate any of my crew trusting in Deity rather than in their own wits and courage. I do not hold to psalm-singing or Bible-reading when there are sails to be trimmed. Only one man I had respect for who knew religion . . . That was Miss Churchill's father who knew sailing as well as I do, if not better. He and I never did see eye-to-eye on God, but he was a practical man in his faith . . . I expect you are that . . . Besides, religion on any ship of sail is a bad omen . . . Do you understand, sir?"

It sounded now as if Julian might be turning him down on those grounds. "If I may add, Dr. Julian," Sebastian took it up quickly before Julian could make a final judgment of him, "your boat is called *The Pequod*, as I was told. That whaling ship of the same name out of Melville's novel *Moby Dick* could have used a little of God. The Devil rode the quarterdeck, sir, in the person of Captain Ahab . . . and the end was hell and destruction for all, as you well know. I do not question your beliefs in these matters, and I respect them . . . But I affirm my faith as practical, and I have proven it to be so. . . ." Sebastian wondered how Backstrom, Alnutt, and Winston would have taken that.

Julian blinked once in his steady scrutiny of Sebastian as if something had tripped in his brain. Then just a faint tug of a smile passed over his thin lips. "Well, some people who sailed with me called me a devil, I can testify to that well enough. But your practical faith will have to be proven to me, Mr. Sebastian. But for now, I will allow it as well enough said . . . What do you think, my dear?"

Sebastian looked at her, hoping for some help. She could certainly testify to what he had said. Her right eyebrow lifted in a familiar salute to the point made.

"Mr. Sebastian will have opportunity to prove it," she answered, "if, indeed, he does qualify." That didn't help. She went back to studying her nails. Sebastian felt the cold in his heart as the distance between them grew wider.

"I should add, Mr. Sebastian," Julian said, "that there was one other person I tolerated who held religion." Then, as his smile became wistful, he asked, "You would know the hymn 'Amazing Grace'?"

Sebastian looked for a hint of the sardonic in that ghostly smile. "I do, sir. . . ."

"The only other element of religion I allowed . . . my darling wife standing at the bedroom window as the sun rose over the harbor, and singing that song softly while I lay in bed watching her . . . She was Anglican . . . Did you know that John Newton who wrote that hymn was Anglican?" It seemed important to Julian.

"I am aware of that, Dr. Julian."

He seemed preoccupied with another time and place for a long moment of silence. Then his eyes returned to Sebastian and the moment was gone. "Well, then, Mr. Sebastian," he said briskly, pushing aside the sailing quiz in front of him, "so far Miss Churchill here and my son, Ryan, are the only crew I've got for this voyage. I don't have time to dilly-dally any longer. Ryan twisted his knee playing tennis yesterday . . . He can sail with us, but will be limited in hopping around the decks. No one else worth his salt has come forward to sail with me. I am a tough skipper, they say. Maybe so. Others just don't want to chance the Horn on a forty-five-footer. I respect them for that. Still others, the veterans, are spooked by the name *Pequod*. They have their right. And others want their five thousand Australian in advance, figuring I won't make Plymouth myself to authorize the payment. They may have a good point there too—maybe.

"In any case, I invite you to join us, Mr. Sebastian. I don't hold much for Yanks these days. You should know that too. But you seem to be a decent Yank at that. But I warn you that we are going to be awfully short of crew to ease the watches and tend the rigging . . . The margins of making it are not all that comfortable . . . We will be four months at least out there, if we get good trade winds . . . If we don't, longer . . . You understand?"

"I do," Sebastian answered. "May I make a suggestion, respectfully, sir . . . I realize the critical matter of an adequate crew . . . May I be so bold as to suggest another man who would very much like to join this voyage?"

"Yes." Julian frowned and looked uneasy.

"His name is Harry Jamison . . . a reporter with the *Morning Herald*. He was kind enough to arrange my stay here . . . He has applied to you before, several times, but was turned down—"

"Jamison?" Julian interrupted, frowning. "Would that be the bloke who did all those news features on my missing daughter? Yes, of course . . . I lost my daughter two years ago, Mr. Sebastian . . . Don't know where she is . . . Australian Security and your CIA and the MI-5 in Britain think she's dead. I don't think so . . . But it was this Jamison fellow who kept the story alive and put pressure on all the international security and espionage gang to keep looking for her. . . ." He paused as if his thoughts about his daughter had crowded everything else out of his mind. Then he continued, "I don't take passengers aboard for this voyage, Mr. Sebastian . . . Certainly not somebody to spend the time shooting pictures or whatever. . . ."

"You're a favorite son now, Dr. Julian," Sebastian insisted. "Jamison only wants the chance to give Australia a look at you on your sentimental journey home . . . to go into the archives, sir. . . ."

"Can he sail? Has he sailed?"

"I can't speak for him on that, sir. . . ."

"Do you know him besides your short time here in Sydney?"

"I met him in Hong Kong some time back when I was there." Sebastian looked at Barbara to see her reaction to the reference. "Spent several days with him . . . He's a good man. I expect Jamison will carry his weight aboard . . . But I leave that to you to determine. . . . "

"What do you think, my dear?" Julian asked.

Barbara glanced quickly at Sebastian as if she wanted to know more about Jamison. She said, "I think you better talk to him . . . We need another crew member, with Ryan not up to par . . . But . . ."

"Yes, yes, of course . . . I'll inform Nagel to call Jamison later today for a talk. Still, I won't have baggage aboard . . . He'll have to pull his weight."

"I understand, sir." But Sebastian hadn't the foggiest notion of just what Jamison could do aboard *except* shoot pictures. Still, he owed Jamison at least a chance at it for the favors he had done and the fact that Sebastian had promised him some kind of story in return.

"So we will check him out." There was a note of finality in Julian's voice now. "We sail at dawn tomorrow, Mr. Sebastian. Nobody knows that. Going to disappear from old Sydney in the morning fog. Saves all the hullabaloo about everybody and anybody with a surfboard escorting me out of the harbor . . . Rubbish!"

"What about security around the house, sir?" Sebastian asked.

Julian gave a spasm of a smile. "Well, Nagel has been monitoring the man at the back at the steps going down to the boathouse ... Every morning at 2, the man gets bored and goes out front to join his other partners for a smoke and small talk ... Only gone fifteen minutes mind you ... but it's enough for us to make the slip if we move lively. We will cross the harbor to *The Pequod* at that time ... I moved her from the Yacht Club yesterday over to the new berth at the Sydney Boat Center at the South Spit Bridge ... That will throw off anybody who may be checking me out as to departure. Where are you staying, Mr. Sebastian?"

"The Old Sydney."

"Hmmm ... Good choice ... Jamison pick that for you?"

"Yes, sir."

"Man has good taste, say that much for him. All right, I want you to stay here for the night, Mr. Sebastian. Just a precaution. You will need to get your gear packed anyway. We will provide it. Dawn comes quick around here. I will send a man for your things at the hotel and pay your bill ... You have the room key?"

"Yes. . . ."

"Good ... and one other thing ..." Julian stood as a sign that he was through. He removed his reading glasses and put one stem into his mouth, concentrating as he studied Sebastian with those luminous eyes. "Do you think you'll collect the five thousand Australian when we get to Plymouth?"

Sebastian wasn't even thinking of the money, but it seemed important to Julian. "I believe you are a 'fair dinkum' man, Dr. Julian," he responded.

Julian's eyes widened as if caught by surprise at the use of the term by an American tourist. Then he smiled and let out a short, genuine laugh. His white teeth, all his own, flashed against the dark tan of his face. "Very good! 'Fair dinkum,' indeed! You have picked up fast, Mr. Sebastian. Better than the Yanks I've met around this town. How about that, Barbara?"

She gave Sebastian a demure smile and said, "Well put." But the mask still glazed over the warmth he once knew in her face. It was as beautiful as ever but almost icy ... not like the face he knew in Kai Tak Airport in Hong Kong when she said, "You are my love forever." No, she seemed locked in a self-imposed facade that did not fit her at all. And she did not look comfortable in it either.

"Well, then, Mr. Sebastian," Julian continued, his voice rising an octave in the easier feeling he had about Sebastian now. He came around the desk to shake hands, still showing the laughter in his eyes over the "fair dinkum" line. "You can be sure we will make it, Mr. Sebastian." His grip was strong in Sebastian's hand. His eyes seemed to bore into Sebastian's, as if he were trying to look into his brain.

"I never gave the money much thought, Dr. Julian," Sebastian said. "But I thank you."

"Good! We will have lunch by poolside after 12 . . . at your convenience . . . Nagel will show you to your room. We will see you later today then."

He abruptly dropped Sebastian's hand and walked back behind his desk. It was done. Sebastian turned and walked toward the door without a further glance at Barbara. He wondered if she approved of Julian's accepting him on board. She showed no signs at all that she accepted his being here. If she was into something bigger here with Julian, she might yet try to talk Julian out of taking him. Anyway, she obviously did not want Julian to know of their past escapades together. Yet three to four months at sea would be a long time to keep from revealing it. The question was: Was she here only on an Interpol assignment to trace possible new evidence on the whereabouts of Julian's daughter? Or something more complicated?

One thing he knew for sure: Something in her had changed toward him, as Bentley had warned. But it did not seem to be the result of the drug overdose. She was deliberately more guarded and distant toward him, that's all.

Nagel showed him to his room. It was spacious, comfortable, and overlooked the harbor to the back. "Your hotel room key, sir?"

Sebastian handed it over. "Will there be anything else, sir?" Nagel asked.

"No, thanks, Mr. Nagel."

Nagel nodded and went out. It was on to 11:30 now. He had no idea how long she'd stay with Julian. So he decided to shower and give her time. He glanced out the window and looked down on the green lawn of the backyard and the high shrubs. There were steps going down to a boat dock and what looked like the roof of a boat house. A man in a gray suit stood by the gate to the steps. Security. All around the place. Too much even for a man of Julian's renown . . . unless, as Bentley said, they were guarding his brains, the brains housing satellite technology. What was so big a deal in that? In any case, again Julian was emerging as a very high-priced Australian commodity.

But was that all there was to it?

At 12:30 he went down to the pool. The only person he saw as he came out the sliding doors was a worker cleaning the pool. Probably a security man in disguise, Sebastian mused. He glanced around, looking for the buffet table. Then across the pool to his left he saw her reclining on a lounge chair.

He adjusted his sunglasses against the sun's glare and walked toward her. He sat in the deck chair next to her. She had on dark glasses, so he could not see her eyes, where her inner emotions spoke the loudest. She did not acknowledge him, so he sat there quietly for a long time, waiting. She wore a red swimsuit that sharply accented her blonde hair, tousled in the wind. Her legs were long, firmly but delicately shaped. The cleanly sculptured muscle tones, the tan of the skin, made him swallow against the pressure rising in his throat. She would be thirty-six years old now. A lovely thirty-six, and in perfect shape . . . narrow waist, flat stomach, all due to tennis every day when she had the time to play and the self-discipline of her lifestyle.

"How did you know I was here in Sydney?" she asked finally, remaining in her lounge chair, her head resting on the back of the chair, her face fixed toward the sun. She reached down beside her chair and took a bottle of sun lotion from the cement, poured some of the lotion in her right palm, and began slowly spreading it on her legs. Her skin turned a luminous sheen.

Sebastian forced his eyes to watch the man cleaning the pool. "I called Inspector Henri," he replied, his eyes dropping back to her again, watching her delicate fingers spread the lotion down her thighs.

"Why?"

"Well . . . it has been more than a year now . . . I didn't hear from you . . . To tell the truth . . . Well, I was lonely. . . ."

He wanted to put that lotion on for her. He thought she would ask him to, as she had once in Hong Kong. But she was not opening up for any such intimacies here. The strand that held them together had become far too delicate in this place.

"Henri isn't supposed to tell. . . ."

"I know. . . ."

"So why did he?" Her voice remained casual, lazy in the sun.

"I told him it was critical."

"What was so critical?"

She was leading him, almost as if he were a little boy. He paused, uncertain of himself with her. "Us. Just us."

She paused in rubbing the lotion on her skin, then put the cap back on the bottle and set it on the cement. Her legs gleamed with the moisture. "Meaning what?"

"Meaning we are running out of time. . . ."

"Jacques fell for that? Gave you classified information on an agent based on that?" Her voice sounded incredulous.

He hesitated. She sounded aloof and judgmental, a side of her he had never known.

"Well, I guess anything critical with us—"

"My dear Sebastian," she interrupted him, her voice heavy with indulgence, "I thought we both agreed a long time ago that this is a life we have chosen . . . There isn't room for the 'critical' in those terms."

"Maybe there's a time to let go . . . Ever think of that?"

She didn't reply immediately. Then, "So you came all the way out here to tell me to let go?"

"It's that important to me, yes . . . And I came to ask you to marry me . . . now."

Seagulls overhead shrilled a mocking commentary to that, almost a derisive sound. She continued rubbing the lotion deeper into the skin of her thighs. "I have a job to do here," she said. "There isn't time to think of that."

He caught the dismissal. "Yes . . . I suppose not," he mumbled, feeling embarrassed. It wasn't an outright rejection of him, he thought, but there was no promise either. "You didn't contact me at Argyle Place last night, or call. . . ."

"You know we can't be seen together. Too many people make the wrong connections, or maybe the right ones. Your showing up at the Sheraton didn't help either. David Julian would suspect both our motives in sailing with him if he knew we were tied to past adventures. You know that once we start moving together anyplace, the wrong things happen . . . People get hurt."

"Some good things happen too . . . We save lives." She didn't respond to that. "OK," he went on, sighing, studying the moist line of her lips where she had added some of the lotion. "Does he know you are Interpol?"

"Yes . . . He has known it for years. He trusts me through my father and for what I tried to do for him in looking for his daughter last year."

He nodded. "Is there something bigger going on here with him?"

"Why do you ask?"

"A lot of security around here . . . at the hotel. . . ."

"He's valuable property . . . to Australia . . . and to just about every other country in the world right now who is thinking of satellite technology. Everybody wants to tap his brain. . . ."

"Or kill him?"

She dropped her sunglasses down on her nose to look at him. Her blue eyes focused on him with a cool concentration, as if she couldn't believe he had said that.

"No dramatics, please, Sebastian," she warned and pushed her glasses back up over her eyes. "We go sailing . . . That's it."

He chuckled. "You never just go sailing for three or four months with anybody, Spartacus," he said, using her Israeli Security code name. "Interpol couldn't afford the expense. Something else is definitely hanging over this thing . . . But, in any case, we'll have enough time together to find out what it's all about . . . A forty-five-foot ketch puts us very cozy together. . . ."

"David Julian is under pressure from all sides for his brain, yes," she admitted, ignoring his jibe. "Sailing is a way to get away from it. . . ."

"The seas are no longer neutral either. Even if we are."

"And what about your man Jamison? David is not so sure he wants to take him. I agree."

"That's his privilege . . . but Jamison is a good man. We'll need an extra pair of hands before the trip is over." She said nothing to that. "I hear you've changed," he said, deciding to get to the core of his concerns. "Frankly, I have to admit I sense it."

Again she waited as if the sun had lulled her mind. He wanted to see her eyes in response to that. She never could hide much from him in her eyes. "What do you mean?"

"Henri told your man Bentley here in Sydney who told me that I should be prepared for a change in you . . . Mainly that you were not well . . . that the drugs forced on you in Hong Kong resulted in some kind of personality shift, something like that. . . ."

She lifted her head off the back of the lounge and slowly took off her sunglasses, the frown digging between her eyes. "You saw Bentley?" she asked, her voice alarmed.

"Something wrong with that?"

"What else did he say?" The storm flags began to show in her eyes. He caught the scent of her lotion, and the pressure to touch her was overpowering.

"That it was dangerous . . . that Julian draws a crowd . . . But he seemed more anxious that I know you weren't well."

"Henri would not have told him that," she said flatly. "Anyway, there's nothing wrong with me . . . He would not have sent me here if there was. . . ." She hesitated, not wanting to go on. "Bentley, we think, has been playing both sides of the street . . . He does quite a bit of point work for the CIA."

"What's 'point work'?"

"He's a bird dog . . . Points his nose at anyone the CIA wants to be sure of for identification . . . Sometimes I think, though Henri is doubtful, that he does the same for the KGB . . . One way to get your condo up on the harbor cliffs before you're too old to enjoy it . . . Anyway, sometimes he will plant alarmist stuff on others to get you running. . . ."

"So I ran to you . . . and you're saying he told me you were not well and in danger and all that to push me to make sure I chased you down?"

"Exactly. The CIA knows we've been together in hot spots before . . . sometimes affecting them too . . . They know either of us would go the extra mile for the other if we knew the other was in danger. . . ."

"They got that right! So why does the CIA want us together . . . For a family portrait?"

"Now listen," she said impatiently. "They probably want us on this boat together with David . . . for reasons, who knows why? They used Bentley to make sure we did. . . ."

"How would they know I'd try to get to Julian?" he argued.

"You were at the hotel . . . Bentley told you it was dangerous around Julian . . . I was with Julian . . . So?"

"The CIA could have called Henri to arrange that—"

"Henri does not deal directly with espionage organizations unless there is a criminal factor, which is Interpol's whole business or reason for existence."

"Does Henri know Bentley plays the double track?"

"He has been suspicious . . . but nothing substantial shows up to prove it. We keep dropping innocuous stuff on Bentley to see if it shows up in the CIA check or even the KGB. We don't have enough to nail him yet, but we are close."

"Suppose Bentley is being used by the KGB for the same reason, to get us on the boat together?"

"If he is, then they'd want us together just to take us both out at once . . . We've been a pain in their necks too in the past, as you well know. But I really can't be that sure."

"But the question remains," Sebastian pressed, "why is the CIA so anxious for us to be on that boat? They could get one or two of their own aboard—"

"David has an instinct about people who operate undercover," she said. "Mind you, he's human too . . . He can't always be sure . . . But his carefulness about that has resulted in his not having the crew he needs . . . He probably turned away some innocent, good sailors on that point . . . As to your question, I don't know why the CIA would want us on that boat . . . Probably to provide some protection for Julian. . . ."

"From whom?"

"I said he's valuable property with what he knows in satellite technology. . . ."

Sebastian mulled it over, still not feeling right about the answer. "You're sorry I came here?" he asked, sensing that she was upset.

"The two of us draw other interests, too many interests," she reminded him again. "Yes, I tried talking David out of taking you for that reason . . . He doesn't know we have a past together . . . But he seemed to think you're OK . . . And he really doesn't have the time to keep looking. . . ."

"Why the rush?"

"The ice starts coming into the Drake Passage at the Horn from the Antarctic around the middle of March, early April . . . He doesn't want to get caught in that."

"Well," Sebastian said, sighing, "at least I know now why you wouldn't acknowledge me at the hotel and wouldn't meet me at Argyle Place. . . ."

"How was I going to introduce you to David at the hotel?" she defended, her voice sounding testy. "Here is my long-time partner in spy-busting? My good friend who teams up with me now and then to scramble the best-laid plans of double drips in the CIA or the KGB? How was I going to walk up to you at Argyle and lay ourselves open for a pickoff?"

"I never saw you angry like this before," he said, smiling at her.

"I'm not angry," she countered. She put her glasses back on, resting her head on the back of the lounge chair again.

"Well, so let's relax and enjoy the cruise to Plymouth," he said, trying to play it light. She didn't rise to that. So he said, "OK, if what you say is true about Bentley and the interest of the CIA or even the KGB in my getting to you, then there is something big going on. And we are in the middle of it again . . . like it or not, right?"

She looked his way, again hesitating about what to say. "To settle your mind, now that you are in," she said condescendingly, "there may be something." She turned to stare out across the pool. "I don't know for sure . . . believe me. Henri sent me here to check on any further clues that David might have as to the whereabouts of his daughter. That's it. But now with Bentley in the picture . . . I don't know."

"Why would Henri send you to check on Julian's daughter after all this time if he didn't have something new he is concerned about?"

"Sebastian," she warned him off again, "I go where I'm sent. I don't ask questions. . . ."

"OK, OK," he soothed. He didn't like the shortness and testiness in her voice. "I hope Henri unloads your Mr. Bentley before he trips more wires . . . I'd be nervous having a man work for me who double drips. . . ."

"In time Bentley will trip on his own wire. . . ."

They sat in silence for a while. Then Sebastian said conclusively, "You don't believe that Julian will be safe on that boat alone, Barb. I can read you on that . . . So I'm glad I came to Sydney and am going with you." She did not respond. "But you have changed . . . you know that? Henri was right on that one. To me, you've changed." She did not pick up on it, but reached down into her bag and took out a comb and began running it through her hair in short, deliberate strokes. It made the gold of it flash in the sun, bringing up the tan in her face to a contrasting luminosity.

"Yes, that is one thing that Henri told Bentley that is correct," she replied, pausing in her combing, her eyes still averted from him. She stopped combing, held the comb in her right hand, and took her time as if careful how to put it. "I felt I lost all personal values a year ago . . . running so long with the Israelis and Interpol. . . ." Her voice was meditative, as if she were still pondering the mystery of that. "I was warned a long time ago that you begin to shift if you stay in the game long enough . . . I was told too that I had to stay out of the clinches, don't get close to anyone. . . ." She paused and looked at him from behind her smoky glasses. "When I left you in Hong Kong, I made up my mind that I could not serve in both worlds—one for Israel and Interpol, and the other for you. I had to choose. Sooner or later you were going to get in too deep, and I'd take too many risks for you . . . even to blowing a high-priority assignment . . . And I knew you'd one day give your life for me too . . . I had to choose between the human values and the larger picture. . . ."

She paused, looking down at the comb in her hands, touching the teeth with one finger. "I talked with Henri about it . . . six months ago . . . He told me I had to choose. So I made the choice. Maybe it's wrong, but I made it and won't or can't go back on it. That's what this change is, Sebastian, what Henri told Bentley to tell you . . . to let you know that it isn't the same with you and me anymore. . . ."

She sighed as if a big weight had lifted, or the crush of it had squeezed her even harder. "So I didn't want you around here when I only made the choice just a few months back . . . I did not want any pressure to compromise my decision to break what you and I were heading toward . . . You make it harder for me here, but I can't change that. But now you know why anyway. . . ."

"God told you to do that?" he asked, feeling alarm in him that she had given him up.

"Sebastian, don't use that on me . . . I prayed . . . Yes, you don't know how much I prayed," she insisted.

"And He gave you peace that it's the right thing to do?"

"How does anyone get that so automatically?" she protested. "I—I mean it's like handing God a blank check . . . If He signs it you're on track . . . If He doesn't, it means it won't fly." She was more tense now.

She sat only a few feet from him. He reached over and slowly took off her dark glasses. Then with two fingers of his left hand he tilted her face toward him. He looked into her eyes. Though obviously troubled, they didn't waver. He felt her warm breath on his cheek. The scent of the lotion was sweet, gleaming traces of it still on her soft mouth.

"If you don't have peace about it, and you don't because you are upset—"

She brushed his hand away. "I do have conviction," she said.

"Again, and your father must have told you, if you don't have peace from God about any decision involving another human being close to you, then it doesn't stand—"

"You're oversimplifying it," she retorted and put on her glasses again in a quick thrust. "Oh, there's David!" She swung her long, lithe, golden-tan legs over the side of the lounge chair away from him and stood. She pulled a red silk beach kimono around her. "Come on, Sebastian," she said, forcing a light tone to her voice. "Time for lunch. . . ." She moved to leave, then paused and looked at him. "I'm sorry, Sebastian," and he sensed the genuineness of that. "I didn't want it to come out this way." She walked around the pool toward Julian, who was standing at the buffet table. Her walk was the same—easy, athletic, with a controlled cadence. It showed a woman of character and breeding. He watched her greet Julian with a hug. Julian waved at him, and Sebastian waved back, lifting an arm that felt like lead.

The sun was no longer warm. The smell of her lotion remained, taunting him. He felt the chill and the dark come at once. Suddenly he wanted to be anywhere but there. He had his answer, what he had come for, all he had come for. Now he wanted to go home. Instead he had committed to three or four months of enduring the distance that she guarded almost vehemently. They would be close in proximity but never again as they once were.

He rose slowly then and walked over to them at the buffet table. *C'est la vie*! Such is life. But he did not take it that easily. The tunnel opened in front of him with no light at the end.

This was not a good day to die.

Seven

They piled aboard Julian's twenty-foot powerboat in the boathouse at 2:30 the next morning. They pushed out quietly, using heavy oars so they wouldn't alert security at the front gate. The floodlights in the dock area arced out a hundred yards or more from the shore.

As the boat slowly moved further out of that circle and finally became enveloped in the darkness over the harbor, Julian kicked over the powerful inboard motor. The quiet of the night cracked with sound. Julian kept the motor running in neutral so that it rumbled and muttered, its powerful screw gurgling disdainfully under the water.

Then, satisfied that they were far enough out, he opened it up slowly, and they began to move, the stern dropping, the bow lifting, the white wake frothing and leaping behind them.

No one, as far as Sebastian could tell, had come to the dock to check.

Julian waited another five minutes, then gave the powerful boat the punch, and the craft leaped forward, shoving them all back with a jolt, the breeze slapping hard at their faces. Sebastian sat in the stern with Jamison next to him. Barbara was just behind the cockpit where Julian and his son, Ryan, sat together.

"He wouldn't let me take my cameras!" Jamison yelled at Sebastian above the roar of the motor. "He made me leave them at the house with that dracula Nagel! I didn't even get to make a phone call to the paper! He said I could use the ship-to-shore phone on the boat once we get clear of the harbor!"

"Be glad you're aboard, Jamison!" Sebastian yelled back. "You wanted your story!"

But Jamison only shook his head in despair. After a minute he lifted his thumb to Sebastian and gave a quick but uncertain smile.

Sebastian hadn't seen Jamison that previous afternoon when he had come to be interviewed by Julian. In fact, he didn't know

Jamison was there at all until he was told by Nagel to get his gear and head on down the steps to the boathouse. Then Sebastian saw Jamison, and he was glad the journalist had managed to convince Julian that he could be of help on the boat. It was obvious that, with Jamison having been turned down for the sail before, Julian really was desperate for that help.

They roared on through the remains of the night until Julian yelled back, "Spit Bridge!" They all looked and saw the span and the lights. That meant they were only minutes away from the Sydney Boat Center where Julian had moved *The Pequod*.

Sebastian watched as Ryan got up and leaned over the windscreen of the boat, trying to get a fix on the harbor entry lights. Sebastian had met him in the afternoon by the pool, an hour or two after sharing lunch with Barbara and Julian. Ryan was a shy kid at seventeen, with long sun-bleached hair and seawater blue eyes that did not change at all when he tried a smile. He was about five foot ten, broad in the shoulders with muscular arms. When he did smile, it was hesitant, as if he were afraid he might have to make a lot of conversation following it. The closeness between him and Julian was obvious. Ryan had a tight, elastic bandage wrapped around his right knee, and while he favored it, he seemed to move around well enough, without too much of a limp. Or maybe he was deliberately trying to impress his father that there was not much wrong with his knee.

"Don't forget your banjo!" Julian had called to him as Ryan had headed back to the house. "I expect the best string-picking east of the Date Line, even west for that matter!" Ryan had paused and looked back, smiled, showing his embarrassment, and then had gone on.

"Buoy marker!" Ryan called out. "Berth straight ahead, Dad!" Julian cut back on the throttle and the motor took to rumbling and gurgling again. The bow swung to starboard. The buoy marker slid by, and they made the approach to the pier. Thirty feet out from the berth, Julian cut the motor and let the boat slide quietly toward the big pilings. The boat bumped gently into the rubber fenders.

"To the lines, gentlemen!" Julian called out. Sebastian was already up with the stern line. Jamison, eager to prove himself, moved forward clumsily around the cockpit to the bowline. Sebastian scooted up the ladder to the pier and pulled the stern inward with the line, then dropped the loop around the cleat. As he turned to check on Jamison, he heard a splash up forward. He looked down and by the dim light of the pier lamp he saw Jamison in the water between the bow and the ladder. Jamison floundered some and finally pulled himself up onto the second rung of the ladder, dragging the line with him.

"Lesson of the sea, Mr. Jamison," Julian called out softly, amused. "When you sail with me, you stay *in* the boat and make the landfall properly!"

"Yes, sir," Jamison replied, coughing on the water he had swallowed but feeling more embarrassed than anything else. He made the top of the ladder, dropped the line over the cleat, and wiped the water off his face. He looked considerably out of sorts.

"All right, let's get the gear aboard!" Julian called out. Sebastian and Jamison went back down to the boat and began carrying seabags and extra cartons of food up to the pier, stacking it there.

Julian and Ryan buttoned down the powerboat and cockpit with a canvas cover, then proceeded up the ladder. Sebastian looked around and in the dimness saw two tall masts across the pier: *The Pequod.* In the buildings on shore lights were on, but Sebastian saw no one moving around.

Julian picked up two seabags and said, "All right, follow me . . . Carry as much as you can. We don't have much time." The sky in the east was now turning a ghostly gray glow. They carried the gear to the two-masted boat across the pier. When Sebastian stepped aboard, he sensed immediately the strong feel of her decks. They piled the stuff forward of the thin aluminum wheel. Sebastian saw that the hull was a dark blue and the dog house, or coach house as some called it, was done up in white. The mizzenmast was six feet back of the helm. There was teak in the decking timber mixed with what had to be pine. The coaming on the dog house above the companionway ladder showed a row of half a dozen instruments.

"Let's get it below," Julian said. "Follow me down."

They each picked up a load and followed.

"Chart room here," Julian said as Sebastian, then Barbara, followed by Jamison and Ryan, jammed in behind him. Sebastian glanced around from the chart table against the bulkhead to his left. A low shelf above the table carried the radio transmitters and what looked like a LORAN receiver used for calculating a line-of-position in navigation, as well as the radar. "Behind you in the stern are two bunks . . . It rolls and jumps a lot in weather . . . So be mindful where you sleep. . . ."

Julian reached down and lifted a hatch on the floor by the chart table, revealing the engine. "Three-cylinder diesel Volvo," he said. "Enough power in there to keep us going around the world twice. . . ."

They moved from the chart room into the galley where there was a four-burner gas stove on gimbals, and food lockers all around on the upper wall.

"Jamison, can you cook?" Julian asked, pausing, flicking on a small lamp to let them see.

"Sir?"

"Cook, Jamison . . . Boil water, make tea, or heat up soup?"

Jamison looked a bit confused. "Well . . . yes, sir, I can do that. . . ."

"Good . . . I think it would be best if you didn't get too close to the water at first. . . ." Julian's voice had a subdued note of amusement.

Sebastian grinned at Jamison, who gave a feeble smile back, feeling the bite of the comment. Barb Churchill was too busy looking around the galley to pay much attention.

They moved on forward through the saloon with its two settees on either side of a narrow teak table in the center of the room. "We'll spend our social and eating times here," Julian explained. Then he moved on through the narrow passage past more bunks, the water closet, and then to the bow.

"Toss your seabags in there for now," he said. "We'll stack the food boxes in the galley and stow them later."

They did as he ordered, then followed him back aft to the afterdeck again. The eastern sky was turning up the lights now.

"I want you all to know that my darling wife and I spent three years seeing to the building of this boat over in Tasmania. For your information, even if you are not interested, but so you know, she is a sturdy traveler. The hull is planked with special huon pine from Tasmania, a tough wood that can take a lot of punishment . . . The heavy timbers are of blue gum, an Australian hardwood . . . Topside and decks are of teak and white top pine . . . The raised planking on the decks is laid over with a quarter-inch of marine plywood covered with soft-insulating and waterproofing compound . . . Just remember that when the seas come over us. *The Pequod*, from stem to stern, from the top of her masts to the two thousand-pound inside ballast and five thousand-pound lead keel, is the safest you'll sail, even if I say so myself. We have 1,050 square feet of sail including the main, the genoas, the jibs, and the mizzen. . . ."

Nobody responded. Julian sounded like a tour guide, and Sebastian wondered why he took the time to explain all of it now. But there was pride in his voice. It was almost as if he were paying special tribute to his dead wife.

"All right, then," he said, clearing his throat, "we'll set the watches later . . . Prepare to get under way . . . Get these boxes of food down to the galley. We'll stow them once we are out of the harbor. . . ."

They cast off the lines at 3:50 A.M. Julian took the helm, started the engine, and backed her out slowly from the pier. Compared to the powerboat, the motor sounded like a Cadillac's engine.

Sebastian carried two boxes down to the galley, Jamison following, Barbara after him. Ryan stood by his father as they navigated out of the harbor and up by the North Heads to the open sea.

Sebastian broke open his box, took out the tins of salmon, tuna, and soups. He reached up and opened a food locker, looking inside. There were a few rows of other canned goods, but not so much as he had expected for the duration of the voyage. He figured that Julian had food stowed all over the place, and he was shifting cargo loads to keep the boat in balance.

He bumped lightly into Barbara as they reached up to put tins into the same locker. He looked into her eyes, only inches from his, felt her sweet breath lightly on his cheek. She had on a yellow oil slicker over a blue turtleneck. He had never seen her in jeans. They were snug to her legs and tight around the waist.

"As I said," he bantered, "it's going to be cozy. . . ."

She did not reply and continued placing tins in the locker.

They went back up on deck. Julian was at the helm, Ryan next to him, watching for the marker buoys in the channel. Sebastian looked back toward the pier they had left. No sign of activity there. They had gone in and come out apparently without notice.

"Clearing Middle Harbour," Julian said, as if it was important to all of them. "Approaching the North Heads now, and then the open sea. . . ."

Sebastian glanced up at the high ridged cliffs passing to port. "Watsons Bay light to starboard," Julian continued, "over in the main harbor. . . ." Sebastian caught the sweeping flash of it. He wondered if security back at Julian's house would have sounded the alarm by now. But if Nagel did his job right, as Julian had ordered, they would not know until about 7 when they did their usual check. Nagel would tighten down the house and make it look normal. But there was always the chance someone had seen them back at the Spit.

The Pequod moved beautifully, majestically, the motor quietly pushing it along, the bow taking the choppy waves without a ripple. As they approached the harbor entrance, the bow lifted more to the incoming ocean surf, but she rode it like a young colt dancing in vigor in the delight of a new day.

Now pink splashed the horizon ahead of them. The dawn's early light revealed the harbor heads and the land contours in bold relief. "Morning light, sailor's delight!" Julian called out, leaning back against the half-circle aluminum rail enclosing the after-end of the four-foot-square cockpit, his hand hanging loosely on the wheel.

Sebastian, not wanting to remain useless altogether, picked up the last box of food on the deck and moved on down the companionway to the galley. He pried off the lid, reached up, and opened a locker above his head. He looked inside. It was maybe three-fourths full. He was surprised that it wasn't jammed with tins. He opened the three other locker doors. Same thing. For a voyage of three to four months, the supplies seemed awfully light.

He stowed what he had, then paused. He turned and walked down the narrow passageway between the bunks, opening lockers as he went. There were clothes and tools. But the few remaining lockers forward and in the sail stowage area were not full either.

He returned to the galley and opened the big freezer box to the left of the stove. There were cuts of ham, chicken, beef, but not many. He found only a dozen packets of frozen vegetables, six packets of pork sausages, another six of bacon, a dozen packages of orange and grapefruit juice. There were ten packages of frozen rye and wheat bread.

He closed the freezer lid, pondering it. He heard Julian describing the sights up on deck, so he slid through the hatch to the stern bunk area and looked around for the diesel fuel locker. Maybe it was back up on deck in the stern. He finally found a stowage locker further back in the sleeping compartment. He opened it. There were a dozen five-gallon jerricans of diesel. Sixty gallons? When they hit the doldrums further south and there was no wind, they'd need the engine to keep going. A trip of this length would need five hundred gallons of diesel at the minimum. He had to believe Julian had more stowed somewhere else on the boat.

He was about to close the locker when he spotted something else, four or five small compact canvas bags back of the diesel cans. He reached and took one out. He unhasped the opening of the bag and looked inside. He saw the timing box, the wires, the canisters that had to contain explosives. Why? All wired up to the trigger box ready for the switch?

Puzzled and a bit troubled, he replaced the canvas bag in the locker, turned, and walked out of the stern section back to the chart room. He glanced at the chart on the table. Julian had drawn his course on a gradual line south, southeast toward the Horn. But it dipped out some to the southwest, probably about a thousand miles down. Julian was not only planning to avoid New Zealand landfall, but he was making a severe dogleg to the west. Strange. Still, Sebastian admitted he was not that good at navigation. Julian had to have a reason for that line.

"Ho, below!" Julian's voice sounded from up on deck. "Mister Sebastian, you're missing the best part of the voyage!"

Sebastian turned and looked up the companionway and saw Julian's face staring down at him. "Yes, sir! I just finished stowing the box of food here. A great boat, sir!"

"The best boat, Mr. Sebastian, to my thinking," Julian replied and gave a quick smile of jocularity.

Back on deck, Sebastian saw that the harbor heads were slowly fading behind them, their humpbacks looking craggy like ancient fortresses. The ocean swells were still light, but the wind had swung around to a little abaft of the starboard beam.

"Well, I think we outwitted the lot of them!" Julian chirped and gave a short laugh. "I wonder what they'll all think back in Sydney when they find out old Julian give them the slip. I think it's time to celebrate!"

With that, he flipped a switch on the console by the helm. Music came up through two eight-inch metal speakers, one on each side of the companionway. Sebastian recognized the Scottish music "Scotland, the Brave" with its quick step.

"Come on, Barbara," Julian called to her as she sat against the dog house wall facing astern. "Your father taught you the Highlander Two-step . . . Let's be about it then!"

Barbara got up with a smile of condescension but not looking too sure. In the six-foot space between the cockpit and the mizzen, Julian faced Barbara with hands on his hips, arms akimbo, and began doing the two-step jig to the quick march. He was nimble, bouncing lightly from one foot to the other, crossing his feet in small jumps. Barbara matched him quite well, and they both began to laugh excitedly in the dance. Julian marched by her, took her by the arm and swung her around to the music, clapped his hands, and did the two-step jig again.

Sebastian, Jamison, and Ryan joined in clapping with the rhythm. The music went on to "Loch Lomond" in the same quick-step march. As they danced it, Julian began to sing the words:

> "Oh, ye'll tak' the 'igh road an' i'll tak'
> the low road,
> An' I'll be in Scotland before ye;
> But I and my true love will never meet again,
> On the bonnie, bonnie banks o' Loch Lomond."

They all sang it with him the second time around. There was an exhilaration in the air that got Sebastian's blood running. For a man of eighty, Julian demonstrated amazing energy and vigor. Barbara's face was flushed and aglow with the dance. Sebastian watched her with the same longing he always had for her, a bit jealous that she knew that kind of joy with Julian and not with himself.

Then the music, in the same march rhythm, moved into a chorus singing, of all things, "Amazing Grace." Julian stopped and lifted his hands to Barbara that he wanted reprieve. He walked over to the mizzenmast, leaned against it, and stared astern to the Sydney Harbour heads turning to misty lumps of gray-blue. Sebastian marveled that the man would allow a hymn to be played on board after the lecture he had given against it. But then Sebastian realized that it was a tribute to his wife.

Julian stood there while the hymn played through, his eyes fixed toward the shore. "Good-bye, Sydney!" he called out, lifting his blue admiral's cap in salute. "Good-bye, my darling wife, Jennifer!" In that moment Sebastian caught the acute point of vulnerability in the highly composed demeanor of the man. Julian was unmindful of any of them. He was alone, with his memories, with the sadness of leaving a city he had known for so long as his home and his "treasure." Finally Ryan walked over to him and stood by him. Julian turned and put his arm around the boy's shoulders. They stood together, facing astern as the hymn played through and ended.

Then Julian put his cap on, tugged on the visor, and turned toward them. "It's to the sails then, mates!" he shouted. "We've got a good reaching wind to starboard! Up with the main! Up with the genoa, the jib, and the mizzen! Give her all the sails we got! Up to it, Ryan! We're bound for Plymouth!" He paused as Jamison scrambled to follow the others forward. "Mr. Jamison," he called out in the sing-song voice he used when addressing the journalist. Jamison paused on his way around the dog house to the forward deck. "Get those wet clothes off, and then brew up some hot tea! Look lively now!"

Jamison hesitated, not wanting to be shuttled into the galley so quickly. Then he looked down at his wet jeans and yellow sports shirt and tan windbreaker. Water still squished from the rubber grip shoes that Julian had supplied to him back at the house. "Yes, sir, Doctor!" he replied, as if just realizing he was wet. He moved on down the companionway.

They met in the Situation Room for the second time in two days. It was 2:30 P.M., December 7. The same players, with the addition of Chief of Staff Jim Brandt; Barney Holt, the president's press secretary; and General William Hescott, Chairman of the Joint Chiefs. Brandt was forty-five years of age, looking youthful with his quiet gray eyes and dark hair. His thin face had finely chiseled cheekbones and a wide mouth that did not smile easily. General Hescott was tall, square-shouldered, fifty-three years of age, a stony face that looked like frozen parchment, and steel-blue eyes that seemed to belong to tax auditors rather than to generals. He looked a bit miffed that he had not been informed of OPAL before now.

The Situation Room down below the White House was built much like the Oval Office of the president, but there was a large round table in the center, rather than a desk. Maps hung on the walls, a movie screen hung at one end of the room, and five phones, one of them red, sat next to Fairfield's left elbow.

They had just sat down when he turned to Mark Townshend and asked, "What about Julian, Mark?"

"He sailed yesterday, Mr. President," Townshend answered.

"Who knew about it?"

"Our man was at the Yacht Club where Julian's boat *The Pequod* was tied up a few days ago . . . but it wasn't there Friday. He couldn't locate it. The Australian Security played it loose around Julian's house, so they didn't really get to serious checking about him until this morning, our time. . . ."

"How do they know he's gone if they can't find the boat?" Fairfield persisted. "He had to go out from somewhere, or maybe he didn't go at all. . . ."

"AOS says the Spit Head berth in Middle Harbour had *The Pequod* registered in berth on Thursday this past week," Townshend explained. "It was gone Saturday morning. . . ."

"Who's on board with him?" Bill Connors asked, his voice brusque and irritable.

"The Churchill lady, the clergyman Sebastian, and a journalist named Jamison . . . and of course Julian's son, Ryan. . . ."

"Jamison ours then?" Fairfield asked.

"Just a journalist, Mr. President . . . We have nothing on him other than that."

"Julian seemed awfully anxious to get out of town without anyone knowing," Yancey Yarborough commented.

"Well, the main harbor is filling up with all types and sizes of racing boats getting ready for the International Yacht Race to Hobart December 25 . . . He maybe wanted to beat it out of there before he got socked in. . . ."

Yarborough did not look impressed with the answer. "What about Interpol? What did Jacques Henri tell you?" Willard Banes asked. Banes sounded snappy and impatient too. As Secretary of State, he was still smarting over the betrayal of the Russians in the OPAL thing.

"He didn't have much to begin with, as he informed us last night," Townshend explained, fielding the jabbing questions that tended to put him on the spot. "So he didn't contact us earlier. But he got a message about two weeks ago through his European network that someone had word on Julian's daughter . . . that some kind of contact would be made with Julian about it. The source then was not identified . . . To play it safe, Henri sent Churchill to Sydney to check it out with Julian and to see what materialized. . . ."

"But still no source for that message?" Connors demanded.

"Henri finally identified it as a double agent out of Moscow," Townshend replied after clearing his throat. There was a long silence as each of them pondered the weight of that.

"So," Fairfield said with a sigh, "she is over in Russia then. Probably handed over her laser technology. And she may be alive or dead. Still no double agent would stick up his head to tell Julian his daughter is dead."

"Yes, sir," Townshend agreed.

"So why out to sea?" Fairfield pursued. "Why would Julian weigh anchor now?"

"Maybe it's New Zealand," Townshend suggested. "Maybe the contact told him to meet him there. . . ."

"But he said he is heading for Plymouth, right?" Vice President Casey asked, adjusting his horned-rims as if to get a better look at Mark across the table. "England, right?"

"Yes, sir," Townshend replied. "But I think maybe that was before he got word from the contact who had the news for him . . . about his daughter. . . ."

"Could be South America . . . Chile . . . Colombia . . . Peru," Jim Brandt offered, staring up at the map of the Pacific, south of Australia, on the wall across from him.

"So maybe we need to get one of our ships out there then," Fairfield said. "Keep dogging him. . . ."

"Mr. President," Connors came in on that, "the entire Seventh Fleet, including ComSubPac, along with SEATO forces, are playing navy war games up around Guam for a week to ten days."

"What about New Zealand?" Casey asked.

"We are not on the best terms with them right now," Connors reminded him, flicking a glance at Casey, as if to say that the vice president should know better.

"All right, then," Fairfield put in quickly, anxious to close with all of it, "Julian will probably put into Auckland even if he intends to go farther south. . . ."

"We have alerted our people there, sir," Townshend responded.

"Time then to take Julian into protective custody," General Hescott said flatly, dogmatically, as if that was all there was to it.

"Well, I tried to get to Prime Minister Jonathan McRay twice yesterday and on Friday," Fairfield said. "He's off in the Australian mountains fishing . . . When his people got through, he was still up the creek somewhere . . . He hasn't called back yet. . . ."

"We did get him, Mr. President," Townshend said, adjusting his gold rims carefully in the way that said he hoped he had done the right thing. "When we heard Jim Brandt couldn't get him for you, we hooked up with some of our people over there and they worked on it and got us through . . . We explained the sensitive situation about Julian and OPAL and that you would talk with him further about it . . . We advised him then to take Julian into protective custody . . . McRay said it would not set well to put a man under house arrest who was recently awarded the Humanitarian and Science Medal from the chancellor of the University of Sydney . . . He said they had the house under surveillance anyway. . . ."

"So much for surveillance," Casey grumbled.

"Well, we have to know where he is," Fairfield insisted. "Can we get McRay to get a fly-over with a helicopter or something? Julian can't be far out after only two days at sea . . . How about it, Bill?"

"I think we can, Mr. President."

"And what about detaching some kind of ship from the Australian yards to find him and stay on his trail?"

"The Australians put everything up into Guam, Mr. President," Connors replied. "They've got maybe a few frigates, World War II class, used for minesweeping then . . . Maybe make fourteen knots maximum, if that. . . ."

"Detach an American Trident sub out of maneuvers in Guam then . . . or Panama," Jim Brandt put in.

"I would not think it wise to do that," Yancey Yarborough countered. "I speak as National Security Adviser here, not military . . . But the Russian sub flotillas nosing around the Guam maneuvers will follow any of ours heading south all of a sudden. Wouldn't want them bumping into each other out there . . . We could get into the Big One before the OPAL threat materialized. . . ."

"Any Russian traffic detected yet in the area south of Australia?" Connors turned to Townshend.

"Sir, I don't handle Navy Intelligence," Mark replied, his voice a bit testy.

"Then maybe we ought to find out," Fairfield said impatiently, the patches of red showing under his eyes again, indicating that his blood pressure was rising. "Bill, you're working with the Navy . . . Maybe you can call over there and see if we've got anything unusual moving around down there."

Connors face flushed now too. He didn't like Townshend's retaliation. But he nodded and got up to go to a classified phone by the wall a few feet away.

"Meanwhile," Fairfield went on, clenching his hands in front of him on the tabletop, "I'll get McRay again and ask him to detach one of those old frigates and get out there to tail Julian . . . at a safe distance . . . Anything is better than nothing. Any other suggestions, gentlemen?"

Connors returned from his phone call and sat down. "No contract with traffic off the southwestern coast of Australia. But I've ordered a radar A-Wacks plane out to do a fly-over . . . If there is anything out there that looks suspicious we should know in a few hours."

"What about Russian subs?" Casey asked.

"I expect our Guam maneuvers drew all of them north . . . But our sub *Bunker Hill* has swept north and south Australian waters for two weeks . . . They've picked up no Russian sub traffic yet."

"Anybody have anything else?" the president asked again.

"Mr. President," Connors said, frowning at his yellow legal pad in front of him, "we have a squadron of five ships in Rio down in Brazil . . . I suggest we move them out around the Horn and at least be in the Southern Ocean area if something does break."

The president frowned at his papers in front of him. "The Russians always seem to know when we move our ships anywhere, Bill," he replied with some uncertainty. "And they get nervous every time and start huffing and puffing with some of their own. I don't want it to get crowded out there . . . Anyway, I think we want to make sure Julian does make his contact. If we start dogging him we could blow it for him. And that will put him out of reach to us forever probably."

"Five ships slipping out of Rio and heading south won't cause a stir, Mr. President," Connors insisted. "I think we should at least start them on the move just in case."

"What do you think, Willard?" the president asked, turning to his Secretary of State.

Banes savored it in silence a few seconds. "Probably wouldn't hurt, Mr. President. But I'd go slow. They'll be watching for any of ours that move that way, you are correct. But Bill is right . . . We probably ought to be ready in case."

Fairfield pondered it a minute, then said, "All right, Bill, detach the squadron. Patrol status. No more. We'll let that Australian frigate go for it for now . . . as best he can."

Nobody added to that. The president then picked out a small sheet of what looked like official stationery from the folder in front of him, the kind embassies used. "You will be interested to know," he said meditatively, "that I just received this message from the Russian ambassador saying they have launched OPAL, which they claim is a pioneer communications satellite."

"That announcement just came over Radio Moscow," Townshend said.

"That means they still don't have their ground guidance then," Banes said in a grousing tone, folding his arms across his chest in a truculent pose. He was still out of joint about how the Russians had made the big jump into space despite all their complaints and threats about the American SDI program. "That may give us time, but for how long? Is there any other satellite scientist we can call on to work UNIVERSE, Mark?"

"No, sir," Townshend responded with a helpless shrug of his shoulders. "Not in this time frame."

The president turned his head to glance up at the map of the Southern Ocean. "Looks as if we have to leave our destiny in the hands of those two people on the boat with Julian . . . Churchill and this clergyman, Sebastian . . . And hopefully *Victor*. Did Henri say anything about how good this Churchill lady is, Mark?"

"He says she's one of the best for something like this . . . He thinks Sebastian is quick on his feet too."

There was a pause then, each man pondering the margins. Still looking at the map, Fairfield said, "Barney, I wonder when we need another press conference?"

Barney Holt was going on forty and looked like a remake of Clark Kent of the Superman legend, broad-shouldered, neatly tailored blue serge suit, dark horn-rimmed glasses, and slicked-back hair. But he knew his job better than most who had been in his spot before.

Barney did not respond immediately. None of them offered to express what they felt. All of them, including Barney, knew how tough the last conference had been two days ago. The president had done some nifty dodging of demanding, pointed questions about the Russian satellite which was confirmed by then by all of the tracking stations around the world. He could only state that he had no clarification of the launch in terms of intent. That he would have to await word from Moscow. But the questions became testier about the purpose of the satellite and why the White House was not informed by the Russians by then. The president could only add the "no-comment-at-this-time" line, which did not set well.

The president looked up at Barney now, his eyebrows lifting, begging the answer to his question. "Well, Mr. President," Barney said, clearing his throat lightly, "I don't think we should have another press conference too soon. I mean, they're going to get suspicious about what's up if we keep throwing it at them, if you'll pardon me—"

" They know OPAL is up there, Barney," the president countered. "And what they're speculating about it is getting scary. The more we hide in our holes, the more the possibility of panic."

"Yes, sir," Barney responded, tugging at his tie. "But I think right now Jim Brandt's morning briefing at 9 is sufficient. At least until we have something more up to date on what we intend to say to the press."

"They'll surely bug us about the laser interference thing, Barney," Jim Brandt offered. "TV sets going blank, telephones dead. They'll want to know why."

"So far we are saying it's atmospheric interference," Barney returned. "We don't know what it is . . . we are checking."

"Tell them Kamiloff is using his electric shaver again," the president interjected with some jocularity to ease the tension. "So, Barney, let Jim handle it for now, but in three days I want to go before the press again. I don't want them blowing this thing up in front of us. Barney, you and Jim and Yancey better stay behind and give me a brief on how to handle it if it gets stickier . . . okay? Meanwhile, Barney, I want the press up front three days from now."

"Very well, Mr. President," Barney replied but not sounding too positive about the decision.

The president rose slowly from his chair and walked over to the map showing Australia and the Southern Ocean. He peered at it a long time, saying nothing. "That's a lot of ocean out there," speaking more to himself, "a lot of ocean to get lost in . . . to die in . . . God help them . . . That poor old man running after what could be a phony contact or a trap to get him in the Russian net, who knows? Yet what father wouldn't run?"

He turned and slowly walked back to his place at the table and stood behind the chair, his hands clenched in front of him.

"What's the time off Australia, Mark?" he asked.

Townshend looked at his watch. "Three o'clock here means it's about 5 or so in the morning over there . . . the eighth. . . ."

"All right, let's all meet tomorrow morning at 9 in the Oval Office . . . By then we should have some updates . . . Better not meet down here too often . . . People snoop too much . . . Arrange your time of arrival at my office so that you don't all arrive together . . . That will start tongues wagging too . . . Stagger it . . . Some of you walk over. . . ."

"Yes, Mr. President," they all said in unison and stood, stuffing their papers into their attaché cases. Then, except for Holt, Brandt, and Yarborough, they walked out through the huge steel door that opened with a soft hiss.

Fairfield said nothing for a long time, feeling the breeze from the air conditioner vent tickling his neck. He felt greasy with sweat. His heart seemed to pound heavily in his chest. He hadn't slept well for a couple of nights. He wondered if the sharp news hounds would notice that tonight. He wondered if the three men before him noticed it too.

"This is the hour that tries men's souls, gentlemen," he said. "No time for summer patriots either. So let's get to it."

The three men sat down at the table spreading papers on the mahogany top. The president glanced once more at the map on the wall to his left and tried to visualize Julian out there with that very inexperienced, far too few crew. *The Pequod* indeed!

Eight

The first six days of sailing with Julian went smoothly. The weather was perfect, sunny, about 80 degrees, with a twenty-five- to thirty-five-knot wind reaching to port or starboard. Now and then when the wind shifted to the stern, they close-hauled into it. *Pequod* bounced more in that sailing mode, but Julian seemed insistent that they "get all the speed out of her in the balmy weather."

Julian set his watch schedule the first day out and allowed Jamison to use the ship-to-shore phone to call his paper. Julian instructed Jamison to tell them that he was on a special assignment and would call them back in a couple of days. "I need lead time, Jamison," Julian said when Jamison protested mildly that his job could be on the line. "Otherwise, we'll have every boat in Sydney trying to dog us to Plymouth."

As to the watch, with the weather balmy, Julian did not set specific times since all of them spent most of the time on deck. But at night from 8 to 2 he matched himself up with Sebastian, Barbara and Ryan taking the 2 to 8 in the morning. Jamison, though looking more pale by the hour even in the lightly rolling seas, consented to stand in on deck until 10; Julian said he would be up and around by then. When the heavy weather came, Julian indicated it would be less sleep for all of them in scheduling watch changes for the full twenty-four hours.

"The self-steering will take the strain off us," he told them. "The computer below will buzz loud enough to wake us up if we go off course."

All went well until the fourth day out when Jamison began to show serious signs of seasickness and took to his bunk amidship. Dramamine did not help all that much.

Barbara spoke only briefly to Sebastian in those first few days and only when directly addressed by him. She kept aloof, although she was polite in answering his banal, conversational-type questions in order not to make Julian suspicious. At other times, rare as they were, she was outgoing, especially when they all ate together in the lounge. But she never let those times carry over, as if she played it all strictly for Julian. She was not going to allow the cioseness they once knew, that was obvious, and it began to chafe Sebastian more and more as the hours at sea wore on. Once he helped her in the galley with the evening meal, working with her silently. He wanted to ask her about the short provisioning on the boat, or whether he should ask Julian about it, but he figured that Julian would have some kind of answer for it anyway.

One night when he and Julian were preparing to go on watch, Julian showed Sebastian the radio and radar equipment. He pointed out the local VHF 2-meg ship-to-ship band, then the 6-meg international distress band. Julian switched on the radar. The concentric circles came up, each circle a new set of distance ranges. The sweeping luminous dial picked out a sharp blip four miles to port, and Julian flipped on the radio to the 2-meg ship-to-ship and said, "*Pequod* calling target, our bearing two-eight-five . . . I see you at four miles . . . how do you read . . . over?"

There was a pause, some hissing on the radio. Then a voice with British accent came on: "Roger, *Pequod* . . . this is *Reliant* out of Singapore with a load of teak for Southampton . . . how are you fairing . . . over?"

"Roger, *Reliant*," Julian responded. "Bound for Plymouth, England, in a forty-five-foot ketch . . . fairing fine at four-zero . . . Good luck, *Reliant* . . . out. . . ."

Julian explained that the Sydney Radio could pick up a call at a three thousand-mile range off the international 6-meg band. "Good thing to keep in touch and make sure they log your position now and then," he added. Julian seemed precise about the radio and the radar as if both were the lifeblood of the boat. Sebastian agreed, but considered the radar to be the key to their survival in terms of other ships.

On the morning of the third day out a helicopter approached them from the northwest, coming in low, and passed over them not more than a hundred feet up. Then it came back for two more passes before heading back the way it had come.

"What's an Aussie helicopter doing out here, and why so interested in us?" Ryan asked, shading his eyes to watch it disappear over the horizon.

"Trying to find us, son," Julian chirped, flashing a smile at him. "They're probably irritated that I gave them the slip in Sydney. They'll do more fly-overs in the next few days . . . Feels rather nice to be wondered about, wouldn't you say, Mr. Sebastian?"

Sebastian looked back at him. Julian had already turned to do some work on the helm, not expecting an answer. Sebastian had noted that the copter carried military markings. He would have expected a coast patrol fly-over if all they were interested in was the whereabouts of a private citizen in a forty-five-foot sailboat.

In the mornings and afternoons they lounged on the decks topside, the weather vane doing the steering for them on the preset wind course. Barbara wore her red bathing suit and sprawled out up near the cabin overhead hatch. Ryan joined her, and they lay side by side, reading and carrying on small talk. Sebastian remained with Julian, sitting in a deck chair in front of the mizzenmast, wishing he himself could have some time up forward with her. The seas were light and gentle and sparkling blue. Jamison made an occasional visit topside, his face showing a green sickly pallor. He tried to be cheerful about it under Julian's prodding.

"You want some story material on me, Jamison," Julian advised, "you better soon get your sea legs, right?"

"Sorry, sir," Jamison replied, trying a smile that faded quickly.

He stayed up maybe a half hour and then was hanging over the lee rail. Julian ordered him back below, encouraging him to "give yourself time."

"He may not make it," Julian added to Sebastian after Jamison went below. "Should have gone into Auckland and let him off. But we are too far down course now to swing back . . . Hope he comes out of it . . . Or maybe we'll happen across a northbound ship to Sydney or Auckland and let them take him in . . . Could get serious for him if he does not come out of it. . . ."

On the evening of the sixth day Julian and Sebastian took the watch on time at 8. The wind was a bit more gusty, though still warm, but the weater vane could not keep the boat on course with the changing wind direction. So Julian switched over to manual steering and took his place at the helm in the cockpit, leaning against the circular rail behind him.

The night was clear, the full moon heavy and bright enough to turn the night into early day, intensified ten times on the sea. The stars clustered across the canopy of the sky, brilliantly splashing diamonds that made Sebastian want to reach up and grab a handful.

"Makes me think of that line in Genesis," Julian said, looking up at the sky. Sebastian was startled by Julian's reference to Scripture. "I think it says something like, 'And God said, Let there be lights in the expanse of the heavens to separate the day from the night, and let them be for signs, and for days and years; and let them be for lights in the expanse of the heavens to give light on the earth; and it was so.'"

"Genesis, chapter one," Sebastian confirmed for him, deciding to push through the crack in the door that Julian had opened. "There's another one that comes to mind for me. It's in the Psalms . . . Psalm 8 to be exact:

> 'When I considered thy heavens, the work of thy fingers, the moon and the stars, which thou hast ordained;
>
> 'What is man, that thou art mindful of him? and the son of man, that thou visitest him?
>
> 'For thou hast made him a little lower than the angels, and hast crowned him with glory and honor.
>
> 'Thou madest him to have dominion over the works of thy hands; thou hast put all things under his feet.'"

Julian did not say anything for a long minute. He glanced up at the sky again and then simply said, "Well put, Mr. Sebastian."

"I didn't know you were a student of the Bible, Dr. Julian," Sebastian added.

"Call me David, Mr. Sebastian . . . We have a long way to go, and I don't believe in titles anyway . . . As for the Bible I am not a student . . . My wife read from *The Book of Common Prayer* every night after dinner . . . Anglican tradition, you know . . . She believed every word of it . . . Made her feel peaceful, she said. . . ."

"And you, sir?"

"Mr. Sebastian, I consider the Bible as literature and not dogma," Julian replied with finality. "Can be interpreted any which way you feel you need it . . . like Dickens or Shelley or Shakespeare . . . Or you don't need to turn to it at all. . . ."

Sebastian let that rest a minute, sensing that Julian was simply making conversation but was precise in his answers.

"Along that line," Sebastian said carefully, "some things have to be taken as dogma, sir. . . ."

"Life is not lived on any dogmatic line, Mr. Sebastian," Julian was quick to cut back. "Science proves that you are always finding new things, experiencing new things . . . Nothing stays fixed."

"But your years in sailing prove one thing contrary to that, if I may be so bold," Sebastian continued, feeling for Julian's pulse, if he had any, in the spiritual area. "You have to hold to the magnetic pole and the fix of the sun and moon and stars if you are to make your way across the seas . . . But if there were no true north—"

"Do not confuse the idea that experience is dogma, Mr. Sebastian," Julian interjected with insistence. "Science can establish the laws . . . Those laws come closest to dogma . . . But if I had no magnetic pole, nor the galaxies, I could eventually steer by my sense of inner direction and make landfall. . . ."

"But true north is still true north to you, sir?"

"So be it . . . for now . . . But don't confuse fixed scientific knowledge with interpretive literature . . . the Bible in question, Mr. Sebastian . . . Forgive me for my skepticism . . . We build our own tracks in the sea, as in life . . . My wife, Jennifer, believed Scripture and we lost our daughter . . . Then she died over that, still reading Scripture, as if the solution were there . . . I have no need to debate the issues, Mr. Sebastian . . . I quote Scripture as I quote Tennyson and Kipling . . . But I don't revere any of it as dogma to me . . . We interpret it as we will or won't . . . I trust I am not too heavy-handed with you on that. I expect you are chained to Biblical dogma as truth by your profession. I respect that. But making Biblical passages into some kind of fetish is contrary to scientific principles and discipline. Anyway, I know of no one who believed the Bible to be dogma who made any difference in his or her life or in my own life . . . That includes my wife . . . I revere her memory and her faith, mind you . . . So then, does that settle it, Mr. Sebastian, inasmuch as I do not take to extended Biblical talk on this boat?"

"Yes, sir," Sebastian replied, backing away from it.

Sebastian got up obediently and went down the companionway to the chart room, turned on the radar set, and watched the gleaming white line make its sweeping circle on the screen. He put on the maximum range to fifteen miles, tuned up for long-range intensification. Nothing showed in the sweeps. But then, at the top right of the outer ring, he caught a glimpse of a small white blip. It might be a ship, but he couldn't be sure. He turned the range back to closer, shorter distance sweeps. Nothing.

He turned to the captain's log and entered the finding, December 12. Then the time. When Barbara and Ryan came on, they could check that blip again.

He went back up on deck and told Julian about the uncertain target ten to fifteen miles at a bearing of 170 degrees. Julian did not comment. He stayed at the wheel, his lower back against the metal circular rail, his eyes moving from quick glances ahead back to the compass.

"Quiet night," he said after a few minutes. "No traffic around us worth worrying about . . . The sailor's delight, Mr. Sebastian . . . a steady deck under foot, the sky full of galaxies, the moon smiling in friendship, the sea a whisper of peace . . . How I love it . . . I truly do. . . ."

Then Julian lapsed into silence. Sebastian felt a kinship to the man as he never had up to then. There was a deep reverence in Julian for life and all that was in it. It rose above the notes of sadness in his voice when he referred to his deceased wife. There was a communion in him with the sea, perhaps not to be found anywhere else. There was deep mystery in him too, a side still hidden away, perhaps never to be revealed. But part of it poked up as he talked about his view of "dogma" and particularly the lack of it except in science. But there was a preoccupation with something else, something not here on the boat or in the star-studded heavens . . . Something beyond time and place . . . It showed up when he raised his eyes from the compass and stared out across the sea to starboard as if he expected his dead wife to appear . . . It was that kind of look.

"Well, Mr. Sebastian," he said with a sigh and a half-yawn, looking up at the sails, checking the wind in them, "I believe you can take her now . . . I am going to retire . . . The years have a way of shutting down the circuits. Just keep her steady on course . . . The watch is due to change in an hour . . . If the wind drops, set the weather vane and turn in . . . We'll know if she wanders off course . . . Good night then. . . ."

"Good night, sir," Sebastian replied and moved up to the cockpit.

Julian, stopping to turn back, said, "Oh, I meant no disparagement of your beliefs, Mr. Sebastian."

"I felt none, David," Sebastian replied. "Thank you. . . ."

Julian nodded, satisfied, and went on down the companionway.

Sebastian stood in the cockpit, his hand resting lightly on the wheel, watching the compass. The boat was beautifully balanced so that she hung to the course without any prodding.

It was nearly 1:30 A.M. when he saw Barbara come up the companionway carrying two cups of steaming liquid in her hands. She was early for her watch. She came up to him and handed him one of the cups.

"Great," he said to her, taking a cup and glancing at her face. The moon brought up her golden hair to a glowing saffron color. She wore a yellow windbreaker and a white turtleneck, and jeans and rubber boots that came up just to her knees. He sipped the hot tea and felt a surging sense of peace and completeness with her beside him. But her deep blue eyes, showing the shafts of light from the full moon, fixed on the sails forward, disregarding his steady gaze at her. He smelled that same sun lotion she rubbed on her skin back at Julian's house.

"Glass is falling," she said to him in a preoccupied tone of voice, looking beyond him to starboard out to the softly rolling swells.

He grunted and turned back to the wheel, adjusting course. She stepped back from him and sat on the port bench a few feet away, sipping her tea, her eyes looking forward.

"We've had it too good out here," he said in response. "Did you check the log and the radar blip we saw earlier?" he asked.

"Yes . . . There's a target about ten miles at one-six-zero . . . I heard David at the chart table earlier . . . Sounded like Morse code coming in . . . And he used the key to answer . . . I wonder why. . . ."

He glanced at her. She seemed detached from him, as always. But her tone of question intrigued him. She never double-checked anything Julian did.

"What's wrong with Morse?" he asked. "Maybe he didn't want to wake anyone with a voice transmission. . . ."

"I suppose," she said laconically. He could not tell if she was convinced or not.

He sipped his tea again, glanced at the compass, adjusted the helm. He hesitated about whether to broach it to her now. Sensing they would not have an opportunity to talk later even if she wanted to, he decided to lay it out. "Something else bothers me though," he began. "I checked and rechecked the provisions of this boat . . . Unless Julian has storage lockers elsewhere aboard, I figure we've got enough stores for maybe six weeks if we watch it. . . ."

"You've been inventorying?" she asked, her voice sounding aghast, and he felt her eyes on him.

He glanced at her. There was a look of disbelief on her face. "Yes . . . I stumbled on to what I thought was a shortfall when I was stowing tins before we cleared Sydney Harbour . . . I counted all of sixty gallons of diesel, just sixty . . . I figure we will need at least five hundred gallons for a trip this long. . . ."

"David wouldn't start with a shortfall of provisions," she countered bluntly. "He knows where he's got it stowed."

"I don't doubt that . . . But maybe we can somehow pose the question to him out of curiosity—"

"I would never embarrass him or myself with that," she said flatly. "To give any hint that I don't trust his judgment—"

"I am not saying he doesn't know what he is doing . . . But one of us should ask him before long. Maybe Ryan—"

"Ryan would not challenge his father on that either. We have to trust him. I do, anyway. . . ."

Sebastian let it go. He was not used to debating with her on anything during the years they'd been together.

He glanced to starboard then and saw the growing squall line moving in a long black shadow across the horizon.

"There comes the dirty stuff," he warned. Just then Ryan came up through the companionway, glancing at the line of clouds. The wind picked up with a puff. The mainsail and genoa snapped full with it. *Pequod* heeled to port. Sebastian adjusted the helm to ease her. The wind was swinging astern, so Sebastian decided to run before it.

"Get the mizzen reefed down!" he called out. Ryan and Barbara jumped to the winches and let out the sheets. Barbara reached for the halyard.

"Hold her there!" Julian's voice pierced the rising shriek of the wind in the shrouds. "Run that mizzen back up! Your wind is close-hauled yet! We need to make up time! Run her up again, Ryan!"

They obediently ran the mizzen back up the mast. The wind puffed again. Then the rain hit them with stinging pellets. The once gentle sea turned black, and the waves grew ugly gray beards.

"Get your foul weather gear on, Sebastian!" Julian shouted, moving Sebastian out of the cockpit with his body.

Sebastian dived down the companionway, Barbara following. She pushed by him to her forward berth while he fumbled for his yellow rain parka. He pulled on a white turtleneck first, kicked off his shoes, and put on knee-high rubber boots. He turned back and glanced at Jamison, who lay in his bunk, eyes wide open.

"What's happening, Sebastian?" he asked, his voice sounding weak.

"Only a blow, Jamison," Sebastian assured. "Tighten down your safety belt! We're going to roll some . . . OK?"

"I've been rolling since I got on this boat," Jamison moaned.

Sebastian moved on through the galley and up the ladder. The sea was everywhere now, boiling in white froth, coming over the bow in huge sheets as the wind drove hard into the sails. Sebastian put on his safety harness and attached the hook to the clew on the steel rail behind Julian.

"This is what sailing is all about, Mr. Sebastian!" Julian yelled, and he let out a loud laugh, almost in childish delight. "Just you and the sea! Nobody else!"

Sebastian tried to view the churning waves around him with equal pleasure. He couldn't. *Pequod* took it all right, but she heeled over heavily to port as the close-hauled seas smacked her hard. Julian expertly kept her head into it, guiding her with the heavy, gradually rising seas that lifted her stern.

Sebastian saw Barbara come up from below. She hooked her safety harness to a clew on top of the dog house roof.

"What's the wind speed, Barbara?" Julian called out to her. She checked one of the instruments above her head on the dog house coaming.

"Going past forty-five knots!" she yelled back.

"Good!" Julian yelled and laughed again. "We'll make nine to ten knots in this one, Mr. Sebastian!"

"Sir?" Sebastian asked, squinting his eyes against a fresh battery of icy rain. "Don't you think we ought to reef the main, drop the genoa?"

"Not yet, Mr. Sebastian! If we have to, we'll reef the mizzen . . . when the wind swings direct astern!"

Sebastian gritted his teeth to the rising fury of the storm. Lightning stabbed snakes of blue light around them . . . Thunder smashed hard, thumping the decks under their feet. They drove on endlessly in a mad world of water and sound, fusillades of rain. Sebastian knew now why few men would sail with Julian. The man had no fear and gave no quarter to wind or sea. *Pequod* began groaning in her torment.

Finally Julian called, "Ryan! Sebastian! Time to drop the mizzen! Wind is on our stern! Hop to it now!"

Sebastian turned and let loose the mizzen sheets from the winch capstan. Ryan got the starboard side. They let the sail drop and wrapped it around the boom, tying it down. "Now is the time to learn the lesson of holding *Pequod* from pitch poling, Sebastian!" Julian called out to him again.

Sebastian glanced at the huge combers piling up on them directly astern. The lightning showed them to be as big as two-story houses; then as they came closer, they loomed as large as five-story apartment buildings tumbling down on them. But Julian stood to the wheel, turning his head now and then to glance almost casually at the mountains of seas. The first huge comber picked them up, the stern rising high with it. Sebastian knew that if *Pequod* stayed bow-forward ahead of that sea, she would dive bow-down with it and possibly capsize or "pitch pole," as Julian had said. But as the boat hung high on the wave, Julian turned the helm slightly to starboard. The boat turned with it at the peak of the wave and began to surf with it, sliding off with a shudder as the wave passed.

"Surfing, Mr. Sebastian!" Julian yelled, his teeth flashing in the triumph of the move. "The only way to keep her from pitch poling! Like surfboarding . . . You got it?"

"Yes, sir!" Sebastian yelled back, but he knew it was a maneuver that only a skilled sailor like Julian could pull off.

An hour later the wind had risen to fifty-five knots. Still Julian would not replace the main with a storm tri-sail nor lower the genoa and go with a storm jib. Julian obviously wanted all the speed he could get out of her.

The rest of the night was a blur to Sebastian. At one point he remembered that Julian ordered them finally to drop the genoa and reef the main. They staggered forward around the dog house to get to it, the wind threatening to blow them over the side even with their safety harnesses clipped to the deck clews. Only Julian's skill at holding *Pequod* to the wind and seas kept them from disaster. He was mastering all the elements, and he had not ordered any of them below to heave-to and ride it out with all hatches battened, as they should have.

At some point Sebastian could not remember, the seas seemed

to slacken some, and the scream of the wind in the shrouds let up. The cutting, stinging rain softened. The sickening gyrating of the boat from bow to stern had eased up even though the huge seas kept pushing her stern and dumping her in skidding wallows to the other side. Each time Julian successfully surfed her through them.

The man and the boat were a pair of indomitable champions!

Sometime, about dawn as best Sebastian could judge, they lifted the slide board closing the companionway hatch against water and staggered down to the lounge. The wind had dropped to thirty knots. Julian put the boat on the weather vane again. They fell into the lounge, lying in their soaked clothes, not bothering to get up, unable to. Sebastian felt almost too exhausted to take a breath. He found Barbara sprawled out on her back next to him. Her eyes were closed. She coughed now and then on the water she had taken in during the storm. Slowly he reached over and unhooked her yellow vinyl parka hood and pushed it back from her hair. She did not acknowledge it. Her eyes remained closed, unmindful of feeling. Across the lounge Ryan was draped on the settee looking as bedraggled as the rest of them.

Sebastian waited for his body to ease up in its aches and fatigue. From somewhere he heard a clinking sound and figured it was a piece of cargo loose, still heaving in the dying storm. "Come now, time for nourishment, then sleep! Up, up! Are you all a bunch of landlubbers?"

Sebastian lifted his head, and Barbara, aware of his move, did the same, almost in agony, groaning softly. Julian stood over them with a tray of steaming mugs looking no worse than having run a few miles for an exercise tune-up.

Sebastian forced himself up from the wet green carpeted deck and reached for the hot bouillon that Julian handed to him. The glint of triumph was still in Julian's eyes. He had won Hobart International Cup again, it seemed. Sebastian reached back and pulled Barbara gently upright by her collar. Her eyes stayed closed. He shook her a few times and her eyes opened, but they were fogged over with fatigue. She took the mug he handed her, staring at it as if not knowing what to do with it.

"We blew the man down!" Julian chortled to them, still standing in the lounge, his legs spread apart, taking the rolling of the boat with ease. He handed another cup to Ryan. "You did well, all of you! Jamison? Rise up, old man, get some of this brew into you! I got some special herbal medicine in this that'll quiet your insides some! Up with you now!"

Jamison peered at them from his bunk in the next compartment. The smell of vomit was strong coming from there, but none of them cared right then. Slowly, under the prodding of Julian, Jamison forced himself upright in his bunk. Julian helped him out of it and to the empty settee behind Sebastian and Barbara. Jamison looked like a ghost.

"You'll be fit in a day or two," Julian promised him and began spoon-feeding the broth to Jamison. "We're going to need you, my friend . . . And you haven't written a line on me yet! So look lively now!" And Julian pushed more broth into Jamison, who looked as if he would pass out any minute.

Sebastian felt Barbara's head fall on his shoulder. He looked down at her. The cup in her hand was slowly sliding from her fingers. He put his own cup on the table and took hers. He pulled her head back to his shoulder, put his back to the settee on which Jamison sat, and let her sleep.

For three days they rolled under a cranky sea and low, heavy cloud cover. The inside of the boat smelled of vomit, wet moldy clothes, and old food. The boat had taken on water through the forward ventilating hatch cover. It sloshed in the bilges. Everything they touched felt wet. The sea continued to boil up now and then under fitful winds that bore the same numbing, icy rain. They made their watches standing to the helm when the wind would not allow the use of the weather vane. Those times on deck seemed endless to Sebastian. Julian again took it all in stride, now and then breaking out in some old sea chant to pick up their spirits.

They scrounged for food on their own . . . mostly cold salmon or tuna on crackers and a cup of beef bouillon when someone would get the courage to try to cook on the gas burner with the boat heeling so often. Sebastian found himself praying that the wind would stop and the boat would cease twisting and rolling.

On the morning of the 15th, well over one thousand miles down the Pacific into the Southern Ocean, they ran into the doldrums. Sebastian woke to a silence that was as deafening as the wind had been in contrast. It was so still it was eerie. It was nearly 6 in the morning by his watch. Barbara and Ryan would have the watch now. He got up and took off his damp, smelly foul weather gear that he had slept in for days. He put on a fresh turtleneck and dry rubber knee boots.

He checked on Jamison, but the man was not in his bunk. Julian's herbal tea or the steady ride of the boat undoubtedly had helped the journalist get some control of his stomach. Sebastian turned and headed on through the galley to the companionway ladder. As he came into the chart room, the engine turned over, startling him. He paused at the bottom of the ladder, listening to it as if it were a symphony of reprieve from the storm. The sucking sound indicated that the automatic bilge pump was running with it.

Out of curiosity he stepped back to check the captain's log. The radar reading taken at 0100 by Ryan indicated that a target showed up steady two miles to starboard and hung close, parallel to *Pequod's* course. He turned to the radar, turned up the close-range intensifier. It was there, looking large and bright within the inner circle range of the screen. Why so close? And why stay with *Pequod*?

He turned and went topside and found Julian already there, standing by Ryan, who was at the helm. Barbara was leaning against the mizzenmast sipping a cup of hot liquid. Jamison sat on the port bench hunched over in his heavy blue windbreaker. His face looked a little better.

"Jamison?" Sebastian said, sliding next to him, putting an arm around the man's shoulders. "You made it up? How long now?"

"More than an hour," Jamison answered, giving a weak smile. "I feel as if I have been dead a long time, Sebastian. . . ."

"Well, you look alive now, Jamison," Sebastian chirped at him. He glanced at the sea. It was almost flat now and greasy-looking, having coughed up its bilge of rage for endless hours and days. There was no wind at all. A misty fog began to close in a couple of hundred yards off.

"Get yourself some hot tea, Mr. Sebastian," Julian ordered, his voice sounding chipper but a bit preoccupied and hollow over the sound of the engine.

"I'll get it," Barbara said. She walked by Sebastian without a glance at him and went down below. Sebastian moved over next to Ryan, checking course. He glanced up at the sails, fully rigged again. They hung limp in the windless air. It felt spooky, the air so flaccid, the fog slowly moving in on them to squeeze them into isolation.

Barbara came back and handed him the hot tea. He tried to

smile at her. She looked up at him and managed a quick acknowledging smile in return. Did she remember sleeping on his shoulder? Well, she would never let him know it anyway.

"If you hated the storm, Mr. Sebastian," Julian said lightly, "you'll come to hate the doldrums even worse . . . You'll wind up pleading for wind. . . ."

"Yes, sir . . . But it's a lot better than wind right now," Sebastian responded, feeling a bit out of sorts. He had not shaved, and the scruff on his face itched. He was conscious of how he must look to Barbara . . . blurry-eyed from lack of sleep, the scraggly beard.

"Ryan, check the radar again and see how close that ship is to us," Julian said, taking over the helm. Ryan went below, stayed there a few minutes, and came back up.

"He's still there a mile or so out, sir," he said respectfully to his father. Julian nodded, turning his head to stare out into the fog to starboard. "Doesn't come any closer . . . Keeps running with us . . . Last night he was behind us a couple of miles, then he passed us about 4 this morning." Ryan's voice carried a note of awe and question at the same time, sounding like a child recounting an encounter with a ghost. "He went on five miles or so . . . stayed there an hour, then dropped back to where he is now right off our starboard beam . . . I tried raising him on the radio . . . No answer."

Julian reached over then and hit the engine throttle. The motor died. They sat in the long, low, black greasy swells of the ocean, the water slurping quietly under the hull.

"Yes," Julian said in a hushed tone of voice. "You hear him now?"

Sebastian strained to catch any sound. Then he heard the faint rumble coming over the water.

"I hear it," Barbara said from behind Sebastian.

"What is it?" Jamison asked, getting up on unsteady legs to lean against the mizzenmast, staring out into the fog.

"His engines, Jamison," Julian replied. "Dead slow to keep pace with us. . . ."

"Why is he staying so close?" Ryan demanded.

"Who knows?" Julian replied. "But he's got a problem in one of his propellers . . . You hear that rickety-tick-zoom sound? Listen . . . there . . . Rickety-tick-zoom . . . Again . . . You hear it? How about it, Mr. Sebastian?"

"Yes, sir," Sebastian said, picking out the break in the rhythm of the rumbling engines.

"I hear it now," Ryan confirmed, his voice still on that tone of question.

"He can't run forever out of sync like that," Julian added, cupping his right hand to his ear to better catch the off-beat engine sound again. "If he does, he won't make much speed with it . . . Could burn a bearing if he doesn't heave-to and fix it."

"Maybe that's why he's hanging close," Ryan offered. "He needs help maybe."

"Hmmm," Julian replied. "Stand by the helm, Ryan . . . Mr. Sebastian, stand with him, and all of you keep your eyes peeled in case he closes in too tight . . . I'm going below to try him again on the radio."

Sebastian watched him go down the companionway hatch, wanting to go with him. Something oddly curious about that ship so close in. Five minutes went by. The fog got thicker, turning to a white, filmy paste in front of them, enveloping the boat so that it was hard to see the masts forward.

Finally, feeling uneasy, Sebastian said to Ryan, "I'm going below to see how your father is doing." The boy nodded. Sebastian moved to the companionway and stopped, looking at the speed guage on the coaming, all the time straining to hear if Julian was talking on the radio. Finally he stuck his head down into the opening. He saw Julian working the Morse key, tapping out a message, fine-tuning the two-meg frequency. Sebastian debated whether to go on down and see what kind of communication Julian was getting. But then it seemed to him the move would appear to be intrusion. Julian wanted to work the radio himself, and Sebastian respected his wish.

Sebastian turned and walked back to the cockpit and Ryan, feeling a bit uneasy but not knowing why.

Finally Julian came back up on deck. "Nothing going on voice radio," he said to them. "A lot of buzzing and squealing . . . So I sent out a Morse message. He might be on a high frequency channel where Morse comes through easier. Anyway, if he's on that, he knows we're here, although he surely can see us on his radar." He turned his head and stared out into the fog to starboard. "He looks a decent size on the radar below." He sighed then and lifted his blue admiral's cap off his head and ran his fingers through his thick, rumpled, scraggly white hair. The rumbling sound of the engines came up a bit stronger and Julian said, "He's speeding up again . . . But that propeller sounds worse."

Sebastian went down to the chart room and checked the radar screen. The target was still in the top half of the inner circle but slowly began crawling up to the second range line. He waited as the blip moved out to four miles ahead of *Pequod* and held steady. Sebastian checked the radio and noted that the VHF light was still on the 2524 talk-between-ships band, indicating Julian had in fact been on it. Out of curiosity he opened the wide drawer at the center of the chart table . . . Only more charts. He looked up at a smaller drawer on top, opened it. He saw the sending key there. He remembered Barbara telling him that Julian had sent Morse to a ship a couple of nights back.

He glanced once at the screen, noted that the target was holding his distance, then went back topside.

"Kick the engine over, Ryan," Julian said as Sebastian approached. Ryan obeyed. The boat's diesel purred again, closing them in to sound. It was a relief to be free of the heavy silence of the fog and the sea. "Keep her on that heading at five knots . . . Mr. Sebastian, if you will be so kind as to stand watch on the radar, please? I want to know if that ship starts coming back again . . . Ryan, stay at the wheel . . . And now, Barbara, my dear, how about you and me cooking up a hot breakfast, hey? How's that sound, everybody?"

"Great to me," Ryan said, giving his father a smile of appreciation. He looked younger than seventeen dressed in his yellow wool sweater, his blond hair flopping around his ears. He looked as if he were more ready for tennis than sailing.

"Jamison, it will do you good too," Julian cajoled.

"Sir, if you don't mind, I'd like to talk to you while you—while you cook, sir," Jamison responded. "I do need to get some copy down on you . . . if you please, sir."

"Well, if you can take the smell of frying eggs and bacon and all that, why not?"

"Come on, Harry," Barbara chirped, trying to lift the journalist's spirits, taking him by the arm and leading him toward the companionway. "Some more tea in you will help. . . ." Jamison looked a bit awkward being led by her, but he managed that same uncertain grin.

Sebastian followed them down and stopped by the radar while the others went on into the galley. He stared at the blip hanging there at four to five miles ahead, a few points off the starboard bow maybe. Just holding, it seemed. He couldn't figure it, and yet something about it forced him to feel growing suspicion. It was like a ghost ship. Silent. Dogging them for whatever reason. He turned to the log again and read Ryan's entries about the target during the night. Same pattern. Four miles behind, coming abeam, four ahead, then dropping back to run a mile off starboard.

He tried the VHF talk-between-ships, hoping to raise her. There was too much static and loud buzzing. He pondered it. When the fog lifted, they would know more. The thought made him more uneasy. Why? The boat's engine throbbed around him like a jackhammer in a cave. The diesel fumes stung his nose and eyes and began lacing a light headache across his eyebrows. But his mind stayed alert, his eyes glued to the screen waiting for the blip to move.

Inspector Jacques Henri walked into his office at 7:00 A.M., an unusual time for him, but only under urgent call from his deputy, Pierre Marquand. It was December 16. When he pushed through the door, he was met by Pierre, a hulking man of six three or so who had the manners of a butler and the efficiency of a mathematician. "Good morning, sir," he said pleasantly enough and then lifted his eyebrow in his way of saying, "This one is a big fish."

"Good morning," Jacques replied and looked around Pierre toward the woman sitting in a black leather straight-backed chair a few feet from his desk. He glanced at Pierre again, whose dark brown eyes widened, as if to say to be prepared.

Henri walked toward the woman and said cheerfully, "Good morning . . . I am Inspector Henri."

She had large blue-green eyes, dark-colored hair, a gaunt pale face, and a colorless mouth that was a straight severe line in her face. She looked familiar. As Jacques leaned against his desk facing her, Pierre slipped a folder of 8 x 10 black-and-white photos to him. Henri scanned each one quickly but with a practiced eye. A small vibration rippled around his heart.

"Your name please?"

"I am Elisa Julian."

Henri looked over his glasses at her, then at the photos again. No question about it. She was thinner with a few cutting, slashing lines of pain around her mouth and under her eyes. But it was undoubtedly she.

"We have been looking for you for two years and more," he said softly, slowly. "And now you come looking for us?"

"I do not have the time to give all the details of my escape from the Russians more than three weeks ago," she said, her words tumbling out in a rush. "I have been working for them the last two years. But it is more important now that I get word to my father in Sydney, Australia, immediately."

"Would you be so kind as to tell me why, *Mademoiselle* Julian?"

"I was supposed to be the exchange for him . . . I go over to the West, he goes to them. The Russians had it set up during the week of the 12th to the 18th of this month, sometime before Christmas for sure."

Henri waited, mulling it, picking his way carefully now. "*Mademoiselle* Julian, your father has already been at sea for at least ten days now. . . ."

Her eyes widened, and she stared at him in disbelief a long minute, willing him to recant the statement. Then her face slowly collapsed in a landslide of tears.

Pierre took a box of tissues and placed it on her lap. "Pierre," he said, turning around and sitting in his desk chair, swinging around to face Elisa Julian, "get Mark Townshend, the CIA director, in Langley, Virginia, as soon as possible . . . special priority and classification."

"Sir!" Pierre replied and went out of the room.

Henri sat back and watched her cry, not knowing what to do to help her. He glanced at his desk calendar, his mind trying to construct the drama that must be going on out there in the Southern Ocean. The final curtain, as Townshend had told him, could have earth-shaking impact.

He felt only sorrow now . . . for the girl, for her father out there beating his way under sail thinking he was giving his daughter a new chance in life. He felt tired then. The years tugged at him, times like these . . . the helplessness, the pain of it all.

"Sir," Pierre said as he came through the door. "Mark Townshend is on the line. . . ."

Henri sighed. Now it begins, he thought as he picked up the phone.

Nine

Late in the afternoon of the 16th Julian told them he was changing the watch. *Pequod* still ran on diesel in oily, low swells under a misty fog that was gradually lifting. Visibility was still less than a half-mile, however.

Julian was concerned that Ryan, who was hobbling more on his twisted knee, get more rest for it.

"Sebastian, you and Barbara got a tough baptism in weathering a northwester out here," he said. "And, quite frankly, I could use the rest later tonight and into the morning . . . I must confess it took a bit out of me too." He was sitting on the starboard bench. Sebastian had the wheel. Barbara was below preparing dinner. Jamison, who had been up most of the day in the quiet seas, leaned against the mizzenmast.

Julian turned toward him. "Jamison, you and I will take the 8 to 2 . . . It's time you had an opportunity to talk to me about that portrait in words you want to paint of me. I guess that's the way you put it to me back in Sydney."

Jamison looked a bit startled that he would be asked to take a watch. Recovering quickly, he nodded, looking pleased.

Sebastian did not comment on the change. It seemed normal enough. He was tired. And by the look of Barb Churchill's face in the last few hours, she felt it too. The storm had torn at their vitals and left them drained.

About 6:30 Julian cut the engine and let *Pequod* heave-to, drifting with the swells. He and Sebastian went down the companionway and checked the radar. There was only that one target blip out about six miles ahead of them, a little to starboard. It had been there most of the day, never moving out of range.

"Well," Julian said, sighing, "he's not coming back anyway . . . Probably nursing that bent propeller of his . . . Right now my stomach calls for nourishment."

They sat in the lounge and dug into Barb's offering of fish steaks, fried potatoes, broccoli, warm wheat bread, finished off by a dessert of strawberries from the freezer. Even Jamison managed to pick at his fish and get it down without his stomach going into spasms. It was cozy in the lounge with the kerosene lamp casting a warm glow and reflecting off the ceiling, creating a soft, mellow atmosphere. The quiet was a relief, *Pequod* lifting just a little now and then with the low swells.

Julian insisted on Ryan "picking the strings" while they sat over their coffee. Ryan was good at it. They all joined in singing a "Row-row-row Your Boat" round-robin. They sang Julian's favorite which he said his wife loved, "Where Have All the Flowers Gone?" His dark eyes went soft and misty as they sang it with him, and he seemed far away. He sat at the end of the table still littered with leftovers and plates and utensils. His blue admiral's cap lay on the table beside him. His white hair looked like tumbleweed ready to blow away, sharply contrasted in color to his yellow rainjacket and green turtleneck underneath. His eyes, usually intent in their blue-gray scrutiny of everything and everyone, were softer and subdued. The memories of other times apparently laid hold of him in the tranquil moment of soft light, a gently rolling boat, and the tunes they sang of other times, other voyages, other loves.

For the first time Sebastian saw obvious traces of vulnerability in the man. A certain fragility now, the years stripping him of the bravado he displayed at the hotel and at his house. It seemed as if Julian were saying good-bye to what he had known all his life, and lines of sadness tugged at his thin mouth and seemed to bend his shoulders a bit.

Sebastian felt a certain apprehension in what he saw in the man. But he did not know why. It was like watching a ship going down stern first, the slow slide into the embracing waters, yearning to join others of its kind in the slumber of the deep.

Then, as if the quiet in the lounge had signaled the message to him, he looked up and around at them almost as if seeing them for the first time.

"Well, then," he chirped, clearing his throat, "what happened? Is everybody half asleep?"

"Dad, it's after 8," Ryan reminded him, putting his banjo aside.

Bewildered, Julian glanced at him as if the time was totally irrelevant. "Ah, so it is," he replied with a sigh. The cracked lines in his face seemed deeper, like rake-plowed sand. He put on his cap, tugged it down over his eyes, then reached over to rub Ryan's hair affectionately.

"Well, let's be up to it," and he stood, his head almost touching the tilley lamp. "Jamison, let's go. Ryan, you can show Barbara and Sebastian here the forward berths and the sliding door that will keep out the diesel fumes . . . Sleep well. . . ."

Without further word, he moved out, Jamison following. Sebastian helped Barbara pick up the dishes and carry them to the galley. Ryan went forward to check on something. Sebastian dumped the remains of the meal into the trash bucket, while Barb was intently busy on the dishes.

Finally he said, "I'd love to know what's going on in that head of yours." The motor kicked over with a muttering growl. She glanced at him, but her eyes did not indicate any concern as far as he could tell. She was good at covering her feelings. The sound of the motor became louder as Julian opened the throttle. It was impossible to talk there, even if she wanted to.

He took the bucket of garbage topside and tossed the contents over the lee side of the boat. He glanced at Julian at the wheel, Jamison next to him, talking to him with the recorder in his hand. Jamison still looked peaked in the light from the binnacle, and Sebastian wondered how long he would stand watch.

He went back below, paused in the chart room to check the radar again. The "target" was still out there at a bearing of about one-nine-zero and six miles out. A strong sense of foreboding went through him like a chill as he looked at it. Something was not right about that ship. He put down the bucket and turned to the VHF. But the static was now full-blown into a shriek. He moved over to get on the long-range 6-meg frequency on Penta Marine Radio in Sydney, hoping at least to test whether he could get through. The same interference was there.

He turned down the volume but left the power on, in case. Inside the galley, Barb was drying the last of the dishes and putting them into the lockers. The diesel fumes were stronger now, and she sneezed a few times. "Let's get forward!" he said to her, raising his voice above the loud clatter of the engine.

She followed him through the lounge and into the forward spaces. Two berths were there across the passageway. Ryan was in one, propping up his right leg on a ledge on the far end of his bunk to ease his knee.

"The slide panel is right there, Mr. Sebastian," he said, pointing to the doorway that Sebastian had just come through. Sebastian moved back, found the latch to it, and pulled. The plywood door slid slowly across the opening and snapped into place. The sound of the engine was quieter now. He reached up, put one foot on the coaming of his bunk, and pushed the overhead sun hatch open. The air was fresh but heavy with the clammy fingers of the fog. But it still felt good.

He watched Barbara head on into the bow section. She removed her yellow jacket and tossed it on the heap of clothes that had not yet been stored in lockers. She lay on it and stretched out. Sebastian knew her mind was turning now as much as his was. She knew more about what might be going on here than he did, he was sure. He longed to have her share that with him.

He unzipped his blue windbreaker and tossed it on the bunk. "You feel OK, Ryan?" he asked.

Ryan lay back, reading a paperback by the light of his flashlight. "I'm fine, sir," he answered politely. "I'll feel better once we get out of these doldrums."

Sebastian chuckled. "I remember that line from Coleridge, your father probably knows it well, that says:

'As idle as a painted ship
Upon a painted ocean.'"

"All of that, sir . . . but . . ." Ryan put his book down on his chest. "I'm not sure what that ship is doing out there . . . still there. Do you, sir?"

"No, I don't, Ryan . . . But I imagine we'll know more when the fog lifts. . . ."

"Yes, sir," Ryan replied, his eyes still doubtful.

"Try for rest, Ryan," Sebastian advised. "When the wind blows up, we'll have to hit the deck in a hurry."

"Yes, sir. . . ."

Sebastian glanced forward to where Barbara was flopped out. He decided he'd make a try. He moved inside and dropped down on some life jackets next to her.

He studied her face in the dim glow from the forward deck hatch marker light. She looked tired. One arm lay over her eyes, as if she were trying to shut out a terrible vision of some kind.

"So what are you thinking?" he asked. She still had not acknowledged his presence. The sound of the motor was muted so far forward, but it was loud enough to cover conversation.

"I'm tired," she answered after a long pause. "Bone tired. . . ."

He sensed she didn't want to get into any personal or heavy

stuff. "So what about that ship dogging us out there?" He rolled over onto his back on the life jackets close to her. She looked fragile in the dim light from the hatch, but the fragility made her look even more beautiful.

"Haven't—excuse the pun—the foggiest," she answered.

He chuckled, glad she could still come up with the quip, showing that she still held some camaraderie with him. "Have you checked the provisions?"

She didn't reply. Then she dropped her arm from her face and glanced at him. He could not see what was there. "David knows what he is doing, Sebastian," she said factually and with finality, as if the conversation was closed.

Her voice sounded resigned and laced with fatigue. He lay a long time, staring up at the overhead, not knowing how to pursue anything with her. He felt the distance from her again, and it was harder now to abide.

He continued to lie there, listening to the motor gargle. He rose and looked down at her. Her eyes were closed, but he knew she was not sleeping. It was her way of telling him she wanted to be left alone.

He stood up in a half-crouch and moved out of the compartment to his bunk, climbed in, and worked at least five minutes to get his long legs properly tucked into the short and narrow berth.

Once settled, scrunched up, his knees halfway out into the passageway, he felt the growing moroseness over her withdrawal from him. It was as if they had never known love for each other—or at least she conveyed that feeling. The pain of his need for her was intense. He wondered why he was there at all, more than a thousand miles from Australia in a forty-five-foot ketch with the woman of his life who apparently did not want to be.

Finally he let the rhythmic beat of the motor massage his brain to sleepiness. That, together with the light lift of the bow into the swells, rocked him into oblivion.

He woke up with a start, staring up at the overhead not more than a couple of feet above. The motor was still running. The deck hatch light poured a misty glow into the compartment. He glanced across at Ryan. He had lifted his head off the pillow as if he had heard something too. Sebastian turned to look at Barbara. Apparently she was still out.

"You hear anything, Ryan?" he asked.

"I don't know for sure, sir. . . ." His voice sounded puzzled.

Instinct borne out of years of catching unbalances of any kind forced Sebastian to swing his legs over the side of the bunk. He pulled on a white turtleneck, blue windbreaker, and blue jeans. He glanced at his watch by the light from the hatch. It was 12:30. He pulled back the sliding door. The diesel fumes came in with a biting acrid odor. He peered down the passageway aft, finally reached for Ryan's flashlight at the foot of his bunk. The boy was half up, leaning on his right elbow, looking aft as well. The light played across the lounge and back through the galley. Sebastian thought he saw Jamison in the chart room at the foot of the ladder leading up to the deck.

"Come on, Ryan," he said and moved forward. He came up behind Jamison, who turned quickly, startled.

"Are you on watch with Julian?" Sebastian asked.

"No, sir . . . He sent me below an hour ago. I was not feeling well at all . . . I'm sorry. . . ."

Sebastian turned and looked at the radar. The target blip within the inner circle was practically on top of them.

He took the ladder in two quick bounds. He saw no one at the helm. He looked forward, then beyond the mizzen astern.

Julian was gone.

"Ryan!" he shouted toward the dog house companionway.

"Right here, sir," Ryan said, coming through the hatch, pulling on a red jacket.

Sebastian went to the helm. He noticed that the automatic computer steering switch had been engaged.

Ryan came up beside him with the flashlight. Sebastian took it, then ran the light over the deck around the helm looking for any sign of a clue that might explain the absence of Julian.

"Cut the engine, Ryan." Ryan stepped to the helm and did so. It was quiet again . . . but there was another sound. A low buzzing like an outboard motor. Off to starboard.

"Where's my father?" Ryan asked, suddenly realizing Julian was gone. His voice carried rising demands of fear.

Sebastian did not respond. He caught sight of a red smear a few feet back by the mizzen. He walked over to it, knelt, and examined it with the flashlight. He touched it, rubbed it between his fingers, then sniffed at it. Blood.

"Jamison, did you hear anything, any sound out of the ordinary, during the last hour?" he asked.

"Heard a thump once, kind of loud, but I didn't think anything of it . . . Thought it was Dr. Julian moving things around up here. . . ."

"What's going on?" Barbara asked, moving to Sebastian, looking down at the red smear that Sebastian continued to study. He played the light farther back toward the stern and saw drops of it there too.

"Still fresh," Sebastian said to her as she leaned over to study the red spots with him.

"Where's David?" she demanded.

"Ryan, take the wheel," Sebastian said, ignoring her question. "Rev up the engine, and give full throttle. Come about to starboard." He walked back to where the boy stood at the helm, the question and disbelief in his eyes.

"Your father has been pirated off this boat, Ryan," Sebastian explained. Ryan stared at him. Sebastian reached around him and hit the starter button for the engine. It came to life.

"But who—?"

"I don't know. Maybe that ghost ship has something to do with it. He's sitting right on top of us out there, no more than a half-mile maybe. Can you take the wheel?"

"Yes, sir," Ryan said, swallowing hard in shock. Sebastian patted him on the shoulder.

"Swing her hard to starboard to two-four-five . . . I'll check radar. . . ."

Sebastian went forward as Ryan took the helm and throttled up. Barbara followed him down to the radar.

"What are you going to do?" she asked, her face close to his as he stared at the radar screen, her breath warm on his cheek.

"I don't know," he said. He noted now that the blip was almost dead center in the inner circle as the *Pequod* swung around to close range with the target. "But I'm going to at least confirm that Julian is on that ship."

He turned, brushing by her, and hopped up the ladder to the deck. He climbed up on the dog house roof and tore the canvas wrappings off the twelve-inch navy searchlight. The lamp rested on a five-foot retractable aluminum stanchion. He crouched down and flipped it on.

The fog had lifted considerably now. It was too hard to tell in the dark just how far. But in the penetrating finger of the powerful light he figured visibility was probably close to a half-mile or more.

The boat's engine pounded them forward in the black, greasy swells, moving them at eight knots or so. Five minutes went by.

Then he saw it. The searchlight caught them.

First the small white lifeboat, more the size of a dinghy, people in it. Then beyond that the size of the gray-plated ship. The small boat was approaching the gangway that had been lowered.

"Give her all she's got, Ryan!" he yelled back.

"She's full out, sir!" Ryan responded.

Sebastian kept the stabbing beam of light on the small boat as it sidled up to the gangway. There were five men. Two scrambled off the boat and onto the gangway, reaching back to the other two and the man that they were half-carrying. That had to be Julian. "God, help him!" Sebastian said, a surge of anger rising within him.

The Pequod moved steadily over the sea, gaining on the ship. Now Sebastian could see the upper decks and the men standing at the top of the gangway, glancing now and then at the *Pequod* as it closed the distance. They didn't bother hoisting the small boat. As soon as everyone was aboard, the gangway was pulled up.

"Hey!" Sebastian yelled. *Pequod* was close enough now for him to be heard, maybe fifty yards off. Sebastian swung the powerful beam of light forward on the ship and saw the name *Minsk*. He swung the light back to the bridge area where he saw a man in an officer's cap and two others alongside him, watching him come on. "Hey!" he yelled again. "You can't do that!" He knew he sounded silly. They had obviously done it! He swung the searchlight to the stern of the ship and saw the flag . . . hammer and sickle. His heart sank, but the anger burned him even more.

As the *Pequod* approached closer, the ship's propellers kicked up foam astern, the heavy beat of her engines cutting the quiet, misty ocean night with hammering sounds. *Pequod* passed close behind her, and the huge mound of her wake slammed into the boat's forward hull. She heeled sharply over to starboard, and the boom of the mainsail slammed with it. The boat hung precariously for a long minute. Sebastian grabbed the stanchion of the searchlight to keep from being thrown over the side.

The wave passed. Ryan was quick to swing the boat around to follow the Russian trawler. Sebastian jumped down from the dog house, leaving the searchlight on.

"That's our friend who's been dogging us for two days," he said to Barbara, who stood by Ryan, her face white in the light of the binnacle, her eyes wide in the realization of what had taken place.

"What ship is that, sir?" Jamison asked above the sound of the *Pequod's* engine.

"A Russian trawler, Jamison," Sebastian yelled back. "They came over in a dinghy and waylaid Dr. Julian off this boat! You got more of a story than you bargained for, Jamison!"

"But why? Why would they do that?"

"Who knows?"

"I'm sorry I did not stay on watch with him, Sebastian," Jamison insisted.

"Forget it, Jamison . . . You couldn't have done much anyway. Too many of them."

Sebastian was conscious of how terse his voice sounded, the outrage coating his words to an added shrillness.

"What can we possibly do now?" Barbara asked, standing a few feet behind Ryan at the wheel.

"I really don't know," Sebastian replied. "But you and I need to talk below!"

She hesitated, unsure of the tone in his voice, what to expect from him, still in shock herself. He reached over and took her firmly by the arm and led her to the companionway. "Stay on that helm, Ryan," Sebastian yelled back.

He faced Barbara in the lounge, forcing himself to calm down. He turned up the tilley lamp. Her face was drawn, eyes still large with wonder and some fear as well.

"Now," Sebastian began, putting both his hands on her shoulders, "I want some answers . . . I want to know all you know. . . ."

"I don't—"

"All you know, Barb!" he insisted, the anger in him not yet assuaged, even with her. "I won't be kept in the dark any longer." She did not respond, so he said, "All right, here's what I think . . . There are not enough provisions on this boat to last much beyond a month, maybe a bit longer if we rationed. That means Julian planned to make a contact out here with that Russian . . . I think it was probably some kind of exchange, had to be. He provisioned enough to get off the boat and allow us to return to Australia. That explains why he sent a message in Morse, the time you heard him tapping the key. He was getting off the signal to that trawler regarding his position and the time he expected to make the exchange. Only now I think it all ran afoul on him . . . The fact that they came aboard and took him away by force, dragging him off like a piece of luggage, says they didn't have the exchange . . . But again only you know—"

"I don't know!" she persisted, her eyes snapping then. "All I know is that Henri said David had a contact to make . . . My job was to check it out, go with him when he made it! I don't know about any exchange of anything! Or anyone! I didn't even know it was the Russians! You've got to believe me on that!" Her voice quivered as something caught in her throat, maybe a sob over the loss of Julian.

Sebastian relaxed his tight grip on her shoulders. He saw the first show of tears in her eyes. He pulled her to him and held her close, her face pressing against his chest. He stroked her hair lightly. He felt the shakiness in his legs, the aftermath of his own anger.

"All right," he soothed. "I'm sorry . . . I didn't mean to shout at you. . . ."

She sniffed and slowly lifted her head and stepped back to lean against the lounge table. She wiped at the tears on her cheeks, cleared her throat, and said, "There's nothing we can do about it now anyway . . . The best we can do is head back to Sydney and report—"

"We're not going back," Sebastian replied calmly, burying his hands in his pockets. He paced back and forth in the confined lounge space in front of her.

"What are you talking about?" she demanded. Her tears were gone. A new shine had come into her eyes, a gleam of protest, of disbelief. "Not going back?"

"No . . . That Russian committed an act of piracy on the high seas," he said. He knew he sounded too pontifical. "That's in violation of international maritime law—"

"You can't follow a motorized ship with a sailboat! He can outrun . . ."

"He's got a bad propeller or screw . . . You heard Julian say that. He can't make much speed . . . That's part of the reason he couldn't get off our radar screen, the other being he wanted to hang around to do this dirty work . . . Once we get the wind, we'll catch him."

"And what then? You think he'll heave-to and talk it over?

They've got the best satellite communications scientist in the world—"

"I know that. But he's also a man, a man who deserves more than that kind of treatment," Sebastian countered. He never liked arguments with her and especially not now, afraid it would break what little they had left for each other. "Sooner or later that Russian has to stop to make repairs."

"Use the radio! Call for help!" she entreated.

"The radio is jammed," he said. "That Russian's been doing it for days. Nothing can come in to us and nothing will go out. We're cut off out here. . . ."

She did not reply, stymied by the sheer audacity of his reasoning. "The Australians, the United States, they'll check—"

"Maybe . . . But we are a long way out now. We've been under heavy weather and fog . . . They wouldn't send recon out in this . . . Later maybe . . . But there's nothing they can do right away . . . Anyway, Julian is already on that trawler. . . ."

"That's what I'm saying," she pleaded, her hands outstretched to him. "We can't possibly change that."

"I'm going to bird-dog him anyway," Sebastian concluded.

Another pause. "With a crew of three?" she prodded him. "One of whom has chronic seasickness, another is hobbling on a bad knee . . . Which leaves you with just me . . . And if you think we can weather another storm like the one we've just been through without the best sailor in the business, then you have to be bordering on—on the imbecilic!"

He paused to look at her. Her cheeks were flushed, her eyes snapping. He smiled at her then. "Never saw you so worked up," he commented. "You're beautiful like that . . . Beautiful without it . . . But when you get your dander up—"

"Please be serious," she said with a groan, putting her hands to her face in despair.

He hesitated, then took out his wallet, found the yellow telex, and walked the few feet over to her. She looked down at the telex. "Read it," he said. She took it and read it quickly, then slowly looked up at him, her face showing confusion.

"They defrocked you?" she said, bewildered.

"That's right. Up to now my chasing in the espionage capers has not been considered 'redemptive' to them . . . So maybe they're right. But now there's an eighty-year-old man out there on that

Russian trawler who didn't ask to be manhandled like that. It's a total violation of his rights—"

"Aren't you being idealistically gallant?" she cut in on him, her cheeks showing patches of red as her own protest mounted. "You would sacrifice the few lives here to prove your ministerial credentials—or maybe to restore them?"

He felt the rebuke. The diesel fumes were strong. He coughed once. He stopped his pacing to look at her.

"I don't want to do that deliberately, no," he defended. "If that's all it is . . . You and I have been willing to sacrifice ourselves before . . . I don't think Ryan will object . . . And Jamison has no choice now anyway. But for once I don't care about Russians, East or West, even ministerial credentials . . . I am after the man. I think God would expect us to try it. It's immoral what that Russian did . . . Right now I am going after that one sheep, forget the ninety-and-nine. . . ."

He caught himself, sensing he was beginning to sound rhetorical, almost sermonic. She just kept staring at him in disbelief, her blue eyes wide, realizing the implications of it all. Before she could respond, Ryan stepped into the lounge, hesitating, not wanting to break in on them. He hobbled to the table and sat on the edge next to Barbara. His face was drawn by the pain of his loss. The glaze of shock still showed in his eyes.

"I don't understand," he said, his voice cracking.

Barbara put her arm around his shoulders. "Ryan," Sebastian said, raising his voice above the sound of the motor but keeping it calm and reasoning, "your father was dragged off this boat by crewmen from that Russian trawler. I don't know why, but they probably want him for his scientific know-how. I want you to know that I intend to chase that Russian all the way around the Horn and straight into Murmansk if I have to. Maybe we won't get that far or very far at all . . . And it sounds impossible and it will be dangerous. I don't even know what we can accomplish by chasing him, or what we do if we catch up to him . . . But I think your father is worth the try."

Ryan stared at Sebastian, unable to compute it all, or its implications. "You can count on me, sir," he said quickly then, his blue eyes glinting with anticipation.

"We are not experienced sailors," Barbara warned him in a reasoning tone of voice. "We only got through that last storm because of your father's skill—"

"He's all I've got," Ryan said flatly, dismissing the entreaty. "He took me in, gave me a chance at life."

"It will be rough, you know that," Sebastian added. "And I can't guarantee we can keep running for very long on what provisions we've got . . . We are low on diesel. . . ." He hesitated about telling Ryan of his father's short provisioning. He decided to let it go for now, not wanting to explain that the rendezvous with the Russian trawler was planned by Julian and the Russians.

"My father always planned well," Ryan said, frowning.

"Yes, well, I think he may have missed the diesel supply." Sebastian dismissed it quickly, in an offhanded tone of voice. "We have no radio either," he went on, eager to get off the provisioning situation. "But I expect Australia Coastal will be looking for us before long . . . and probably the Air Search Group . . . But it's an awfully big ocean—"

"Sir, I'd rather keep running after my father and die trying than to turn back," Ryan said adamantly.

Sebastian paused, looking from him to Barbara. Her eyes still showed disagreement with his decision. She removed her arm from Ryan's shoulders, looking resigned to the inevitable. But her eyes continued to protest Sebastian's action. He knew she would not argue it further. But in those eyes he also sensed that he may have broken the thin strand that held them up to now. He was forcing an issue beyond himself for what appeared to be an attempt on his part to balance the books with Backstrom, Alnutt, and Winston. She was too disciplined as an agent of Interpol to allow that cause to force her into hopeless idealism. Or selfish motivations. He sensed he had been wrong to spring the telex on her and make it the basis of his decision. It would have been better simply to base it on an attempt to get back a man who had been pirated. Period. She did not agree with his decision in any case, but with Ryan's plea, she had no choice but to defer to him. Yet skepticism and the deadly coolness to Sebastian showed in her eyes.

Just then there was a rattle in the mainsail boom topside. "Wind," Ryan said and moved eagerly away from the table to the chart room companionway.

"I need your help now to start rationing the food," Sebastian told Barbara before following Ryan. "Heavy breakfast, soup and crackers and vitamins for lunch, easy on the dinner . . . We may have a long way to go."

She did not respond. He wanted to take her in his arms and feel her touch of confidence in him. But she kept behind that veil of aloofness, intensified now by her disagreement with his decision.

He turned then and walked out and up on deck. Jamison looked forlorn and green around the gills. Sebastian ordered him below. Jamison looked relieved and stepped away from the wheel.

"Cut the engine, Ryan," Sebastian said. Ryan hit the switch on the console. It was quiet again. The wind was chasing the fog out now. It blew stronger by the minute out of the northeast. "Put her over on self-steering and let's get sail up," Sebastian added. Then they tacked the boat into the freshening breeze, sheeting up the sails. *Pequod* took to it with a snort of her bow into the suddenly rising sea.

It was now 3 in the morning. Sebastian remembered that it was about 12:30 when he woke up. He went below and checked the radar again. The Russian was about eight miles out front, but he wasn't gaining on them all that much. With full sails and a good wind, *The Pequod* could make close to eight knots. If the Russian could not run faster than that, *Pequod* could stay on him. It all depended now on how much speed the trawler could get on a damaged propeller or a faulty engine or both.

He stood next to Ryan, checking the compass. The boy sniffed once and turned his head to stare away into the darkness starboard. Sebastian turned and fussed around the mizzen, allowing the boy to have his moment to mull over the loss of his father.

Then he moved on next to him in the cockpit again. He reached over and put his right hand on the boy's shoulder as the wind slammed the sails. *The Pequod* rose to it with a new spirit. The fog vanished, and the morning stars showed in the dying night. There was cause to doubt his action now, Sebastian knew. He was leading them on a chase that could be destructive for them all. But all he could think of was the lined face of an old man who had suffered the worst indignity any man could.

"He's not gone from us yet, Ryan!" Sebastian called out as the wind shoved the boat with a heavy hand. "We've got a fair wind! And the Russian is hurting!"

"Yes, sir!" Ryan replied and tried a smile that was game enough in the dim glow from the binnacle.

Sebastian slapped the boy on the back to encourage him. But a stitch of worry clawed inside. Another storm like they just had could be a nightmare without Julian aboard.

On that, Barbara was exactly right.

Ten

Mark Townshend took the helicopter to Camp David, where President Fairfield had called the "Situation Room" meeting to avoid any contact with the press. It was a little past 4 in the afternoon of the 16th.

They all sat across from each other at the ten-foot-long, five-foot-wide polished oak table in the lounge of the game room. In the center of the table was a large, flat, inch-thick square plastic map of Australia and the Southern Ocean. The map was as wide as the table and five feet long. A cardboard replica of *The Pequod* sat on the dark blue expanse of the Southern Ocean, about six inches down from the southernmost tip of Tasmania.

The president waited for Townshend to get settled in his chair directly across from him. Everyone in the room sat quietly, frozen in a still photo posture, eyes fixed on the CIA director. He cleared his throat and, with his right hand, swiped at his short, blond crewcut and glanced at the written notes on his yellow pad. He had already called the president at 7 that morning on the classified line into the White House Oval Office to tell him about Julian's daughter showing up at Interpol.

"I don't know how much of this you want, Mr. President," he began.

"Short and to the point, Mark," Fairfield said with a quick smile of encouragement.

Townshend nodded. "We received an hour-long tape of an interview Inspector Henri of Interpol had with Elisa Julian yesterday," he began. Then he went on to state that the Julian woman had defected at the International Electronics Trade Show in Prague, Czechoslovakia, more than three weeks earlier. She had gone there with a delegation of Soviet scientists to look for any navigational electronic components that might adapt to OPAL's ground guidance needs.

"What embassy did she defect to?" Yancey Yarborough interrupted, frowning in suspicion.

"She didn't try the embassies," Townshend replied. "Too risky . . . The Russians would have covered the American and British immediately, the only place she would risk trying for. . . ."

"Fill in the cracks, Mark," Fairfield urged, tapping his yellow No. 2 pencil on the plastic map cover in front of him.

"Yes, sir . . . Anyway, she made contact with a Russian Jew electronics engineer inside the OPAL complex in Murmansk . . . six months ago; his name is Igor Asmiroff. She found out he is doing forced labor on OPAL for being affiliated with a Russian Jew dissident group. After watching and testing him for three months, she made her move to cultivate his friendship. . . ."

"Why?" General Hescott cut in skeptically. "I thought she sold out to the Russians . . . After all, she went over on her own—"

"Let's save those questions until later, General," Fairfield insisted. "We don't have a lot of time for it. . . ."

Hescott backed off and leaned back in his chair, his face going expressionless.

"I think I should answer that right now, Mr. President," Townshend said, glancing at Fairfield, who simply jerked his head forward, allowing it. "She had grown sour on OPAL, General. She had gone over to them expecting to work on a communications satellite that would give the Russians dominance in space in that kind of technology. When she found that it was a military offensive weapon, she wanted out."

He paused and glanced at Hescott to see if that satisfied him. Hescott did not respond. "At any rate," Townshend continued, "the result of her friendship with Asmiroff led her to ask him if he knew a way out. She told him that she was to go to Prague for the electronics show. Asmiroff said he would try. It took three weeks to complete the contact on the outside. When the Julian woman was at countdown on heading out to Prague, the dissidents set up a contact for her at the exhibition with a man named Borg, a member of the East German delegation. Borg is an electronics man but runs courier for British MI-5 now and then. When she got to Prague, she made contact with Borg."

"Where was her Russian security?" Connors said, sounding suspicious.

"They were on her most of the time, but as long as she stayed within the Warsaw countries' exhibits she felt no real pressure. Contact with Borg led him to arranging for her to go out of the exhibit hall through a steam tunnel. The tunnel entrance was down the hall from the women's public washroom. Security was lax when she was in that area.

"The steam tunnel led to a manhole four blocks away from the exhibit hall. She came out into the waiting arms of a Czech underground group posing as sanitation workers. They didn't waste any time. She hadn't been out of that manhole five minutes before the streets were alive with Russian security looking for her. So there was no way they could try going over the East German border to the West without being picked up. And as I said, chances of making a friendly embassy for asylum were out as well, since Russian agents would be covering them first to pick her up before she could enter the gate. Their only chance was to cut across Czechoslovakia south and over the mountains into Austria. It took them a week or more.

"Once in Vienna, she was put into the hands of an American salesman of farm machinery whose name is Straub. He did some covert work on the side just for kicks. But he was a proven cover man. He spent another week looking for ways out of Austria for her to Switzerland. Finally he paid off a friend who ran traffic in the freight train martialing yards south of Vienna. They got on a train heading for Zurich. Straub accompanied her in the empty boxcar along with a Czech bodyguard with Austrian papers. Once in Zurich, Straub contacted a Swedish diplomat's courier who got her the necessary documents to cross into France. She rode in the back of a truck, hiding under bags of onions all the way to Paris. And then to Interpol headquarters where she is now. . . ."

Nobody said anything for a long minute. "Sounds almost too simple," Connors said with some skepticism.

"I haven't gone into the details of how close the Russians were to her all the time, sir," Townshend countered. "They spent three days on that boxcar, stalled on a side spur, their food gone, no water, and very cold . . . They could hear voices calling to each other all that time . . . Had to be Russians checking the yards. . . ."

"Seems security on her was far too lax, considering she was a big number in their plans," Jim Brandt added.

"They had no reason to suspect her coming over," Townshend replied. "She had gone over to them in the first place. If they were suspicious, they would not have taken her to that exhibition in Prague."

"They must have seen her with Asmiroff in the OPAL complex," Connors insisted.

"Henri did not go into detail on that . . . But he did say at one point that she and Asmiroff worked together on laser developments on a regular basis. It would not be difficult to talk about other things without their knowing."

"Did she give the Russians the lasers?" Connors pursued.

"She did."

"Then can she make the counter-laser scramblers for us?"

"Given the time, she thinks she could," Townshend replied. "However, as Henri said when I asked that of him in a follow-up phone call last night, she is not too comfortable in that area . . . That is not her specialty. She says that her father knows more about that, including ground guidance systems that the Russians need for OPAL. . . ."

"How much time would she need?" Casey asked.

"Too long . . . Three to four months at least."

"So her only reason for defecting back here," Jim Brandt put in, "is disenchantment with the OPAL operation?"

"One other important point, sir," Townshend responded quickly. "She said the Russians told her back in October that they were going to allow her to return to the West at the proper time . . . in the near future . . . That they would be in touch with her father about it. She didn't know what that meant for her or for him. She knew her father would not come over voluntarily. But she also knew he would come if it meant she could go back home to Australia. She told Henri that she had a feeling some kind of exchange would be made perhaps around the middle of December . . . They had told her she would be home by Christmas if all went well. So the thought of her father locked into OPAL, forced to use his scientific genius for a military project, was too much. It had almost killed her. That's what moved her to make the chancy jump at Prague."

"A lot of youthful idealism shattered, I'd say," General Hescott sniffed.

"Better the awareness of it while you are early enough in life to do something about it," Willard Banes responded, a remark intended for no one in particular.

"I take it she is buttoned up in Paris?" Yancey Yarborough asked.

"She's out in a country estate under heavy security," Townshend assured him. "Interpol will not chance flying her here or to Australia . . . and I agree . . . Not now anyway."

"All right, then," Fairfield interjected with a heavy sigh, staring at the replica of *Pequod* on the map in front of him, "that brings us to the matter of the sighting of this Russian trawler heading into the Southern Ocean, Bill. . . ."

"Yes, sir, Mr. President," Connors responded quickly, eager to get to the military strategy. "Australian Coastal spotted one heading south-east fifty miles off the southern coast, going twenty knots, full out. She's the *Minsk*."

"You're saying the trawler may be the contact for Julian?" Jim Brandt asked, frowning at the map.

"Safest way for them to go," Connors replied.

"Why not a sub?" Brandt asked, moving a cardboard replica of another ship on the map about four inches down from the southern coast of Australia.

"If they move a sub down there, they know we will have one of our own on their tail to check them out," Connors countered. "Russian trawlers, though, are usually all over the Pacific and don't draw that much attention from us. That's what they want . . . little or no attention for this operation."

"But you're still presuming," Casey said with some doubt.

Connors' dark eyes took on a flash of sparks. "My presumption is not without credence, Mr. Vice President," and his words had bite in them now. "The Russians have nothing else out there—"

"All right, gentlemen," the president cut in with a deliberate mollifying tone, trying to soothe the two men who made no pretense about their dislike for each other. Still it came off a bit sharp, evidence of his growing impatience now. "Somewhere out there Julian is waiting to make an exchange for his daughter, if her hunch is correct . . . And it could well be . . . Only now David Julian is out there waiting to make a deal that won't come off. Not for him anyway. What's the latest on *Pequod*? Do you know where she is?"

Connors shrugged. "There's been a four-day front over the Southern Ocean, Mr. President. Closed down solid two days ago. We have our A-Wacks radar planes high above it, but though we pick up three or four blips of ships down there, we can't be sure until we do a visual. There have been three days of force six winds . . . followed by fog thicker than a double malt . . . Julian was last heard from five days ago when he called Penta Marine Communication in Sydney for a weather check . . . Now we can't seem to raise him at all . . . frequencies jammed. Sounds as if the Russian is throwing up a lot of sand to clutter the channels."

"Can you do a visual recon now?" Yarborough asked.

"We logged out two A-6 Intruders from Melbourne a few hours ago," Connors replied. "They'll be over the area we figure Julian would be about now if he stayed around the position he logged in with Penta Communication. . . ."

"So what do two Intruders do if they spot *Pequod* and the trawler?" Willard Banes asked, sitting straight back in his chair, his arms still folded across his chest in the posture of a disgruntled Indian chief. "What will they prove? They can't radio down to *Pequod*, and if Julian is already over on that trawler, which we don't know—"

"We will at least know *Piquod* is still afloat," Connors appealed. "And it will give the Russian something to think about with our planes over him."

"So we assume that Julian is probably on the Russian trawler by now?" Fairfield asked.

"No doubt," Connors said conclusively. "They would have been ordered to get him off as soon as they knew the daughter left the Prague Exhibition."

There was a long silence as they all pondered the implications of that. To Mark Townshend the room seemed heavy with tension and foreboding. The president looked haggard and red-eyed. His press conference a week ago had been a tough exchange with reporters who stayed on OPAL most of the time. The president insisted that the only information he had was that it was a new communications satellite. He begged "no comment" about other tracking stations indicating a different configuration in OPAL.

That led to more grilling about the matter of the blackouts of televisions around the country, together with phone lines going dead for no apparent reason, which brought out the hound instinct in the reporters again. Fairfield simply replied that there was some kind of "atmospheric disturbance that had to do with weather passing" which scientists were checking out.

And just when he thought he had put them at bay, they brought up the subject of the cancellation of the visit by Soviet Premier Kamiloff by the Russians. Did it have anything to do with the satellite? Fairfield had been taken aback by Kamiloff's cancellation too when he found out just prior to the press conference. Townshend explained to him that the Russians probably did not want Kamiloff in the United States at this particular time with OPAL so close to becoming their big ace; and, two, they didn't want Kamiloff under the gun with demands by Fairfield as to what the Russians intended with OPAL.

All the president could say to the press was that he had no idea as yet why Kamiloff had canceled, except that the Russian ambassador indicated that the premier was not well. It was a weak excuse, he knew, but he did his best to restrain the press from speculating until there was further clarification from Moscow.

But Mark sensed the press was not satisfied at all with the president's answers. The president himself was convinced afterward that they had zeroed in on the real possibility of a Russian offensive weapon in space. The more they turned it over, Mark knew, as the president did, the more they dug around, the more pressure there would be on the White House. Fairfield looked almost desperate now in his attempt to find a way to ease it all before the cap blew off and the panic began.

"How would the exchange between Julian and his daughter work?" Jim Brandt asked. As Chief of Staff he was forever trying to tuck every piece of information into his brain. "Would Julian go over to the trawler and only then would the Russians release her?"

"Julian would be too smart to go that way," Connors refuted in his usual dogmatic tone of voice. "He'd insist his daughter be passed over to him first . . . You can bet on it. That's the way I would do it."

"One better than that," Willard Banes added with a sniff. "He'd wait for the Russians to run her over at least halfway and only then get into his own boat and go over to them . . . The main thing is, Julian won't get off his boat, if he has any sense, until he's sure his daughter is visible and close enough to make the transfer."

"So now we don't have his daughter in it," Yancey Yarborough cut in impatiently. "What do they do now?"

"They take him," Townshend said quickly, because he had turned that over in his mind all night.

"You mean pirate him off?" Casey asked with astonishment.

"Of course," Connors replied with a half-snort of disdain for Casey's naiveté. "When the sea is calm or in the doldrums, certainly at night, they heave-to, send over a boat. Julian hears them coming, has arranged the time by radio, thinks his daughter is coming over . . . Before he can tell, they are on him. . . ."

"So let us now come to grips with the possibilities of that event," the president cut in, reaching for a walnut in the wooden bowl by his left elbow. He placed the nut carefully between the jaws of the aluminum nutcracker. "Let's say that Julian is now a captive of that Russian trawler . . . What now?"

Jim Brandt reached over and put on the map another cardboard replica of a ship that represented the Russian trawler, placing it a few inches to starboard of *Pequod.*

Nobody said anything for a long time. The log fire popped a shower of sparks.

"If they take Julian, they'd have to take the crew members too." Yarborough finally broke the silence, his voice subdued in the weight of his concentration.

"Why speculate on that?" Banes said, dismissing it with a huff. "The Russians would not take anybody besides Julian anyway. No point. Whoever is left on *Pequod* can't do anything after that fact now."

"The point is," Connors insisted, his voice sounding petulant and impatient, "what do we do now? We received word last night that a Russian sub is on its way south from snooping around our Guam maneuvers, Mr. President. I did not pay much attention to it until this morning when our own sub, *Bunker Hill*, tracked it going by the Great Barrier Reef off Australia, full out at twenty knots straight south. He's wasting no time to get down there."

"What are you suggesting, Bill?" General Hescott asked.

"That we deter *Bunker Hill* to follow him down," Connors answered. "Get in the way of that Russian sub if he tries to pick up Julian off that trawler."

Jim Brandt put out another cardboard boat on which he printed "Russian sub" with black marking pen. He placed the boat north up the coast of Australia.

"How long, then, before that Russian sub gets there, the approximate position of that trawler now?" Fairfield asked, his voice a bit subdued as if he were working on a problem in algebra.

"Probably four to five days if he keeps his present speed," Connors replied. "If he dives, he'll go faster . . . which he will do. . . ."

"Where is that Australian frigate Jonathan McRay promised me?" the president asked, lifting his eyes toward Connors across the table.

"Took two days to get repairs completed," the Secretary of Defense replied. "Last report we had she was three hundred miles south of Sydney going full out at thirteen knots. She's old, remember—"

"Well, the Aussies have guts," Fairfield cut in abruptly. "Her skipper will get her there and do what he's asked to do. McRay is sending the best of what he can deploy. . . ."

"Couldn't he move one of his modern destroyers out there instead of an old World War Two minesweeper, Mr. President?" Casey asked.

"Australia doesn't want to get caught in the middle of a big one right now," Connors countered. "McRay isn't about to send out a high-powered man-of-war, one of the few they kept back from the exercises up in Guam, and maybe provoke action they don't want. I don't blame him."

"So what exactly is this old frigate going to do out there, Mr. President?" General Hescott asked, making it polite but sounding a bit skeptical at the same time.

Fairfield looked up at Connors and lifted his right eyebrow as if to say it was the Defense Secretary's question. "Well," Connors replied, shifting in his chair as if to get leverage for his answer, "all she's got is a three-inch up forward, one astern, and a few popguns in between. But I guess she could create some kind of presence out there."

"Like a pup nipping at your heels?" Hescott offered with a ghostly smile of incredulity.

"Better than nothing," Connors cut back in a grousing tone. His cheeks were red now as he built up a head of steam over the cross-checking. "I did recommend we move elements of our fleet over there a week ago—"

"So where would the Russian head now?" Yancey Yarborough broke into the exchange. "Given that they have Julian already . . . around the Horn then? Seems we could have our ships waiting on the South American side anyway. . . ."

"He probably won't go that far," Connors replied. "Not with Julian aboard. He might head for the Magellan Straits, which are closer. They may arrange for an air pickup there. Still, the Russian sub could catch up to them quickly enough . . . There's nothing pushing that trawler now anyway."

"Maybe . . ." the president came in, sensing the testiness in the room. He finally squeezed the nutcracker in his right hand. The walnut broke with a loud sound in the room, sounding like a tree limb snapping. "So let me try this one out on you, gentlemen," he went on, peeling the husk off the walnut. "The Russian will take Julian off and leave the crew of *Pequod* . . . Miss Churchill, Sir Sebastian, Julian's son Ryan, and the Australian newspaperman . . . And it puzzles me why Julian would take a journalist, of all people, knowing he was going to make the exchange out there . . . I doubt the good doctor would want his betrayal documented for the hometown folks."

Nobody responded to that, apparently unable to provide any wisdom. The president stood up then and leaned his hands flat down on the map, as if he wanted a better look at the players in front of him. He pushed his glasses up on his forehead, squinting intently at *Pequod*. "The trawler, given our asumptions about her, will go on taking it easy south until that Russian sub catches up and they transfer Julian over . . . Without the daughter to exchange, the Russians are going to feel uneasy with Julian on a slow boat to Murmansk . . . What do you think, Mark?"

Townshend quickly looked up, as if caught thinking of other things. "I would say that squares up about right, Mr. President," he said, clearing his throat.

"Bill?"

Connors frowned at the map, hesitating. "Well, Mr. President, I'd have to go along . . . I agree that they have to make the switch as quickly as possible . . . They would know by now, and especially when our air recon does a low fly over them, that Julian's daughter has blown the exchange . . . I don't think they'd want Julian hanging out there if we decided to send a couple of fast destroyers after him."

"Hmmm," Fairfield said, looking down at the map again. "OK, then, what are the chances of *Pequod's* crew pushing to stay on that Russian's tail?"

There was a long minute of silence as they pondered that. "Mr. President," Connors finally said, his voice rising to a note of entreaty, "*Pequod's* crew will surely turn around and go back to Sydney now. What can they accomplish in following that trawler anyway?"

"Nothing maybe," Fairfield admitted, standing up again and folding his arms across his chest while he continued peering at the map and the cardboard models of the trawler and *Pequod*. "But did you ever see a horse come to attention when a single bee begins to buzz around its tail? Just the presence of one gets him moving. Why? Because the horse knows one bee will draw other bees . . . And that could create, shall we say, a situation?"

"Yes . . . the horse starts running faster hoping to leave the bee behind," Yancey Yarborough added. "And that pushes the trawler to speed up or make some silly mistake—"

"Why would the trawler captain want to outrun his own sub?" General Hescott asked in some bewilderment. "He needs that sub of his to catch up and get Julian off."

"A Russian sub can go forty knots submerged," Connors interjected. "He will catch up to that trawler in a hurry regardless of how fast the trawler goes, which is all of twenty knots."

"You miss the point, General Hescott," Fairfield added, giving a mollifying smile. "We've got to crowd the trawler . . . I don't think they want any of our people hanging around them when they transfer Julian to that sub . . . Am I correct, Bill? Willard?

"No." Banes came in quickly as if wanting to upstage Connors' command of the conversation. "They don't want us to know they made the transfer . . . You may have the strategy, Mr. President, though it may not affect the situation . . . The more we pressure that trawler, the more possibility of that captain making a mistake. It's all we've got in any case."

"Why would the trawler captain be afraid of a forty-five-foot sailboat?" Connors argued, making his challenge to Willard Banes rather than to the president. Banes continued to sit stoically with his arms folded across his chest. "Just remember that the trawler probably is running on powerful diesels . . . *Pequod* has to depend on wind . . . That trawler can outrun that sailboat . . . Or if he has to, he could run right over *Pequod*."

"Okay," the president cut in, sensing the rise of heat in the room. "But we have to do something . . . We can put our Intruders over them, but they know we can't keep recon up forever that far down the line . . . We'd have to have refueling planes following . . . I don't know how fast we can get that operation going anyway . . . So how much range do they have, Bill?"

"Enough fuel to get down to where they are now and back," Connors replied.

"So, enough fuel to get down there and back to Sydney," Fairfield went on. "No time to play around down there . . . but if we keep *Pequod* on him, we could make him feel even more nervous . . . or make him keep looking over his shoulder not really sure what *Pequod* has in mind . . . That kind of back trail watching can make you push the gas pedal a little harder . . . You ever try to get headlights out of your car mirror, gentlemen? Or to come back to my original analogy . . . the bees buzzing . . . What do you think?"

"I just can't put that much hope in *Pequod*, Mr. President," Connors insisted. "Not with the crew left on her . . . no, sir. . . ."

"OK, may it be farfetched," the president conceded, "but we do know that Russian trawler captain is going to be anxious to get Julian onto that sub . . . That can make him push, and I'm gambling on it . . . Our job right now is to make sure somehow that he can't get Julian off easily, or at all . . . And I want to do that without a nuclear missile shoot-out taking place."

"Well, we can't communicate with *Pequod* yet, Mr. President," Connors continued in a pessimistic tone. "There's no way we can know what has happened or what the remaining crew intends to do . . . There is no question in my mind that Julian is off that boat and already on the trawler, and the remaining crew is pushing *Piquod* back to Sydney."

"Your air recon should establish that one way or the other," Willard Banes suggested.

Connors' white bushy eyebrows lifted in acknowledgment, but he did not respond. Fairfield savored that for a long time, continuing to stare down at the map.

"Bill," he finally said in a meditative tone of voice, "where is that squadron of ships we dispatched out of Rio?"

"Last fix yesterday they were around the Horn and steaming northwest . . . heading in the direction of the trawler. . . ."

"How far away?"

"About a thousand or so miles off . . . But they've been shuttling along at only about twenty knots."

"Can they get to the trawler in a couple of days then?"

Connors frowned down at his yellow pad. "They can push it at thirty knots, Mr. President. They may not get there in time for tea but surely for the main course . . . One thing is sure, they'd be in close enough to be picked up by the trawler's radar. They'd know our ships are coming."

Fairfield nodded. "OK then, we'll count on *Pequod* to push that Russian trawler captain hopefully into the arms of our ships and to neutralize him . . . Or get him confused . . . maybe panic him . . . if that Russian skipper is the type. Or maybe we can get him to deal with us and put Julian over to us?"

"Mr. President," Connors interjected, his voice straining with control, though his red cheeks gave evidence of his rising blood pressure, "if you will permit me . . . if we close in, they will kill Julian before giving him to us . . . They'll dump him overboard and say they know nothing of any pirating out there—"

"I would agree with that, Mr. President," Mark Townshend confirmed quickly. He caught his own break of decorum, and his face flushed.

"Go ahead, Mark," the president encouraged.

Townshend cleared his throat uncomfortably. "Well, Mr. President, they won't give him to us . . . and they won't be found with him aboard . . . That's the way they are . . . as you know, Mr. President."

Fairfield gave him a quick smile of acknowledgment, dropped his glasses back over his eyes with a swipe of his right hand. He walked behind his chair and leaned his arms on the back of it, squinting down at the map. "We've got to continue to crowd the trawler," he concluded, his voice sounding hoarse and heavy with fatigue. "Whether that sub catches up or not, and he probably will, we may make them all hesitate long enough in making the transfer to allow us a stroke . . . any kind of stroke to prevent Julian going over. Mark, I take it this clergyman, Sebastian, and the Churchill woman have a yen for that kind of action?"

Townshend had checked and rechecked both Barbara Churchill and Sebastian through the case log back at Langley. "Churchill is a tough lady, Mr. President," he said factually. "She'll go the extra mile regardless of risks if her assignment calls for it . . . and sometimes even if it doesn't . . . This Sebastian at the same time is the type who will go ten miles if there is the human factor involved. He's not much on sticking his neck out for Cold War games . . . But he goes for the underdog every time . . . It's his theology, I guess."

"So then," Fairfield pursued, staring at his clenched hands in front of him, "would you say that this Sebastian fellow would probably get up a head of steam if the Russians did pirate Julian out from under Sebastian's nose?"

Townshend hesitated, frowning at the map and the cardboard models there in front of him. Then he looked up at his Commander-in-Chief and said, "I don't want to be dogmatic about it, Mr. President. I don't know what they are facing out there. But my guess is he'd probably chase that Russian just over the principle of the thing. Yes, sir."

The president chuckled, and all of them looked up quickly, never expecting to hear that sound from him in the mounting tension in the room. "Good for him! And Churchill will follow . . . She doesn't have much choice if he elects to do so anyway . . . But between those two, as you told me, Mark, I'd say they've got a chance of making that trawler captain uncomfortable."

"Excuse me, Mr. President," Connors interjected, his voice carrying doleful tones, his cheeks flushed, his blue eyes looking hard. "Are we going to place the future of the free world on the backs of a few people on a forty-five-foot sailboat? The chances of them surviving, even if they did give chase, without Julian, are extremely marginal. And beyond that, there is little they can do to that trawler in any case—"

"Bill," the president responded quickly, and there was that no-nonsense look in his eyes now, the red spots under them spreading wider like an inflamed rash, "that sailboat is as tight as a battleship if what I read about Julian this past week is correct." He picked up the book from the floor beside his chair and slid it across the slick surface of the map to Connors. Perplexed, the Defense Secretary looked at it, unable to see the relevance of that to his argument. But he politely picked it up and began thumbing through the pages, though his mind appeared not to be into it. "That's all about Julian, the man who won the International Cup from Sydney to Hobart twice . . . Yes, without him the rest of the *Pequod* crew may find it tough going . . . But they've got one of the best seagoing ketches for the job, so I think they'll do OK, and if they opt to crowd that trawler, they'll provide the pressure we need. . . ."

He paused and reached out with his yellow yardstick and nudged *The Pequod* a notch ahead to put it directly behind the trawler. Connors put the book aside, concentrating on the map again. The rest of them studied the position of the two cardboard models of *Pequod* and the trawler, their faces mirroring the uncertainty of what was being posed here.

"I'm putting some money on that Australian minesweeper *Vic-*

tor too," Fairfield added, and he turned and pointed his stick at the replica which was ten inches or more behind the other two. "I may be grabbing at straws, gentlemen, but I don't have many viable options here . . . unless you all think we ought to have the shoot-out down there, which would destroy any hope of keeping the Russians and OPAL at bay a little longer. . . ."

"I don't wish to sound truculent, Mr. President." Connors continued to dig, but kept his voice polite even though the furnace of his emotions poured more heat into his face. "I don't see *Victor* making it down there in time. We will have a confrontation then between the Russian sub and our *Bunker Hill*, somewhere out there when the trawler attempts the transfer. I have to be fair in warning you, Mr. President, that we cannot afford to allow Julian to get out of our hands and to the Russians . . . It will demand a maximum effort on our part to prevent it . . . and a maximum effort on the part of the Russian sub to pull it off."

"They surely won't go to a nuclear launch down there," Jim Brandt argued, his face turning pale.

"They have to go for broke," Connors argued. "They are too close to making OPAL the hammer that will beat us to our knees. . . ."

"You've got hound-dog torpedoes and conventional missiles without nuke warheads," Banes interjected. "That can stop the Russian sub as well as any . . ."

"Willard, it's who draws first with the biggest punch," Connors retaliated. "The Russians have the most to lose if they don't keep Julian. Besides, *Bunker Hill* is an old converted *Poseidon* sub used for communications patrols . . . She can crank up a bundle out of her missile wells if she has to, but her conventional use of hound dogs is not all that proven . . . I'd say go with caution but keep the finger on the firing key. . . ."

"So we exchange nuke warheads down there," Banes went on doggedly, his eyes snapping at Connors, "and who wins? As soon as we unload one on the Russian sub, we take everybody out . . . the trawler with Julian and *Pequod* and all the fish at sea . . . and what then? The Soviets unload their nuclear attack on us and with our nuclear retaliatory capability neutralized by that laser interference, where are we then?"

Connors caught the invective in Banes' voice and he backed off, not wanting to take on the Secretary of State when he was in that mood. "Just want to lay it all out, Willard," he said. "We are dead either way . . . If it takes a nuke strike, let it begin out there, that's all I'm saying. Better that way than sitting around allowing the Russians to make us crawl—"

"Gentlemen," Fairfield cut in, rubbing his eyes with the heels of both hands, straightening up behind his chair to do it. "Let's not talk nuclear war . . . yet."

"As long as we are on the laser interference," Jim Brandt asked, "do the Russians know yet that they have mucked up our missile navigation systems?"

"Apparently not," Connors replied, still sounding grousy and petulant. "If they knew we were having problems or even chronic dysfunctions, they'd be crowding us by now."

"But how long before they know?" Casey asked.

"Who knows?" Connors said with a shrug. "The press reported our blackouts on TV and telephones. But the Russians can't know the full extent of that interference on our missile capability yet. Otherwise, as I say, they'd be closing in on us by now. One thing we did find out, Mr. President, is that the laser interference is erratic, not constant. There are times when our missile navigational systems work fine. That means their lasers only bother us when OPAL is in a certain position in orbit. Once we find that out, we can take proper measures to activate our nuclear capability. . . ."

"The press is bound to get inside the missile problem," Hescott warned.

"Or the Russians may have one of their agents inside one of our missile bases or even in NORAD," Yarborough commented gloomily.

"Which only emphasizes the limitations of time," the president interrupted the exchange. "Now that Julian's daughter is over here, and the Russians know it, and they have a sub chasing down there to get David Julian, what can we expect the Russians to do about activating their fleet in that area? Any signs, Bill?"

Connors frowned at the map as if growing more irritated with the demands. "We've spotted a small flotilla of Russian warships coming out of the Indian Ocean just a bit north of the western coast of Australia . . . We are watching them. As yet they have not changed course south . . . But I would guess, Mr. President, that once they know we are sending five ships around the Horn, they will head full out down there. . . ."

Fairfield said nothing for a long minute. The room had gone

deathly still as all eyes remained fixed on the map, each man creating his own battle scenario of what could be in a few days. Their faces were drawn and pinched by the tension.

"So . . ." Fairfield picked up again, sitting down in his chair and leaning his elbows on the map. To Mark Townshend, Fairfield looked as though he had aged ten years overnight and another coat of weather-beaten paint had been added in the past hour. "You know that Kamiloff is not coming. And you know the reasons Mark has suggested for that. I don't blame the man for not wanting to be over here with OPAL about to become operational. And I wouldn't want him to come under the demands I would make of him about that."

"The press is beginning to put it all together, Mr. President," Jim Brandt offered. "Kamiloff's cancellation because of illness, together with the presence of OPAL up there, has them all speculating. . . ."

"So be it," Fairfield said with a sigh. "All we can do now is put it all on *Pequod*, gentlemen . . . and *Victor*. Not very good odds for us . . . Maybe, only maybe. But let's keep cool heads. Bill, I leave it to you to make certain the captain of *Bunker Hill* does not go to the firing button unless fired upon . . . He's got to hassle that sub to the point it can't surface and get Julian . . . I know the risks of a shootout . . . But tell the captain to bite his lip before going to countdown."

"Very well, Mr. President," Connors replied, still disgruntled.

"What about the Cabinet meeting tomorrow, Mr. President?" Jim Brandt asked. "We've gone more than a week with OPAL and have not filled them in. . . ."

"Yes, we do it tomorrow," Fairfield replied. "I imagine they will be a bit miffed . . . But we had to keep this thing as close to our chests as possible."

"And the National Security Council, Mr. President?" Yancey Yarborough added. "I've had a lot of calls in the last week asking me about OPAL and the cancellation of Kamiloff."

The president frowned at the map. "I'm having a dinner party tomorrow night at the White House for the U.N. Security Council delegations. That's at 7. Invite our Council people . . . When the others are gone, we'll meet in the Cabinet Room. And as for the Joint Chiefs, General Hescott, you better get them clued in right away too. . . ."

"I think any military decisions should go to them first, Mr.

President," Hescott said, miffed himself now. "I don't think we should allow our five ships around the Horn or even move *Bunker Hill* in pursuit of the Russian sub without conferring with the Chiefs."

"You want to lose more time waiting for them to come to consensus?" Connors interjected with some impatience. "You are the chairman, and you speak for them now . . . Otherwise we've lost any edge we might remotely have. . . ."

"He's right, General," Fairfield added. "Call your people together, brief them on my decision, and do what you can to calm them down."

"Yes, sir," Hescott replied with a depressing note in his voice.

"We have to update Barney about how to handle the press, Mr. President," Jim Brandt came in again. "They are on his tail day and night, like a pack of hounds. . . ."

"He'll have to stall them, that's his job," Fairfield said shortly. He was beginning to sound waspish now under the increasing tension. "It's now 5:30, gentlemen . . . do you know where your nuclear missiles are?" He gave a short, grunting sound as if he wanted it to be a chuckle, but it came off sounding sardonic. "Dinner at 7 . . . I will be off in my copter back to the White House at 6 in the morning. I expect the rest of you to be at Cabinet on time tomorrow. Before we adjourn, gentlemen, remember what I said: cool heads prevail. We are not down and out yet. OK?"

"Yes, Mr. President," they all said in unison, trying to put it on a high note though their voices lacked conviction. They all got up then and stuffed papers into their attaché cases and walked out slowly. Their conversation was a mixture of questions, some argument, some doubts. A few remained glumly silent including Bill Connors and Willard Banes, who were more preoccupied with the immensity of the growing crisis.

The president stayed behind in his chair, staring at the cardboard replicas of *Pequod* and the trawler, then the Australian minesweeper further behind them and the Russian sub up the coast of Australia. They were all coming together very fast, he thought. He heard the sound of Christmas carols coming from another room in the house, drifting through the open door.

"Silent night," he repeated, his voice heavy. "But for how long? Holy night? Unholy night out there. . . ."

He continued to stare at the map, the heaviness in his chest feeling like a hand pressing down. He stood up slowly, still staring at the map as if expecting the cardboard mock-ups to move.

"Go with the wind, Sebastian," he said finally, his voice hoarse and hollow in the empty room. "And God go with you!"

Eleven

Captain First Rank Ilius Aviloff had it out with his political officer, Comrade Second Rank Ovar Romonovich, an hour after they brought a groggy David Julian aboard the *Minsk*.

"I do not as captain of this ship condone unnecessary violence, comrade," Aviloff said with a biting tone in his voice. "I forbid you ever again to withhold necessary information about any assignment I am to undertake while in command. Your boat was all the way to *Pequod* before Comrade Zugonski handed me the message from Leningrad Naval Command stating there would be no exchange . . . That made it too late to abort. . . ."

"Abort, comrade captain?" Romonovich said, pausing in his eating of a cup of caviar. He was a bulky man, almost rotund, no more than five foot eight inches in height. His face was puffy and blotchy from too many digestive explosions inside. His gluttony for vodka and sausage was well known among his fellow officers. He was no more than thirty-eight years old but looked twenty years older than that. Because of the ballooning effect, his dark eyes were mere slits, forced into a squint. His short goatee was scraggly, like a squirrel's battered tail. "May I remind you, comrade captain, our orders were not to abort in any case," and he went back to gulping his fish eggs. "Our assignment was to get Julian. We did that. As to violence, comrade captain, that is sometimes our way of life when the stakes are high."

"There is the matter of honor," Aviloff argued. "Julian gave his word to come over to us in exchange for his daughter . . . The daughter is already over to the West . . . So we have committed a totally dishonorable act in breaching that agreement."

"Honor?" Romonovich gave a lifeless smile, a mere spasm of his fat lips speckled with the black caviar. "Which honor is that, comrade captain? The honor you knew in the days of the siege of Stalingrad perhaps? Or escorting American supply ships through the Baltic to Murmansk in 1940? That honor in your days, if you will pardon me, comrade captain, no longer applies. It is bourgeois."

"Let me remind you, comrade," Aviloff countered, feeling the rising disgust for the man's slovenly demeanor and his piglike gulping of the caviar in the presence of his commanding officer, "that you are under my command."

"Oh, of course, of course, comrade captain," the political officer was quick to affirm, putting down the cup of fish eggs on the captain's desk and smacking his lips. "I mean no disrespect . . . But it is my assignment to protect Mother Russia's interests in terms of what we consider political situations. You are, comrade captain, the chauffeur, and I pick up the merchandise. Not a bad analogy, is it?"

"It is close to insult," Aviloff said crisply, keeping his eyes boring into the political officer's face.

Romonovich gave that quick sardonic smile as if he were amused by the exchange. As political officer, his role was in effect to do as he said—to carry out the assignments that were of a "political nature" as Leningrad and Moscow declared. Like picking up Clay Bird off the Australian coast a few days ago. Romonovich had never explained who the man was or why he boarded *Minsk*. He had been waiting on a thirty-foot fishing boat twenty miles off the coast.

Aviloff watched him come aboard . . . a heavyset man dressed in rumpled gray slacks and an open-necked sport shirt, carrying a windbreaker over his shoulder. His eyes were hidden behind sunglasses. He came up the ladder, gave a quick grin to Romonovich that flashed with the sun, then was led below to his quarters. The political officer had not explained him or allowed him to take his meals with the officer's mess.

Aviloff did not bother to question Romonovich about the man; it was his domain anyway. And as KGB connected with Naval Intelligence, Romonovich had no reason to share any of his doings with Aviloff unless it affected the safety of the ship. Yet, any political officer would be careful to maintain proper protocol with the captain lest he risk insubordination . . . such as right now.

"Comrade captain," he went on in that overdone diplomatic tone of voice as though he were speaking to a child, "we have in our hands the one man who can make our satellite OPAL fully offensive. I refer to Dr. David Julian, of course. There is no room for a discussion of honor when it comes to that. Honor is in the completion of our assignment in whatever way is necessary. Sentimentality about methods is outdated and unworkable. In all due respect," and he said that with a tone of extravagant deference, "let me remind you that political assignments take precedence over your command. You get this ship where it is to go. My task is to fulfill my orders when you get me there. So then," and he picked up his half-filled glass of vodka, "I drink to your expert navigation, comrade captain." He lifted his glass and swallowed the contents in one gulp, put it back on the desk, belched, and nodded his satisfaction.

"*The Pequod* continues to pursue us," Aviloff warned, anxious for some counterthrust to punch a hole in the facade of fat and the false obsequiousness of the man.

Romonovich's laugh was a short cough sounding like a bark, his small front teeth showing dark stains from the caviar.

"Excuse me, comrade captain, but it worries me that you feel that little boat is any consequence to us . . . We have a 130-foot trawler under us . . . sixty thousand tons of steel against a forty-five-foot ketch. The wood chip is of no bother to us. . . ."

"He is a pointer, Comrade Romonovich," Aviloff argued. "We have taken down our colors . . . There are other ships in the area moving north . . . If there is air reconnaissance, *The Pequod* will target us."

"So?" the political officer replied, lifting his eyebrows. "We will leave him behind . . . He depends on wind . . . We have diesel. If that is not enough, you can turn on him . . . roll over him . . . Whatever is necessary, comrade captain, to protect our passenger, Julian, you will do . . . at least until our submarine *Gorky* catches up to us and we transfer him. . . ."

"I remind you, comrade," Aviloff kept burrowing into the pompousness of the man, "that we have a bad bearing in the starboard engine. We should heave-to and repair it."

"Heave-to?" Romonovich looked aghast. "We keep moving, comrade captain! To stop draws attention."

"If we stop, the *Gorky* catches up sooner," Aviloff advised.

"Yes, and whoever else is behind us, comrade captain. The Seventh Fleet may be in Guam, but a matter of so sensitive a nature as capturing Julian will bring speedy action by the United States and the Allies. For all we know, there are American ships pursuing us now . . . perhaps a submarine or two . . . So we can be sure we will see ships coming down on us. . . ." He paused and belched again. Aviloff felt the heat rush up into his cheeks. "By the way, comrade captain, I do not like what I see in your executive officer's demeanor lately. Second Rank Comrade Popov shows all the signs of preoccupation with his self-pity. I suggest you properly orient him as to his loyalties . . . or it shall become my duty to do so. Now then, may I say good night, comrade, and my gratitude for the excellent caviar and vodka." He nodded, then walked to the door, paused, and turned back. "May I suggest, comrade captain, since you are such a skillful player at chess that you invite David Julian to a match. We have word that he is very good at it. Give him some recreation, get his mind off his circumstances . . . yes?"

Aviloff did not give him the benefit of a reply. The political officer turned and walked out.

Aviloff stood there a long time, feeling the backwash of the odors that accompanied the political officer. He turned and walked to his desk, feeling the burning acid in his throat over the way Julian had been treated. Romonovich was right. The old school who still remembered Stalingrad and convoy escorts in the Baltic, like himself, were going off the scene. Now it was the new rank, the Romonovich class, the unfeeling apes of the Party who knew no morality or honor—only the need to get it done for *Rodina*.

He thought of Julian, remembering his being carried aboard the *Minsk*, his bleeding head wrapped with a crude bandage. The man looked fragile, but he was feisty enough to punch a seaman on his way up the ladder from the small boat. The man had to be in a fury. He had agreed to exchange himself for his daughter. Now it embarrassed Aviloff that he was part of so cruel an event, the dishonoring of a man of dignity.

Then suddenly Aviloff became curious about the man. Perhaps he would have him brought up, as Romonovich suggested. They could converse in English. Aviloff was of the old school where English was mandatory when training for the navy. It would at least be a way to show Julian that not all Russians were like Romonovich.

Lieutenant Commander Robert Sperry, captain of the Australian frigate *Victor*, looked out across the gathering seas, the two-day fog now dissipated, giving way to a chilly sun. The pounding of the frigate's engines on the deck plates beneath his feet was both a comfort and a cause for concern. They were making only twelve knots, maybe thirteen. Not enough.

He was fifty-two years of age, had served a hitch in the Australian navy during the Korean War commanding an escort vessel for United Nations supply ships. He had joined the Australian Coastal ten years ago. He was an expert yachtsman and seaman all around.

He was a tall, thin, wiry man who was browned to the texture of leather by the years of sun and sea that was Australia. He had deep, blue eyes, a slightly hooked nose, and a wide mouth with lines of humor at the corners. He was a laid-back commander, but no one bucked him or tried to use him. When he snapped an order, the fifty-two crew members jumped to it.

He was worried now though. The storm that had slammed into them four days ago had sprung some leaks in the old hull of the frigate. She had not been used to long runs out into the Pacific, keeping mostly to in-shore rescue operations, never more than twenty miles out. In the past few days she creaked and groaned in the rough sea, and there were reports of some flooding in the engine and supply spaces.

Right now he wished he were home with Megan, his wife, and their granddaughter, Crystal, who was five. They had planned a picnic at Bondi Beach, a favorite outing for Crystal. And it was becoming more of a pleasure to himself as well. He was beginning to long for more days at the beach, sprawling lazily in the sun.

But what made him even more uneasy now was the uncertainty of his mission. All he had been told was to find *The Pequod*, Dr. David Julian's ketch, somewhere along a projected course of which nobody was quite sure. The last radio check was more than a week ago, and after that . . . silence. But Commander Ward Griffin of Coastal put it to him straight: "Just find him, Bob. All the heavies are up in maneuvers around Guam. Find him and stay with him until we get further orders from upstairs."

Sperry wondered then why Ward would even think of "heavies" for this mission. So he asked over the phone, "Is there a bogie crowding Julian, sir?"

Hesitating, Ward had said, "Rescue for now, Bob . . . If it changes, we will radio you. Just find him and stick with him, all right?"

Sperry still felt uneasy. The *Victor* was not a top ship of the line, even for Coastal. She was too old. Some kind of flap was on for the top brass to reach this deep into the reserves for a job that seemed to carry dimensions of deeper magnitude. He thought of Megan and Crystal again. His daughter, Jan, and her husband, Bob Dane, were off on a biological field trip with their science department colleagues at the University of Sydney. He loved Crystal. He and Megan felt their lives had taken on new beginnings with her around.

They were obviously disappointed when he told them he had been called back on watch with Coastal Rescue. And Megan had looked at him with that question in her eyes, the same that had nibbled at him since he put *Victor* out of Sydney Harbour. What was so important in Coastal that they had to pull him back on watch? They had other people on watch schedules, men younger than he, and certainly as competent.

But even more, when he saw they had *Victor* out of the yards and waiting for him at the pier, rather than the seventy-foot light riggers usually used for rescue, he knew that there was something different in the wind. No one else in Coastal had experience in bigger tonnage ships like the corvette he had commanded during the Korean stint.

He thought of David Julian, the man who was the "favorite son" for many Australians, including himself. Sperry remembered reading Julian's books in school, on the new physics, then astronomy, which led to the five books on satellite technology theory later at university. Julian had become some kind of folk hero. And brassy. He had to be to take a cruise at eighty to England.

But the fact that he cut out of Sydney without telling anyone was odd to Sperry. The city had been waiting for weeks to give the man a proper send-off. Now the top brass were anxious to find him out in the Southern Ocean. And for Sperry the orders were strange: "Stick with him." Why?

He turned and walked aft on the bridge to look out the windows astern. He glanced up at the single stack. The smoke kept puffing out at intervals. Sperry disliked a stack on any ship coughing out carbon in black mushroom clouds which at times obliterated the stern.

He felt the vibration of the engines increase under his feet. The old turbines were going into arrhythmia again. He turned to his executive officer, Dick Cornfield, and said, "Number one, take the bridge . . . I'm going down to the engine room."

"Aye, sir," Cornfield replied.

Sperry descended into the bowels of the old, creaking frigate, ladder by ladder, until he got down to the steaming, bellowing, hissing engine room. The turbines were booming a raucous, desperate sound. He slid down the rail of the last block of iron steps to the deck, glancing up at the steam gauges.

"Mornin', captain!"

Sperry turned to see his chief engineer standing a few feet away. His name was Butch Call. He had served in War II, the last part of it on a tanker running the Atlantic convoys to Britain. After that, he had a year or two on a destroyer escort. He knew steam turbines well enough. He was in his late fifties at least. He was short, pudgy, with a quick ready grin that showed a gap in the lower line of his teeth. He had large brown eyes, a pug nose, and a perpetual sheen of engine grease on his face. He should have retired by now, taken his years and pay and lolled out on a beach and forgotten ships and Coastal Rescue. But he was of the old line . . . he would go until he was incapable or was politely ordered out.

"Sounds rough!" Sperry yelled to him above the sound of the grinding turbines.

"You bet, sir!" Call yelled back, wiping his oily hands on the smeared blue rag. "Her plates is too thin, her seams is splittin'. And her turbines is knockin' on bad bearings, sir! She oughta be put to sleep, if ya don't mind my sayin' it. She did her duty in War Two at Coral Sea . . . Got her Royal Citation too, sir! She needs a decent burial, that's what . . . Not poundin' her heart out like this, sir! If ya'll pardon me, sir!"

Sperry glanced toward the oil-fed furnaces and boilers that rumbled out the sound of flame and steam. Above that was the continual thumping of those turbines coughing hissing gasps with each turn.

"Can you get any more speed out of her?"

Call's eyes went wide with that. "Sir, she's puttin' out all she can turn now! If I open her a notch more, she'll rise to it, sir . . . But she'll give her last gasp with it! Like a stroke, sir . . . Ya know what I mean? She'd blow her main arteries . . . She don't belong out here fightin' to stay afloat, ya know what I mean, sir? What she doin' out here on rescue for, sir, mind if I ask?"

"Got a big one down the ocean in trouble," Sperry said, and decided to leave it at that. Then he added, "I may need a few more knots out of her some time along the way, Butch."

"I understand, sir," Butch said, but his eyes showed his reluctance, as if he were being asked to "put her asleep" himself.

Sperry turned to go back up the ladder, then paused. "We're trailing a lot of smoke out of the stack! Any way to control that?"

Butch rubbed his hands on the rag, frowning as if he thought it was a picky point. "In the old days she could make a lot of smoke up the extra pipes when asked for it as a screen . . . But the filters to hold that back are worn now, sir. You'd get more smoke if I didn't go lean on the oil feed and keep the carbon down. Nothin' more I can do, sir. I'm sorry."

Sperry felt awkward in asking about it. "OK, let it go, Butch. We have nothing to hide anyway. Keep them turning."

"Right, sir!"

Sperry started back up the ladder, leaving the choking, dying sounds behind him. Back on the bridge, he checked course and position. He guessed he was four to five days behind *Pequod*. He hoped he would face no more storms in the old ship. If so, her turbines might give out. As he looked over the sun-whipped swells ahead, he could only pray there would be no more heavy weather. For himself and for *Pequod*. Something was going on. He caught it in Commander Ward's voice. Something bigger than a rescue operation. He wondered if *Victor* was making her last run after all. That thought made him more contemplative.

Yet somehow he knew David Julian and *Pequod* were going to need him.

David Julian sat across the small round table from Captain Aviloff, saying nothing. He had been sitting there a long fifteen minutes in silence, a deliberate protest of Aviloff. His dark eyes were carrying the smoke of the smudge fires of anger that were ready to puff into flashing flame at any minute. The bandage around his head looked like a dirty sweatband. His rumpled blue admiral's cap was pushed up from his eyes, revealing the twigs of white scrambled hair that added to the defiance and pugnaciousness in him.

Aviloff had put the chess board on the table between them. Julian showed no interest. His smoldering eyes stayed on Aviloff's face.

"Dr. Julian," Aviloff finally said with a sigh, speaking English slowly and precisely. "I understand how you feel. I did not support the order to take you bodily off your boat. We have a political officer aboard who commits me to those actions . . . He has the authority to do so in certain situations. I am sorry—"

"I dishonored myself to my country," Julian cut in abruptly, his voice heavy with the bite of insult he had experienced. "And myself . . . I did that because I thought I had a gentleman's agreement with you Russians that I would get my daughter back to the West in exchange for myself. I have been betrayed. I hardly think it is the time for games, captain."

Aviloff nodded. He debated whether to tell Julian that his daughter was already in the West. But he backed away from it, knowing it could complicate matters with Romonovich. Though he did not fear the political officer, he knew that if it got back to the Admiralty at this point, it could go against him. He thought of Soya and his sons. It was not worth creating pressure on them, even though he could not imagine that it would. Still, with a man like Romonovich, who looked for cause against anyone, it was better to play it close.

"Dr. Julian, I have two sons in the navy back in Russia," he said then, deciding to take the only tack he had left. "I would do anything to protect them and provide for their happiness . . . I sympathize with you in this sordid business with your daughter. But if it is any comfort I would have done as you did . . . and I would be just as angry to be cheated as you are right now." He paused and touched a knight on the chess board with his right finger. "But all the more reason to share together something we have in common on this reasonably neutral ground here . . . this cabin . . . for neither of us can do anything about our circumstances. . . ."

Julian still did not move. He continued to sit across the table in his pose of truculence. Finally Aviloff reached over and picked up the coffeepot from the hot plate and poured two mugs full. He pushed one across the table. Julian ignored it. Aviloff sipped his own, then waited.

It was an hour before David Julian reached for his cup. Aviloff reached for it. "Let me warm it up for you, doctor," he said softly. Julian's eyes dropped to the cup as if surprised he had picked it up. Then he extended it slowly across the table.

Aviloff took it, got up, and poured the cold coffee out into the sink in the corner, poured a fresh cup, and handed it back to Julian.

Julian held the cup a long time, his eyes remaining on Aviloff, still not sure he should yield to any amenities here. Aviloff pointed to the chess board.

"You may begin, doctor," he said and smiled.

Julian hesitated, then put down his cup and stared at the board.

He won the first two games, and Aviloff saluted him by pouring more coffee.

"You play well and straight," he commented.

"I always have," Julian replied categorically, and there was a deliberate jab in his voice. He took off his blue admiral's cap and placed it on the table by his right elbow. "In all areas of competition I play fair and straight. I expected you Russians to do the same. You tell me you are not responsible. But you are still captain of this vessel. I have always taken responsibility for my boat."

"When it comes to the safety of this ship and her crew, I do," Aviloff replied, feeling the bite of Julian's words.

Julian looked up at him. His eyes were not as smoky or as close to flash point now. But his chin still jutted out in his continuing anger. "Just remember, captain, you cannot get my brain without my heart. You have shut away my heart by not delivering my daughter to *Pequod*."

Aviloff nodded. "I appreciate that . . . It appears, however, that you have a heart for chess. And your brain obviously is in it with unusual alacrity. Shall we go another then?"

They conversed between moves. Julian talked about his background, his deceased wife, his daughter, then Ryan. Aviloff shared about his life with Soya and their two sons. And there were long silences when both men concentrated on their moves on the board.

The time went by quickly. Finally when Aviloff looked up from his concentration on the chess game, he saw shafts of sunlight coming through the ports.

"Sun is up, doctor," he said, leaning back to stretch and yawn. "I am partial to watching the sea at sunup from the deck of a ship. Would you join me?"

They walked out on the porch facing the stern. The sea rolled in long, easy swells under a brisk northeasterly breeze. The air was fresh, and both men took in deep breaths of it to revitalize their lungs and hearts.

Out of habit, Aviloff had carried his binoculars with him, putting the strap around his neck. He lifted them and searched the horizon, then swept to port and starboard, came back again to fix on something that moved a few points astern portside.

He lowered the glasses, lifted the strap from around his neck, and handed them to Julian. "Five degrees to port, about one-seven-five bearing, doctor," he said.

Julian took the binoculars and stared through them. "*Pequod*," he said, a note of surprise in his voice, and a tinge of disappointment. "He should be heading back to Sydney! They can't fight this ocean by themselves . . . Provisions are low . . . Besides, my son is on that boat. . . ."

He handed the binoculars back to Aviloff. The captain took them, put the strap around his neck again.

"So why does he keep coming?" he asked. "Who commands her, and what can he hope to accomplish following us?"

Julian did not comment for a long time. Then he said, "It's a question of dogma, captain," his eyes intent in the direction of *Pequod* some miles back.

Aviloff lowered the binoculars and glanced at Julian. "I don't understand."

Julian grunted what sounded like a half-chuckle. "Dogma," he repeated, and a thin smile crossed his lips as if he had a secret. "Like your Marxist-Leninist dogma . . . Only this one who drives *Pequod* lives by Biblical dogma. You know anything about that, captain?"

Aviloff continued to look at him. "Biblical?" Immediately he thought of Soya.

"Yes, sir," Julian said with a sigh, his voice carrying a lilting tone as if he found it amusing. "He believes in True North for everybody. True North to him is God. I told him there are no fixed True Norths . . . Everyone finds his own. He said there has to be, if a man is to know where he is going in life. Rather a plebian view . . . But if he's anything like my wife who held to that kind of dogma, and I think he is, you can be sure he'll keep coming after you, captain. Or drown trying."

"True North?" Aviloff asked, still bewildered.

"Yes, you see, to him God has cut trails all over the place for a man to follow," Julian went on, almost reciting. "The stars, the winds, the currents . . . He even believes God has walked the seas and left His mark for man to follow . . . That's his idea of True

North. . . ." He paused, shading his eyes with his right hand to stare out toward the last position of *Pequod*. "He's a naive clergyman, captain. . . ."

Aviloff lifted his binoculars to study the boat, a flash of blue-and-white canvas in the distance.

"Clergyman?" he responded in some wonder. "It is he who pursues us? A man of the church?"

Julian chuckled again, amused at Aviloff's astonishment. "Your world would consider him the weakest, captain. But not his kind. My wife used to refer to 'the hound of heaven.' God, she said. God is 'the hound of heaven' who pursues every man and woman until we all yield and take His love He offers. It's all about God, captain, and those who believe in the myth and the legend. Those 'hounds' bark and make a lot of noise, but nothing changes. And now that silly dogmatist, the 'hound,' is leading my son to his death . . . I knew he might do just that too . . . I knew it when I took him on as crew . . . I thought I had taken special measures to make sure he would not, could not pursue . . . But yet he comes anyway . . . Nothing worse than a religious fanatic to compound already existing complications . . . Do you agree, captain?"

Aviloff could not answer immediately. He was confused and dumbstruck by what Julian was saying. "Unless he is a Marxist fanatic," he finally offered. Then he lowered his binoculars again but continued to stare astern at the pursuing boat. He thought of Soya. How could it be true? Someone who would believe the Book enough to go that far?

"What does he think he can do?" he asked Julian. "Does he think he can rescue you? That we will turn you back to him?"

Julian's laugh sounded a bit harsh over his attempt to be jocular. "He jabs your conscience, captain. Or at least he thinks he does. To him, you have committed an injustice to another human being . . . me. It's immoral in his credo. His mind says you have to make it right or face the judgment of God . . . So he thinks he is acting for God now . . . You must give me back or be judged . . . Or else you take the forgiveness that he believes God has for you and then you will give me back. The true evangelist, captain. I had it all from my good wife when she lived . . . It is all nonsense, but it will drive him beyond his limits for his cause. . . ."

Aviloff heard the bells announcing the change of watch on the trawler. He felt that a part of his universe had shifted. His devotion to *Rodina* had been the only "True North" for him. As much as he liked the Book, there was no demonstrable act of the characters within it that could measure up to the Marxist-Leninist statement of behavior and action. To sacrifice oneself for another person made no sense . . . If it was sacrifice for the State, yes; for the masses, yes.

"You do not sound as if you respect anything he believes or what he is doing," he said to Julian.

"I think he should use common sense and turn around and go home," Julian replied flatly. "I respect him only in the same way I did my wife for the same silly beliefs . . . But I hold to no Deity, captain. It is a myth. And myths cannot be depended upon."

Aviloff pondered that for a long minute. Then he lifted his binoculars again and studied *Pequod* pushing under full sail. "He is good with sails?"

Julian grunted. "Still green, captain," he replied. "That is what I am afraid of now. None of them is competent enough to hold her in a big blow. My son, Ryan, knows the most, but he has a game leg."

Aviloff lowered the binoculars and glanced at the horizon. "His myth will soon be put to the test," and he pointed at the smudge of clouds on the northeastern horizon, still looking harmless but gathering the familiar cirrus swirls of a storm. "I think we should see what is shaping up."

They stepped back into Aviloff's cabin. He went to the barometer on the wall, Julian following. "It falls quickly," he said in a somber voice. "It will be bad later today for your *Pequod* and crew."

"So I see," Julian said, his voice subdued. "Yes, I am afraid Sebastian will now test his True North . . . I just hope his God will give him luck and show him the way. For my son's life . . . and for my long-time friend's daughter as well. . . ."

Aviloff continued to feel the disturbing ripples in his chest. The Book was now being acted out in his world, the sea, the same trackless sea he had plowed all his life. And one man dared to believe that God left the marks to follow? Soya would be ecstatic if she knew. But as for himself, all he could conclude was that the clergyman would need more than tracks in the sea to come through the storm that formed up in the northeast.

The trawler's siren sounded even as he continued to study the barometer needle. The warning was to the crew to begin lashing down any loose deck equipment. The day would go fast, and the storm would be on them by afternoon or early evening.

"It is time for you to return to your quarters, Dr. Julian," he said. "I shall now have to take command of the bridge. It has been a good night. I will speak to you again and perhaps share another chess match."

"My privilege," Julian said. But his voice carried some dragging notes of worry, thinking about *Pequod*. He pulled his blue admiral's cap down over his eyes as the guard came into the room on Aviloff's signal.

Aviloff stayed in front of the barometer a long time after Julian left. He felt confused, out of balance. He walked back to the porch aft of his cabin again, stepped outside, and stared astern toward the 175 bearing where he had last seen *Pequod*. He lifted his binoculars and scanned to the left and right of the bearing. He finally picked up the faint flash of her white sail, looking like a sea gull banking her wing in the sun, aft on a 180 bearing.

He stared at it a long time, unable to comprehend what the clergyman manning her now was thinking. None of what Julian had told him had made sense. Finally he turned and walked back inside, still troubled but not knowing why. Romonovich was there waiting for him just inside the door, extending a yellow signals paper in his right hand.

Aviloff moved to him and took the paper without a word, conscious of the reek of vodka on Romonovich's breath. He looked as though he had slept in his clothes. Aviloff scanned the message:

> COMMANDER ILYUS AVILOFF
> SUPREME SOVIET SHIP MINSK
>
> PROCEED IMMEDIATELY TO DISTANCE
> YOURSELF FROM PEQUOD. MAKE
> ALL SPEED.
> ADMIRAL KARKOV
> LENINGRAD

Aviloff looked up quickly at Romonovich, who showed a certain gleam in his squinting eyes, the spasm of a smile forming on his fat lips, as if he had given the order himself.

"You told them about *Pequod*?" Aviloff demanded.

"It is, as you know, comrade captain, the duty of the political officer to report all possible political situations that may interfere with the delivery of Dr. Julian."

"I thought you said *Pequod* was an inconsequential wood chip, comrade," Aviloff jabbed, a flush of heat beginning to burn his neck.

"I also said, comrade captain, that you could outrun him on diesel. . . ."

"You know I have a bad starboard engine that needs repair. If I have to increase speed, there is a very good chance I will lose that engine . . . That puts us almost dead slow to save the other one."

"Comrade captain," Romonovich replied imperiously, "the Admiralty does not want anyone around when we transfer Julian to our submarine *Gorky*. They do not want the United States, Australia, anyone in the West to know that we even transferred him . . . Do you understand that, comrade captain? That includes *Pequod* . . . The Admiralty gave the order—"

"You lifted our radio scrambler to talk to the Admiralty about this?" Aviloff continued to lean verbally into his political officer, disregarding the warnings that Romonovich would like nothing more than to report the captain's arguments back to Karkov. "You were not authorized by me—"

"Comrade captain," Romonovich replied in that insultingly ingratiating tone of voice, his lips parting in what was supposed to be a smile but looked more like a sneer, "I have my duty—"

"By lifting that scrambler you could have allowed *Pequod* to get a signal out!" Aviloff berated him. "If Australian monitors got through, they will have air reconnaissance over us in no time!"

"Comrade captain, I am only doing my duty—"

"Then you do so as I order you!" Aviloff took to walking rapidly in small circles in front of Romonovich, his hands clenched behind his back, head down. "I remind you again . . . You will not take any action of any kind on this ship without my permission. Is that understood, comrade?"

Aviloff stopped and turned his head to stare into the squinting dark eyes of the political officer. "Comrade captain," Romonovich said venomously, "I serve the KGB and the GMU as well as Navy Intelligence . . . My first duty is to them. . . ."

"The safety of this ship and crew is my responsibility . . . and you will abide by that! Speeding up our engines could mean complications and place Dr. Julian in danger . . . Mark it well, Comrade Romonovich, I will have you in front of Admiral Karkov for insubordination if your breaking radio silence and increasing speed result in disaster to this ship. Is that clear?"

The political officer's eyes were mere slits, and his cheeks seemed to puff out like a frog's. "Do not exaggerate the case, comrade captain—"

"I do not exaggerate!" Aviloff began walking in his tight circles again, fighting for control, not wanting to press too far over the line. "I need Comrade Popov up here immediately."

"He is under confinement to quarters, comrade captain," Romonovich said flatly.

Aviloff stopped short again in his circling and stared at the political officer. "Confinement? Why?"

"He is too negative among the crew . . . He always talks about the bad engine . . . He is not to be trusted. . . ."

"You make my executive officer a prisoner on this ship on your own cognizance?" Aviloff demanded, ignoring the warning beats inside him now. "You can note for certain, comrade, that you are logged in as being totally unfit to carry officer rank on any ship of Russia. When and if we get to Murmansk, you will stand trial for that too. Do you understand?"

Romonovich blinked, but other than that there was no sign in the bloated face of any feeling about it one way or the other. But the sloppy smile playing on the fat lips and the narrow slits of the eyes indicated his usual contempt for Aviloff's authority.

"I repeat the order, comrade captain," he said, his voice carrying a certain smugness. "We increase speed and leave *Pequod* behind."

"And our own submarine as well?"

Romonovich grunted a sound of disdain. "Comrade captain, you know that our submarine *Gorky* moves very fast . . . She will be on us in a few hours no matter how fast we go. Our assignment is to leave that sailboat behind, correct?"

Aviloff knew the political officer had scored the point. There was nothing else to do. He turned and walked to his desk to get away from the stench of the man. "You will get Comrade Popov up here immediately," he said, leaning his hands on the desktop and staring at the yellow signals message, "or we will not increase speed. He alone has the engineering charts and knows how much that starboard engine can take without breaking down. Julian's safety is at stake, may I remind you, comrade? If you wish to play with that fact, then it is your own responsibility."

The political officer seemed to go very still, like a bird dog sniffing a sure prey.

"As you wish, comrade captain," he said, but his voice carried the note of final judgment he felt he now owned. "But when you are finished with Comrade Popov, you are to return him to confinement."

"Do not test me further, Comrade Romonovich."

Aviloff moved away from the desk, folding his arms across his chest, stopping a few feet from the political officer, staring into the slits of his snakelike eyes. An enemy had now surely been born, and Aviloff knew it. And making an enemy of a KGB or GMU intelligence officer was asking for serious complications back in Russia.

Romonovich hesitated as if he wanted to say something more. But then that sloppy, false, ingratiating smile crossed his puffy lips. He bowed stiffly and, with a curt nod of his head, turned and walked out.

Aviloff let out a heavy sigh. It was a shaky one. He had lost control. The anger still coursed through him, forcing a heavy beat in his chest. Something about the political officer aroused in him the carefully banked emotions he had felt for some time about the new order in *Rodina*. Now it was out. Romonovich saw it all too well.

He looked up as a knock sounded on his door.

"Come!"

Popov opened the door slowly and stepped inside. The second-in-command looked even more forlorn now. He carried the roll of engineering charts under his right arm.

"Come in, Popov," Aviloff said, trying to sound upbeat. Popov said nothing as he put the charts on the desktop.

As Aviloff spread them out, he thought of what Julian had said about the clergyman who captained *The Pequod*. "The hound of heaven"? Well, with the *Minsk* about to increase speed, and the storm quickly approaching, it would take quite a feat and certainly a good scent for the clergyman to stay on them now.

Twelve

Sebastian tapped the barometer glass on his way aft. It was still dropping. It was 2 in the afternoon of the 17th. He chewed on some crackers and salmon, all he would be allowed in the rationing menu Barbara had given him. A swallow of fresh water and a half-dozen super food supplements on top of it. That was it.

Barbara had the wheel while Ryan slept. Jamison was in his bunk, unable to lift his head due to the seasickness. The man's face was gaunt, his eyes hollow. He had to be down ten to fifteen pounds at least.

The radar showed the trawler up in the outer circle of the screen eight miles ahead. She stayed on that range consistently, as if she could care less that *Pequod* was following. But he was afraid now that the coming squall might throw them off. He would find it hard keeping track of her on radar with possible high seas cluttering the screen. He tried the radio again, wondering why the VHF frequency had come clear from its heavy zooming interference during the 4-to-8 watch. Ryan heard it lift from where he stood by the dog house coaming. They heard a Morse key working loudly and clearly. The Russian trawler apparently had to make a top-priority signal to some other ship in the area. Sebastian rigged up the key that Julian had used. While Ryan took the wheel, he kept sending out his position on the Penta Marine Communication 2182 band to Sydney. Then he went to voice, but he could not get an answer. Before he could try again, the zooming and hissing scrambled the frequency. The trawler had jammed again. He had no more than one minute to send his position and a word about Julian being on the *Minsk*. But he wasn't sure he had gotten through at all.

The wind was coming fully astern at twenty-five knots when he went back up on deck. *Pequod* was making a snappy eight knots, all sails flying. The sails were tight with the wind, and *Pequod* took it smartly. Rising swells pushed water over her forward decks. The water was a pristine blue under the bright sun, temperature at 78 degrees. It felt good to be in his tennis shorts, feeling the warm sun and salt air pump in a vibrating kind of vigor. For those moments he found reprieve from concentrating on the Russian trawler and the tight margins of carrying out the chase for very long and still surviving.

He moved forward to check the sheets to the genoa, ran his eye over the jib. Even as he let his eye run up the masts, he felt the wind turn a bit chilly. He glanced over his shoulder toward the line of milky gray clouds beginning to darken on the northeast horizon. By evening it would be on them. And it could be a big one, judging by the barometer readings.

He had slept a few hours after coming off the watch at 8 that morning. Sebastian had told Ryan after the watch to stay down to give the ailing knee time to recuperate.

He turned again and walked aft where Barbara stood at the wheel. She was wearing yellow shorts and a halter.

"We ought to reef the main," she said as he came toward her. "That mast is beginning to vibrate with the wind already. . . ."

"Too early," he replied. "We need all the sail we can hold up to keep anywhere near that trawler." They hadn't conversed much at all since he had made his decision to go after the Russian. It was still a sensitive point with her. He knew it was not because she didn't care about Julian. Nor was she merely concerned for her own life, for that matter. But her years of discipline with Interpol taught her never to go beyond the parameters of her assignment if the odds were stacked against her. And she had made it plain enough that was the case. She had measured their chances on *Pequod* without Julian and figured it was too long a bet. She didn't say that to Sebastian directly, but her refusal to discuss it further was her way of saying she disagreed with him.

Sebastian checked the sheets on the mizzen, saw that they were all right. He wanted just to talk lightly with her, to find what they once had, to rekindle it. He wanted to put the helm over on the weather vane now and just reminisce with her about their adventures and their love in the past. He was growing more depressed by being close to her and at the same time not having her really with him or communicating to him. She kept her distance with a certain maddening intent. Even when they all took their evening meal together in the lounge, the *Pequod* running on automatic steering, she kept Ryan strumming his banjo to provide a diversion from any light banter Sebastian might want to strike up with her. Sooner or later, though, he knew he had to have it out with her directly.

He glanced at her from where he stood by the mizzen, off to her left a bit. The wind ruffled her honey-colored blonde hair, whipping it across her forehead at times. She would toss her head to throw it back, then reach up to adjust her dark glasses. Her skin had turned a deep tan, contrasting her hair, bringing it out into cascades of gold. She stood to the helm in an easy balance against the increased roll of *Pequod*. The muscles in her shapely legs rippled some as she eased her body into the pitch of the deck.

Finally, unable to stand forever as spectator to one with whom he had once known love, he moved up alongside her at the helm. He caught the clean smell of the ocean on her, mixed with the sweet odor of the suntan lotion. She kept her eyes ahead, not acknowledging him at all.

"Keep her close on one-four-five," he said, hoping to get her to respond. She dutifully corrected the helm a couple of degrees. "You've been on watch a long time," he added. "Put her over to automatic and relax . . . We're all going to need all the rest we can get for what looks like a mean blow coming up behind us. . . ."

"She gets too squirrely on the weather vane," she said politely.

"She'll settle down," he cajoled. "Go on, put her over and relax."

She hesitated. Then finally she put the wheel on self-steering and leaned back against the rail of the cockpit. They stood there not saying anything. She pulled on her blue windbreaker against the increasing wind and the slight drop in temperature.

"I was remembering," he began, clearing his throat to make the overture, "the time we were in the Arctic together . . . I dreamed about it last night again . . . The time I left you in that igloo bleeding from that shoulder wound and went on ahead to the ice station . . . My dream was strange . . . You kept running after me, and I couldn't hear you because I was on the snowmobile barreling it along . . . You remember that time?"

She leaned back against the rail and folded her arms, glancing up at the mainsail. "That was a long time ago," she said in a factual tone above the whine of the wind in the rigging. A wave pushed *Pequod* abruptly to starboard. He fell into her and put his arms around her to catch himself. He made no move to let her go. Her face was only inches from his. She turned her head toward him, but even that close he could not see her eyes behind the sunglasses.

"You're trying too hard, Sebastian," she said laconically. He looked at the moist line of her lips glistening from the lotion.

"So are you," he replied. And he felt like he wanted to clear his throat again; her closeness always did that to him. "And it doesn't make sense—"

"You want some coffee?" she cut in on him, pushing him off the subject. She moved a step off the rail to the helm. He let his arms drop and leaned back, watching her no more than a few feet in front of him. She would not retrace the past to what they once had. He felt even more dismal then.

He was about to say he would get the coffee for both of them when Ryan hobbled up the companionway from the dog house. He got around well enough with that knee, but Sebastian could see the signs of pain in his eyes more often lately. He came forward to where they stood by the helm, glancing at the northeast horizon, frowning some.

"The trawler seems to be pulling away," he said to Sebastian. His face was pale, and his blue eyes showed a glaze of fatigue even though he had slept five hours since coming off watch at 8 that morning. The shock of losing his father held a steady, unrelenting grip on him.

"She was still steady at eight miles ahead when I came up a few minutes ago," Sebastian said.

"Well, the blip is moving up high on the ring now, sir," Ryan replied. "She probably picked up speed. . . ."

Sebastian moved toward the dog house to go down to check the radar when he heard a loud sound like thunder. He glanced at the northeast sky, but the clouds were too far back yet to give off any squall noises. Then he saw the two jets coming straight at them dead astern low to the water. They shot by wing to wing a hundred yards to starboard. The pilot in the nearest jet had his hand lifted. Then they were gone, barreling south.

"Australian Intruders!" Ryan yelled with excitement above the continuing echoing thunder of the jets as they flew on.

"Military?" Sebastian called out, shading his eyes against the sun to watch the jets disappear south.

"Yes, sir!"

Sebastian knew then that the authorities were aware of something going on with Julian out here. He turned without further word and walked aft to the storage locker, opened it, and pulled out the triangular red signal pennant canvas. He grabbed the bucket of yellow paint and the brush and went forward of the helm, laying out the canvas on the deck.

"They'll be back," he said to Ryan and Barbara. "Gone to look for that trawler south . . . I'm going to put something on this pennant and run it up the mainmast . . . They have to know Julian is gone—"

"I'd put it down, Mr. Sebastian."

Sebastian had the brush poised over the paint can when he looked up to his right. Jamison was standing with his back to the dog house coaming, a few feet from the companionway near the starboard rail. He held a gun in his thin right hand.

Sebastian stared at him, not believing the gun. Jamison's face seemed to have turned greener now as the boat rolled heavily with the rising swells.

"Jamison?" Sebastian said, standing slowly to his feet, still holding the brush in his right hand. "You've got something in mind?"

"Mr. Sebastian, I want you to turn this boat around . . . now. . . ."

"Look, Jamison . . ." Sebastian figured Jamison might be suffering from a form of dementia that often accompanied severe dehydration in seasick victims.

"Mr. Sebastian, don't make me use this," Jamison warned, lifting the gun. It wavered in his hand, so he put both hands on the butt, steadying it. It was a German Mauser as Sebastian could tell. A no-nonsense weapon that looked far too big for Jamison's hands.

The thunder of the two jets came on loud again above the wind in the rigging. One of them climbed for altitude as it approached *Pequod*. The other stayed lower and did one pass over the boat, the pungent smell of its spent fuel pouring down on them from its afterburners.

Jamison looked up at it, then lowered his hands and the gun, watching the others intently. The Intruder banked around and came back, making a slower circling pass around *Pequod*.

"I'd let him go, Mr. Sebastian," Jamison called out in warning. "Go ahead and give him a nice wave . . . but that's all!"

The Intruder did three circles around *Pequod*, the last one close in so the pilot could look down on them from a hundred feet. Sebastian knew he was either counting how many were on deck or looking for Julian among them. There was nothing Sebastian could do but lift his right hand in salute.

Finally the jet banked off to the north, wagged its wings, and shot skyward, climbing after its partner above the clouds in the northeast.

Sebastian turned back toward Jamison, who had the gun on them again. "Tack around, Mr. Sebastian," he ordered, "and set the course back to Sydney . . . I would move quickly, sir!"

Sebastian let out a slow breath and dropped the paintbrush on the canvas pennant at his feet. "Ryan," he said, "let go the sheets to the main. . . ." Ryan stepped back to the winch and undid the sheets, letting them play out.

"Mr. Jamison, you can't be one of them," Barbara said incredulously.

"It's what has to be done . . . Sorry, Miss Churchill," Jamison replied, his voice cracking some as he tried to speak above the sound of the wind in the shrouds.

As Ryan let out the sheets further, the boom of the mainsail flopped loosely with a clatter. The sail rattled uselessly, empty of wind. *Pequod* lost some headway and wallowed bow down into the swells.

"Bring her around, Mr. Sebastian," Jamison called out again, the gun still in both hands and pointed directly at him.

"Jamison," Sebastian appealed then, "you're too sick to keep a gun on us all the way to Sydney."

"Mr. Sebastian . . . " Jamison pulled the hammer back on the gun slowly but deliberately.

Sebastian hesitated. He saw the boom of the mainsail beginning to swing with the slack sheets. Jamison remained with his back to the coaming of the dog house. Then a sudden gust of wind picked up *Pequod* from the port beam. It caught the mainsail and snapped it, making a sound like a cannon shot. The boom catapulted to the right. Jamison, sensing the movement, turned his head toward it. He was too late. The boom caught him in the head before he could duck. He staggered to his left, caught his foot on a deck cleat, and fell over the low restraining lines.

The gun fell from his hands and clattered on the deck even as he fell over the side. Sebastian made a lunge for him, but it was too late. Jamison hit the water, went under, came up, and opened his mouth to yell, terror like a live animal in his eyes.

Sebastian reached down and grabbed the life preserver hanging on the dog house coaming and threw it over the side. Then he picked up a yellow life jacket by the cockpit and pulled it on. He found a safety harness, clamped it around his waist, picked up the end of a coiled nylon rope used for warp lines, and attached the clip to the hasp on the harness.

"Take the other end of the line around the winch, Ryan!" he called. Ryan picked up the line and ran it around the self-tailing winch. Sebastian figured there was a good hundred feet of line. "Now start tacking her around! Barb, drop the mizzen! Now!"

"What are you going to do?" she yelled to him from the helm. "That sea is rising!"

Sebastian looked astern and saw Jamison's head bobbing in the blue-black water fifty yards back. "He's got to know something that we need to know!" he yelled. "Just be sure to bring her around to starboard and pick me up!" Then he jumped over the side and began swimming toward the stern to the spot where he last had seen Jamison's head bobbing in the swells.

The water was cold and pulled at him with a crosscurrent. The nylon line held firm to the clasp on his safety belt, which meant Ryan was keeping it tight to the winch on *Pequod*. That helped Sebastian in his attempt to stay on top of the waves that seemed mountainous as he swam. He glanced back once to see both Ryan and Barb working the sails as they began to tack around. But the boat seemed to grow smaller in the distance as he swam away from it. If they didn't get around in a hurry, the hundred feet of line would start dragging him back.

He raised up to look for Jamison in the peaks and troughs of the water ahead of him. Nothing. Then when he rose high on a swell, he caught sight of the journalist ahead maybe thirty feet. He was floundering in a trough, trying to keep his head up, arms flailing. He would be too weak to fight that for long.

Sebastian swam on but felt as if he were losing ground to the onslaught of the sea. He glanced back on the top of one high rise of water and saw that *Pequod* was tacked around now, bow on to him but seemingly still too far away. The nylon line tugged on him again, restraining him. He waited for the slack and went on swimming toward the spot where he last saw Jamison. The waves were coming in a gyrating crisscross, trying to twist and suck him under. Only the line kept him from floundering.

He pushed on with breaststrokes, his breath coming hard, gagging and coughing on the seawater that rolled over his head.

He felt the nylon line jerk him then, and he knew he was as far as he could go until *Pequod* gained on him. He glanced back over the high, breaking wave. The boat was coming on but seemed slow in closing with him.

He turned and faced toward where he had last seen Jamison. He was nowhere in sight. Then to his left Sebastian caught sight of the journalist's head floating on the surface of a crest; Jamison was as lifeless-looking as a piece of flotsam. He was still twenty yards away. Sebastian twisted around to see if *Pequod* was gaining. A hundred feet didn't seem that far off. But now he had little time to debate what to do. If he didn't get to Jamison immediately, the reporter was going to drown. To get to him in time, though, Sebastian knew he would have to unhook the line to *Pequod*, the one safety margin he had in this sea. That would leave him with only his life jacket. It would be tough to carry Jamison with only that to hold him up. If Jamison was KGB, wouldn't it be just as well to let him drown?

As he hung there, he caught a flashing vision of Backstrom sitting in that deep chair in his Chicago apartment . . . Alnutt with his condemning dead gray eyes . . . Winston's lifeless smile . . . "Not redemptive"?

Sebastian slowly reached down and unhooked the line from the clip in his belt. Immediately he felt the sea grab him in a fist, trying to pull him under. He went down, the water smashing over his head. He fought back out of panic, coming up gasping, snorting, his chest burning with the exertion.

He felt numb from the cold water, his muscles cramping with it. He rose up on a swell and looked around. He spotted Jamison being carried up to the high peak of the next wave. Sebastian slid down into the trough and up the next mountain, then tumbled back with the rush of the wave. He felt a bump briefly in the trough, and he reached out blindly hoping to get hold of Jamison. His hand brushed the wet shirt, and he closed his fist quickly on it.

As they rose to the next wave, he took off his life jacket and got it around Jamison and tied the strings tightly around his waist. The journalist seemed unconscious, floating dead in the water. Sebastian got behind him and put one hand under Jamison's chin, pulling his head up, using his left arm to push against the sea back around toward where *Pequod* was coming on. But he felt the water pull at him more now with Jamison's weight pressing on him. Each time a new swell came up and smashed them both into the trough, he was finding it harder to come back up. He swallowed more water, choked, but held on to Jamison's life jacket though the water tore at his grip.

"Not now!" he yelled once in prayer as the rising sea threatened to take him down. "I still have to talk to her! And, God, what about Julian?"

The heavy mist was forming on his brain as the water squeezed with a death grip. He made one more lunge upward, dragging Jamison, hoping he had the strength to hold on. Then through a fog of wind, current, and the sucking of the sea, he saw the blue hull of *Pequod* just about twenty yards away. It looked like ten miles to him. The main was slacking off along with the genoa as Ryan tried to slow her down. The jib was all that took the wind. Then he saw the lifeline snake out from the bow, a life preserver on the end of it. He saw the yellow life raft go over the side amidship. Then Ryan jumped down into the sea to climb into it.

Sebastian grabbed the preserver ring, still holding tightly to Jamison's life jacket. He was so tired now he didn't care if he stayed up or not. He forced his brain not to yield. "Jamison!" he yelled. "You have to help me! Try to move your arms . . . Swim or we'll both go under!" Jamison's head came up slowly from the water. His eyes were shut against it, but he tried gamely to respond, lifting his arms and punching at the water. It helped some to ease the full weight Sebastian had to carry.

As a green film began to smother him, Sebastian felt the bump of the life raft on his head. He pushed upward with all he had left, coming up coughing. He felt the hands on his arms, strong and pulling. He maneuvered Jamison around. Ryan caught hold of the journalist under the armpits and pulled upward. Sebastian pushed him on the rump.

"OK, sir!" he heard Ryan yell from a long way off. "Heave up as we go up on this crest!"

Sebastian waited as they rose to the height of the wave, then gave one last shove upward with it. Ryan's hands gripped Jamison, then pulled Sebastian by the arms up and over.

They lay on the deck of *Pequod*, he and Jamison, coughing up water. Barbara was working over Jamison, who was flat on his stomach. She kept pushing on his back with her hands. Sebastian lay there on his stomach trying to get his breath. Ryan threw a blanket over him. It felt good. The wind was chilly. The fatigue numbed his brain. He could hear the whine in the rigging. He opened his eyes and glanced northeast. The clouds were darker now, giving off brilliant flashes of lightning. The sunlight was slowly dissolving behind a growing milkiness across the entire sky.

Slowly, then, he stood up, holding the blanket around him. "Tack around," he called out to Ryan at the helm. "I'll take the wheel! Barb, Jamison will be OK . . . Give Ryan a hand with the sails. Once we're tacked around he can go below. That storm won't be on us full-force for an hour at least!"

She stood up from her work over Jamison, who had come around now and slowly crawled over to sit up against the bulkhead of the dog house, holding his head between his hands, the gray blanket draped around him.

"How's his head?" Sebastian called after her as she moved around the dog house forward with Ryan.

"He's probably hurting," she called back but not turning to look at him. "I can't tell how bad it is. You sure you want all sails up in this wind?"

"We lost too much time on that trawler," he replied. She hesitated, as if wanting to turn around and argue with him, but instead she went on to help Ryan.

Sebastian saw Jamison's Mauser still lying on the deck where he had dropped it. He reached over and picked it up and stuck it in the belt of his wet tennis shorts. He went to the wheel then and held her steady on until Ryan and Barb sheeted up the sails in the tacking maneuver. At the right time Sebastian swung the wheel fully to port. She came around smartly, but slammed her bow hard in the cross-waves. He got her on course 145 and waited until he had the seas coming directly astern, then set the weather vane.

He moved over, helped Jamison up, and led him down the

passageway to the lounge. Barb and Ryan followed in a few minutes. Jamison plopped down, his back to the settee. Sebastian lay half-prone on the settee, propping his head on his elbow, pulling the blanket closer around him. Ryan took a seat at the teak table nearest the settee. Barbara sat on the edge of it a few feet away, looking down directly at Jamison. She held the big orange beach towel close around her against the chill. Her blue eyes carried sparks of anger. Ryan just sat, staring.

"That was very noble," she finally said in a controlled biting tone. "But a stupid waste of time and energy and possibly life. If you insist on this crazy business of chasing that trawler, do you have to play martyr by saving a Russian agent at the same time?"

Sebastian coughed a half-laugh. He loved her when she was angry. It made her look even more beautiful, bringing out the deep blue of her eyes, pink spots splashing her cheeks some. Her full, curved lower lip showed a bit white, either from the lotion or from the mounting anger within her.

"Jamison's got some answers, right, Jamison?" he said. "I'm curious to know . . . And forget the martyr stuff, Barb. You know by now after all we've been through that I am reluctant in that department." He shifted on the settee and looked at Jamison again. "How's your head feel, Jamison?"

Jamison sat immobile, still holding his head between his hands. He looked forlorn, half-dead, and confused. "I still hear the bells ringin', sir," he mumbled. He coughed harshly, the water in his lungs sounding like gravel. All visages of the good-humored, rather sassy, and certainly robust man he was in Sydney were long gone. He looked gaunt, almost skeletal. His hair was plastered to his head by the water, dripping down his cheeks like greasy sweat.

"All right, then, you owe me one, Jamison. How does it feel to work for the KGB? Or CIA? Which?"

Jamison coughed again. "I—I wouldn't know about that, sir," he replied, wincing some as the boat heeled to starboard. "I'm no KGB or CIA or anything like that . . . Just a gumshoe reporter, Mr. Sebastian . . . Not very good at that either. . . ." He took a deep, shaky breath, swiping at the wet twigs of his reddish mustache with his right hand. His once-studious, crystal-blue eyes were shrouded in purple curtains of fatigue, blinking some as the water kept dripping down his forehead. "You know, sir . . . about Julian . . . I would never have made this boat as crew on my credentials . . . I told you that back in Sydney . . . I didn't get but ten questions on that sailing quiz the way I figured . . . No, sir . . . Actually Julian wrote out a check for me the night we left his house . . . in my name for three thousand quid . . . I could pick it up when I returned to Sydney with you all and his daughter aboard. . . ." He coughed again, and it was hard and gagging, sounding like a cold engine in winter.

"Daughter?" Barbara interjected, her voice rising in alarm. "What about his daughter?"

"Well . . . only thing I was to do was make sure you turned around and didn't try to follow him . . . on that trawler . . . when he got off. . . ."

"His daughter, Jamison!" Barb snapped at him again. "What about his daughter?"

"He . . . he told me he was going to exchange himself for her . . . with the Russians . . . That's all he said. . . ."

Sebastian glanced up at Barbara. Her face had taken on a mask of incredulity. It was getting darker in the lounge as the cloud cover outside began to wipe out the sun. "Ryan, light the tilley," Sebastian said. Ryan obeyed. The kerosene light threw weird shadows over them as it swung with *Pequod's* roll.

"Is his daughter on that trawler?" Barbara continued to hammer at Jamison.

"That's what he told me. . . ."

"So where is his daughter now?" Sebastian cut in. "If there was supposed to be an exchange . . ."

"That I can't tell ya, sir . . . The Russians didn't deliver their end, seems to me . . . Or maybe they never had her . . . Julian never did tell me when he was going over . . . So I didn't expect anything to happen that night he was taken off by them. . . ."

"So he gave you a gun and a promise of three thousand Australian to make sure once he made the exchange we would turn back to Sydney?" Sebastian pursued, feeling the boat rise again to a heavy wave, bow on.

"I can't believe Elisa was in Russia at all, certainly not all this time," Ryan put in for the first time, his voice dragging in his disbelief.

"We don't know she ever was, or for how long, if she was, Ryan," Barbara countered, trying to ease it some for him. "Maybe she was held prisoner there and forced to work for them. . . ." She paused and looked at Jamison again. "Jamison, why would he think we wouldn't turn back once he was off *Pequod* and his daughter delivered over to us?"

Jamison pulled the blanket tighter around him as he shivered some. "Well . . . he felt uneasy is all I can say . . . He wasn't sure how Mr. Sebastian would react to it all, being a clergyman and all . . . He said Mr. Sebastian was too much like his dead wife . . . *Messianic* is the word he used . . . He said he would not have taken Mr. Sebastian aboard either, especially since he felt uneasy about you, sir, except he had no time to look for other crew members . . . Even with his daughter back on board, he told me he had a hunch Mr. Sebastian might try something foolish and muck it all up trying to get him back off that trawler . . . He said I would be his insurance against that . . . if I was willing . . . If I wasn't he said he'd kill me . . . That's the way he put it to me . . . just like that. . . ."

There was a pause, none of them quite believing a David Julian who would make such a threat. "Well, so he had it right," Barbara commented, not bothering to hide the quip in her voice. She did not look at Sebastian when she said it. She continued to lean against the table, her arms folded, eyes fixed on Jamison, goose pimples showing on her tan legs as the chill clamped down harder.

"He could have told Barbara about the exchange," Sebastian added, ignoring her jab at him. "A close friend and all. . . ."

Jamison shrugged, indicating he had no idea about that. "Well, he knew I was Interpol," Barbara admitted. "He probably figured I'd try to get to Henri with the word or maybe someone local . . . He probably felt if I knew I might foul it up for him. . . ."

"So why did you wait so long to try to turn us around, Jamison?" Sebastian asked, feeling the boat slide off under another roller.

Jamison began to look green with the heaving boat. But he cleared his throat against it and said, "Well . . . when I realized the Russians just came on and grabbed Julian off this boat . . . no daughter in exchange as he expected . . . Well, sir, I thought it was right to chase that Russian as you wanted . . . Anyway, I was so sick, sir, that when I stood up I was about to pass out . . . But then last night I lay here so tired I didn't know my name . . . And I thought of that money in Sydney . . . And I knew I couldn't ride on this pitchin' boat another day . . . afraid to die, afraid I wouldn't . . . And after all, I did promise Julian, sir. . . ." Jamison seemed eager now to get justification for his act. "Well, anyway, I thought what was the use of chasing the trawler anyway? That's what I said. What would it accomplish? So I decided, sir, to try to turn you around. . . ."

"I know my father would do anything to get Elisa back," Ryan spoke up. He had been sitting quietly, his eyes staring at the deck between his feet. His elbows rested on his thighs, hands clenched loosely in front of him. His voice sounded confused, and there was still pain in his eyes. He wanted to say something more, but instead he took to frowning back at the deck as if unsure how to express himself.

"If she's still aboard with him, we can hope we can get them both back, Ryan," Sebastian offered, ignoring Barbara's warning glance about any further promises. "There are people looking for us . . . Those two Australian jets coming over us proves it . . . They won't let us sit out here alone for long. . . ."

"So how much do they know?" Barbara challenged, attempting to get him to see the reality of their situation here. "We got no message out to them . . . thanks to Mr. Jamison. . . ."

"I—I'm sorry," Jamison said, his voice cracking some again. His head sunk further in his hands.

"Well, I did get a couple of minutes of transmission out this morning on VHF," Sebastian responded. "Meant to tell you . . . Just got caught up in other things . . . But the trawler jammed . . . I heard them sending Morse earlier . . . Ryan heard it too on early watch about 4 . . . I sent out our position . . . But I'm not sure they got it."

"Well, I'm glad you remembered to let us in on that timely piece of information," Barbara said.

"I'm sorry . . . As I said, I just forgot. . . ."

"If you insist on dragging us all on this chase, then I think it behooves you to remember things like that . . . We've all been waiting for a break in that frequency—"

Sebastian lifted his right hand in appeal to her. "I admit my error . . . But I don't know if I got out any word . . . Still, maybe I did . . . The point is, there is some hope. . . ."

Pequod leaned to starboard, then slid off as another heavy wave slammed her on the port beam. The warning buzzer gave off a raucous sound from the chart room, indicating that the weather vane was not holding her on course.

Sebastian glanced at Barbara again. She looked peeved. He

didn't need that in her now. He tried the smile of entreaty, but it did not get her eyes to soften.

"Well, Jamison," he finally said, kicking his legs over the side of the settee, "I'm glad you're not KGB anyway . . . But I never knew you would be up for sale to anybody. . . ."

"Sir," Jamison responded quickly, defensively, "that's a lot of money for a reporter in Sydney. . . ."

"Well, with the story you've gotten out of this you'll probably get international fame and a lot more money than that," Sebastian added.

"I doubt I have a job with the paper now, sir . . . They probably feel I left them high and dry . . . Anyway, I don't think I'll write the story now, all things considered, ya know what I mean? Who's to say I'll see the end of this voyage . . . I'll surely die from seasickness in another day, at this rate."

"The end you will see anyway, Jamison," Sebastian assured. He took the gun from the waist of his tennis shorts and pulled the ammo clip from the butt. "Not a bullet in this gun, Jamison," he said, lifting the empty clip to the light.

Jamison looked sheepish. "I have no truck with hurtin' people . . . leastwise you all . . . I can't even kick a cat, sir . . . I was hopin' to bluff ya all the way, Mr. Sebastian. . . ."

Sebastian tossed the gun on the table. They remained silent for a long time. The warning buzzer sounded again.

"We should get to it," Sebastian said, standing up and balancing himself against the heave of the boat.

"And if I do make it, sir," Jamison was hasty to add, "I have you to thank for it . . . You saved my life out there, sir . . . I was a goner . . . I don't know how to repay that. . . ."

"Well, right now put on some dry clothes and boil up some tins of soup," Sebastian replied. "That is, if you have the stomach for it?"

"I'm game, sir," Jamison responded quickly, and he stood unsteadily, refusing help from Ryan who had reached out toward him. He looked as though he might pass out. But there was a look of intentness in his eyes, a desire to make amends to all of them for what he had done. He turned slowly and walked out of the lounge forward toward his bunk, staggering some as he went.

"I better see to the helm," Ryan said and got up and hobbled aft out of the lounge.

Sebastian continued to stand in front of Barbara, balancing

himself with the roll of *Pequod* that was increasing with every minute. She continued to lean against the edge of the teak table, her eyes down on the deck, her face peaked in the dim light of the tilley. He stood, holding the blanket around him, not sure if he wanted to say anything or not. The boat heeled to starboard suddenly, and she was thrown against him. He put his arms loosely around her, letting the blanket drop to the deck. She did not try to push him away. Instead, she put her forehead on his chest. He felt the wetness of her tears on his skin, but no sound came from her.

"It's so wrong," she protested, her voice muffled. "Wrong for what they did to him . . . The Russians . . . Wrong for him to take Jamison and make a deal to be sure we'd get back to Sydney . . . Wrong that he did all that for his daughter, betraying himself to his country . . . And now she's not even in the picture . . . Probably not even on that trawler for all we know . . . Probably back in Russia. . . ."

He continued to hold her as she sniffed against the tears. He wanted to tighten his arms around her, to comfort her, but he knew she was still sensitive to any closeness to him, even though she allowed this moment of vulnerability. "There are no perfect equations," he said, though it sounded inadequate. "You know that by now. . . ."

She sniffed again, then suddenly, as if she had become aware of what she was doing, she moved back quickly from him, dabbing at the streaks of tears on her cheeks with her right hand.

"I suppose you think it changes things," she jabbed at him, pulling a crumpled Kleenex from her jacket pocket and swiping at her nose. "You think chasing that trawler is just fine now with David Julian an unwilling prisoner aboard her? Well, remember . . . the Russian KGB probably knows we are on this boat. They would dearly love to get us both now that we are out in the open against a ship ten times our size and power . . . And on top of that, if we keep crowding them, they will have to do something about us . . . To say nothing of what they could do to David if we keep pushing them . . . And even if we could come up with some cockamamy idea as to what to do when we do catch up with them, we wouldn't get an opportunity to change David's chances for life . . . So now while we have sense and enough provisions aboard to make it, let's get back to Sydney!"

He leaned against the lurch of the boat, hearing the water

smack her on the bow, then gurgle on down the scuppers topside to the bilges below. "There was a time you'd fly a paper airplane to the North Pole and back if you had to for somebody's life, no matter what the chances," he said with entreaty, unable to keep his voice from going sharp in the irritation he felt toward her. "Henri was right—you have changed. I don't know what has poisoned you about the larger picture of things, but it is beginning to unnerve me some."

He left her there to think about it and went forward to his bunk, then into the water closet, got out of his wet tennis shorts and put on blue jeans, a heavy white turtleneck, and a yellow vinyl storm jacket over that. He pulled on rubber boots and yellow waterproof oils over his jeans. He felt both disappointment in her and yet that same aching love. He had lost control with her for the first time he could remember since he had met her. She didn't deserve that. But right then he had no second thoughts about taking it back. *The Pequod* began shuddering under the pounding of the rising seas. His mind had to go to the hours ahead, ticking off the checkpoints that would prepare him for the unexpected. But he was no David Julian in sailing. That bothered him now.

And how far ahead was the trawler? How far had he fallen behind her? He had to be wary of her too . . . A storm at sea had a way of bringing ships close on into collision course. The trawler could chew them up in one bite. The radar would not show her either, the screen cluttered up from the rising seas.

He opened the door of the water closet and stepped out into the passageway. She almost bumped into him as she made her move forward to change. She did not look at him as she squeezed by. He paused to watch her go on forward to her quarters in the bow, wishing now that he had not been so sharp with her.

Finally, knowing he could not undo that now, he turned and walked back aft, checking all loose gear, tying some down, making sure the fresh air hatch over the lounge and the one by his bunk were battened down and locked. When he got to the galley, he saw Jamison doing his best to whip up hot soup in a black iron pot on the gas stove. He wore a white apron that was smeared red from the soup, and he had dumped quite a bit around the galley deck. But he was still emptying the contents of another tin into the pot. He staggered with the roll of the boat, trying to hold the tin out steady in his right hand to keep it from spilling.

"You got any of that in the pot yet, Jamison?" Sebastian asked, feeling admiration for the man in his attempt.

Jamison turned and tried a grin, but it was lost in the pallor of his face. "Yes, sir!" he called back. "You'll be havin' something hot on deck in a jiff, sir!"

"Fair dinkum, Jamison?" Sebastian jabbed lightly. Jamison's eyebrows lifted, and his shaky grin came through a bit brighter.

"Fair dinkum! Yes, sir!"

Sebastian gave him a thumbs-up as he moved on through the chart room. He paused and switched on the radar. *The Pequod* started going into twisting gyrations from bow to stern. He was knocked off balance and grabbed the chart table to keep from being tossed. He heard a banging in the galley and wondered if Jamison had lost the soup altogether.

He straightened up, concerned now with the intensity of the wind roaring in the rigging topside and the possibilities of a force ten gale. He tapped the barometer. Down to 987 millibars. It was going to be bad with a register that low.

He steadied himself against the pitch and roll and looked at the radar screen. Nothing. All green grass from the sea. He reached out and switched it off, decided to save all the power he could. He would not know where the trawler was now anyway until the storm blew out.

The radio was hissing and zooming as usual. He tried other frequencies, but got the same thing. He finally gave up on it.

He staggered up the companionway to the deck and felt the full rush of the wind and the pressurizing grip of the storm. When he stepped out on the deck, he could imagine nothing closer to what hell must be like.

The seas were mountainous, piling on top of each other, climbing with each gathering. Giant black-green monsters came at *Pequod* like a charge of cavalry out for vengeance. The white teeth of their tops reached out to snap *Pequod* with one crunch. Rain and blackness the color of ink contrasted with jagged streaks of lightning. Swirling waterspouts born on the slashing points of wind inversions sucked up water into a gyrating funnel with a rumble that sounded like some ocean beast was ready to emerge from the deep. The world was in an agony of sound and force as he'd never known before.

He staggered out of the companionway hatch, groping and

stumbling his way toward Ryan who was hanging on to the wheel, blurred behind the screen of rain and seawater flying over the fantail.

Sebastian knew that the storm was mounting to a force eight even as he slid alongside Ryan in the cockpit and hooked the safety clip to the belt on his harness hanging tight around his shoulders and waist. The sails were gut-full of the wind, and the sound of the mainmast vibrating under it was a rapid fire tattoo punctuating the scream of the gale, like the sound of a jackhammer.

"We've got to reef the main and genoa, sir!" Ryan yelled into his right ear. His words were caught by the banshee-sounding wind before he got them out of his mouth.

"I'll see to it!" Sebastian yelled back and unhooked his safety belt to move forward, grabbing what he could to keep from sliding with the heavy roll of *Pequod* to starboard. A giant comber came over the fantail and slammed across the cockpit, burying Ryan, then came on tumbling over Sebastian and down the companionway into the chart room.

Sebastian felt the pull of the water take him skidding along to starboard until he slammed into the coaming of the dog house. He hung on to a deck cleat until the water passed. *Pequod* seemed to stagger under that one, her bow staying down under the tons of water far too long.

He pulled himself up and saw Barbara coming up the companionway in her yellow rain slicker, buttoning up her safety harness. "Hook on to the cleat on the dog house!" he yelled to her, pointing to the roof. Her face seemed ashen white as she caught the mayhem of the storm around them, her eyes going wide with it. But she struggled up to the dog house roof and hooked up the safety line to the harness. "Main and genoa!" he yelled to her as he scrambled alongside her, pointing up at the straining sails.

They both moved forward then, trying to hold balance against the pitching boat that seemed to twist in agony again as the waves began that huge cross running toward them. Sometimes the seas came directly astern, lifting *Pequod* up and plunging her down the far side of the wave. The boat went steeply bow-down, racing slam-bang into the trough, burying her forward decks under water. Each time she seemed more reluctant to come back up . . . but she did. Julian had put a spirit in her that refused to bow to the elements.

Ryan had managed to let go the mainsheets from the winch a

few feet away from the helm. Barbara unhooked the main halyard from the cleat. They worked together to keep the sail from booming out with the wind as it came down. Sebastian would have liked to remove the sail altogether and stow it below, but it was too late for that now.

They got the sail wrapped around the boom and lashed it as tight as they could with thick nylon ropes. The *Pequod* bucked again and heaved as a huge comber took them on the stern. They clung to the mainmast as the boat rose high astern, the bow going down for the plunge forward.

Sebastian reached out to grab Barbara as she began to slip on the tilting deck. He debated now whether to batten everything down and lie-a-hull, strip her of her sails, and ride it out below decks. *Pequod* would lie beam on to the seas, but there was a chance she could roll with the waves and stay afloat better than this way. It was a highly debatable question, because they could capsize under those conditions.

He went forward with Barbara and got down the genoa. They bundled it up and jammed it into the deck sail locker Julian had improvised forward of the air hatch.

"Let's take down the jib, and try to rig up the storm jib!" he yelled at her. "We've got to have steerage!"

"I'll get it!" she yelled back.

"No! I'll get Ryan!" He turned and worked his way back to the dog house. By now *Pequod* had slowed with the two mainsails down. Only the jib gave her some headway. Ryan stood at the helm that was mostly useless now. Sebastian yelled to him, "Go below and get the storm jib!" He had to repeat it over the scream of the wind.

But as Ryan headed for the companionway, having locked the wheel to the weather vane, Sebastian saw the huge comber coming at them from astern. It was so big that it cast an extra dark shadow into the already black shroud of the storm around them.

"God help us!" he yelled, turning around to see where Barbara was. She was hanging on to the mainmast with both arms, her lifeline hooked up forward.

He turned to get back to her even as the huge, monstrous wave picked them up, giving off a rumbling sound as tons of water rose in a mammoth fist to smash them.

Thirteen

Captain Aviloff hung on to the compass stanchion in front of the helmsman on the bridge of the *Minsk* as the ship shuddered under another huge mountain of rolling sea. As the trawler's stern rose high with the next crest, shoving its bow down, Aviloff cocked his ear. The ship's screws were out of water at that point, thrashing uselessly until she settled back down in the trough. At that point he sensed the vibration in the deck plates under his feet. It seemed more noticeable now.

It was going on to 1800 hours in the early evening. The off-watch crew had gone to mess. But Aviloff knew most of them would not find the food very appetizing as the *Minsk* continued to roll and toss while running before the wind. The storm had struck more than an hour ago, winds rising already to sixty knots and climbing. Under Romonovich's prodding, the engines had been run up to get fourteen knots, but Aviloff knew that the starboard engine was not going to hold with that speed.

He finally turned to Popov, who was leaning against the bulk-head a few feet to his right. "What do you think, Comrade Popov?" Aviloff asked, keeping his voice guarded from Romonovich who stood in the middle of the bridge hanging on to the bridge support stanchion six feet or so behind them.

Popov pushed his cap higher on his head, revealing sweaty brown springs of thinning hair. A frown dug between his eyes as he pondered. "She cannot take this speed, comrade captain," he said finally. "She sounds out of sync already with the port propeller. The engine room reports there is a loud vibration in the starboard diesel!"

Aviloff was conscious of Romonovich shifting around behind him, partly due to the heaving decks of the trawler under the lash of the storm, but also in his anxiety to hear what Aviloff was saying to Popov. He had protested Popov's presence on the bridge earlier as Aviloff ordered, claiming "Popov was confined to quarters unless given special permission." Aviloff had won that disagreement on the grounds that his executive officer was the best judge of the ship's ability to perform in her engine capacity.

Aviloff weighed what his next decision would do to incur the wrath of his political officer. But as he listened to the vibration under his feet, he realized he had no choice.

"Comrade Ilyich," he said then to the young navigation officer standing by the engine telegraph, "reduce speed to eight knots."

Ilyich glanced quickly toward Romonovich expecting a rebuttal. "Reduce to eight knots, comrade captain," he said obediently. He rang down the order and stood back.

"Comrade captain," Romonovich interjected quickly, a warning note in his voice, "we are not to reduce speed. I remind you of the order—"

"Comrade Romonovich, you are not authorized to make decisions countermanding the orders of the captain of this ship," Aviloff replied, keeping his voice calm, not wishing to make a dogfight of this in front of the other officers and crew on the bridge. Still, he wanted them to be witness to what he was saying to the political officer in line with his authority as commander.

"We must make distance between us and that boat that pursues us," Romonovich insisted. "I too am under orders—"

"The safety of this ship is my order, I remind you again, comrade," Aviloff snapped. "I will not increase the danger by forcing our starboard engine to malfunction!"

"I protest, comrade captain! Admiral Karkov—"

"I will deal with the admiral in good time, comrade—"

"And there is our man Clay Bird below who is not exactly a lightweight in the KGB—"

"Clay Bird is your responsibility, comrade. If he wishes to argue the case with me, let him do so. Now I must order you off this bridge, Comrade Romonovich, in accordance with procedures at sea, Article Twelve in the captain's manual produced by the Admiralty," Aviloff went on, keeping his voice calm but putting the snap of command in it while holding back the pot of hot lead bubbling up in his chest. He turned his head to look squarely at the political officer. The slits of his eyes were widening now to show the black pits of his eyeballs. Romonovich hesitated, his eyes darting to the left and right, sensing the other officers and seamen on the bridge watching him. Aviloff knew that Romonovich had the power to create considerable mayhem back in Russia over that order with so sensitive a "cargo" aboard as Julian. And he saw it in Romonovich's eyes too, a light dawning there of both hatred and vengeance even as he turned and stomped out of the bridge through the starboard hatch.

"Steady at your helm, comrade quartermaster," Aviloff said calmly, glad to have the stench of the political officer off the bridge. The other six members of the bridge watch stood steady, leaning with the heeling of the trawler, eyes straight ahead, faces blank. He knew what they were thinking: their captain had dared to tangle with a KGB-GMU connection aboard. They knew what happened to anyone who did that, officer or not, Article Twelve or not.

Aviloff turned his head and glanced at Popov. His second-in-command stared at the deck, arms folded across his chest as he leaned back on the bridge bulkhead. His face was even more clouded now with the implications of the captain's action. He looked as if he were about to sink into a morass of hopelessness and despair. He looked up at Aviloff, his eyes showing the pain of what all of it could mean to him in the end.

Aviloff walked over to him, grabbing on to the stanchion to keep from being toppled by the sudden dip of the trawler to starboard. He withdrew his hand from his vinyl foul-weather jacket and opened it, extending it slowly for Popov to see.

"Two keys, comrade," he said above the scream of the wind outside the bridge, but keeping his words guarded from the others. "One is for Julian's cabin . . . If we are in danger of sinking, I will set off the ship's siren. That is a signal to you to use the other key, which is to unlock your door from the inside. Get to Julian's quarters immediately. Otherwise the political officer will get there and make sure Julian does not live. Then lead Julian to the forward escape locker. You know what to do there."

Popov frowned at the keys in Aviloff's palm, as if he did not yet understand or was afraid of the implication of Aviloff's words. "Comrade captain," he said, glancing quickly around at the others on the bridge to make sure he was not heard, "there is a guard on Julian at all times. And I know there is one that goes by my door regularly—"

"If it is not possible, I will find a way," Aviloff assured. "In any case, stand alert to the intercom in your quarters. I may call you at any time depending on what is happening up here on the bridge. Do you understand, Popov?"

The second officer swallowed with some difficulty, sensing the mounting complications of the action being posed.

"Is it worth risking everything for Julian then?" he asked, his eyes continuing to dart around the bridge.

Aviloff looked up at him quickly, fixing his eyes on Popov's. "You forget, Popov, it is your life too. Correct?"

Popov's eyes lowered to stare at the deck, sensing the mild rebuke of his captain. The trawler heaved sharply to port under a heavy comber, and there was a groan of metal through the ship.

Popov frowned again, his eyes going wider in the pressure of the moment. "What is to happen to us now, comrade captain?" he asked.

"We will make our history or be victims of it, Comrade Popov," Aviloff replied, then gave him a quick smile of assurance and turned away to move back toward the helmsman. He heard Popov go out the bridge hatch a few minutes later.

"Message from the submarine *Gorky*, comrade captain," the communications officer said, handing over a yellow signal paper.

Aviloff took it and glanced at it quickly:

> ON COURSE 28 HOURS AWAY FROM RENDEZVOUS MINSK. FINAL CONTACT SCHEDULED PRIOR SURFACE AT 1600 HOURS 18TH. PREPARE TRANSFER WITH ALL DUE HASTE.
>
> CAPTAIN BOLOVARICH
> SUBMARINE GORKY 999774

"Very well," Aviloff said to the communications officer. "Acknowledge the message and confirm the time, providing this storm blows out."

"Aye, sir."

Aviloff turned to look out at the rain-spattered windows facing forward. It was coming down to the final hours then. He had no doubt that Romonovich would have him transferred to the sub as well. The political officer had his claim of interference with sensitive matters concerning the OPAL project. Besides, he had the agent Clay Bird to back him up. Aviloff was not sure how much weight Clay Bird carried on board. He had not seen the man since he had joined the *Minsk*. But two KGB of at least equal weight could make it difficult for him.

He felt the trawler shudder again under a smashing blow from a comber. The feel of the vibrating engines under his feet was less since he had reduced speed. But he also knew the starboard engine couldn't hold long in this kind of sea.

He thought about *Pequod* then for a reason he could not determine. He was sure that "the hound of heaven" had long since succumbed to this force eight gale. He felt strangely sad about that. And for Julian as well. But he pushed the emotion aside as irrelevant to his duty now.

He wondered what Soya was doing.

Submarine Gorky

Comrade First Rank Omar Bolovarich moved into the communications department just forward of the control room. The Russian builders of the thirty-thousand-ton modern nuclear submarine had skimped on space so that the radar, fathometer and echofathometer and sonar panels were jammed together in an array of dials, wires, and computers.

Bolovarich was thirty-eight years of age, heavyset, five foot nine in height. He had a round face and sleepy gray eyes that portrayed him often as a soft, aloof commander. But behind that indifferent visage was a sharp, almost ruthless competitive mind and personality. His father was a retired schoolteacher in the Urals. His mother had died five years ago from pneumonia. He was an only child. Growing up alone had taught him the necessary disciplines for survival. And no quarter.

"What have you got, Comrade Atoff?" he asked the sonar operator in a beguiling, disinterested tone of voice.

Comrade Lieutenant Gregory Atoff continued to listen to the sounds in the sea around *Gorky* through the phones he pressed tightly to his ears. He was twenty-six years of age, blond, with brown eyes and a long, narrow face. Finally he sat back and faced the captain.

"I am not sure, comrade captain . . . It is not a clear signal that I can isolate . . . But it could be another submarine."

Bolovarich grunted. He would not be surprised if the Americans or the Australians had sent one of theirs to follow. Probably the American submarine he had detected when he passed the Great Barrier Reef. If there was a sub out there at all, it would be that one.

He took the extra pair of phones off the desktop and put them on. He listened to the usual sea noises, then the hum of his own reactor and the high-pitched turn of *Gorky's* propellers. He waited to catch the sound that would indicate the presence of another submarine, the high whine of the screws in particular. If it was an American sub, the sound would be hard to detect. They had a way of running quietly, unlike the Russian tractor engine sounds that pounded signals in all directions.

"It comes every twenty seconds or so," Atoff offered. "Just a trace of a propeller sound. . . ."

Bolovarich glanced at the second hand of the clock on the sonar panel wall. At thirty-five seconds he heard it faintly, like a power saw coming on and off. Still, it did not stay long enough for him to conclude it was a submarine's propellers. The sound was unlike that of any American sub he had heard when he was patrolling them in the North Atlantic.

"It does not come in clear," he said, handing the phones to Atoff. "What does your computer say?"

"Not enough identifiable sound to determine, comrade captain."

"He may be directly astern in the cone of silence," Bolovarich commented. "We would not hear him there . . . So we will begin a thirty-degree turn to starboard and port. If he is there, you will hear him then with our sonar directly on him. Let me know if you pick him up. . . ."

"Aye, comrade captain."

The captain turned and walked forward to the control room, stepped over the hatch coaming, and proceeded to his command station. There he took out his signals logbook. The last message in code from Admiral Karkov was clear in one sense, not specific enough in another:

UTILIZE STANDARD DEFENSE MEASURES WHEN NECESSARY IF PURSUED. RENDEZVOUS AND TRANSFER

TO BE COMPLETED WITH NO WITNESSES. CHOICE OF WEAPONS AT YOUR DISCRETION. AVOID NUCLEAR UNLESS ORDERED.

"Comrade Komileski," the captain said, returning the message log to its place.

"Comrade captain?" his second officer replied a few feet from him.

"Begin turns of thirty degrees to starboard and port for the next hour . . . Reduce speed and control reactor noise."

"Aye, comrade captain."

If it was an American in pursuit, what then? Karkov's orders were precise enough for him to take action. As they moved closer to rendezvous with the *Minsk*, it was a necessity. They wanted no interference or detection.

He turned then and picked up the phone, pushing a button. "Fire control?"

"Aye, captain."

"Stand by with sensor torpedoes one and two . . . Possible target information for your plot at any time. . . ."

"Aye, comrade captain!"

Bolovarich hung up the phone and stood there frowning at the deck. He had never expected in his twelve years of submarine command to be in the position of firing on an American submarine or any of their vessels of the line . . . if indeed there was one somewhere behind them. He knew about OPAL, of course. He had not thought much about it since information from Naval Intelligence was slim on what it was or its final purpose. Or else Moscow was keeping it under wraps, which was probably the case. But it appeared that it was big enough to warrant a shoot-out with the Americans.

The thought of that did not trouble him all that much. He was committed to Russia and its military dominance. He had fought his way alone all his life against all odds. He had bloodied plenty of noses while hammering his way to the top, sometimes merely to survive. He had learned to accept pain and inflict it with the same stoicism. To win was his all-consuming passion, to win over any enemy or any challenger. That's what had brought him the command of *Gorky* at so young an age. He had no friends in or out of the navy. He treated his crew fairly but as necessary functional pieces to make his own command reach perfection. And they rose to it so that *Gorky* became one of the top submarines in the flotilla operating in the Atlantic and the Pacific.

He felt the submarine beginning to lean a bit as it made its first thirty-degree turn to starboard. Perhaps now was the moment to go for the big win?

USS Bunker Hill

Lieutenant Commander James Holland had been sitting with Sonarman Second Class Joe Kelley for five minutes or more. Kelley was twenty-two years of age with freckles sprinkled across his nose that intensified his bright blue eyes. He was a graduate in Oceanography Electronics from MIT. He enlisted in the navy to pay off his college loans and used his education to gain experience in his field. His real love was to listen to the sound of whales under water, and for the six months on *Bunker Hill* he had spent a lot of time doing just that.

"Can you isolate him?" Holland asked, which must have been the fifth time already. Kelley had summoned him to the communications shack because he had been tuning in on the Russian's possible maneuver change.

Kelley continued to work the dials, the phones tight to his head. He said he had a "glitch" or a possible change in course by the Russian, who was about fifteen hundred yards ahead of them. Next to Kelley was the computer that collected all the noises that came through the sonar. At any time he could pause in his attempt to determine the identification of a certain sound, punch the "go" button on the computer. The machine would read out what the sound meant against the program of one thousand possibles to be heard in deep ocean cruising.

Finally Kelley pushed the phone off his right ear and said to the captain, "He's changing course, captain. He's moving to starboard on a sharp turn. Either coming around to check us for a better sound identification or heading out to some other destination."

Holland picked up a set of phones and put them on. There was no mistake in the swishing, somewhat grinding sound of the Russian sub. They always had trouble muffling their reactor and propeller noises. They had been tailing her for two days now, sometimes moving up to within one thousand yards of her stern. But the Russian had never deviated from course nor turned around to get a sonar sweep just to make sure. She stayed on twenty-five knots, backing down a few times maybe to listen.

"OK," Holland confirmed. "He's probably going broadside to check us out. He is maybe suspicious even though he can't get a clear fix on us in the baffles." The "baffles" was the area of the cone of silence, twenty degrees either side of the stern of a sub where its sonar could not pick up the sound directly behind. Holland wondered why the Russian had suddenly become suspicious. Still, even in the "baffles" sound waves could spread out at times, just enough to send out a peculiar alien ripple a smart sonarman could pick up but not necessarily identify.

"She's a Delta class, sir," Kelley said. "That's the sound signature. The computer confirms, sir." Holland glanced at the screen and saw DELTA printed out in big white letters.

"So we have a boomer then," Holland added. A "boomer" was loaded with nuclear Skyhawk missiles and supersensor torpedoes that could search and find anything metal within three thousand yards and blow it up. That complicated any cozy pursuit.

"What's his depth?" Holland asked.

"He's at six hundred, sir . . . We're still at seven. . . ."

"Speed?"

"He runs at thirty knots for a few hours, then drops back to twenty-five, probably to do some listening . . . He's at twenty now, sir, which allowed me to pick him up again. . . ."

Holland nodded. In order to hear and fix sounds through sonar, *Bunker Hill* had to cut speed to twenty knots. The last sound fix was twenty-four hours ago when the Russian slowed down to eighteen knots. At that time Kelley zeroed in on them at three miles ahead.

"Well, he can roll forty knots out of that power plant whenever he wants to," Holland commented. "He could leave us back here blowing bubbles any time he feels like it . . . if he knows we're here. . . ."

Holland felt patches of sweat forming on his forehead. He had received the priority message from ComSubPac two days ago to start the chase after the Russian. And with that came the "condition yellow," which meant he could go with his hound-dog torpedoes if the Russian became warlike. That meant a possible search and destroy. He had read the message about David Julian and the attempt of the Russian sub to make the transfer. But he knew too that his own hound dogs were not as efficient as what the Russian

Delta sub carried. The rebuilt Poseidon class he commanded was really for patrol and communications, not trading torpedoes or missiles with a "boomer" Russian.

Holland was a gangly six foot three, with dark bushy hair and a meditative demeanor about him that said he did a lot of thinking before he acted. He was thirty-nine years of age, with twelve years in sub service. He had received commendable merits for his commands of the Trident sub *DelRay* in the Atlantic two years ago. Before that he had skippered a Poseidon, the *Walrus*, on North Atlantic and ice-cap patrol near the Pole. He had expected more than command of the rebuilt *Bunker Hill* six months ago. To skipper a communications picket sub was boring duty, the kind the navy gave to a lieutenant to break in on. He never really knew why he did not get a Trident based on his experience, but it was the same with a lot of other qualified sub officers.

But he was here now nevertheless. No Trident, but in an "attack mode" he never dreamed he'd experience. Only now he wondered about the ability of *Bunker Hill* to come up to it; and he wondered about himself as well. He kept thinking of his wife, Sandra, and their daughter, Melissa, eight years old last month . . . It was Christmastime and he wanted to be home . . . Yet it was Sandra who cheered him up when he felt so morose over getting assigned to *Bunker Hill.* "Piece of cake, darling," she told him in that usual confident tone of voice. "Besides, you'll have lots of time to write all that poetry you always wanted to do. . . ."

"Hold it, sir," Kelley cut in on his inner musings. "I got another signature . . . The kind that goes with Russian subs when they arm their supersensor torpedoes or go to their muzzle hatches. . . ."

Kelley reached over quickly and hit the "go" button on the computer. Holland wiped again at the sweat itching his forehead, stood up, and leaned over Kelley to stare at the computer screen.

FIRING LOCKING DEVICE ON SUPERSENSOR TORPEDOES ON RUSSIAN DELTA CLASS SUB

"Is he serious, sir?" Kelley asked, clearing his throat against the tension. "When he's sure we are here, is he really going to unload on us? I've been tracking subs for a while now, mostly Russian . . . They never went to the firing button before . . . Sir?"

"Wait and see, I guess, Joe," Holland replied, trying to keep his voice calm. "He's coming around anyway to see if we are for real." He picked up the phone from the panel in front of him and punched the button. "Control?"

"Bell here, sir. . . ."

"OK, Marty," Holland said to his executive officer Martin Bell, "our Russian has caught on to us . . . Come to port 10 degrees, increase speed by ten knots. Let's see if we can stay in close to his stern, hide in the baffles. . . ."

"Aye, skipper."

Holland hung up the phone and looked at the computer again. It was time to tell the crew what was going on. Joe Kelley was showing some concern behind the studious veneer of his face. Holland remembered the message sent to him by ComSubPac a few days ago: " . . . Pursue Russian sub heading for rendezvous with Russian trawler *Minsk* . . . Take all measures to prevent transfer of human cargo Dr. David Julian from *Minsk* . . . Use discretion . . . Hold to yellow readiness . . . Fire only when fired upon . . . Avoid nuclear confrontation unless condition red declared by Commander-in-Chief. . . ."

What did "all measures" mean? If the Russian fired his sensor torpedoes, that was only one step from the nuclear missiles in his muzzle hatches. Holland had shared that with Martin Bell earlier. And "fire only when fired upon" was a little late against Russian sensors anyway. In any case, this was no drill. Kelley knew that. Holland remembered his training with ComSubLant in the North Sea and the Atlantic. He would travel with five other subs and track an "enemy" group of his own submarines in war games to test their proficiency in tracking. They went through all the battle attack procedure, *except* they never fired a hound-dog Mark-48 torpedo or a missile or so much as sneezed at each other.

But this was now approaching a shoot-out. He had dreaded the moment for himself, though he had always thought it was remote. The Russian had the edge . . . He was bigger, faster, and had the sophisticated weapons, conventional and nuclear, to do the job on *Bunker Hill*. Just how far would the Russian captain go? How far would Moscow let him go? But even with what little he had received on Julian and the OPAL project, he figured Russia would go all-out to get the scientist.

At the same time, if the captain of the Russian sub had any

sensitivities to what a shoot-out could mean, they could just play games here without blowing the cap on it. But if the Russian had a streak of the Ivan Syndrome, the type who was aching to prove something good about himself, then it was going to be messy.

"He's trying to ping on us now, sir," Kelley said.

"Is he bouncing a signal on us?"

"Not yet, sir. . . ."

Holland picked up the phone again. "Control? Take her down to nine hundred . . . Under the thermocline, that's right . . . Marty, stick her nose down fast . . . I got the Russian pinging. . . ."

Going to the thermocline meant they would be under the line where warmer and cooler water came together. That line tended to blunt any sound waves and meant that *Bunker Hill* would be difficult to detect by the Russian's sonar.

In five minutes Marty called him to report they were under the nine hundred line and leveling out.

"He's making the circle, sir," Kelley said, holding the phones tighter to his ears. "And I don't hear him getting a bounce on us through his sonar search. He can't get through the thermocline. . . ."

"Well, he can't hang around all day," Holland commented more to himself. "He's got a mission down the line somewhere." Kelley flicked his blue eyes at his captain, not sure he understood. Holland said nothing further.

They waited. Holland continued listening with the extra pair of phones. The Russian chugged along two hundred feet above them, doing slow turns to port and starboard, his pinging sonar signal muted some by the thermocline.

Then Holland picked up the phone again. "Control? Marty, all engines stop. Pull the rod on the reactor . . . I want it dead silent aboard."

"Aye, sir!"

He hung up and punched another button. "Fire control, who's on watch?"

"Chief Breyden here, sir." Breyden was a twenty-year veteran, steady as a rock. He was from Boston, had a wife and three sons.

"OK, chief," Holland said, "stand by hound dogs two, three, and four . . . Wait for the countdown to arm."

Breyden did not even pause to savor that. "Aye, sir," he said dutifully, sounding as if he were asked simply to choose the movie for tonight.

Bunker Hill went very quiet then as it floated in limbo nine hundred feet down, engines stopped, reactor down. All they heard was the slurping of the sea against the hull and the low hum from machinery on reduced power. The sound of the Russian's propellers and reactor could be heard even under the thermocline.

"He's swinging back around to starboard, sir," Kelley said, and the computer, tracking the sub through the sonar panel, threw up the green glow line on the grid in front of Kelley. "Going the other way, sir . . . Back on course seems like . . . He's probably giving up on getting a fix on us. . . ."

"Let's hope," Holland commented.

The Russian was probably listening for engine sounds more than anything else. And doing his pinging up rather than down. And even if he tried to penetrate down, the thermocline would discourage him.

"Depth?" he asked.

"Still at six hundred, sir. . . ."

And a moment later, "Going over us again, sir . . . Some Ivan we got here, sir. . . ."

"He's trying to sucker us into starting our reactor," Holland said. "He heard us once undoubtedly, but now he can't find it. . . ."

"There he goes, sir!" Kelley cut in. "Just poured on the soup to his reactor . . . Shoving the rod, sir . . . He's decided to keep going. . . ."

Holland picked up the phone. "Marty? The Russian is heading back on course . . . Take five minutes and kick over the reactor . . . He's burning to get after that trawler . . . If he opens up his reactor he can outrun us . . . I want all the speed we can get to stay with him." That would be twenty-eight knots. The Russian could go forty full-out. At least.

Meanwhile Holland had to consider "all measures" to prevent the Russian from completing the transfer of Julian off the trawler. Did that mean to stop the Russian dead? Harass him? Did "prevent" mean spitting on him, ramming him, shooting at him—what?

He called again and got Marty. "Marty, get me up to antenna depth . . . Got to send a classified to ComPacOps."

"Excuse me, captain," Marty said, a note of hesitancy in his voice, feeling perhaps he shouldn't ask. "We are still at stand-down, sir. Do you want to go to battle-ready?"

"We'll radio in our situation first and ask for clarification in our approach to the Russian," Holland replied. "We have to tell Operations that the Russian has armed his sensors . . . ask what's our move—wait and see, or get in our punch first? . . . OK?"

"Stormy topside, sir. . . ."

"I think we can get up our ultrafrequency antenna without feeling too much of it. . . ."

"Aye, skipper."

Holland reached over then and took the intercom mike off the hook on the panel, hit the button that would carry his voice throughout the entire sub.

"Attention . . . this is the captain speaking. You should know now, if you aren't aware, that we are pursuing a Russian sub which is heading south to pick up an Australian scientist held on a Russian trawler. We are on a condition yellow unless fired upon or ordered to full attack. We do not anticipate a shoot-out. But I am ordering you to man battle stations in about sixty seconds. Our job is to prevent the transfer of that passenger from the trawler to the sub in any way we can without hitting the firing button. I will keep you informed."

He put the mike back, glanced at Kelley, and smiled. "Thank you, sir," Kelley said. His blue eyes were just as studious as always. But his tongue darted out once to moisten his lips that had suddenly gone dry.

Holland stood up and patted Kelley on the shoulder. "Stay on him, Joe," he said. Kelley nodded, but the freckles that splashed across the bridge of his nose seemed to stand out like crumbs of chocolate cake against the increasing paleness in his face.

Holland turned and walked back to the control room. He was relieved the Russian captain had decided to cut out, try to outrun *Bunker Hill* and complete his job at the rendezvous. But the fact that he had armed his torpedoes said he intended to use them if he had to. But how much further would the Russian go? to his Skyhawk nukes? It depended just how valuable the Australian scientist was to them . . . And right now it appeared that he constituted a "go for broke" cargo.

As Holland took the captain's station in the control room, he noticed that the faces of the watch were impassive, very still, very preoccupied now. Each man knew what the risks were.

It had happened at a Bunker Hill at another place, another time, long ago . . . the shot heard round the world. Was it about to happen again, on this *Bunker Hill*?

He desperately hoped not.

The Victor

Sperry grabbed the chart table to keep from being thrown against the bulkhead as the *Victor* did a wild roll to port. Second Officer Dick Cornfield was pushed full up against the table where he was trying to use the calipers to plot a course line to *Pequod.* Communications Officer Bill Langley stumbled back against the bulkhead and slid to his rump on the deck.

"A bit of a wag we've got, sir," Langley said as he stood to get back to the table.

"I'd say," Sperry replied. It was 1500 hours now (3:00 P.M.) on the 17th. They had been in the plot room, set off from the radar, radio, and sonar shack by a bulkhead and a closed hatchway. Third Officer Jim Banfield was Officer of the Deck on the bridge.

"If the signal is correct, sir," Cornfield went on, using the calipers again on the chart, his voice rising now above the shriek of the wind outside, "I'd put us about twenty-four hours or so from *Pequod*. The Russian trawler would be a little ahead of him. I think this storm will hold them both up, allow us to close the gap more."

"If we can keep up this speed," Sperry added, listening to the creaking, banging noises in the old ship's plates as each new wave jarred her. He had called both Cornfield and Langley into the plot room to share the classified message that had come an hour ago from Commander Ward Griffin. The normal frequencies were cluttered, but they switched to the UHF receiving antenna. The other piece of wizardry was the laser transmitter which locked into the PacSix satellite. With both pieces of high-tech equipment they could send or receive without being detected by any other ship. Or interfered with. The *Victor* was old in every way except for her communications shack, which had been newly outfitted a few months ago.

The yellow signals message lay on the chart table just above Cornfield's calipers where Sperry had dropped it after reading it to his three line officers:

PROCEED ALL SPEED INTERCEPT RUSSIAN TRAWLER AT APPROX POSITION INDICATED BELOW. USE WHATEVER HARASSMENT YOU CAN PREVENT TRANSFER DAVID JULIAN, SYDNEY, FROM TRAWLER TO RUSSIAN SUB CLOSING FOR RENDEZVOUS APPROX LATE THE 18TH. IMPERATIVE DO NOT LOSE JULIAN. DESIST USE

OF FIREPOWER UNLESS FIRED UPON. PEQUOD REPORTED IN SAME AREA OF TRAWLER. GOOD LUCK.
COMMANDER GRIFFIN 777844

When Sperry finished reading it, both men frowned, then stared at the deck, puzzled. It was Cornfield who finally asked, "What's Julian doing on a Russian trawler?"

Sperry shook his head. "Haven't the foggiest, Dick."

"So what does harassment mean, sir?" Langley added.

"Whatever imagination we have, gentlemen, to muck up that trawler captain's intent to transfer Julian, as the message says," Sperry replied.

"And the Russian sub, sir?" Cornfield pursued, perplexity in his eyes. "We are not a man-of-war, sir . . . We are Search and Rescue. We've got some big ones back in Sydney—"

"Most of them in Guam," Langley corrected.

"They've got a few heavies for backup," Cornfield argued, trying to get some logic out of the message. "Seems to me they could have anticipated. We were sent out on a rescue run, sir—"

"They wouldn't use a heavy," Sperry explained. "Government house does not want us to play the matador out here. It's probably somebody else's wag to do that."

"Like who, sir?"

"The bloomin' Yank Navy . . . or the Brits," Langley commented wryly.

"Yes, well . . . we've got it now regardless," Cornfield insisted. "Excuse me, sir, but if they want Julian that bad, then I should think—"

"Don't, me lad," Langley cajoled, giving Cornfield a wink. "You'll go bats tryin' to reason the minds of the brass. . . ."

"He's right, Dick," Sperry said. "We've got our orders, and you know what that means . . . Go for it."

Cornfield was thirty-four years old with no experience in any kind of "harassment" duty on the high seas, especially with Russians. He was a broadly built man, five foot ten or so, dark hair and gentle brown eyes that went with a meditative air about him. He reminded Sperry more of a veterinarian than a ship's officer. But he had served three months on an Australian destroyer five years ago before finishing his hitch in the navy and transferring over to

Coastal. Griffin probably figured any man who had some experience on anything resembling a "heavy" should be aboard. Cornfield had a wife expecting in three months back in Sydney. So he had a reason to be carpy.

Bill Langley was going on forty and had done six months duty on an Australian frigate a bit smaller than *Victor*. "Ran a thousand cases of Coca-Cola to the Solomons once a month, sir," he had said to Sperry when he reported in. Langley had seen no high seas action either, though he seemed a bit enthralled by the prospect. He was six foot two, well compacted, a tennis buff on shore. He had salt and pepper hair, eyes the color of gun metal that carried shafts of humor in them.

"We going to throw pots and pans at that sub, sir?" he asked, leaning into the chart table as the ship dipped for another roll.

Sperry smiled. "Well, we've got a few rounds of 3.5 ammo in the locker for the three-inch . . . I imagine it could bark a few times, but it won't scare off the wolf . . . So we harass. Put your minds on that, gentlemen. . . ."

"But can we get there in time, sir?" Cornfield asked, putting aside his grousiness over the message and the assignment. "I mean in this blow?"

"Maximum effort . . . You know the book, Dick," Sperry replied as he picked up the phone and punched the button to the engine room.

"Butch Call here," the chief engineer's voice came on, sounding petulant and somewhat distant in the banging noises going through the ship.

"Butch, what's our speed?"

"Eleven knots, sir . . . And she's barely keeping her clothes on, sir! The bow plates sound as if they're going to buckle!"

"I need thirteen out of her, Butch," Sperry shouted back. "I have a priority message from Coastal. We've got to get to our target at maximum speed!"

"Sir, I'm taking water down here!" Butch shouted back. "And the pumps ain't helpin' much . . . We got more comin' in 'tween decks! If ya want to get there, sir, I advise we hold speed or even slow down."

"Try her at thirteen, Butch!" Sperry yelled into the phone again, the sound of the gasping turbines cluttering up the background. "If she shows signs of cracking, we'll fall back!"

"I'll need a little time to shore up the bulkheads down here, sir!" Butch bellowed, his voice almost pleading as if he were being asked to put the ship under. "I—I'll ring up when I'm ready, sir!"

Sperry hung up and grabbed for the chart table again, sensing the somberness in the two officers now. "Bill, when did you last get that target on the sonar?"

"Before the storm hit, sir . . . about 1430 hours . . . The target went pretty fast and deep, sir, heading on our course, sir . . . Then he came back around the other way, made some turns, and then barreled ahead again, sir. Then we picked up another blip behind him in ten minutes, heading in the same direction . . . Nothing since, not in this storm, sir. . . ."

"Two subs," Sperry said, frowning at the table. "I wonder if they're both Russian?"

"Gettin' crowded like the Hobart Race gatherin' in Sydney Harbour, sir!" Langley replied with a grin.

"I hope one is ours," Cornfield commented. "Even it up some . . . I hate to go up against two Russians . . . Even one gets my liver flappin', I don't mind sayin' it, sir!"

Sperry nodded. *Victor* shuddered again as it rose stern high with the sea. There was a lot of banging of falling gear throughout the ship. She went bow-down with a crunch that rattled her from stem to stern. Cornfield slid over the chart table to the deck on the other side. Langley grabbed at a stanchion and hung on. Sperry spreadeagled himself across the table, hanging on to the edges with his hands.

The ship slowly came back up, vibrating again as she did so. "You all right, Dick?" Sperry asked. Cornfield got up slowly and brushed at his blue jumpsuit, pulling his blue cap with COASTAL RESCUE across the visor back on his head. He smiled sheepishly and grabbed on to the bolted-down chart table across from Sperry.

Sperry leaned against it as another roll pushed *Victor* over hard to starboard. She hung over a long time, then slowly, ever so slowly, came back again. "We don't want to run over *Pequod*!" Sperry commented, raising his voice above the scream of the wind in the rigging on the signals deck. "We got no radar in this weather . . . Not enough to see him anyway . . . And she may be lying-a-hull in this kind of gale, if the skipper is smart! Dead in the water, crew riding it out below . . . We'd be on her before we knew it!"

"Whoever is skipperin' that ketch, sir, is either a looney or King

Neptune himself," Langley offered, clutching at the support stanchion a few feet from the table.

"So why'd he stay out here?" Cornfield asked, leaning with another heave of the ship. "If Julian is gone over on that trawler, why hang around?"

"You can ask him when or if we see him!" Sperry shouted as the wind rose around them. *Victor* shuddered with the smash of the seas on her delicate, old hull plates.

Sperry didn't know himself if *Victor* would make it, let alone *Pequod*. He felt the uncertainty now of the elements, the storm, but also the subs in the area, the trawler . . . It was no longer a rescue mission. Now it was a confrontation of a different sort. Loaded with danger. He longed to know what was behind Julian being on the trawler, even as Cornfield had asked. He longed to know why *Pequod* stayed out here in this murderous gale. He thought of Megan and Crystal, wondered if he would ever see them again.

But the skipper of *The Pequod* crowded in around them. Who was he? The man had grit, he'd give him that. Or as Langley intimated, maybe he was just naive or a bit crackers. If *Victor*, all two hundred and twenty feet of her, was taking a pounding like this, what was that forty-five-foot ketch doing now? He hated to think of it, even as he felt the ship under him tremble and shudder again, leaning far to port and being beaten to submission by the elements.

The phone buzzed. He leaned against the bulkhead as he picked it up.

"I've opened her to thirteen, sir!" Butch Call's voice crackled through the line. "I don't know how long we can keep her plates from bustin', sir! But you've got your speed!"

"Thanks, Butch! Keep your eyes and ears open! Call me if you see she might be taking in more water!"

"This ain't no normal gale, sir! The man who plowed this paddock has a lot to answer for! Wind's strong enough to blow oysters off a rock, sir! I'll ring ya back if I catch the sound of her dyin' on us, sir!"

Butch hung up. Sperry turned back to the hatch and stumbled out to get to the bridge and relieve Banfield. It was going to be a long night.

Fourteen

The monstrous wave, carrying hissing froths of white swirling water, smashed into *Pequod* over her fantail. Sebastian glanced behind him to see if Barbara was ready for it. She had grabbed the mainmast even tighter with both arms. He noticed her safety line attached to the deck cleat behind her.

Pequod's stern rose high to the wave. It was like going up a roller coaster track slowly to the top just before the plunge over the other side. As the boat rose, he could see the gouging sea on both sides of the boat. He felt like a spectator watching a film in a movie theater.

Then the water came crashing down on the boat, slamming across the afterdeck, plowing over the cockpit, boiling over the dog house and rolling forward. Sebastian was knocked off his feet by the force of it. As he went down, he wondered if Ryan had seen the huge comber coming and had pulled the wooden hatch shut over the companionway. If he hadn't, the lower decks would be flooded.

He fought off the pull of the water, rolled over and stood up, glancing back toward Barbara. The mast had broken the full force of the water, but she was on her knees, arms still wrapped around the base. She looked so fragile, so small, the vinyl jacket making her look as delicate as a yellow butterfly clinging to a vine.

Pequod's bow went down with the wave, speeding headlong into the trough ahead of it, burying her nose deep. Tons of blue-black water poured over the bow, boiling back up the forward decks all the way to the dog house. Barbara was buried under it, but she still held gamely to the base of the mainmast. Sebastian saw the constricted look of fear and uncertainty on her face. "Hang on!" he yelled at her, struggling against the pull of the water. The wind took his words and flung them aside. Then the boat's bow slowly came up again, the water spilling off her decks over the side, a lot of it draining down into the bilges.

When Barbara managed to climb back onto her feet, Sebastian

turned aft as Ryan came up, carrying the storm jib folded in his arms. Sebastian waved him back down. It was too late to try to rig the storm jib now. They'd have to go with the regular jib until the wind quieted, though he noted that the sail was flopping, a couple of shrouds hanging loose. He tried yelling to Ryan to go back below and close the hatch. Ryan could not hear him. So Sebastian gestured with his thumb down and added a pumping motion with his hands to indicate that he should start working the manual bilge pump to get the water out. Ryan waved and went back below.

Sebastian knew he had to get back to the wheel and hold *Pequod* straight on with the stern to the heavy, monstrous seas continuing to pile up behind them. Even as he made his move to do so, he saw another huge comber, looking more like a tidal wave, coming at them astern. *Pequod* had hardly recovered from the last smashing blow of water. This one looked mean enough to break her.

He turned around and pointed at the wave to Barbara. She nodded her head, put her arms around the mast again. Even from where he stood, ten feet or so away, he saw her eyes widening under her yellow hood. He wished he could get her down below out of this weather and sea, but there wasn't time. His other concern was to get to the wheel. It was locked on the weather vane automatic steering, but he wondered if it would hold under the next smashing fist of the sea.

He finally decided to unlock his safety belt and get back to Barbara, give her support as much as he could. He stumbled back to the mast, locked his line into a cleat a few feet away to the left of her. He had hardly gotten it fastened when *Pequod* started that familiar rise stern-first as the huge comber moved on her. The water came on top of them in a torrential rush. He felt himself picked up by it and thrown off his feet into the mast a few feet away. His right shoulder slammed into the base of the mast. He felt the stabbing pain and wondered if his shoulder were broken. The water knocked him around again, and then he felt himself lifted with it and flung along like a piece of flotsam.

He flew over the port rail into the sea. The safety belt pulled him up short; otherwise he would have been sucked under. He fought his way back up through the biting cold water, snorting and coughing as he surfaced, looking around for Barbara. She was not at her place by the mast. Panic jabbed him sharply. Did she loose her safety line?

He fought his way back to the port-side restraining lines that were half-buried under the water. The boat leaned heavily over to port, yawing some in the sea, swinging around toward a beam-on position with the ocean. His mind told him she would broach if she caught another wave that size. That would surely finish the boat and them. But all he could think of was Barbara. And with that came the agonizing thought that he may have made a big mistake after all in insisting on trying to chase after Julian with so little understanding of how to handle the Southern Ocean. She had made that statement to him both in appeal and in anger . . . and now he felt a pang of guilt and remorse as he shuddered at the thought she might have been lost.

He crawled back up the careening deck, looking in every direction for some sign of her. Then he caught the quick flash of her yellow vinyl jacket in the boiling water off the port side ten feet away. He jumped over the restraining lines and swam over to her, ignoring the grinding pummel of the heavy sea. He reached out and pulled her head up from her facedown position in the water, yanked at her safety line with his other hand. It was still tight to the deck cleat. Her white teeth flashed in what must have been the start of a scream, the water streaming down her face. "I've got you!" he yelled above the banshee sound of the wind and the continual rumble of the sea gone wild. He dragged her in by her safety line, the other hand pulling on her jacket.

Pequod was beginning to rise from the staggering blow of the wave, leveled out again, her port rails slowly lifting back to steady-on. Sebastian managed to get Barbara over the rail, shoving her up the slanted deck toward the mainmast. He crawled up after her and lay down on his stomach beside her, breathing heavily from the exertion of fighting the sea and the fear of having lost her. Her lips were blue from the cold water, and they trembled as she lay there. He put his left arm across her back to assure her she was OK. His face was only a foot from hers. Her eyes were closed as if to shut out the horrible vision of water that had buried them.

Pequod continued righting herself, the water pouring back off her decks. But one glance aft showed another line of huge combers marching down on them. He knew he had to get the boat around and her stern into them or she would capsize. He put his mouth next to her ear and shouted, "You have to get below! In a hurry!" She opened her eyes, red from the salt water, and stared into his. He saw both the fear and the shock there and maybe condemnation too for what he had committed all of them to. But she lifted her head and looked beyond him aft and saw the rolling waves coming toward them.

She got up slowly. He unhooked her safety line as well as his own and led her across the pitching deck, around the dog house, and down to the companionway. Ryan had put the hatch in place after all. Sebastian slid it open and waited for her to descend.

"You can't stay out here!" she yelled at him, resisting his hand on her arm urging her down below. She glanced at another monstrous comber coming at them off the port quarter.

"I've got to try to get her around to run before it!" he shouted. "We'll be on beam's end if we don't!"

"Then let me help—"

"Nothing you can do! Get below and tie yourself down in your bunk!"

She reluctantly turned and went down the steps at his urging. She glanced back at him as he moved to slam the hatch shut. It was as if she were looking at him for the last time. He caught something in her eyes then, perhaps more of what he was trying to see, a look of remembrance, of the years that had passed them, times of being welded together in danger and even in love.

"I'll be all right!" he shouted down at her, knowing he didn't have the time to speculate. He closed the hatch and turned, staggered back to the cockpit and the wheel. He glanced at the comber coming like a runaway freight straight at him, a galloping wall of water bent on burying the boat once and for all. He knew it would happen if he didn't get *Pequod* around and stern-on to it.

He stood to the wheel, pushing it hard over to starboard, hoping to correct her yawing to port. The jib up forward was flapping with the wind now, of little use for headway. Still, there might be enough in the sail to help *Pequod* swing about . . . he hoped.

The wave came over him even as he tied his safety belt to the cleat near the cockpit. It knocked the breath out of him. But he saw *Pequod's* bow coming about to starboard slowly even as the water knocked him flat. He was slammed against the wheel as he went down, the water burying him again.

He came up thrashing at it, thinking he was knocked overboard. But he felt the deck of the cockpit under him, and he grabbed the wheel and pulled himself up, coughing and gagging on the green water that plowed on over the dog house. The wave had caught *Pequod* as her bow swung slowly to starboard. She heeled hard over to port, and he found himself hanging on a 30 degree list, grabbing the cockpit rail for dear life.

The boat held up shakily to that first rush of water on her bow, then swung around sharply to starboard in the wave's backwash, her bow rising with it and then beginning to plunge down the other side. Sebastian remembered then how Julian had angled her bow to the wave's crest and got her surfing harmlessly with it. But could he do it? He never had before. But first he had to get *Pequod's* bow turned back more to port, get her stern more directly around to the seas and wind. He jammed the wheel hard over, hoping whatever was left of the jib might help him.

He felt, rather than saw, *Pequod* obey slowly under the prod. At the same time, he felt her rise from the stern with the new onslaught of the combers. He put the helm hard to starboard, hoping to angle her some across the wave's crest. He felt himself picked up and shoved forward with increasing speed like going down a roller coaster dip. Then, as he braced for the bow to do a deep dive into the trough, *Pequod* suddenly caught the wave's passing peak and skidded back into the backwash.

He didn't take time to celebrate the maneuver. The chances of making another one like that were remote. He could see enough of the towering waves coming behind him to overwhelm the boat, and there was not enough steerage to get her around or keep her running before the sea. All he could do was try to keep her from turning helplessly beam-on to starboard. The air around him was a kind of swirling black-purple, smelling of the electricity from the lightning, that ozone pungency that burned off the neons along crowded Rush Street in Chicago. The wind was a continual scream, trying to pick him up and fling him bodily out of the cockpit. It was the worst madness of nature that he had ever known or could ever imagine.

He thought then that he ought to get a storm jib up to give the boat some necessary steerage to keep her stern to the seas and wind. But he also knew it was too dangerous right now for any of them to try handling sail. All he could do was try to hold her with the wheel and hope what was left of the regular jib forward would give him the extra he needed.

The minutes of frenzy he felt in battling the seas seemed to stretch into painful hours. He tried peering through the flying spray and peppering rain to catch a glimpse of the jib forward by the dim light of the forward deck hatch. He couldn't. Once he saw the forward companionway hatch open, and a head poked out for a moment. Then it ducked back in again, as a comber swept over the stern and headed pell-mell for that open hatch. It was slammed shut just in time.

And then, feeling the pounding ache of the fatigue and biting cold and wondering if he could hold out at the wheel, he felt the wind shift. It swung more to port, backing away from the stern, turned and shoved *Pequod* roughly so that she swung hard to starboard again. He fought to keep her straight on before the wind and sea using the wheel. But she would not respond. Finally he took the chance, unhooked his safety belt, reached for the flashlight in the locker under the helm, and ran forward to the coaming of the dog house. The beam from the flashlight picked up the jib, flapping uselessly like a piece of laundry in the wind. Without it, he could not possibly hope to hold the boat from sliding beam-on to the sea starboard. Their only hope for survival then was to strip down that battered jib, get below, and ride her out lying-a-hull.

He hesitated, glancing around once astern to where the seas were coming from. He sensed then that the wind and seas had definitely shifted to a more easterly tack, and it seemed less cold. Maybe the storm was blowing out? Or maybe a new front?

Finally he stepped down and slid the companionway hatch open and yelled, "Ryan!" But Ryan was already standing at the foot of the steps, his life jacket on over his safety harness as if preparing to come up anyway. "We have to pull down the jib and bare-pole it! We can't keep steerage in this wind!"

"Right, sir!" Ryan yelled back, taking a safety line from the hook by the door of the companionway hatch and moving up toward Sebastian. Barbara looked up through the hatch, a question in her eyes. Did he want her topside?

"Stay below, Barb!" Sebastian shouted. "It's too rough up here!" She gave him a look of chagrin as if she'd been insulted. Then he slammed the hatch cover back into place.

He turned and followed Ryan up over the dog house roof and forward toward the jib. Another rumbling comber came up on them even as they fastened their safety lines to the deck. The boat heeled heavily to starboard. Ryan grabbed for the mainmast shroud instinctively, but the sea tumbled him to the restraining lifelines. Sebastian reached out and grabbed him before he went over, dragging him back up the steep incline of the listing boat.

Sebastian unhooked the flashlight from his belt, lifted the beam upward toward the torn jib. He kept the light in his left hand, helped Ryan work the jib down with the other, all the time listening for any more sounds of a comber coming in. When Ryan got the jib down and unsheeted, another wave came climbing over the port side like a pirate ready to storm the bridge. They hung on to the base of the mainmast as it tore at the rigging, hissing over them. The jib was torn from Ryan's arms and carried over the starboard side.

"Forget it!" Sebastian yelled at him. "We better get below!"

They lurched their way back to the companionway hatch. Sebastian slid it open, and he and Ryan half-tumbled down the steps into the chart room as another comber slammed into the *Pequod,* from the starboard side this time, as the boat swung around beam-on to the seas. Sebastian reached back and slammed the hatch shut again, and as the wave came over he could see the planking of the hatch bend with it. The water went over them with the sound of a grumble, as if frustrated at being cheated. He turned back into the chart room, where the water was now ankle-deep.

He was surprised to see Jamison hanging on to the radio console with one hand, a cup of steaming brew in the other extended toward him. The only light came from the tilley swinging from the overhead, casting bats of shadow here and there.

"Good show, Jamison!" Sebastian yelled above the wind, trying to sound upbeat, taking the cup from the journalist and gulping the hot broth quickly, glad for the burn of it in his stomach. Jamison's face was still as green as a spring apple. His blue eyes were red-rimmed from lack of sleep, wide with some apprehension as the seas pounded the decks overhead. But he gamely managed a hesitant grin in response, pleased that he had done something commendable.

Sebastian glanced at Barbara who was holding on to the chart table with one hand, the cup in the other, swaying with the heavy rolls of *Pequod* to port. "Better drink up!" he shouted to her. "We're lying-a-hull, beam-on to starboard! We better climb into our bunks pretty quick and ride her out!"

"Can we get sail up?" she shouted back, clutching at the console as she was shoved by the boat's sharp heel to port.

He shook his head, draining the last of the hot soup from his cup. "You can't stand up out there at all! And the seas are coming right over her! We'll have to wait. Where's Ryan?"

She did not respond immediately, her eyes getting larger in the prospect of lying helplessly in the boat before the pounding seas. Her face looked pale and drawn in the dim light. Her lips still showed that tinge of blue from the cold. Her wet, golden hair was plastered to her head. She still looked dazed from the shock of her experience with the sea.

"Ryan?" he shouted at her again above the growing racket in the boat as the seas belted her hard again.

Her mouth moved once, but no words came. "He went aft, sir." Jamison picked it up for her. "To check on any leaks in the forward hatch!" Sebastian nodded and looked at her again. Her face looked white, almost pasty, in the dim light from the chart room light on the bulkhead over the radar console. He moved on by her and peered at the barometer on the bulkhead over the radio. The indicator showed it was still holding steady on force eight. He reached over quickly to grab the console table for support as *Pequod* slid off to port again. He was thrown forward into the console table, and he felt the pain jab in his right shoulder. He winced against it, suddenly remembering the jolt the shoulder took against the mast when he had slid into it.

Barbara put her cup down on the radio console and moved over the few feet toward him. "You all right?" He nodded. "You better get that sweater off so I can look!'

He removed his yellow vinyl jacket, then his pullover. There was a mean swelling high on the shoulder. She touched it with the fingers of her right hand, pressing to see if anything was broken. He glanced at her. She was only a few inches from his face as she studied the wound. He caught the concern in her deep blue eyes, still glazed some with fatigue and shock. The bluish tinge on her lips had faded, revealing the soft, tender natural pink and the curve of her mouth.

"Not broken," she said to him. She put her left hand on his chest to help balance herself against the roll of the boat. The warm softness of her touch more than compensated for the pain of his shoulder. "You'll need a bandage on that," she said finally. "It's got an abrasion an inch long." He shivered in the cold. "And get those wet clothes off," she ordered, stepping back to the console. "You'll catch pneumonia!"

He tried to grin, but she did not respond. Just then Ryan came into the chart room from the galley carrying a small wrench in his right hand. His limp seemed more noticeable. He glanced uncertainly at Sebastian, noticing the shoulder.

"We have a lot of water in the bilges!" he shouted as the wind rose in a scream in the shrouds again. His face was gouged with pain from his knee. His blue eyes showed no fear from the seas pounding *Pequod*, but a perpetual frown streaked a furrow of dark scratches over his nose. That was enough to say he was worried. Undoubtedly he had done enough sailing with his father to know; yet there was no judgment in his eyes when he looked at Sebastian for being committed to this growing sound of death around them. His mind had to be on his father; he'd go down trying rather than not trying at all.

The boat heeled sharply over to port again, hung there a long time before coming back. "We better take to the bunks!" Sebastian yelled at them. "When she lets up at all out there, we'll run up a storm jib and get steerage back! What say, Ryan?"

Ryan nodded, looking up at the ceiling as if trying to detect the sound of another comber. "Right away, I think, sir!" he shouted back.

"Let's go!" Sebastian added, prodding Jamison to duck down in the stern berth area. For some reason the journalist found it easier riding for him back there. "Tie yourself down, Jamison!" Sebastian warned him. The journalist nodded and disappeared. Sebastian half-pushed Barbara forward through the galley and the lounge, both of them tossed rudely to port again as another wave slammed *Pequod* with a shudder. They got into their bunks, Ryan just forward of the two of them.

Sebastian was glad to ease his aching bones into the bunk, even though he felt the alarm bells going off inside him over the punishment the boat was taking lying helplessly beam-on to the storm. He glanced across the aisle to Barbara. She was lying back, staring up at the ceiling, the safety belt tight around her waist. She turned her head slowly to look at him, but he could not see much of her face in the darkness.

Sebastian lay there for what seemed a long time, bracing for the pound of the combers, feeling the helpless boat groan as it heaved again over to port, shuddered from stem to stern as it tried to come back. Each time she heeled like that, she seemed to stay over longer.

It was after one of those long, listing, sickening rolls to port that he felt Ryan get out of his bunk behind him.

"We've got to get some sail up, sir," he said, leaning over Sebastian to be heard over the wind. "She can't keep from going over if we don't."

"Okay," Sebastian said and pushed his long legs over the side of the bunk. "I'm thinking about that trawler out there somewhere, Ryan," he added, pulling on a dry blue turtleneck sweater he had stuffed under his pillow. "I'll get the sail," Ryan said, ignoring the remark.

Sebastian moved on aft, feeling Barbara behind him. He reached up to one of the overhead lockers in the lounge and pulled out a red windbreaker, which he put on as he continued walking, half-staggering aft. He stopped at the radar and flipped it on. A lot of the green grass splashed across the screen, but as he continued to study it he thought he could see a bright blip, somewhat faded, almost blending with the green tentacles of storm interference. He put the pinpoint of light at about four miles. That startled him some.

He felt Barbara come up close to him, grabbing for the console table as the boat slid off into an agonizing dip again. She handed him a few Ritz crackers and some yellow cheese. It tasted soggy and stale, but he was glad for it anyway. He couldn't remember when he had eaten last. He glanced up at the clock on the wall. It showed 2100 hours, the 17th. They'd been battling the storm for five hours already!

He saw Ryan come through the door from the galley, the red-colored jib folded in his arms. "Got something, sir?" he asked, putting his free arm against the bulkhead alongside the radar to brace against the rolling boat.

Sebastian put his finger on the tiny blip on the screen. Ryan studied it, frowning again. "I'm not sure, sir. But if that's a target, he's coming our way, looks like!"

"Why is he so close then?" Sebastian asked. "He must have radar!"

"Clutter on his screen too probably. But we're lying dead here now . . . He could run over us if he stays on that course! We have to get sail up, sir!"

Sebastian nodded. He glanced at Barbara. "You game?" he asked.

She was zipping up her yellow vinyl jacket, then tied her hood tightly with the drawstrings around her head, then pulled on her life jacket and safety harness. "Are you kidding?" she snapped back in some disdain.

"It's going to be rocky up there," he reminded her. "We better stay close!"

He opened the hatch and climbed on deck to the battering wind and pounding seas. It definitely was not as cold now. And the rain seemed warmer on the skin. But the seas were the same, rising like mountains in the dark over them and smashing down on *Pequod* with a seeming vengeance. Still, Sebastian thought they might not be as big as before, if that meant anything considering the punishment they gave out to *Pequod*.

They worked their way carefully over the dog house roof, got beyond the mainmast, and faced the headstay. They clipped their safety belts down. The rolling of the boat was even more extreme as they continued wallowing beam-on at the mercy of the wind and sea.

Sebastian unhooked his flashlight from his belt and played the beam up the headstay. "Small storm jib, sir!" Ryan yelled at him, lifting the red sail to hook on the halyards. "Enough to give her steerage, but not too big to wreck the headstay!" Sebastian nodded. It was testy rigging the small storm jib in the wind as the twisting boat rocked heavily over to port under the hammering of the seas. They finally sheeted the sail in place, and the wind gutted out in her immediately. The boat slowly came around, but it seemed too slow.

"Get the helm!" he shouted at Barbara. "Put her hard over to port if she's not locked on already!" He regretted asking her to go then, because it was a dangerous crawl back to the cockpit. But she went, staggering, lurching against the heeling deck. Sebastian kept his light on her until she was in the cockpit and had put the helm over to port. Then he turned forward and watched the bow slowly come around.

He and Ryan continued to watch the jib to make sure it would hold. Satisfied, Sebastian shouted, "We better get back to the cockpit!" Ryan said nothing but followed him aft.

They got to the cockpit as another comber went over. Sebastian took Barbara by the arm and led her to the companionway hatch. She was reluctant to go. "Get on the radar!" he said. "Watch for that blip on the screen! Let me know if it gets inside the inner ring!"

She hesitated a moment, wanting to protest being sent below.

Finally she moved on down the steps as he opened the hatch, then patted her lightly on the back as she went down. He closed the hatch after her and went back to the cockpit.

When he got back next to Ryan behind the helm, he felt a continual throb of apprehension. Partly because he wasn't sure he should try to keep that jib up in this kind of wind and sea. Maybe it was better to ride "bare poles" and hope the boat would survive it all right beam-on. But there was something else crowding his mind. If there was a ship out there to starboard as the radar seemed to indicate, they had no chance lying dead in the water.

He glanced around at the seas and noticed that they came at them criss-cross now. The wind was not holding to any particular direction, forcing a boiling, gyrating effect in the combers, chopping them up or sometimes joining others in a partnership of destruction. It was impossible to run before a wind that did not stay on a permanent tack. But what worried him more was that the erratic seas could do more damage than the steady, even rolling ones. It was like falling into the jaws of a whale and being shaken apart.

"I'm going to turn on the searchlight and take a look!" he shouted at Ryan. Ryan nodded. Sebastian moved to the dog house roof. The navy lamp stanchion was bent some by the combers, but it still worked. He turned on the light, played it over the seas to port and starboard, then aft. He was right. The green-black, white, bearded sea giants were stacked up, jumping at them crazily, twisting *Pequod* each time they hit, grinding the hull.

He turned off the light and made his way back to Ryan at the helm. He felt uneasy again. He knew so little about this kind of sea, how to sail in it. But what it posed held a certain foreboding in his mind.

As he stood by Ryan, he felt the boat shudder more with each wave. *Pequod's* bow stayed down longer each time. She was waterlogged, unable to rise as quickly against what she carried in her flooded bilges.

For the first time, Sebastian began to close with the grim reality of the situation. They probably could not survive unless God did a miracle. *Pequod* was fighting bravely, her hull still intact, her masts still standing—thanks to Julian's construction genius. But the continual shuddering in her hull after each comber now indicated she was close to breaking up. He knew now why Julian went to such extremes to get Jamison to force them back to Sydney. The farther south they moved on this ocean, the tougher the storms and seas. It took more than their own game but mostly amateur efforts and sailing sense to match it.

And yet, while he felt a strange sense of sadness for all of them, he knew he had to try to hold it together. To save them if nothing else. The pursuit of *Minsk* had been a driving compulsion for him. It had nothing to do with Backstrom, Alnutt, and Winston. Not anymore. It was his own charge to carry or lose. He had gone too far, committed them to too much, not to run right up that Russian's rear end and at least make some kind of point. As silly and pompous as it seemed, he felt he had been right. There was no vengeance in him so much, but a sense of necessary justice in his action, the need to make some kind of statement. For himself? For God? Had he driven them all to this insanity simply to ease his own sense of battered conscience then? Perhaps. But as the seas laughed at him, tore at him, pummeled *Pequod* to her knees, he knew he hung on now because he really had no choice. The sea had grabbed him hard and forced him to fight for his life and theirs. Perhaps that was the greatest and only demand that pushed him now. But in that, he only hoped that in doing so, he might have declared something . . . but what? As Barbara said, there was not much he could do even if he did catch up with the Russians. Nothing for Julian or anybody else.

So what justice now? The sea had the last laugh, the last pound of the gavel. And as he glanced at Ryan hanging on to the wheel, he felt a stab of guilt . . . even of condemnation. Was he Captain Ahab on the quarterdeck of *Pequod,* driving them on this destructive journey to fulfill a sense of vengeance on that trawler captain? He had told Julian that Ahab needed a little of God on the quarterdeck with him to possibly avert the disaster that overtook that crew in Melville's *Moby Dick*.

Well, how much of God rode him with now? Sebastian sensed that his motives maybe were not exactly pure . . . And maybe Backstrom, Alnutt, and Winston still jabbed him about his sense of calling. Yet, as long as one act of injustice was done to one human being, was he not bound to try to right the balances? Even as the boat shuddered from stem to stern under another crushing wave, it seemed all too altruistic.

Still, he was committed. The storm might very well win. He was not experienced enough in sailing to anticipate emergencies.

He lacked the skill and instinct of Julian. He felt helpless most of the time in how to make the right moves to keep the boat upright. Ryan was equally unsure. They were playing a "hunt-and-peck" game and hoping they were hitting it right. And he knew he wasn't.

He wanted to go below now to be with Barb when the end came. He did not want to be swallowed up without telling her one more time that he loved her. To hear her say it to him.

He thought then of that prayer he had memorized years ago in some tight situation.

> Stay with me, God. The night is dark,
> The night is cold: my little spark
> Of courage dies. The night is long;
> Be with me, God, and make me strong.

"Sir?" Ryan's voice screamed in his right ear. Sebastian turned toward him. "I saw lights out there! Looked like running lights, sir!" Ryan waved his right hand toward the starboard beam. Sebastian stared into the dark and rain in that direction, the wind slamming stinging water into his eyes. He saw nothing. But he began to feel something was there.

He left the cockpit and worked his way to the dog house, up on the roof to the searchlight. Fighting off a heavy sea that dragged at his legs, he grabbed the light and swung it around to starboard.

The beam stabbed into the black curtain.

Then he saw it. Just the red lead line of her hull as it rose to the seas . . .

She was not a large trawler, but she carried tons of equipment, he knew that much. But now she seemed awfully big as her bow went down into the troughs and came up building a huge wave in front of her that joined the rest of the maddening, churning sea. That could push a swamping comber on to *Pequod* that could severely damage her.

The *Minsk*.

Moving now on a course straight across *Pequod's* bow to starboard. A collision course.

He turned to yell at Ryan to put the helm to port. But he knew Ryan had already done that, feeling the boat under him lean that way.

Sebastian left the searchlight on, turned in the direction of the trawler, hoping someone on the bridge watch might see it and change course to avoid the collision. He jumped down to the deck just as the companionway hatch slid open and Barbara stepped up and yelled, "I've got a target in the inner ring!"

"I know!" Sebastian replied, and he waved his right hand toward the trawler out there in the darkness. "Get your life jacket on! You hear?"

She hesitated, her face white as she stared up at him, not comprehending. Then he slid the hatch cover back in place and staggered back to Ryan in the cockpit. The searchlight kept stabbing into the ink of the night. But the shadow of the trawler kept coming, her bow wave rising higher now in front of her, mixing with the churning criss-cross seas and building a wall of water that soon would barrel down on them. Why couldn't they see the light? Sebastian kept shouting it in his brain.

"Our only chance is that the jib will give us what we need to get out of her way to port!" he yelled at Ryan. Ryan nodded. Sebastian glanced starboard along the line of the searchlight's path. The trawler was beyond it, coming on steadily. He caught her running lights again on collision course with *Pequod's* bow. If they missed, it wouldn't be by much!

The *Pequod* plunged bow-down into another trough. The *Minsk* was lost from sight then. But in a minute they would both come up on top, straight on to each other. Unless *Pequod* had enough steerage to swing to port in time.

"Get below, Ryan!"

"Sir?" Ryan shouted back the protest.

"Get below! No use two of us getting caught up here!"

Ryan opened his mouth to argue, but then thought better of it, moved out of the cockpit, and ran forward to disappear down the hatch. Sebastian locked the wheel to port and ran to the dog house, climbed up on the roof, and hooked his safety belt to the cleat. Then he swung the searchlight around forward. He saw the trawler going by just about five points off the starboard bow of *Pequod,* no more than fifty yards away.

He saw the rising form of the wave off her bow mixing with the swirling, pointed cliffs of the seas. It seemed to grow larger like a mountain being born from some cataclysmic explosion deep under the sea. It had the shape of a killer. Sebastian figured it would hit the boat a few points forward of her starboard beam, a vulnerable spot for a boat already lying low to port and dragged over by her waterlogged bilges.

He turned the light up to the jib. He thought he should take it down or reef it, but the boat needed the push to get around to port to avoid the worst crush of that oncoming wave. There wasn't time now to do anything about it anyway. He saw the wave looming up to starboard, lifting a huge white beard like the bared teeth of a monster. He turned then and jumped down to the deck, opened the hatch, and dove down the companionway, shutting it behind him.

"Get into your bunks and tie down!" he yelled at Barbara, who was working the bilge pump handle. "Now!"

He moved over to her, grabbed her wrist, and pulled her through the galley and lounge to the bunks. He shoved her into one, then leaped into another opposite her. He felt, rather than saw, Ryan take the next one forward of them. He hoped Jamison was still tied down in his bunk aft.

"What is going on!" she yelled at him.

"Buckle your belt!" he shouted back, hearing that rumbling sound of the huge wave like thunder. "And pray!"

He felt *Pequod* rise on her starboard side, lift to a steep incline as though she was going to go over. She hung there a long time it seemed, then plunged over to port, her list growing so steep that Sebastian felt himself jammed against the port bulkhead. He thought he heard Barbara give off a muffled cry just before the boat was slammed hard by the comber. The bow went down suddenly, like the boat had been mortally wounded. Then the slant of it took her into a dive so steep that Sebastian felt his feet suspended straight up over his head.

Everything that hadn't fallen inside the boat up to then let loose, sounding as if someone had unloaded a truck full of broken rock on a hardwood floor. Then *Pequod* went straight down, and she rose high stern-first, tumbling end over end, her masts pointed down, her keel to the sky.

In the few seconds before they settled completely down into the sea, Sebastian flipped on the flashlight he still held tightly in his left hand when he came down the hatch. In the glow, he glanced across the aisle at her. There was no fear in her eyes as she looked back at him, only resignation. Like himself. But it seemed the memory of the years they had together passed between them without comment

. . . and he thought he saw a softness in those eyes as she took the time to remember. There was no time to say anything. But she seemed to be trying to gather it all up like a bouquet and hand it to him.

And then he braced himself for the plunge into the deep.

Fifteen

Sebastian felt suspended in the eerie insides of *Pequod*, staring down at the ceiling where the deck of the boat was before they pitch-poled. He heard the diesel engine shift on its mount with a loud thump. He hoped it wouldn't break loose and careen through the boat, knocking holes in the ceiling. Objects of every size were banging around, falling, sliding, clanging together in mad ricochets of sound. It was dark.

He fumbled around for the flashlight. It wasn't there. He unhooked his belt and fell to the ceiling awash with water. He put his hands down in the half-foot of it, feeling around. His hand brushed the handle. He grabbed it and pulled it up, flipped it on. The light was strong enough for him to survey the water and everything floating in it.

He looked up to see Barbara trying to get out of her safety belt. He reached up with one hand and held on to her as she dropped down. She fell into him, grabbing him around the waist with her right arm and holding on. He put his arm around her shoulders to steady her, played the light around.

"Ryan?" he called out, his voice sounding muffled in the weird atmosphere of an upside-down world.

"Here, sir!"

Sebastian played the light forward. Ryan stood in the passageway looking soaked from the water, swiping at it as it streamed down his face.

"Jamison!"

There was no response from the after-section. Sebastian figured Jamison had not heard above the creaking, banging sounds in the hull above them.

"Are we going to sink then?" Barbara asked in a calm, factual tone of voice, her arm still tight around Sebastian's waist.

Ryan had moved up close to them. "She'll come back over," he said. "Just be ready for it." The sea sounded far off for some reason, just a low rumble in the distance. "The keel will flip us back," Ryan added, looking up as if begging the keel above to do its work. Another long tense minute. Nothing happened. The bow of *Pequod* lurched downward, and Barbara's arm went tighter around his waist. "We're still lying in the backwash of that big one that knocked us over . . . The next comber will probably do it."

Sebastian began to pray for the biggest comber in the Pacific to rise up now and do just that. There was the sound of water trickling in from somewhere above, gurgling out of the bilges and into the cabin.

"We've got a five thousand-pound keel on this boat," Ryan went on, as if he was talking to the boat itself now, reminding her of the point. His voice cracked a little in the intensity he felt.

Sebastian glanced down at Barbara, then tightened his arm around her shoulder to encourage her. She lifted her head and looked at him. He could not see her face very well in the fading light from the flashlight. "It'll come," he said to her. He saw a faint smile show. He wanted to kiss her one more time, blow away any of that self-imposed distance she had maintained for so long. But then he felt the boat shudder from stem to stern, a rising rumbling sound coming with it.

"Hang on!" Ryan warned. "This one will do it!"

The boat shifted downward again as if about to make a final plunge to the deeps. It hesitated, as if uncertain which way to go, teetered, and then lurched sharply to starboard. With a sigh and a clatter, she staggered again and began to come upright.

The water came down on them again as they tried to take the flip back by hanging on to the bunk stanchions. There was the sound of more falling objects, some groaning and creaking deep in the boat's innards. Sebastian and Barbara were thrown into the bunk as the boat came back over. Ryan hung on to the bunk stanchion with both hands.

Then the boat settled, heaving some with the seas. Sebastian helped Barbara out of the bunk. He didn't think he could feel more wet than he was. He found his flashlight, anxious to survey the damage and to find out how Jamison came through it. He felt the water higher now, almost up to his knees.

"She's waterlogged," Ryan said, moving toward the stern. "We have to pump her bilges if we can, sir!"

"Jamison!" Sebastian called out again, following Ryan aft. Again no answer.

They moved on through the galley that looked like a tornado had hit it. The stove, bolted to the bulkhead and hanging on gimbals, still hung in place miraculously, but its gas plates were probably clogged with water and dirt. The propane gas tank still clung to the wall, though a bit bent. There were stalks of celery and lettuce floating in the water, which meant the freezer lid had popped open, spilling everything out. Sebastian wondered how much food they could salvage with all the water that had come in.

As they came into the chart room, they saw Jamison standing unsteadily by the radio console. He looked confused, soaked, and distraught in the dim glow of the flashlight.

"You alright, Jamison?" Sebastian asked.

"Yes, sir." His voice sounded hoarse, like maybe he had swallowed a lot of salt water. "But beats me why, sir!" His teeth began chattering against the wet and the cold or maybe the fright of all of it at once.

"I'll work the bilge pump!" Barb offered and moved through the water like she was in a slow motion scene. As she pumped the handle there was the sound of sucking bilge drains.

"Sound clogged," Sebastian offered. Ryan nodded.

"Find pots and pans, Jamison," Sebastian said. "We've got to get this water out. You up to that?"

"I take no fancy in drownin' in this soup, sir!" And he reached down and grabbed a cooking pot floating in the water.

"I'm going to open the hatch," Sebastian said to Ryan standing by the radar console, hanging on. "I'm going up for a look-see! When I'm up there, start throwing the water out the hatch on deck. But keep a lookout for a comber coming at us and close the hatch before it comes in on you! Are there any other flashlights aboard that maybe didn't get lost in the capsize?"

"Only place possible is in the emergency hatch on the fantail!" Ryan replied. "That's usually locked down pretty tight!" Sebastian nodded and then reached up and slid the hatch back and climbed up on deck. What he saw in the dying light of his flashlight made his heart sink some. He moved aft toward the emergency hatch. He noted that the mainsail sheets, along with the mizzen, were a tangled mess. The mizzen itself was bent to the left, probably unusable.

When he got to the stern, he played his light over to look at the rudder and the weather vane. As the boat tipped up stern-first with a wave, he noted that the rudder was still looking solid. But the weather vane was a loss. He pulled it up and tossed it behind him on the deck.

He undid the bolt clamps on the hatch and opened it, rummaged through and found another good-sized flashlight. He threw in his wasted one, slammed the hatch shut.

He turned and moved forward, the heavy bright beam of his flashlight taking in the damage forward. He noticed that the headstay that carried the jib was hanging slack. Her shrouds had been pulled loose from the deck, her sheets loosened and balled up into a snarling mess. The sail hung there, but it had taken a beating in the capsize. The boat was still slowly moving around to port, so he half-crawled back to the cockpit and put her helm hard over to starboard. The almost useless jib picked up some of the wind, enough to nudge *Pequod* around out of her beam-on to port.

He flashed his light forward again surveying the damage, as much as he could see from the cockpit. The mainmast was leaning some to port, and two loose shrouds were flapping in the wind. The boom was still there but hanging at a crazy angle to the mast. The bow pulpit was a battered mess. The restraining lifelines, both port and starboard, were gone. He flashed his light up the mizzen and saw that the radar and reflector were still in place, miraculously. But the antenna wire was loose and swinging with the wind. It had probably been pulled loose from the clamp on deck that guided it down through the deck, through the stern, and into the chart room. He would have to see to that right away. Without the radar, he couldn't possibly track the trawler. He noticed as he swept the light around forward again that the searchlight had been swept away, and the stanchion as well.

He half-skidded forward to the companionway hatch. It was open as Jamison and Ryan heaved water out onto the deck with their pots. He heard the rumble of another comber behind him and shouted, "Look out below!" He slammed the hatch shut. He clamped his safety belt hurriedly to a cleat on the deck as the comber slammed him hard as it came over the side, then muttered off through the scuppers. He shook his head to get the water out of his eyes, coughed on it, then turned and worked his way back to the cockpit again.

The helm was still over to starboard. He worked it back to keep the bow straight on with the seas, more to the stern. The boat seemed to ride heavy with the water. He knew the damaged jib would not give them steerage for long either. He felt the wind definitely on an easterly tack now. It was warmer too. He hoped it was not another front brewing. A southeasterly would do them in for sure in that case.

He got the boat on a staggering 045 degree heading. He needed another weather vane to replace the damaged one. He went forward to the equipment supply locker in front of the main. The cover had held with one slide bolt. He undid it and looked inside by the beam of his flashlight. He found the smaller weather vane, pulled it out, and slammed the cover back down. He went back astern, dropped the vane into the slot next to the rudder, hooked up the line to the helm. The boat responded. She was on self-steering. Enough time hopefully for him to get below and help bail.

He went down the companionway, carrying the larger damaged weather vane with him, not wanting it to be bouncing around the decks topside. He slid the hatch open, glancing behind him. He neither saw nor heard any big comber on its way; so they could throw out more water in the lull. When he got down into the chart room, he saw Barbara still pumping the bilge handle. But she wasn't gaining much. Had to be clogged drains. The water was higher, up over his knees now. They had to gain on it or the boat was gone. He found a couple of gallon-sized plastic buckets floating in the galley. He handed her one and said, "Forget the pumping! She's got plugged bilge lines! Use this!"

She took the container, staring at it in confusion. Her face was flushed from the exertion of pumping. Her hair showed the dirt and grime of the boat, and some of it smeared her forehead. Fatigue lines cut deeply under her eyes and mouth.

"So bail!" he yelled at them and threw a gallon of water out the hatch. He knew it was like trying to empty the Mississippi, but it was all they had now. And they went at it, sensing in him a certain kind of fanaticism in the bailing that said enough of the danger. They scooped and half-shoveled the water out the open hatch, closing it when they heard a comber rumbling in on them. As time wore on, their faces showed the strain, the killing fatigue. Sebastian had hung the flashlight on the bulkhead over the radio console. The light cast weird shadows in the chart room, forming bizarre silhouettes of them as they worked. As time went on, their movements became more sluggish, slower. Sebastian jabbed at them, barking the warnings. "Bail and pray!" he shouted time and again. After every fifty buckets or potfuls, they rested a little. They found a place to lean against and just stood, sagging, heads falling to their chests, eyes closing, breathing heavily.

During one break Sebastian sat on the steps of the companionway trying to get his breath. He glanced up once and peered through the light at the clock still bolted over the radio console. He saw the luminous second hand still turning. The clock showed it to be 0200 and the calendar said 12-18. How long had they been at this?

Ryan found a plastic container of strawberry jam floating on the water. He twisted off the top and passed it around. It tasted good and seemed to revive all of them.

Sebastian sensed, as they doggedly continued the bailing, that the seas were not coming on as destructively. They still continued to close the wooden hatch, but the water did not smash into it as much. Some time around 0300 they had gotten the water down to no more than an inch or two on the deck. It was a slimy, gritty mess smelling of battery acid, oil, grease, and food. Charts, tools and bedding were strewn everywhere.

Sebastian and Ryan were finally able to clear the bilge pump intake. Ryan took the first round of hand pumping. Sebastian paused and looked at Barbara and Jamison. Their faces were smeared with grime, cheeks gaunt, eyes swollen and red. Sebastian patted Jamison on the back. The journalist was too tired even to acknowledge it. Barbara leaned against the radar console table, head down on her chest, the grime of the boat on her sweater, face and hair. He moved over to her and put his arms around her, lifting her head gently.

"We did it," he said. "We're OK for now . . . You need to lie down. . . ."

She jerked awake, staring at him as if not comprehending who he was, where she was. Her eyes were almost unseeing in her fatigue. "What?" she responded sharply, frowning up at him.

"Sleep. . . ."

"So? Who doesn't?" she snapped back. "You don't look so good yourself, you know. Like a ghoul . . . a ghoul . . . You got something else for . . . for me to do?"

"You've done enough—"

"Oh?" Her head slumped down to her chest again. "You know . . . one thing if . . . we get out of this . . . I have . . . to meet Backstrom . . . Alnutt . . . and Winston . . . Who are those guys?"

He smiled, glad that she still had the pluck to find something jocular in this madness. "I'll put a sail sheet on a bunk," he urged.

"No . . . I . . . want some hot chocolate. . . ." Her eyes were closed, and she fell against him, just about out.

"You can't . . . not now. . . ."

She straightened quickly, her eyes snapping. "Who said?" Her voice challenged him with a berating sound.

"There's a half a tin of Ovaltine I found floating around," Jamison offered. "It's up there on the radio console, sir."

"We don't have a stove working, Jamison," Sebastian countered. "All the gas jets are clogged and wet."

Barb stared at him, as if not comprehending what that had to do with it. Then her lower lip trembled as though she might cry in her disappointment. The grueling fatigue was doing that to her now. He reached into his back pocket and pulled out the unbroken jar of peanut butter he had found on the deck. He broke the seal on the cover and handed it to her.

"Find a spoon and we'll eat," he said to her with a smile, keeping his voice calm even as he spoke above the wind outside. She took the jar, acting as though it wasn't up to hot chocolate. He knew it wasn't. But then she went into the galley, moving unsteadily, dragging her exhaustion. She came back with two spoons, wiping the grime onto the sleeve of her sweater. They paused and ate, too tired to make conversation, sharing the spoons.

Sebastian took time to check the barometer bolted on the wall next to the clock. It was still registering 997 millibars. But when he tapped it lightly with his knuckle, the needle rose four points. "Glass is rising!" he said, lifting his voice in a tone of optimism. "I think, through the miracle of God, we beat the force eight!" They all looked too glazed by their fatigue to realize what he was saying. "Ryan, we've got to get sail up!" he went on. He glanced up at the repeater compass. "We've been wandering off course for the last hour or more. Time we got back on track. That trawler is getting away from us!"

"I'll get the ghoster and another jib," Ryan said, and he moved out of the chart room to go aft.

"Maybe that bent mizzen might take a sail too!" Sebastian called after him. But he knew that was pushing it on a damaged mast. Still, with the wind reaching to port, maybe they could at least try it. The main thing was to get up some speed, try to pick up the trawler again.

He went back on deck. The waves were running about twenty feet or so, he surmised, playing his flashlight over the side to port. They were long swells, not the crisscross mountains that had rolled them over earlier. A few gray beards were among them still, meaning they weren't through with *Pequod* yet.

He set a new compass course of 245, figuring the trawler would probably be easterly given the course she was on when she passed *Pequod's* bow earlier. He'd have to get the radar checked and the antenna repaired to be sure.

Ryan came up the companionway with the sails in his arms. They untangled the mainsheets and reran them through the winches. They repaired the loose chain plates holding the shrouds to the headstay, realigned the boom on the mainmast, tied down the loose shrouds to it. They they ran up the light ghoster, sheeted up the new storm jib after taking the battered, useless one down. *Pequod* took the slap of the wind in her sails with a jaunty lift of her mangled bow. Ryan advised not to try a mainsail until the wind died some because of the damaged mast. Sebastian agreed.

They checked the radar antenna line, and found it had pulled loose from the deck clamp just as Sebastian figured. They reran the lead through a new clamp back into the deck.

They checked the mizzenmast as to how much strain it could take, if any. They decided not to try it until the wind abated. Then with the boat on self-steering, they went below again to check out the radar. Both the radar and radio were bolted tightly to the bulkhead with double-strength steel clamps. If they hadn't been, they would have pulled loose in the capsize.

Sebastian tried the radar. The screen showed only a dim glow, impossible to read. "Power is down," he said to Ryan. "Can we give the engine a turn?" Ryan lifted the floor hatch off the engine bed. They both crouched down to look at the engine in the dim light. It was still bolted down to the bed, though one bolt had been sheared away. The engine seemed to be sitting crooked on the bed, and the wiring showed watermarks. Ryan hit the starter button. The diesel coughed and gasped but wouldn't fire.

"Battery terminals and bushings wet," Ryan said. "Maybe the emergency supply locker on the fantail would have some dry silk signal pennants." Sebastian went back on deck, rummaged through the locker, found a couple of the pennants, went back below. They both worked on wiping off the battery terminals and the bushings. Ryan cranked up the engine again. More coughing and gasping, and then it fired. It clattered and vibrated on its wooden bed, but after a minute it settled down. Ryan let it run for ten minutes, enough to get up enough battery power. And enough to bring the radar screen up to some level of luminosity, though it was still dim. There were a lot of zig-zag lines mixed in with the green clutter of the storm interference. "Components are wet," Ryan advised. Still, they could make out enough of the concentric range circles and perhaps a sign of a target.

"There," Sebastian said finally, putting his finger on the faint blip in the scud on the screen. Ryan wasn't sure. They waited. Sebastian felt Barbara come in from the galley and move in behind him. He turned and glanced at her. Her eyes showed hard blue now behind the redness of the fatigue, as if she was feeling revulsion for that interminable blip.

"Maybe," Ryan finally conceded, grabbing the console as the boat slid hard to starboard under a heavy sea. "That puts him at ten miles or more, sir. You'd think they'd have gotten farther than that on us by now."

"Well, maybe that engine is giving him trouble," Sebastian replied.

"You still think we can catch him, sir?" Ryan asked hopefully, his blue-gray eyes coming alive through the cloud of fatigue there.

"Why not?" Sebastian replied. "We need to change course some to two-five-zero. But we need a little sleep . . . some fixing up of the boat . . . get the bilge lines open. But this boat has a lot in her yet. The wind is down to forty knots in gusts. The seas are turning to prairie out there. The big green cliffs are dying off."

Barbara began wiping the bulkhead down with a wet cloth in aimless movements. She turned then and dropped the rag on the console next to Sebastian.

"Well, if that will be all . . ." she said, her voice sounding heavy with exhaustion, though she tried to put a snap into the tone of it, trying to show her own feelings about that trawler. She opened her mouth to say something more. Then her eyes fluttered, blinking rapidly as if she were trying to clear her vision. She began to sway though the boat was not jumping much right then. Sebastian reached out in time to catch her as she slumped forward on the console.

"We'll get her to her bunk," Sebastian said, picking her up in his arms even as Jamison stepped into the room from the galley. He stared at her, then shook his head. "If you find anything dry in the boat," Sebastian said to Ryan as he moved through the door into the galley, "bring it . . . This lady is in shock."

Sixteen

President Fairfield strode into the Oval Office, a bundle of stuffed manila folders under his left arm. The members of the Situation Room Task Force stood as one from their chairs, then waited until he got behind his desk.

"As you were, gentlemen."

The president sat in his chair, opened the top file folder, and scanned it quickly. The day seemed long to him already since he had awakened at 4:00A.M. at Camp David to catch his copter back to Washington. He looked at them, sitting in a semicircle in front of him: Connors, Banes, Townshend, Brandt, Casey, and Barney Holt, his press secretary. Yarborough had convened the National Security Council at 7:30 earlier, and General Hescott was going at it now with his Joint Chiefs at the Pentagon.

President Fairfield knew the decision had to be made *now*. He could tell it by the heavy atmosphere in the room. And he could see it in their faces. The cutting lines of strain around the eyes, the sallow color of the facial skin, the grubbing shadows of fatigue around the mouth. There was also that certain sense of melancholia hanging over them in knowing that no matter which way they moved now, somebody was going to be hurt or killed.

The question for him was whether he could decide without full concurrence from the Security Council and the Joint Chiefs. And there was Congress as well. His meeting with the Cabinet at 7 A.M. had not gone well; too many noses out of joint that he had waited so long to bring them up to speed on the OPAL situation. And he knew Yancey Yarborough and Hescott were probably having it hot and heavy in their meetings as well.

He felt old now as he sat in his chair behind the desk, and he knew he looked it. He hadn't slept much in three nights, maybe a week. How long had he been at this thing? Years, it seemed. He reached over to the silver coffeepot by his right elbow and poured his fourth cup of the morning. The caffeine was already pounding in his head, but it at least helped shake off the tentacles of fatigue that squeezed his brain.

"All right," he began, sipping his coffee, breaking off the low murmur of conversation among them, "quick and dirty . . . Barney, update us on the press."

"As you may well know, Mr. President," Barney began politely, "the papers and TV networks are playing OPAL as a definite military offensive satellite . . . They're trying to smoke us out for a confirm on this . . . I've told them we have no official word from Moscow yet . . . But they are beginning to charge us now with a cover-up or lack of decisiveness in handling the situation . . . And there are blackouts across the country from that laser, with more reports of the same from everywhere across the world. The pressure is on us to come clean on what we think and what we are doing about it all. . . ."

The president grunted a neutral commentary, adjusted his silver-rimmed glasses as he continued to study the file in front of him. "Well, you all know I've tried to get the Russian ambassador, Alexi Putin, to confirm that OPAL is military," he said. "I even asked him what he was doing in the Southern Ocean, and that made him blink. Anyway, Putin says there is no military intent with OPAL . . . So print that, Barney. And he also says he knows nothing about a trawler and so on. But he is lying, of course. You can always tell with Putin . . . He chainsmokes when he lies." He paused, then took another sip of coffee, holding the cup halfway from his mouth as he glanced up at Barney. "Hold them off, Barney, a little longer . . . We have no confirm from Russia . . . And keep UNIVERSE ONE rolling in front of them. I want the Russians to wonder if we are serious about launching our satellite. . . ."

"Yes, Mr. President," Barney replied but not sounding happy with it.

"OK," the president said, putting his cup down and sighing, "I have the updated information from the Secretary of Defense. Here's how it looks, and correct me, Bill, if I drop anything. . . .

"One, *Bunker Hill* has been tailing the Russian sub *Gorky* for a few days now. They played tag for a while . . . Then the Russian got tired of it and armed his torpedoes. Which means they are not fooling around down there and will go to any extremes to knock us out of the game. *Bunker Hill* is at battle stations, condition yellow, ready to take action when fired upon. . . .

"Two, Bill, you speculate along with Mark that the Russian sub will rendezvous with the trawler by dawn of the 18th . . . tomorrow . . . You say they'll want to transfer Julian under cover of darkness or early dawn?"

"Mr. President," Connors offered, "given the Russian sub's speed of thirty or forty knots, we projected the time off that. If they get there and that force eight gale is still kicking up a heavy sea, they'll have to wait . . . That means they'll have to transfer when it is light, which they don't want to do . . . But it's go or no go for them now. . . ."

"What does Weather Ops say?" Jim Brandt asked.

"Melbourne says it will clear by dawn," Connors replied. "At least they expect it to. . . ."

"Will *Bunker Hill* be able to keep up with the Russian?" Willard Banes asked.

"She can make twenty-eight to thirty knots, but she'll be behind the *Gorky* most of the way . . . maybe an hour or so," Connors explained.

"And *Victor*?" Banes pursued.

"Still plugging along, Willard, but this storm will slow her . . . She's eight hours at least from the trawler as of midnight last night . . . And I don't think she can do much when she gets there against a Delta-class Russian sub anyway. . . ."

"What time is it there, Mark?" Fairfield asked then.

Townshend was ready for him this time. "Past midnight of the 18th, Mr. President."

"You also say here in your report, Bill," the president continued, "that our five-ship squadron coming around the Horn is six hours away and moving full speed . . . And what about that Russian flotilla last moving eastward up the Pacific?"

"Changed course last night, Mr. President," Connors said. "Heading straight south and all-out for the party at the trawler. . . ."

The president cleared his throat harshly as if all of this were beginning to make him gag. "So then . . . how about *Pequod*?"

Connors hesitated, looking up from his yellow pad full of notes, and stared blankly at the president. He had considered the boat out of the picture long ago and irrelevant to events taking shape now. "Well," he said, shifting in his chair, "if they survive the force eight—and I say *if*, which is not likely—they'd be in the trawler's area. But I don't think she figures into the situation any more than *Victor*, Mr. President . . . Far less than *Victor*, in fact . . . This is a full-blown military confrontation now. . . ."

"Our sub against theirs?" Jim Brandt asked.

"I have six F-15s ready to scramble out of Melbourne," Connors said.

"And what will they do?" Banes interjected, his face frozen in a pose of truculence whenever military options were discussed.

Connors glanced at his pad again, never liking to take on the Secretary of State. "We use them if we need to, Willard . . . And we just might have to."

"Well, do they shoot when they see the whites of the eyes of the Russian crew members on *Gorky* or what?" Jim Brandt jabbed at Connors.

"That's up to the Commander-in-Chief," Connors countered, bristling. "I simply deploy the players as the Joint Chiefs authorize under the president's mandate."

"Looks as if I better get Kamiloff on the hot line," the president said, closing the file folder. They all glanced at him, surprised. That was usually the last resort, meaning a serious confrontation was at hand. "We have to try to back him off any action down there that might precipitate the big one. . . ."

"In all due respect, Mr. President," Banes appealed, "all Kamiloff can do is proceed with *Gorky* if he intends to get Julian safely in his hands."

"Well, we've got to try, Willard," the president snapped, showing the frayed side of himself now. He got up then from his chair and walked slowly back to the windows overlooking the White House lawn. He stood there a long time, his hands behind his back, ignoring them.

Then he heaved a heavy sigh as if he wanted to throw off the weight of a decision he had just made. He turned and walked back to his desk, hands behind his back, eyes on the floor. He paused behind the leather chair, leaned his elbows on the top edge of it, dangling his hands down in front, which was his pose when he began to debate the choices or come to a conclusion.

"Gentlemen," he began slowly, choosing his words carefully as if he thought any one of them would blow up in his mouth, "as I see it, tell me if I am wrong . . . we've got millions of people in the free world balanced against one man out there in the Southern Ocean.

God knows I hate to put people into balances . . . But I have no choice but to compute on that basis." He sounded as if he were making an appeal for their understanding. "Unless Kamiloff responds to my appeal, and you're right, Willard, he will probably not . . . then I have to do it . . . Bill, order the captain of *Bunker Hill* to proceed at all speed to the target area . . . and then sink that trawler . . . with David Julian aboard. . . ."

The room went still. The loud, ponderous ticking of the grandfather clock was the only sound. Finally Willard Banes unlocked his folded arms, shifted in his chair, and said, "That constitutes an act of war, Mr. President." A note of incredulity dominated his voice.

"I have the War Powers Act," the president replied calmly as if anticipating the challenge. "Truman used it to put troops in Korea . . . Kennedy used it to mount the Bay of Pigs. . . ."

"Excuse me, Mr. President," George Casey interrupted. "But Congress will raise bloody hell," and the vice president tore off his black horned-rims in a gesture to indicate his disapproval. "The Party could lose its shirt in the next election—"

"If the Russians succeed, George, there won't be any election!" Connors countered with an unusual ribald tone of voice, his tired eyes taking on sparks of flame.

"The Russians will make propaganda hay of it," Banes warned.

"The Russians are already making hay with OPAL," Connors jumped in, eager now to side with the president.

"I thought we agreed earlier that we need Julian alive for our own UNIVERSE ONE," Banes argued, his blue eyes snappy, his cheeks taking on a pink hue. "He's no good to us dead."

"He's no good to the Russians either, Willard," Connors cut back. "That's the point now. If we can't get Julian off that trawler, and the Russians will kill him before allowing him to come over to us, then we can't let him go over to them either!"

"Can *Bunker Hill* make it in time before the transfer?" Jim Brandt asked in an academic tone of voice.

"She'll run herself to the limit short of a meltdown," Connors stated flatly. "Anyway, if *Gorky* has to wait for the seas to calm down, we've no problem with *Bunker Hill* getting there to do the job."

"We are still the aggressors in what could precipitate a nuclear war," Banes intoned, lifting his pudgy hands in appeal.

"What choice—"

"Gentlemen . . ." The president interrupted the exchange that was beginning to rise to hostility. "Let's not reduce ourselves to a barnyard brawl here." He looked at his clenched hands in front of him, squeezing them tightly as if they were cold. "I would again be derelict in my duty to protect free people everywhere if I did not take this course. I do not know how far I can press an aggressive act such as this . . . I will keep trying Kamiloff . . . But I think he'll risk the shoot-out down there. . . .

"I know the War Powers Act requires me to consult with Congress on any military action that can be construed as an act of war, George," the president added with a mollifying tone for his vice president. "But while the Act allows consulting with Congress and is firm in that resolution, it also allows flexibility to the president to take swift action if circumstances warrant, especially to defend this nation from attack . . . OPAL's presence as a military satellite poses enough of a threat . . . We're into a time bind now anyway . . . Events move too fast . . . We don't have the luxury of going through the motions with Congress . . . I take full responsibility for this action, and it is already on tape to that affect. . . ."

"May I ask, then, Mr. President?" Casey replied, still sounding carpy, "if the Foreign Relations Committee has discussed this?"

"They've been aware of OPAL and the action forming up in the Southern Ocean for over a week," Willard Banes said in a gruffy tone of dismissal. "Even then, most of them are gone on Christmas break, as is Congress."

The president glanced at his watch. "Jim, get Yancey Yarborough out of his Security Council meeting and call Hescott at the Pentagon to see what the atmosphere is."

Jim Brandt rose and walked out.

"The Russians aren't going to love us for what we do, Mr. President," George Casey continued, his voice sounding waspish. "They could retaliate . . . In fact, I wager they will. . . ."

The president nodded, continuing to stare down at his hands. "I have to chance that, George . . . Or maybe I can talk Kamiloff out of being trigger-happy. The Russians don't want the kettle to boil over on them because of one ship . . . They stand to lose as much as we do in a nuclear war. . . ."

"But what about our missile capacity, Mr. President?" Banes desperately reasoned, both hands held tight to the arms of his chair, leaning into his questions. "Do we have the power to retaliate with that laser jamming us?"

"The interference is not consistent," Connors replied. "We might very well get a strike off anyway . . . When OPAL is in a certain orbit she doesn't have the same effect."

"But what if the Russians know we are neutralized by now anyway?" Casey mumbled skeptically.

"If they were sure, they wouldn't need Julian, would they?" Connors sniped back at the vice president.

"As I said," the president cut in calmly, "we have to chance it."

Just then Jim Brandt walked back into the room. "Hescott said the Joint Chiefs are in favor of a limited military action," he said, taking his seat. "Yarborough said the Council is still arguing it out . . . May take all day, maybe all night. . . ."

"So we let the shoot-out occur down there in the Southern Ocean," Connors concluded confidently. "The president has made a wise decision. Better a contained battle between two subs there than allowing them to keep Julian and pull the curtain down. . . ."

"If you can contain it, Bill," Willard reminded him.

There was a pause then as if the argument had succumbed to the fatigue every one of them felt. The president slowly took off his glasses and tossed them on the desk in front of him, a gesture of frustration. The once-pink hue of his face had turned to a pale-gray pallor.

"Bill," he said quietly, turning to face the grandfather clock, staring at it, hands behind his back, as if computing time or begging time, "don't commit your F-15s yet. But I think you better order our ships back from the exercises in Guam. That Russian squadron won't get to the trawler in time to change events . . . But we should be ready in case."

"Yes, Mr. President," Connors replied, his face showing beet-red now in his tension.

"Mark," the president continued, "I want you to arrange to have Elisa Julian in Sydney immediately. Have Interpol fly her back on a private government jet to provide security . . . She ought to be home at a time like this."

Townshend opened his mouth to say that Henri would not go for that, but he let it go. "Yes, Mr. President," he said.

There was another long pause. The immensity of the implications of the committed action left them numb, unable to form arguments or commentary.

"Barney," the president went on, rubbing at his swollen red eyes with the heels of his hands, "I want the TV networks blocked out for 8 o'clock tonight. I am going on the air. Time to tell the American people what's going on . . . By then something will have been settled down there in the Southern Ocean."

"Are you going to tell them about the military action we are taking?" Barney asked.

"Why not? Kennedy told the people about his fiasco with Bay of Pigs. Anyway, I don't want the people to have to read it in the morning papers, OK?"

"Right, Mr. President," Barney replied.

"Any final words, gentlemen?" Fairfield asked, turning back to lean his arms on his chair. "Willard?"

Banes would have the last word as he usually did in sensitive foreign situations. But he and the president were old friends, had been through tough ones before, though not quite so implicating as this. He knew now that the president had had his mind on this decision for a while; so the action would stand.

"I wish we could explain to the Australian Prime Minister, Mr. President. Julian is their star, their hero. But there isn't time, as you say." He paused, then shrugged. "So we are down to zero then . . . Someone once said, 'If wishes were horses, beggars would ride.' The choice is made . . . I can only hope, feeble as it is, that Kamiloff might yet back off. . . ."

The president nodded. There were slashing lines of pain in his face now as he continued to lean on the back of his chair. But he gave a ghostly smile of appreciation for Willard's concession. "If any of you are praying types, gentlemen, I suggest you put in some time with the Almighty," he said. "I like to think of myself as a Christian man . . . But I'm not a good one. Maybe this office is not the place for a Christian of any kind . . . But we are at the place now where only Deity can alter the course of history." He paused, then said, "Bill, I expect you to contact *Bunker Hill.*" Connors nodded. "Who's her skipper?"

"Commander Holland, Mr. President."

"Good man?"

"Good fitness . . . Just not room for him to squeeze up the line to a Trident . . . So he's got a refitted Poseidon instead."

"Well, he's squeezed up, I'd say . . . Jim, get Kamiloff on the line immediately . . . Good day then, gentlemen."

They sat for a minute without moving, unable or unwilling to leave. Then one by one they rose and went out.

Jim Brandt was the last one out the door. He paused and looked back at his chief. He had moved away from the chair and stood facing the clock, hands behind his back. His shoulders seemed more bent. This was the moment of extreme exposure for a president, when all the finery of office was stripped and only the raking fingers of destiny tore at his innards.

Brandt closed the door. Fairfield heard it but did not turn. He continued to stare at the clock, trying to visualize what it was like now out there in the Southern Ocean, past midnight, dark, a wild sea running. And his mind went to *Pequod* . . . the smallest ship in the game. He wondered about Sebastian and Churchill . . . if they were still alive.

Then his mind slipped back to the silence of the office around him. It was almost as if he could hear the groans and whispered prayers of presidents past who had faced their heavy hours here . . . alone. And the feeling that dragged on him led his mind to Kipling:

> "The tumult and the shouting dies,
>   The Captains and the Kings depart;
> Still stands thine ancient sacrifice,
>   An humble and contrite heart."

"Dear God," he said out loud to the clock, "if I was never humble or contrite before, and I wasn't, I am now nothing but a child in the dark . . . Lead me home, dear God, lead me home."

Captain Aviloff knew the starboard engine was about to go. He could feel the change of vibration on the bridge deck plates under his feet. A few minutes later the engine room rang up and Popov said, "The starboard engine is smoking, comrade captain. If she continues, we will burn her up. Permission to shut down?"

"Permission granted, Popov," Aviloff said. "Comrade, it is now 0415 in the morning. We have made contact with *Gorky*. She is ten miles behind at a bearing of one-six-five, waiting to surface. We will have to hold at least another hour or more until this sea settles down for them to come up and to transfer Julian safely. Also, *Gorky* thinks there is another submarine behind him, and we should not wait too long. I am going to my cabin to get a little sleep.

Wake me in forty-five minutes. When you come, bring Dr. Julian with you. . . ."

"Comrade captain, I don't think—"

"I will arrange for Julian to come up with the guard."

"Romonovich—"

"He is passed out in his bunk from too much vodka, comrade."

"Very well, comrade captain."

Aviloff hung up. "Quartermaster, the starboard engine has been stopped. Ease your helm to port to compensate to stay on course."

"Aye, comrade captain."

"Comrade Ilyich, you have the bridge until the next watch at 5. I will be in my quarters."

"Excuse me, comrade captain," Ilyich said. "We have a signals officer's report of seeing a boat close on our starboard bow around 0100 hours. Do you wish to question him on it, comrade captain?"

"Boat?" Aviloff asked. "Why did he not report it then?"

"He was not sure, comrade captain, at first . . . Then he thought he'd better log it in later . . . But we were too busy to check on it. . . ."

"Yes . . . Very well, send the signals officer to me in the radar room immediately."

A few minutes later Aviloff faced Third Rank Moshoy Balantov. He was about twenty-five years of age and looking a bit uneasy in what to expect with his late report.

"What did you see, Comrade Balantov?" Aviloff questioned.

"First a light in the storm, comrade captain. I couldn't be sure at first . . . Then it came on a little stronger. Then I saw the boat, a sailboat, two masts, comrade captain . . . hanging heavy bow-down and heeled over to port. . . ."

"Did you identify her, comrade?"

"I am sorry, comrade captain. We were on her too quickly . . . I tried to get a searchlight on her from the signals bridge, but I lost her, sir. . . ."

"Did she carry any sail?"

"Just a jib, sir . . . All I could tell, sir, was that she was in a bad way. . . ."

"Did you see anyone on deck?"

"No, comrade captain . . . No one was on deck . . . But it was dark and raining—"

"All right," Aviloff said, but he felt a strange jab of apprehension run through him. Could it have been the *Pequod*? "Comrade, make sure you have the details of the sighting logged in with the Officer of the Deck," he said and turned and walked on up the stairs to his quarters. How could *Pequod*, if it were indeed she, be so close on them? Radar had reported no sightings either. Surely with that boat coming so close something would have showed in the clutter of the storm. He paused inside his cabin, slowly taking off his jacket. He sensed an eerie feeling, as if it were a ghost ship floating out there . . . Julian had called the captain "the hound of heaven." Nonsense! In any case, it was probably gone now for good if Balantov's description was correct.

He walked over to the barometer. It was definitely on the rise. The wind was down, at twenty-eight knots now. With a sigh, he dropped down on his bunk. He was so weary that his eyes burned and watered, his bones ached. He glanced out the port over his head. A dim gray pallor began to show against the scudding clouds, which seemed to be breaking up. The sun would be up in an hour or so.

He had just begun to feel the sleep start to clamp down on his brain when a knock sounded on his door. He lifted his head with a start. "Come!" he said, not bothering to hide his irritation at being interrupted so quickly.

The door opened. He saw a bulky form of a man silhouetted against the passageway light. The man moved inside, closed the door.

"Yes? What is it?" Aviloff demanded.

The form moved into the room and stood over him. Aviloff rose on one elbow and looked up, peering at the face. He turned and flipped on the light over his bunk. The man was broad in the chest, a bit rotund in the middle. He wore a blue rain jacket and a dark turtleneck underneath. His face was round, his gray eyes coldly neutral. His smile showed small teeth that seemed pointed.

"Comrade captain, my apologies," he began, his voice carrying a forced lilt. "I am Clay Bird."

Aviloff cleared his throat. "Yes. I recognize you now from the day we picked you up off Australia. . . ."

"Permit me to properly identify myself, comrade captain." He took out his wallet, flashed the KGB identification. Then he extended a name card. "My cover name in Sydney, comrade captain."

Aviloff took it, read it. "Bentley? Interpol?"

The man chuckled, but it had the sound of a hyena.

"Yes . . . I have been under Interpol's blessing for five years, comrade captain. I don't think they ever knew."

"You have something in mind now, comrade—?"

"Mikelich," the man answered for him, returning the wallet to his hip pocket. "Dubrin Mikelich. May I sit here, captain?" He proceeded to pull out the desk chair and dropped his heavy bulk into it with the grace of an elephant. "Now . . . I have the message from the bridge about *Gorky*. It is imperative, comrade captain, that we transfer Dr. Julian off *Minsk* as quickly as possible while we have some darkness. . . ."

"That, as you surely know, is impossible with these seas running," Aviloff replied. Why was it that this KGB and his political officer, Romonovich, expected ridiculous achievements? "We cannot launch a small boat until we get down at least to five-foot seas."

"You predict how long, comrade captain?"

"I am not a weather forecaster, Comrade Mikelich. In an hour or two, perhaps."

"It will be light then. . . ."

"Of course. . . ."

Mikelich shifted in his chair, folding his arms as if he were going to stay and argue it for a while.

"Comrade captain, I am concerned that we make the transfer of Dr. Julian as quickly as possible," he went on again, his voice taking on a sharp tone of authority, so much like Romonovich's. "I am also ordered to make certain there are no witnesses besides ourselves . . . There is another submarine somewhere behind *Gorky*, but a good hour behind, as the *Gorky* captain indicated. That means, comrade captain, that we will have to risk some high seas to keep the cover of darkness."

"And risk losing Julian in the transfer?"

"You are a skilled seaman, comrade captain. You will think of a way to assure his transfer even in risky seas."

Aviloff grunted at the pomposity of the statement and the total illogic of it. Like all KGB, he concluded. "I cannot launch a boat successfully over eight-foot waves, Comrade Mikelich . . . That is very risky at best. To insure Julian's life I would prefer to go with no more than five-foot seas."

"It may take some time for it to level off," Mikelich challenged.

He paused. Then, "There is one other assignment I have. The first part I arranged in Sydney. Julian's boat *Pequod* was sighted behind us yesterday . . . Is that correct?"

"Correct. But how did you know that, comrade?"

The toothy smile again, the pointed teeth. "I, too, was looking, comrade captain. I was surprised to see her . . . I was almost certain they would have turned back after we took Julian off her. But knowing the two people on that boat, I am not all that surprised either. You see, I am ordered to make certain that *Pequod* is destroyed, by us if possible. There are two people aboard that boat whom the KGB would dearly love to have out of the way for good . . . One is an Interpol agent, a woman; the other a clergyman named Sebastian . . . Both have managed to muck up some of our sensitive operations in the past. I have worked hard in Sydney to make sure they were on *Pequod*, and once having arranged it, I was ordered to join you to make certain that those two people do not come out of this alive. . . ."

"My signals officer sighted a sailboat last night in the storm," Aviloff replied, feeling irritated now with the man. "We just about ran over her, not more than twenty yards to starboard . . . She was in a bad way, floundering . . . So maybe the storm did your dirty work for you, Comrade Mikelich."

"I will need evidence that she is gone, comrade captain," Mikelich insisted, his voice carrying a sharp, authoritative tone.

"Evidence?"

"Some proof she did indeed sink . . . These two people have been written off before as dead and have showed up in another part of the world spitting in our eye. . . ."

"I cannot possibly produce—"

"We will backtrack this ocean once Julian is transferred, comrade captain, and look for wreckage."

"Comrade, I have engine trouble here. And I need to heave-to to repair it if I am to keep this trawler afloat! Is that understood?"

"I am not interested, comrade captain, in the picky problems you have with this trawler." The big man stood, towering over Aviloff. "I expect your full cooperation in these matters. It begins to show light already outside . . . We do not have much time now. In thirty minutes, captain, we will talk again, and I trust you will be ready to transfer Julian over . . . I want *Gorky* notified before then to surface and stand by. . . ."

"Thirty minutes will be too soon," Aviloff warned. "We have twenty-foot swells out there yet. . . ."

"Thirty minutes, comrade captain," Mikelich repeated and ambled out of the room, closing the door sharply behind him.

Aviloff continued sitting on his bunk, rubbing the stubble of beard forming on his cheeks. He dropped slowly back on the bed, wanting desperately to get sleep now. But he seemed suddenly alert for some reason. Why would a clergyman and a woman mean so much to the KGB that they would want evidence of their demise?

His mind wandered. He thought of Soya. He remembered the mornings when they had awakened beside each other, before dawn like now. And she would read from the Book by the light of the flashlight under the covers. He loved to hear her soft voice next to him, the warm touch of breath on his cheek. And she read the words as if each one was a key opening another lock to the mysteries of the universe. What would she think of that clergyman, Sebastian, the "hound of heaven," but who now had succumbed to the ravages of a force eight?

She would find something to say from the Book on that, he was sure. He felt sad about it. For Soya? Maybe. Or was it just the commiseration all seamen had for others who were lost in the ocean storms? He didn't know.

He half-dozed, listening to the straining port engine thumping an uncertain beat throughout the ship. The trawler lifted on the swells, creaking and groaning after her night of torment.

He awoke with a start and glanced at his watch. It was nearly 0500. The light was somewhat brighter coming through the port now. Soon Mikelich would be back.

He swung his legs over the bed and stood, glanced out the port over the bunk. The gray pallor began to brighten. Flying fish were skimming the waves. The seas looked high yet, and the trawler still rolled heavy with them. But the wind was down, the rain gone . . . They would have sun before long.

He pulled on his jacket, slung the binoculars around his neck, and walked out onto the porch facing the stern. The air was brisk and clean-smelling. He did a casual sweep of the horizon with his binoculars as was his habit. There was a good mile or more of visibility now, and the foggy, dissipating clouds were lifting.

He raised his glasses one more time, scanned astern to port and starboard. Then he stopped. *Impossible*! He kept his eyes on it for a long time to be sure. Then he turned quickly back into his cabin, picked up the phone, and rang up the Officer of the Deck. He recognized Ilyich still on the watch.

"Comrade Ilyich? I want Comrade Popov and David Julian in my quarters immediately. . . ."

There was a pause. "Comrade captain," Ilyich said hesitantly, "I have orders that both Popov and Julian are not to leave their quarters without permission from Comrade Romonovich—"

"This is your captain speaking, comrade," Aviloff snapped. "I order you to bring them to my quarters now . . . It is time to plan for the transfer of Julian. Do you understand?"

"Immediately then, comrade captain."

Aviloff paced his quarters, hands behind his back, then stepped out onto the porch again and looked through his binoculars. He felt unnerved, shaken inside. He heard the door open and turned to look inside. Popov and Julian were there, and Ilyich as well, looking a bit uncertain. Aviloff stuck his head inside the doorway and said to Ilyich, "Leave us. And thank you, Comrade Ilyich!" Ilyich hesitated, caught between the orders of Romonovich and his captain. Then he turned and went out.

"Come out here," Aviloff said to the two men. They went out and stood by the rail, waiting. Julian had on his blue admiral's cap as usual. He looked a little pale and red-eyed as if he too hadn't slept much that night. The storm maybe. Or worry about *Pequod* and his son. Aviloff lifted his binoculars from around his neck and handed them to Julian.

"Now tell me, doctor, that there are no tracks in the sea. At bearing one-seven-five . . . tell me what you see."

Julian took the binoculars, glanced at Aviloff with puzzlement, and scanned toward the bearing. Then he stopped and stood still a long time, staring.

"I can't believe it," he said, his voice carrying a tone of incredulity along with excitement and relief. "It's *Pequod* all right . . . I'd know the cut of that bow anywhere . . . All beat up looks like, hanging heavy to port, probably waterlogged. . . ."

"So 'the hound of heaven' continues to pursue?" Aviloff pressed him. "That boat was sighted floundering by one of my crew last night . . . just off our starboard bow . . . She was as good as gone . . . Now she is there . . . still coming. I have sailed all my life, Dr. Julian, and I know that no forty-five-foot sailboat could come through a force eight gale with such an inexperienced crew as you claim them to be. Am I correct?"

Julian lowered the binoculars, his eyes still intent on the bearing where *Pequod* came on. Then he turned his head and looked at Aviloff. "I would say so, captain, yes. But—"

"As you told me yourself, Dr. Julian," Aviloff went on hurriedly now, knowing Mikelich would be coming soon, "a clergyman on that boat believed there were tracks in the sea . . . that God put them there for His own to find . . . True North you called it . . . I have never believed or experienced True North before . . . But what of him now?"

Julian made no response. He glanced through the binoculars again as if unsure of what he had seen. *Pequod* kept coming on, disappearing in the troughs, then bobbing up top again. "Fifty years of sailing won't allow me to go that far, captain," he finally said. "But it makes for an interesting subject to ponder. . . ."

"But let us then be honest to some degree," Aviloff countered, his voice demanding. "If you can agree that we are also men who admit the unexplainable . . . that could be God then . . . If so, then my wife, Soya, is not wrong. Your dead wife is not wrong in her belief about 'the hound of heaven' . . . That means the Book is right . . . Would you consider that to have some logic?"

"Expert sailsmanship, I'd say," Julian contradicted, but not with the dogmatism he usually lent to such matters, "and a lot of guts."

"But is he alone capable of it, of bringing that boat through and staying with us?" Aviloff persisted.

Julian handed the binoculars to Popov, who studied the boat. "I would be hard put to agree that he could do it . . . by himself," he said diffidently. "But I am not sure I am prepared to admit that there is a God who accounts for it. Still, Sebastian once said to me back in Sydney that Captain Ahab needed God with him on the quarterdeck if he intended to save himself from destruction . . . whatever that means. . . ."

Aviloff stared at him as the first smears of pink showed on the eastern horizon, stabbing long fingers through the breaking cloud cover. He appeared as though he had come to a devastating moment of truth.

"Then we do not have much time for what we must do," he said conclusively, taking the binoculars from Popov. "There is danger here now, and we must act quickly and decisively!"

Seventeen

Aviloff took out the blueprints of the compartmental structure of the trawler and spread them out on the chart table. He moved quickly. "Dr. Julian, Popov here can follow English but slowly," he said. "So I will switch to Russian now and then, because there is not much time. . . ."

"Time for what?"

"For you and Popov to get off *Minsk*."

"Off?"

"Yes . . . Popov has dreamed of defecting for more than a year. . . ."

"Well," Julian protested, "if my daughter is in Russia, I'd rather—"

"She is not in Russia, doctor. She escaped from my country a couple of months ago, showed up in Paris two weeks or so ago . . . That is why there was no exchange. . . ."

"Now, see here—"

"No time . . . I'm sorry," Aviloff replied brusquely. "I am going to try to get you both off . . . and I need your cooperation." Julian stared at him for a few seconds, a frown digging between his eyes. Then, realizing Aviloff was serious, he pulled the brim of his cap down lower over his eyes.

"Whatever you say, captain," he said simply.

Aviloff then proceeded to show the location of the shaft tunnel three decks below in the trawler, under the communications deck. "The ladder down to it is outside the stern ventilator hatch, Popov," he went on, pointing at the area on the blueprint.

"I know of it, comrade captain," Popov said.

"All right . . . You both go down there . . . Follow the tunnel forward to the port supply locker . . . It should take you no more than five minutes to make your way. . . ."

"And when we get there, comrade captain?" Popov asked, his dark eyes going wider in the complications he foresaw.

"You have the key to the locker," Aviloff went on. "The emergency release inside the bow hatch will knock out the panel. Put on your life jackets, throw out the rubber raft, and jump in after it. . . ."

"When, comrade captain?"

"When you feel the port engine stop. We will be dead in the water . . . Then you jump . . . it is safest then."

"But Romonovich will shoot us in the water, comrade captain. . . ."

"A chance you take, Popov. Better chancing it out there than here . . . You try to get to *Pequod* . . . It will be close to us by then."

"I don't fancy your people will allow us to make it or to stay on *Pequod* if we get to her," Julian commented.

"There is another submarine around," Aviloff added. His brown eyes were dilated, showing the fatigue and red streaks in them; but there was something else in them, a certain light either of excitement of the moment or anticipating danger, or perhaps the release of some inner wellspring that had been locked for a long time. "She can't be one of ours or we would have been told . . . She could be American, Australian . . . Anyway, there is a chance out there despite the odds, Dr. Julian." Aviloff turned and spoke rapid Russian to Popov, who nodded but looked hesitant, unsure, rubbing his thumb along the edge of his lower lip in a pose of troubled concentration.

"You are coming, I presume, captain?" Julian asked.

Aviloff glanced at him. A faint, sad smile crossed his thin lips. "I am still captain of this ship, doctor," he said factually. "I have responsibility for the crew . . . And you know what that kind of responsibility demands. Anyway, it is perhaps one last point of honor I have left . . . And I want to see my wife, Soya, and my two sons again. I have much to share with Soya. . . ."

"They will put you in Siberia, comrade captain!" Popov protested.

"And it could mean your life," Julian added.

"One of us must make it happen for the others," Aviloff concluded with finality. "It is time now." He turned and led them to the porch overlooking the afterdeck. Popov hesitated at the ladder, not sure he should go. He turned and looked at Aviloff, the anguish clouding his eyes. "Drink lots of Coca-Cola for me, Popov," Aviloff said and embraced his first officer, giving him an encouraging smile.

"Comrade captain . . . my wife . . . will you visit her for me?" Popov asked. "Tell her . . ."

"I will visit her and explain it all," Aviloff assured him. "Now you must hurry. . . ."

Popov, with uncertainty still dragging on him, turned and descended the ladder. "You won't reconsider, captain?" Julian asked.

Aviloff shook his head, took the hand Julian extended. "You are a good chess player, my friend," he said. "But you must remember that the best calculated moves fall short in the larger issues of life. We need another hand on ours then, doctor. Good luck."

Julian paused, unsure of how to respond. Then he nodded and took the ladder down where Popov waited. The dawn was beginning to flood the decks with a pale glow, outlining the two men below.

"By the way," Aviloff softly called down to Julian, who paused to look up at Aviloff, "you tell that 'hound of heaven' I am grateful . . . I would like to meet him someday . . . But at least I have forgiveness now, doctor . . . As you said, I get it when I give you back, correct?"

Julian stared up at him, looking a bit perplexed by the remark. Then he touched the brim of his cap with his right hand in salute. "That's what my wife always told me, captain," he said. And then he followed Popov down the ventilator shaft and disappeared.

Aviloff waited until the stern hatch cover was closed over them. Then he quickly went back inside his quarters. He found his diary in his desk, unlocked it, and went to the pocket inside the cover. Soya always put quotes out of the Book there, despite his protests. Not many. He had told her not to bother, that it might be dangerous for him if someone found them. But he remembered one of the passages there that had particular meaning now.

He searched through the few small pieces of paper and pulled out the one he remembered:

> "If a man has a hundred sheep, and one wanders away and is lost, what will he do? Won't he leave the ninety-nine others and go out into the hills to search for the lost one? And if he finds it, he will rejoice over it more than the ninety-nine others safe at home! Just so, it is not my Father's will that even one of these little ones should perish."
>
> Matthew 18:12-14

He read it slowly three times, then sat back to ponder it. Yes, *Pequod* carried the man . . . but God was there, or the God-man then? Following to seek the lost sheep? Was it not himself? Soya said it was. But he had never believed it, never understood it . . . until now.

Slowly he put the paper back inside the cover, closed the book, and put it back into the desk drawer. A few minutes later a knock sounded sharply on the door.

He got up, walked over, and opened it. Romonovich's face greeted him, his black eyes burning with accusation. Mikelich stood behind him, towering over the political officer.

"Where is Julian?" Romonovich demanded, looking around Aviloff into the room.

"He is not here, Comrade Romonovich."

"Then where is he?"

"You should check his quarters, comrade."

"But he was here," Mikelich cut in, pushing by Aviloff into the room, then out onto the back porch.

"He was here, but he is not anymore," Aviloff said, following Mikelich to stand a few feet from the big KGB man on the porch.

"Comrade Romonovich, turn out all of the crew not on watch and search all the deck spaces immediately for Comrade Popov and Julian," Mikelich ordered. "Every nook and cranny, comrade."

"Right away, comrade," Romonovich responded as he left.

"This could go very hard on you, comrade captain," Mikelich went on, turning to stare out astern of the trawler. "It would be better for you to tell me where you have hid Popov and Julian or what you intend to do with them."

"As captain of this ship, comrade, I have the right to ignore the question as not in keeping with my role here," Aviloff commented.

Mikelich looked at him, one eyebrow lifted in surprise, his lifeless gray eyes turning to slits. "It is as you wish then . . . But that only aggravates your situation even more." He turned and looked astern again, his eyes toward the bearing of *Pequod*. Aviloff could see the boat now and then coming up out of a trough of a wave, then leveling out again. "I see we have our little pigeon flying straight toward us," Mikelich said.

"Comrade Mikelich, I am needed on the bridge," Aviloff reminded the bulky KGB officer.

Mikelich did not reply immediately. "Well, then, you will take the bridge, comrade captain . . . And you will follow my orders when I tell you to run over that boat . . . She does not run with heavy sail . . . So she will be slow and vulnerable . . . Do you understand, comrade captain?"

"I understand," Aviloff replied, wondering if Julian and Popov had made the forward supply locker yet. It wouldn't be long before the crew found them.

"Enjoy the time you have," Mikelich concluded. "Life dribbles away far too quickly for you, comrade. . . ."

Aviloff did not honor the statement. He turned and walked back into his quarters and out the door to the bridge. He felt no fear, sensed no regret. Soya would be happy and proud of him. His only concern now was that Julian and Popov get off the trawler . . . immediately.

Sebastian woke up with a start. He could not place himself in time, and he lay there a few minutes reorienting himself. The pink of the sun streamed a shaft of promise through the port onto the bulkhead above him. He glanced across the passageway. He saw her looking at him. He tried a grin. His face almost cracked with it, the salt water digging his skin.

"Morning," he said. His shoulder ached, and his mouth felt as dry as wool.

"Morning."

"You look like soggy Cheerios," he quipped. She looked cozy, though, under that canvas tarp he had found a few hours ago in the forward sail locker. It was only half-dry, but the coat of waterproofing on it kept it from feeling wet. He had put that over her to try to keep her warm.

"You look like yesterday's flapjacks," she countered. "What happened?"

"You passed out . . . about three hours ago."

She turned onto her back to stare up toward the ceiling of her bunk. "It feels calm now . . . The boat isn't jumping . . . Wonderful feeling."

"I think I smell coffee," he said then, and his stomach began to respond. When had he last eaten or drunk anything? Any of them? He swung his legs over the side of the bunk. He still had on his jeans and blue turtleneck.

"How can anyone make coffee?" she asked in a lazy voice, but she began to stir, pushing the tarp off, rising to the possibility of something hot in her stomach as well.

"Who knows?" Sebastian said. He went on down the passageway into the galley. He almost bumped into Jamison who was standing by the stove, taking a pan of hot, black liquid off one of the gas plates. "What's this, Jamison?"

Jamison grinned. "Been cleaning the jets with a toothpick and some wet string dipped in alcohol, sir . . . Still not workin' good . . . Only one burner . . . But I got me some coffee for ya, sir."

Sebastian grinned at the journalist as he poured into two mugs. "What's that?" he said pointing at a plate.

"Corned beef, sir . . . I got a lot of tins, sir."

Jamison pointed to the left and a stack of tins he had apparently salvaged in the last few hours.

"You're some kind of miracle-worker, Jamison," Sebastian said, taking the cup of hot coffee and sipping at it. It was weak but hot.

"Got some tins of pears, sir," Jamison went on, his voice sounding pleased. And he poured the contents into a small bowl and set it down by the coffee. "Ain't much, sir . . . But maybe it will stoke up the furnace some."

Just then Barbara came into the galley. She had pulled a comb through the snarls in her hair and despite the grime still showing, it had taken on some of the familiar golden glow. She had slept in her clothes and, since there was nothing dry on the boat, she still wore them. She had put on her yellow vinyl windbreaker to keep warm.

"Jamison, you are a dear," she said, reaching up to give the journalist a hug. Jamison grinned and swiped at his sandy red hair in some embarrassment.

"If ya'll pardon me then," he said, "I promised Ryan a cup of this brew."

Sebastian watched him go up the companionway ladder to the deck. He turned then and handed her the other cup of coffee.

"Hmmmm . . . Glorious."

"Get some of this in you," and he handed her a saucer of corned beef with some pears dumped on top of it. They ate quickly, hungrily, then paused to sip their coffee again.

"Where are we?" she asked, leaning against the frame of the door to the lounge.

"Dunno . . . Just about to check. You feel OK?"

She glanced at him over the rim of the steaming coffee mug held close to her mouth in both hands. As if she were trying to place him in all of the stormy events of the past hours.

"Yes. How's the shoulder?"

"Aches some . . . Be OK." He swallowed the rest of his coffee, feeling the hot glow of it spread through his body, chase the cold. Despite her taciturnity, it was good to stand with her there, sharing the meager breakfast, the strain of the storm gone.

"You dragged me out of a lot of water," she offered.

He glanced at her. "No charge," he said and grinned. She looked at him, caught the banter, but did not respond to it. He didn't mind. He just wanted to stay there with her now . . . the smell of coffee in the galley, the boat sliding along comparatively easy with reduced seas. The temperature was feeling almost balmy compared to the icy wind and rain they had known for more than twelve hours.

"I guess I haven't been exactly civil to you," she said in an offhanded tone of voice. It caught him by surprise, that she would take that tack with him all of a sudden.

He reached over and poured more coffee in her cup, handed it to her. "Civil, yes . . . Politely civil, yes . . . Intimate, no . . . Not even politely intimate . . . But then I am trying to understand and accept the fact that you have removed yourself from all of that. . . ."

"Trawler ho!" It was Ryan's voice coming from topside. Sebastian tossed the empty pan into the sink and turned to move quickly out of the galley, through the chart room, and up the companionway to the deck. He felt her right behind him.

He glanced at the swells coming at *Pequod* astern. They were slicked out now, maybe fourteen feet or less, no gray beards among them. The water had taken on a more peaceful bluish tone, a good portent of fair weather. The gray pallor of dawn was giving in some to the rising sun.

He turned at the coaming. The wind speed instrument showed gusts of twenty-five knots. *Pequod* took the seas easily and moved along under the light ghoster and main at six knots.

Sebastian glanced forward, looking for the trawler. He caught Jamison standing a few feet to the left of the companionway, arms resting on the coaming, staring forward.

"Good breakfast, Jamison!" Sebastian said to him.

Jamison turned his head and tried to smile. He looked better now, though some green still streaked shadows under his eyes and around his chin.

"Thank you, sir," he replied.

"You feeling more fit?"

"I think I might be wantin' to live, Mr. Sebastian."

"Good!" Sebastian turned and stared forward again. "Where is she, Ryan?" he called out.

"Five points off the starboard bow!" Ryan called back from his place at the helm. "Try these, sir!" He lifted a pair of binoculars. "I got them out of the storage here at the helm . . . A bit beat up, but they might do!" Sebastian went back to pick them up and returned to the dog house. Barb sidled up next to him, holding the cup of coffee in her right hand.

Sebastian scanned the bearing ahead through the binoculars. Finally he spotted the trawler. She was more than a mile away. "Not moving very fast at all," he commented, more to himself than to Barbara. "Ryan?" he called. "Bring her around to come at the trawler from her starboard side!"

"Yes, sir!"

"So what are you going to do when you catch up to him?" she asked. He handed her the binoculars. The question was more academic than challenging.

"Not sure," he said. He did not look at her, though he sensed her lowering the binoculars and looking at him. "Maybe just slide alongside and ask the captain to give Julian back . . . How's that sound?" He tried to make it jocular, but he knew she would not rise to that.

"You going to cozy up with him all the way to the Horn?" she demanded.

"Couldn't even if I wanted to," he replied. "We're running low on supplies. And the boat is hurt too much. But the Russian can't make the Horn either unless he stops and makes repairs on his engines. So we dog him for a while, see what he does. I still think that those two Australian Intruder pilots who did a passover on us back there knew something was not right here . . . They had to . . . So we wait for them to come back, crowd that Russian some while we do. . . ."

"Well, if that Russian has engine trouble, he's probably called for help himself by now . . . Did you think of that?"

He glanced at her. She was looking through the binoculars again. She was jabbing him some, in that prickly-pear way of hers that had been so much of her behavior all of this time.

"If I were he, with Julian in custody, I'd ask for an assist in a hurry, yes . . . He probably knows that it might get crowded out here before long . . . He saw those Aussie jets too. . . ."

She lowered the binoculars, placed them on the roof of the dog house next to him. The wind ruffled her hair and cascaded it over her face. The pink hue of the sun, breaking through the thinning cloud cover, brought up the pale tones of her cheeks to a blush that contrasted her sleep-clouded eyes.

"You think that trawler captain will let you get close to him?" she asked, meditative doubt riding the question.

"That part worries me some," he admitted. "But I don't think we should sit back here waiting for one of his own to come charging in and close the door completely. We didn't come all this way, through a force eight, to ride away with a yawn . . . Is that what you want to do?" He put the question to her mildly.

"So when you cozy up to him," she said, ignoring the bait, "he might jolly well put a cannonball through us."

"That is a thought," he quipped, and she glanced at him. She did not respond, leaning her arms on the coaming instead and staring intently toward the direction of the trawler.

"Ryan, set the weather vane and come below!" Sebastian called out. Ryan had brought *Pequod* around so that the Russian was now a few points off her port bow. "Jamison, you look as if you could use some nourishment," he said to the journalist. Jamison blanched, but he nodded with a weak grin and followed them below.

They gathered around the radio and radar in the chart room. "I think we need to talk it over," Sebastian said. He reached over and turned on the radio power switch, hoping there would be a lift from the Russian jamming.

"Sir?" Ryan interjected, pointing his right finger at the radar screen near the top. "I think we have a ship coming up behind us. . . ."

Sebastian glanced at the bright blip on the lower circle of the screen. "Maybe a freighter?" he asked.

"A little fast for a freighter, sir," Ryan replied.

"Russian, maybe?" Sebastian suggested. "Could be the trawler's assist . . . Or maybe one of ours? I figure she's about ten miles or more back. Right, Ryan?"

"About that, sir. . . ."

Sebastian tuned to the two-meg ship-to-ship frequency on the radio. The jamming was not there. Instead, there was the heavy beat of Morse coming over, skipping along like the fever pitch of war drums.

"That's very close," Ryan said.

"You think it's the trawler sending?" Sebastian asked.

"I can pick up letters, sir, but no sense to them," Ryan replied.

Sebastian turned to Barbara on his left, a foot away, sipping at her coffee. "OK, lady, you studied Russian . . . Do your thing."

She hesitated. "That was a while ago," she defended.

"Better than nothing," Sebastian urged.

Reluctantly she stepped around to the console and took the crumpled piece of scratch paper he handed to her, along with the stub of a pencil. She listened to the Morse, frowned, shaking her head at the rapidity of the message. Then she wrote:

> . . . PERMISSION SURFACE FOR . . . TRANSFER. GORKY.

Sebastian was reading it over her shoulder as she wrote. "*Gorky*?" he asked, scratching the itchy stubble of his beard. "Has to be a sub . . . Russian . . . That's his assist . . . They want to get Julian off the trawler. . . ."

She lifted her hand for silence as she began copying again.

> . . . SEAS PREVENT TRANSFER NOW . . . THIRTY MINUTES . . . WILL INFORM. CONTACT AGAIN 0510. MINSK.

"Ah-huh," Sebastian said. The Morse stopped and the whistling, zooming interference of the jam cut into the frequency. "He's pretty sure of himself, going over a two-meg local to send that kind of message."

"A sub?" Ryan asked in awe.

"They're going to transfer your father off, Ryan," Sebastian said. "Seas too high to make it right now. . . ."

"What do you have in mind, sir?" Ryan asked, frowning at this new complication. "If they get my father off the trawler and over to that sub, he's gone forever. . . ."

Sebastian leaned his hands on the console, head down, not knowing how to meet this one. "All we can do is get in the way," he said then. "Try to complicate it some for that trawler captain . . . If that ship behind us is one of ours, maybe we can give her time to catch up. . . ."

"It'll take more than waving our hanky at him, sir," Jamison said. Sebastian turned his head and looked at the journalist. It was the first time he had contributed anything since Sebastian had dragged him back on board two days ago.

Sebastian nodded to him. "Right on, Jamison." Sebastian glanced at the radar screen again, watching the blip. Then he said, "Ryan, in Sydney your father brought aboard five canvas bags that contain explosive charges. I saw them when I did a quick inventory some time back. What did he intend to use them for?"

"When we ran into a school of whales, sir, he would toss them over to scare them off . . . Whales can damage a boat hull if they get to running. . . ."

"Are they timed devices?"

"Yes, sir . . . from five to sixty seconds . . . Just compressed gunpowder on a fuse, sir . . . Doesn't do much damage, but makes a lot of noise . . . My father never wanted to hurt the whales, just scare them."

None of them responded, each of them computing the possibilities and the impossibilities of the proposed action forming in Sebastian's mind. He glanced at Barbara, who had put her back to the wall next to the radio console as if withdrawing from any of the implications. Her eyes carried skepticism, but she was allowing him now to let it out for them.

Sebastian turned and leaned his back to the console, folded his arms, and looked at them. They were all weary, eyes red and swollen from lack of sleep, their bodies battered and suffering from the storm they had fought. They had followed him through wind and water beyond their imagination. They had been turned to mush by the elements and the battle to keep *Pequod* alive. Their minds could not compute readily what this new possibility would demand. Sebastian was not sure himself.

"I say we go for it, sir," Jamison spoke up then.

Sebastian looked at him. The journalist still appeared as gaunt and peaked as ever, but there was a light in his clouded blue eyes now. "I'm tired of being sick, sir, and thinkin' about it all the time . . . Tired of puke and lyin' like a pollywog in my bunk all the time. I need to get my mind off it, sir . . . A bit of action is my cup of tea now, sir . . . I see no sense dyin' all the way out here and not havin' a go at that Russian. . . ."

"And I say we can't let my father be dragged over to that sub, sir," Ryan chimed in, the curtain of fatigue over his face dissolving under his intensity. "He's my father . . . Maybe I have a bigger stake than anyone here in going for him, or trying to anyway . . . Otherwise we came all this way for nothing."

Sebastian nodded, then looked at Barbara for a response. She put down her cup on the console and jammed her hands into the pockets of her windbreaker. "You know I want David Julian back, as much as any of you," she said positively. She looked as if she might want to caution them about the odds. But then she said to him, "You're the captain."

"OK then," Sebastian said, rubbing his right hand over his mouth, still pondering how to do it. "Ryan, you and Jamison take three of those charges up to the bow. The weak spot for that trawler is her engine propellers . . . One of them is dead in the water already, looks like. That captain is going to get nervous if we start dropping charges around his fantail. So it will harass him . . . Maybe make him start thinking more about us than Julian or the sub."

"That may be asking too much," Barbara reminded him tartly. "I mean, won't he get nervous enough to go to gun action?"

"If he's got one," Sebastian replied. "But we play it as it comes, I guess . . . All I want to do now is make him delay. Ryan, the barometer is coming up fast, the seas are going down. We'll keep sail up until we get on to the trawler . . . Then we drop the ghoster, stick with the jib, and try to add power with the engine . . . Don't know, though, with the sea still high, the engine might not work . . . exhaust won't come out of the water, she could stall . . . What do you say, Ryan?"

"Might be tough working the engine, yes, sir," he said. "But the jib can do a lot . . . if you're figuring to slow down enough to stick with the trawler and fast enough to maneuver . . . Well, sir, the jib could do it."

"All right then . . . Barb, you stand by the radio here . . . Stay on the two-meg channel . . . That Russian may lift the jamming long enough to get a contact with whoever is behind us. We need to know . . . friend or foe . . . I'll take the helm. Any questions?"

None of them responded. They looked pitifully tired, close to the jagged edge, but they were game. "One thing more," he said to them. "I happen to believe God gave us the miracle that got us through the storm . . . and I believe He's still with us . . . Let's go with that."

Jamison and Ryan nodded, then turned and went astern to get the charges. Barbara turned to the radio, reaching for the earphones. He wanted to say something more to her. He needed her now, some word that said she was with him all the way on this one. About God going with them. They had had agreement about their faith being an integral part of their survival in the tight spots they'd been in before. But even that seemed to be hidden behind the strange distance she kept from him. It made him feel all the lonelier.

She put the earphones on and began tuning the radio. He turned and went on up the companionway to the helm. The plaguing doubt of what he was about to do hung on him. Even as he felt when he committed them all to chase the trawler in the first place. They had come through the storm. But going up against the trawler with a Russian sub sitting out there looking on was considerably different. Surely not to God! But was he pushing God and them too far? Should he wait for the appearance of the ship behind them, hoping it would be one of theirs, capable of creating the action with some authority here?

He feared for them now . . . For her mostly, perhaps. Of losing her by this clumsy kind of action that begged, as she warned, some hot action by the Russian trawler captain or the sub or both. The stakes were too high for that Russian and the sub to allow him to get too close or to get in the way of the transfer.

"Keep your hand on us, Lord," he said as he took the helm off the weather vane and glanced ahead to where the trawler churned on slowly, getting larger now as they gained on her.

Gorky

Captain First Rank Bolovarich was beginning to feel testy. He was holding *Gorky* at five hundred feet waiting for clearance from

Minsk to surface. It was already 5 in the morning. The sun was up. He stood in the control room facing the periscope shaft, tapping his fingers on it impatiently as the submarine made its slow circles a mile off the trawler.

"Control, sonar!" He heard Atoff's voice on the speaker over his head. "I have a surface bearing at 175, comrade captain!"

"I will come," the captain said and moved forward to the sonar shack. He glanced at the computer behind Atoff's right elbow. Nothing. "What is it, Atoff?"

"Heavy screws, noisy . . . I can't determine it . . . He is moving at thirteen knots, comrade captain. . . ."

"Range?"

"Eight miles. . . ."

Bolovarich picked up one of the spare phones, put it to his right ear. He listened, then put the earphone down. "That is no freighter," he said mildly in a meditative voice. "Keep me informed, Atoff."

"Aye, comrade captain."

He went back to his station at the control room. It was quiet, with only the low humming of the machinery and the reactor noises aft, and now and then a subdued voice from an officer asking for a helm correction. It was getting tense. And where was the American submarine? Somewhere back of them . . . He hoped it was too far back to make a difference here now. There was no time to hang around. He had to surface.

"Comrade Komoleski," he said to his second officer, "up to periscope depth. We need to check the weather. And prepare to surface."

"Aye, comrade captain."

It was too big to lose now. Too big a fish on the surface. His assignment was to get that scientist off that trawler with no witnesses. He had hoped to do it before dawn. Now he was going up to the sun, the worst thing for that.

"Control, sonar!" Atoff's voice again. "I have another target . . . Sounds of heavy screws from the south-southeast, bearing three-four-five."

"How many screws, Atoff?"

"I cannot tell, comrade captain . . . They come on fast. . . ."

Bolovarich did not like that. He had been warned of the possibility of five American ships reaching him from around the Horn.

"And I have the sound of screws, deep water, behind us at 190 bearing . . . Fifteen miles . . . Closing rapidly. . . ."

"The American sub, Atoff?"

"It is him, comrade captain . . . The computer verifies a Poseidon class. . . ."

Bolovarich grunted. Poseidon? Slower than the Tridents. How well was he armed?

"Comrade Komoleski, up to periscope depth."

"Aye, comrade captain."

He heard the hiss through the boat as the ballast tanks were emptied. The *Gorky* rose. In two minutes Komoleski said, "Periscope depth, comrade captain."

The periscope rose up the well in front of the captain. He took the handles, snapped them in place, peered through the scope. The water was high, but he finally got clear. He mulled the predictable against the nonpredictable now. He had two targets astern of him and another force coming at him from the south-southeast. He would have to close near enough to the trawler to make the transfer of Julian possible. And he had to move now before the American sub closed on him.

He made a 360-degree sweep of the horizon first. He caught the trawler in the scope off to port. He swung aft. He saw the two masts come into view. He focused the scope to get a better look. A sailboat? One sail up. What was it doing moving up toward the trawler's stern? What was it doing here anyway? Here was the unpredictable. One more element to keep in his mind, to ponder. That boat would have to be cleared out of the way . . . But of what significance was it? Still, a witness was a witness. Gun action would take care of it.

He focused the periscope aft looking for the surface target. "Sonar! What is the disposition of the surface target at one-seven-five, range and speed?"

"Range four miles . . . Now showing at bearing one-nine-five . . . Speed still at thirteen knots."

Good. Bolovarich could not see it on the periscope yet. She would not get into the action here soon enough to prevent the transfer.

"Sonar, what about the American at one-nine-zero?"

"Seven miles and closing . . . Speed at twenty-eight."

Yes, he would have to pay attention to the American. The force coming from the south-southeast would not be in it for a while.

"Surface!" he barked the order. Immediately hands flew to the consoles. The Klaxon bellowed the warning. The sub vibrated as the tanks were fully blown. "Set the battle watch! Watch B to the bridge! Prepare to take on passenger! Stand by for deck gun action!"

Eighteen

USS Bunker Hill

Lieutenant Commander James Holland stood by Joe Kelley's chair in the sonar shack of the *Bunker Hill*. He had reduced the speed of the sub to twenty knots so that Joe could get proper target bearings on the sonar. The computer began spitting out the signature immediately, identifying the screw sounds of the Delta-class Russian boomer sub. The range was closing to three miles now.

"Reduce speed to ten knots," Holland said into the box over his head.

"Ten knots, aye!" the voice came back from the control room.

"I have another surface target I'm pinging on, sir," Joe said then.

"Which one?"

"The one bearing at 265, sir . . . She's making about thirteen knots. Sounds like a clunker, sir."

"What do you mean?" Holland picked up the extra set of phones and listened, holding it to his right ear.

"We have no software to get a signature on those screws, sir . . . They sound as if they belong to an oldie, sir . . . Maybe World War Two?"

Holland listened and caught the thumping sound of the screws. He nodded. Joe was right. That could be the Australian frigate he had been alerted to earlier by ComSubPac.

"Will he get in the way, sir?" asked Lieutenant Martin Bell, his executive officer.

Holland looked at him. They were both aware of the priority message that had come in four hours ago: *Sink the trawler with Julian on board*. It was signed by the Commander-in-Chief. It had stunned both men, though neither of them showed it. Holland had had a sick knot in his stomach ever since. Still, it was an order. It was not up to him to weigh the rights or wrongs of it. His was to successfully complete the action.

"Where's that frigate heading?" Holland asked.

"Still on our course, sir," Kelley answered. "Heading into the pit with the rest of us, seems like . . . Hold it, sir . . . The Russian is blowing tanks . . . He's surfacing, sir!"

Holland reached up and pressed the button on the transmitter on the shelf over Kelley's head. "Control, get me up to periscope depth!"

In twenty seconds the ballast tanks were blown and *Bunker Hill* began to rise. "We still have heavy seas up there, skipper," Bell reminded him.

"I know, Marty . . . but I have to get a look . . . If Julian is on his way over to that sub, we've got a different action on our hands, which nobody has authorized from ComSubPac . . . So we better see what we've got. . . ."

He returned to the control room and the periscope station. The scope slid up the tunnel. He grabbed the handles, focused. He was up and under the water. Then he had the view he wanted.

He caught the Russian sub to starboard just beginning to settle on the surface, her decks awash with the rolling seas. She was half a mile off the trawler's starboard beam. He turned the scope left and saw the trawler. He studied it for a couple of minutes. There was no sign of any preparations for a boat to be lowered as yet. The seas were still a bit high for that, he figured. He rotated the scope to port and caught the "oldie" target of Kelley's. She was an old frigate, maybe a minesweeper of World War Two vintage.

"I got that 'oldie' up there, Marty," he said to his executive officer. "Kind of beat up from the storm . . . Listing a bit to starboard." Holland wondered now what the intention of the vessel was. He finetuned the lens on the scope and caught the ship's name on the bow. *Victor*. "Yeah, that's him . . . what ComSubPac radioed us about . . . Australian Rescue . . . I hope he won't foul it up for us, Marty. He's heading straight into that trawler's territory!"

Holland swung the scope around to the trawler again. Then he saw the two-masted sailboat.

"All engines slow!" he ordered. The beat of the engines eased off. "Five degrees right rudder!"

"Five degrees right rudder, sir!"

"Steady on! That's *Pequod*! Right under the trawler's nose! What's he doing in that slot? He's got the trawler tight on his port beam and the Russian boomer looking down his throat to starboard!"

"Any sign of transfer action on the trawler, sir?" Marty asked.

"Not yet . . . Give me a firing solution, Marty. We've got to get a proper angle. Wait! Looks like the trawler may be beginning to swing to port. All engines dead slow!"

"Engines dead slow, sir!"

"We'll have a better angle on him if he keeps making his turn, Marty," Holland said. "We'll go for a bow shot. No sign of transfer activity yet, but the trawler captain must want to unload off his port side instead of starboard."

"The Russian sub, sir?" Marty asked again.

Holland swung back to focus. "He's making a turn outward, probably to meet up with the trawler as she completes her port swing. Or else he's coming around to get some gun action on that Aussie frigate closing in . . . Set your stopwatch, Marty, to two minutes and give me a firing solution on bearing three-two-zero, five hundred yards on that trawler!"

"Aye, sir, firing position now in the computer, sir."

"Down scope!"

The periscope slid down the well. Holland felt the sweat soaking the back of his shirt. He had been sweating ever since he got the order to go for the trawler. It was not a simple firing position in terms of both the target and the possible retaliation of the Russian sub. He knew that when he sank the trawler, or laid the first Mark 48 torpedo into her hull, all hell could break loose. How far and extensively that would reverberate across the world, he couldn't tell. But people were going to die out here, that much he knew. Not only one innocent scientist named Julian, but a lot of others. And then when would the dying stop?

"What's the range on our ships coming from the south?" he asked Marty.

"Last contact . . . eight miles . . . speed thirty knots."

"If that Russian sub makes his move, they won't be here in time . . . Firing time?"

"One minute and ten seconds, sir."

Holland thought of his wife back home probably just waking up. She was as vulnerable as the whole world now to a nuclear war. Maybe only seconds away?

"Up periscope! Stand by torpedo tubes one and two!"

Sebastian opened the throttle on *Pequod's* diesel and angled the bow toward the stern of the trawler twenty yards dead ahead. They had taken down the genoa sail, left the jib up. He told Ryan to dump the first charges as close as possible to the trawler's propellers. One of them, he could see, was not turning in the water. The other seemed to be thrashing sluggishly, and an engine was being overworked to compensate.

"Let her go!" he yelled to Ryan and Jamison up at the bow. Ryan threw his square canvas bag toward the trawler's stern. Then Jamison followed. The explosions shot a geyser of water high enough to splash over the trawler's fantail. Immediately Sebastian saw men jamming the starboard wing of the bridge, looking back at them.

Jamison began doing a jig, lifting his hands in the air as if he had scored the winning goal in the Australian soccer championship. The one propeller kept turning in spite of the explosions, however. But Sebastian figured they had at least diverted the trawler captain's attention.

Then as he steered *Pequod* out and away to line up more directly to the starboard side of the ship, she began to make a turn to port. "She's running, sir!" Jamison yelled back to him from the bow. Sebastian moved his helm to port, and the engine sputtered and quit. They had been moving miraculously on the engine as it was, with the seas still up. But that left him with only the jib and no time now to rig new sail. He glanced to his starboard beam and saw the Russian sub on the surface, making a wide turn to come around. She looked awesome!

Barbara stuck her head out of the companionway, waving at him. "It's an Australian frigate!" she yelled at him. "Named *Victor*!" She pointed behind him. He turned to look. The ship was still a silhouette in the sun, too far back yet to catch how big she was. But he felt a surge of hope . . . She could still make some kind of difference! Maybe!

He turned to line up more on the trawler's starboard side, following her around. He heard Ryan shout back to him, but he couldn't make out the words. Suddenly he heard a loud slap and a whining sound overhead. He felt a thump in *Pequod's* hull to starboard; then a geyser of water shot up twenty feet.

The trawler was firing on them!

"Ryan, get on back!" he shouted. He waved his hands to the two men on the bow, signaling them aft. At the same time he swung the helm sharply to starboard to throw off the range to that stern gun crew on the trawler. The trawler kept making her turn to port, leaving him behind. Sebastian decided to swing completely around and pick up the trawler as she completed her turn. He glanced back toward the Russian sub which was coming around slowly, bow on. Then he ran forward and dropped the jib.

Then they all went below to the chart room. "Jamison, put those two remaining charges back in the stern," he said. "We have an Australian frigate coming up on us . . . Get ready for some action. Ryan, take the radio and see if you can pick him up again. Barb, you come with me forward to the galley and help me check on any damage from that shell."

Barb followed him, helped him lift the floor hatch leading into the bilge. "Water coming in," he said. "Hole is not too big . . . Have to run the bilge pump off the engine. . . ."

But then he heard the sound, that same whining, rattling sound as before. Another shell was coming in. He put his arms around her and held her close. This one sounded as if it were coming straight in.

Minsk

When Aviloff heard the stern gun bark behind him, he ran aft through the passageway of the bridge and out on the porch. He looked down to see the gun crew loading the three-inch again. Mikelich and Romonovich stood over the crew, giving orders.

"Mikelich!" Aviloff screamed the warning. "I gave you no order to open fire on that boat!"

"This is not your command now, comrade captain!" Mikelich yelled back. "I have my orders to sink that boat! If you intend for Julian and your man Popov to make that boat, comrade captain, it is too late!"

So the wise old fox knew then! So be it. Aviloff turned and ran back to the bridge. "Hard to port, helmsman! Quickly!" He hoped to get the bow swung farther over to throw off the range for the gun crew. It was too late. The gun let out a bellow. Aviloff watched *The Pequod*. The shell cracked into the mainsail on deck at its base. He watched in shock as the ninety-foot mast was ripped off its base plates and went slamming through the dog house, the top of it cutting through the stern deck and cockpit. Debris flew up in a shower.

"Stop engines!" He had to signal Julian and Popov to make their jump for it now, if they had not been discovered as yet. The trawler stopped. Aviloff glanced at *Pequod* again. "She is finished," he groaned. "They are all finished!"

Victor

On the bridge, Lieutenant Robert Sperry surveyed the line of players in front of him, less than a mile away now. He saw the trawler open fire on *Pequod* with its stern gun. The shell hit below the waterline of the boat. The sailboat had no business getting in the middle. Whoever commanded her was brave but foolish.

At the same time, he saw the trawler swing to port to make a circle back around, angling toward *Pequod*. Was she going to ram the boat? He could see no sign of a boat being loaded to get Julian off. But he saw the Russian sub coming around toward the trawler.

"Sir, I'm picking up a target to starboard, bearing zero-six-zero, sixty fathoms," the sonarman called from the communications shack aft of the bridge.

"That's the other sub, sir," Dick Cornfield advised.

"We have identification on him yet?"

"Not yet, sir."

"OK . . . Not our problem now . . . Not yet anyway." Sperry moved forward on the bridge to check the situation ahead through his binoculars. He saw the trawler gun crew let go with another round. It caught *The Pequod* at the mainmast, toppling it. It was time to make his move.

"Russian gun crew on deck, sir!" Cornfield warned.

Sperry went to the phone and punched a button. He heard the sound of the laboring turbines, then Butch Call's voice.

"Sir?"

"Butch, it's time to do what we agreed to do!" Sperry yelled into the phone over the raucous sounds of the turbines in the background. "Open her up, Butch!"

"Aye, sir! Permission to order my crew topside, sir! I don't want them here when the boilers go, sir!"

"Permission granted! You get out of there too, Butch!"

"I'll sit with her, sir, until I'm sure she's goin'!"

"Don't wait too long, Butch!"

Sperry hung up the phone. Immediately he felt the jump of *Victor* with the new shot of steam into her turbines.

"Gun crews standing by, Dick?"

"Fore and aft . . . We have only six rounds apiece, sir."

"When the Russian opens up on us, and only then, we make every shot count! Helmsman, bring her to starboard five degrees and run straight down that slot between the trawler and that ketch!"

"Aye, sir!"

Sperry moved to the starboard wing of the bridge then and watched as the range to the trawler and the fatally wounded *Pequod* closed rapidly.

Minsk

David Julian and Popov stood in the port supply locker. The trawler's engines had stopped. They could hear sounds of the searching crew on the other side of the compartment. It would be only a few minutes before they broke in.

"It's time now, Popov!" the Australian said. He reached up and pulled the release lever. The hatch blew out and fell into the sea eight feet down. Julian looked out. The swells were only about six to eight feet. Then he saw *Pequod*, about sixty yards out, and he groaned. He saw the mainmast down, buried in the dog house. He saw no movement on her decks. Were they all caught below? He had heard the sound of the trawler's gun, figured the *Pequod* was the target. The captain did not order that. But he knew someone aboard had gone for *Pequod*, figuring he and Popov might be trying for it. Or maybe just to get it out of the way.

"Dr. Julian?" Popov said then in English. His face was pale, eyes fearful. Julian pulled the life raft toward the hatch. "We will be shot if we jump into the water! They are waiting for us on the bridge—"

"Who?"

"Romonovich, the political officer . . . Also the man called Clay Bird! KGB!" Julian glanced at him, realizing now who had authorized the gun action.

"They are ready to break in here any minute, Popov!" Julian warned. "You can stay here and get shot or try to make a swim for it!" Julian pulled the air release on the raft. It began to inflate immediately. He pushed it toward the hatch opening, then looked out. Popov was right. They'd be under fire as soon as they hit the water.

Then he saw it. The ship was coming toward them, full out, kicking up a powerful bow wave. He blinked at it, not sure. Then he saw the Australian colors flying from the bridge mast. Out of its stack poured a huge cloud of black, thick smoke, laying an impenetrable curtain over the water, fifty yards either side.

"There's your answer, Popov!" Julian yelled with jubilance, pulling Popov by his collar until his head was hanging out the hatch. "Take a look!" The *Victor* rolled on by, not thirty feet away, smoke pouring over them. "Hallelujah, you Aussies!" Julian shouted, lifting his fist in the air. "Jump, Popov . . . Jump, man, jump!" Julian gave Popov a shove out the door and followed him into the sea.

USS Bunker Hill

"Never saw a barnyard like this before," Holland said, staring into the periscope. "But the trawler's forward bow hatch is gone! I think old Julian may be going over! But it sure isn't by the book! Oops! There goes *Victor*!"

"Firing solution set, sir," Martin Bell said. "Thirty seconds to target, angle on the bow two-six-zero. Fire control standing by!"

"This crazy Aussie is chasing down the slot between the trawler and that sinking sailboat!" Holland went on, his voice rising with excitement. "He's coughing out a ton of smoke . . . Can't see a thing! Belay the firing order! Stand by to surface! Gun crew on deck!"

The siren sounded for surface and battle stations. "Range to our ships south, Kelley!" Holland called into the speaker overhead.

"Close in now, sir . . . About two miles!"

Holland wondered if Julian would make it out of that trawler's hatch. The question was whether he was being rushed off by the Russian crew or doing it on his own. He couldn't tell. The sky was blacked out by *Victor*. The sub surfaced with a sigh. The hatch was cracked, and Holland clambered up the ladder to the sail deck. The hatch forward on the deck opened and the five-inch gun rose on its platform. The gun crew was on it and cranked up within a minute.

Holland stood on the conning tower straining to see through the thick cloud of smoke that blotted out everything ahead. "That was the most beautiful and craziest 'oldie' I've seen!" Martin Bell said from his side.

"A lot of crazies out here today," Holland replied. "The question is, did Julian get off? Stop engines!"

They sat quietly in the low swells, waiting for the smoke to lift. Holland felt vulnerable now. Uncertain. "Where is that Russian sub, radar?"

"Bearing one-one-zero, sir! Range fifteen hundred yards. She's going under, sir!"

"What? Why'd she do that? I saw no transfer!"

"She lost sight of the trawler maybe, sir," Martin Bell offered. "Maybe the transfer was aborted, sir."

"Thank God if it was . . . What about *Pequod*? Let's start engines slow and move toward where we saw her last. She is probably in trouble. . . ."

"Aye, sir."

Sebastian felt the mast more than saw it as it slammed through the roof of the galley and the chart room with a terrible crunching sound.

He felt himself being thrown back against the bulkhead of the galley, the mast jamming him hard against it, knocking the wind out of him. He blacked out. When he opened his eyes, he saw the mast across his chest. He looked beyond it to Barbara opposite him, trying to get her arms up over the mast to hang on or to hoist herself up. He felt the water around his knees, and it seemed to be rising.

The mast had pulled the upper deck around them, jamming them tight and wedging them into an unmovable position. "You all right?" he asked. She looked at him from across the ten-inch width of the mast. She coughed once. A bloody smear showed over her right eye, trickling blood down her cheek.

"I—I think so," she said and coughed again, straining to get her arms up over the mast. She slipped back. He reached over and took her hands in his and held on. Sebastian looked up and saw the heavy smoke over them. It was slowly dissolving, and the morning sun broke through it, warm and balmy.

"Great day for a sail," he quipped.

"I think I feel water coming up around me," she said. "Do you?"

"Probably from the hole in the hull where that first shell from the trawler hit," he said. He didn't want to pursue what it meant. "Can you move at all?" he asked.

"No," she said, and she put her forehead on the mast, her hands still held tightly in his.

"Can you move downward at all?"

"No . . . I'm just stuck tight. . . ."

"OK," he said, keeping his voice calm. "First time I got to hold your hand the whole trip. . . ."

"Oh . . . Sebastian," she said, her voice trembling some, her head down again. "Don't give me any graveside farewells—"

"Farewells? Graveside? What are you talking about?"

Pequod lurched, her bow dropping. Sebastian felt the water come up higher to his waist. Barbara let out a shaky sigh. The blood from the cut on her forehead seemed to run more, and her eye was filling with it.

"Ryan?" he called out then.

"Back here, sir," Ryan yelled from the chart room. His voice sounded muffled.

"Can you move?"

"No, sir . . . I'm pinned to the companionway steps!"

"Jamison?"

"He's in the stern . . . He got caught by the top of the mast . . . Can't move either. . ."

"Well, hang on! Help has to come soon! That Australian frigate is out there somewhere!"

"Can't keep my head out of the water, sir!" Ryan called back. "And it's rising . . . I'm half lying down in here as it is!"

"Just hold on, Ryan! Tell Jamison the same!"

"Yes, sir." Ryan's voice sounded more muffled then.

"Well, I guess I mucked it up proper for us all," Sebastian said then, taking a tighter grip on her hands. "So much for Backstrom, Alnutt, and Winston. . . ."

She chuckled, and he glanced over the mast at her. She lifted her head to peer at him, her right eye slightly closed against the blood. "Who *are* those guys?" She tried jocularity on him. He laughed with her, and then he saw tears coming down her cheeks.

"Remember Hong Kong?" he asked. "Kai Tak Airport?"

She didn't answer right away.

"I mean . . . when I kissed you good-bye," he added, feeling the water rising on him. "I should have asked you then. . . ."

"What?"

"To marry me. . . ."

She put her forehead back on the mast again. Her hands were slippery in his. He felt she was sliding away from him.

"I would have turned you down," she said.

He paused and looked up again at the smoke clearing above his head. "Tell me one thing then," he went on. "You know I love you . . . I went to Sydney to ask you to marry me . . . You know that . . . Just tell me now . . . Did you ever love me?"

Her head did not move from where she rested it on the mast. Then she slowly lifted her head and looked at him.

"I always loved you," she answered, and the tears streamed down her face, mixing with the blood. "And I thought you were glorious as captain of *Pequod* . . . And you didn't muck it up for us . . . not for me . . . I tried to change toward you . . . I had to . . . I—I was afraid. I couldn't stand your dying somewhere with my love so strong for you . . . You have to understand I had to try to distance myself . . . Selfish of me . . . but I didn't want to mourn you the rest of my life . . . Or you me. . . ."

He pulled her hands up closer and kissed the ends of her fingers. She cried softly, tried to move up toward him but couldn't.

"Mr. Sebastian?" It was Jamison's voice, sounding even more muffled coming from the stern of the boat.

"Yes, Jamison?"

"Sir, we can't get out from under this mast unless we can get the top part of it out of the way . . . I'm pinned under it . . . If I could get this end pried loose, I think she'd bounce back up through the hole above me. The mast is pinned under the debris below me . . . Bent like a bow, sir."

"What do you want to do, Jamison?" Sebastian hollered back, not sure what the journalist was trying to say.

There was a pause. "Sir . . . once back in Sydney . . . I asked you why . . . why a clergyman got into this tacky, bloody hell of a world anyway . . . Remember, sir?"

"Right, Jamison."

"You said . . . our Lord came into this world two thousand years ago . . . He didn't fit in either . . . But you said you thought you were in good company for all He accomplished."

"I did, Jamison," Sebastian yelled back.

"Well, sir . . . I just want to know if I can join that company!"

Barbara lifted her head slowly and looked at him. Her eyes showed some wonder then, almost unsure of what Jamison was asking. "Just ask God to let you in, Jamison!" Sebastian called back. "Just put all the past right before Him . . . and let Him take it Himself . . . That's why He came into this bloody hell of a world!"

There was a pause. *Pequod* creaked and grumbled deep in her vitals. "Thank ya, sir!" Jamison finally said. Another pause. Then, "I have to tell ya, sir . . . I got one of Julian's explosive packages sittin' within arm's reach under the mast . . . Sittin' on a tool box . . . I . . . I just armed her, sir. . . ."

"Jamison—"

"I figure I owe ya all one, sir!" Jamison interrupted. "For makin' your lives miserable . . . and for your savin' my life!"

"You don't have to do that, Jamison! Help will be coming—"

"No time, sir! We'll all be goin' under any time now!"

Barbara kept her eyes on him, waiting. Her right hand slipped from his, and he reached out frantically and grabbed it again. The water was coming higher.

"How much time on it, Jamison?" he yelled.

"Ten seconds and counting, sir. . . ."

"Turn it off, Jamison!" Ryan's voice came in, sounding even more muffled. "This boat won't sink yet—"

"You're a good lad, Ryan," Jamison replied. "Ya do your father proud—"

The explosion sounded like a paper bag popping in the stern. There followed a creaking, grinding sound as the mast slowly rose, the top part of it in the stern sprung loose by the explosive charge. Sebastian felt the mast shift some in front of him. He pushed at it, trying to get more leverage to squeeze his body upward. With his right hand he felt a shelf of some kind behind him, and he used it to push himself up. At the same time he saw Barbara's head disappear under the water.

With a bellow of protest, he pushed the mast another notch from him and shoved himself downward in the water. He saw her flailing her arms, trying to get back up. He reached out and put his left arm around her waist, using the other to stroke himself upward, kicking his feet as he did so. He broke through and reached out to grab the mast with his right hand, trying to find a grip. She coughed and gagged as her head came up beside his. He pushed her left hand up to the mast.

"Hang on!" he said to her. but she looked like she might slip away from him again.

"Take the line!" he heard someone shout from above him. He looked up and saw Julian staring down at him from under his blue admiral's cap. Sebastian reached out and took the heavy rope, tied it around her waist. Then Julian and the other man, whom Sebastian did not recognize, began to pull while Sebastian pushed. Once she was on deck, he climbed up on the mast and hoisted himself up, Julian's hands reaching out to help him.

"Ryan," he said, gasping for breath. "In the chart room. Jamison's in the stern . . . I—I don't know if he's alive. . . ."

In a daze, he found himself on the splintered afterdeck of *Pequod*, sitting next to Barbara who clutched the gray blanket close around her. She leaned against him, and he put his arm around her shoulders. She was trembling some in shock. He looked up once and saw a massive gray wall hanging over them. After a while he realized it was the hull of a submarine no more than twenty yards away. It seemed to stretch endlessly upward to the sky, lost finally in the black smoke still hanging over them. He saw hoses snaking over to *Pequod* and realized in his tired brain that they were pumping water out of her.

Someone passed in front of him, and he asked, "What about Ryan?"

"He's all right, Mr. Sebastian." Sebastian glanced up to see Julian standing over him.

"Jamison?"

"Got beat up some . . . I don't know how bad yet. A doctor is coming over from that American sub."

He let it go at that. He pulled Barbara closer to him. Someone wrapped another blanket around them both. It felt good. But the touch of her hair against his face was even better.

Gorky

Time was running out, Bolovarich knew. The five American ships were already in the area, their long sonar fingers poking around, searching for the *Gorky*. As he peered through the periscope, he could not see much. The smoke from that frigate still hung in the air. He could not tell if Julian had come off the trawler or not.

"Can you raise the trawler yet, comrade?" he asked of Komoleski for the third time in five minutes.

"No, comrade captain." The captain pondered it. Why wasn't the trawler on radio standby?

"All right, let me have the firing solution," he said.

Komoleski hesitated only a fraction of a second to indicate his hesitancy to obey. But when the captain glanced at him, he immediately made the calculations.

"Range twelve hundred yards . . . Bearing zero-five-zero . . . Angle on the bow, twenty degrees . . . Ready to fire in twenty seconds and counting. . . ." The fire control computer had run out the figures, working the sonar readings that brought the trawler into a proper target angle. No longer was it necessary to see the target to hit it. The genius of the new technology, the captain mused.

"Do I have a clear track to target?" he asked, thinking of the American submarine and that silly sailboat out there somewhere hanging around the trawler. Or even that Australian frigate.

"All clear, comrade captain," Komoleski replied.

The captain continued to stare through the periscope in the direction of the trawler, hoping the smoke would lift so he could make sure. He had lost the big one then. It irritated him. By a mixture of unpredictable events, he had been robbed. A small sailboat and that Australian frigate had humbled him. He hated to lose. But if he did, he always hoped it would be to larger forces.

"Any radio contact with *Minsk*?" he asked again. There was none.

He had his orders: Get Julian off that trawler or see to it that he didn't get off at all. They could not afford to allow him to fall into the hands of the Americans. He would have liked to be sure that Julian was still on that trawler. But there wasn't time. The American ships were closing in on him. He caught sight of the American submarine then, sitting off to his starboard, half in, half out of the smoke. It would be easy enough to sink her as well right then. But his orders did not allow for that.

He held *Gorky* steady, engines slow, as he awaited the countdown to zero. He debated how many torpedoes to fire. Two fish would make sure she sank quickly, no survivors. Or could he count on the political officer aboard the trawler to finish Julian? He chose the one fish, allowing them to get off the ship. He had never sunk one of his own before. He tried to rationalize his decision on that. Even then the trawler would not stay up longer than ten minutes or so.

"Ten seconds to fire, comrade captain."

"Fire only one," he ordered.

"Aye, comrade captain."

Was he going soft? Maybe.

"Torpedo away, comrade captain."

At the same time he saw the twin green lights show up on his periscope to confirm it. Bolovarich could not see what the torpedo would do. He could only listen for the sound of explosion. It came fifteen seconds after the fire command. The dull, echoing sound indicated he had hit his target.

"Strike, comrade captain!" Komoleski said. "We have the sound of screws approaching!"

It was time to go down deep. He could come back later to take a look to make sure. He felt no victory in this thing. But he had done what he had been told to do. That was what he lived by all of his life.

Nineteen

Captain Aviloff was on the bridge when he saw the torpedo coming. Its white foam track was easily seen in the shallow shooting angle the submarine captain had chosen. It tracked back along a bearing where the *Gorky* had last been reported.

A stabbing sense of rage and sadness pierced deep within his heart as the torpedo struck the bow of the trawler. There was no honor in shooting your own kind. He had never been able to absorb the enormity of that which had become standard protocol in the Admiralty's Book in Leningrad if the issue called for it.

But that emotion passed as the trawler began to settle slowly forward, the water pouring in through her broken plates. He had been in some form of collusion that had brought it about anyway. When the Australian frigate had barreled by them pouring out smoke, he had gone aft and clipped the radio antenna on the roof of the bridge just aft of the signal platform. He wanted to make sure the submarine captain could not make contact and be told that Julian and Popov were off the *Minsk* and on *Pequod*. It would have been certain death for that boat, her crew, and the two men he had gotten off the trawler.

But he felt no remorse in that action, even as he felt no judgment for his own submarine captain. He had made a decision that constituted an act of treason to the Soviet navy in engineering the escape of Julian. And treason to *Rodina* as well. He was no less guilty, then, of a crime than the submarine captain. In fact, the submariner had only obeyed orders. As for himself, he had deliberately violated them.

But in the doing of it, he had preserved a life caught in innocent circumstances. And provided hope and a new beginning for one of his own officers who was dying from the constriction of depression born out of the hopelessness of endless nights in Soviet Russia.

Did the charity balance the treason? He did not know.

He turned back inside the bridge and hit the red alarm button on the bulkhead. The siren went off, screaming through the decks and ordering the abandoning of *Minsk*. He noticed the bow of the trawler beginning to take on a sharper angle downward. There would not be much time. He ordered the cargo nets over the side to make it easier for the crew to get off. The life rafts and small boats were already being lowered into the sea.

"Comrade Ilyich, what of the crew in the lower decks?" he asked of his third officer, who remained at the engine telegraph next to the helmsman.

"Last report, comrade captain, a minute ago said they were all out," Ilyich replied. "Except the forward compartment, second deck . . . just aft of the supply locker on the port side, comrade captain. . . ."

Aviloff knew that Mikelich and Romonovich had gone there when members of the crew reported the hatch cover blown out. The torpedo had struck very close to that area.

"Keep trying to raise them," Aviloff said.

He saw a couple of American destroyers moving up fifty yards to starboard to take on survivors. Two others had begun to make a sonar sweep of the area, looking for *Gorky*. A third ship slid slowly by on his starboard side, close enough for Aviloff to look across the twenty yards that separated them to see the captain on the bridge wing facing him. It was the Australian frigate. Smoke boiled up from her stern, indicating she had boiler damage or her turbine bearings were gone. She still had enough to keep her moving, though she was not far from being finished.

The Russian walked out on the starboard wing and looked at the captain across from him. He looked young. Aviloff lifted his hand in salute, got one back. That captain deserved a medal for what he had done today. Aviloff watched as the frigate moved slowly on out and away, disappearing in its own smoke.

He turned back into the wheelhouse and walked to the other side of the bridge. He studied *Pequod* still sitting fifty yards off the port beam. He saw Julian wearing that familiar blue cap, standing on the battered stern of the boat, hands on his hips, watching him as if he were waiting for Aviloff to get off the sinking trawler. Up forward, standing apart from the others, was Popov, hands straight at his sides, the intensity in him obvious as he stared back at Aviloff. Behind him on the stern were three others . . . a blonde woman, a smaller built man, and a tall one, standing head and shoulders over the others. Would that be "the hound of heaven"?

"All hands cleared, comrade captain!" Ilyich called to him. Aviloff walked slowly back inside the wheelhouse, hands behind his back.

"What of the forward compartment, Ilyich?"

"The torpedo hit under it, comrade captain. I do not know if any of them got out."

"Very well . . . Time for you to go now, Comrade Ilyich." The bow of the trawler lurched downward, and the sea began to lap over her forward decks.

"Comrade captain?" Ilyich protested gently.

"Go now, comrade. That is an order. And thank you."

Ilyich bowed his head, saluted, and walked out of the bridge and down the steps to the boat deck.

Aviloff walked slowly back across the bridge and out in front of the wheelhouse. He turned as he heard a noise to his left. He saw Mikelich stagger up the steps from below. Blood stained the front of his blue shirt. He had a gun in his right hand, hanging down along his leg.

Aviloff waited. The KGB officer was mortally wounded. But his gray eyes fastened on him with deliberate intent. "You . . . you betrayed *Rodina*!" he accused, his mouth showing blood as he talked.

"Get on with it, Mikelich," Aviloff snapped. "If you are to shoot me, please do not dishonor me by wasting time with rhetoric!"

Mikelich leaned heavily against the bridge rail, trying to get his gun up. Aviloff waited calmly. The gun rose shakily in his trembling right hand. Then the man folded, his head going to his chest, his legs buckling. He crumpled into a heap.

Aviloff did not wait to check on him. He turned instead and walked quickly back through the bridge to his quarters. He found the diary in his desk and wrote the few words in the front.

TORPEDOED AT 0910 HOURS BY RUSSIAN SUB GORKY.

Then he wrote in the date and signed his name. The Americans would not have to take the blame for it now. He wrapped the diary in a plastic bag, then tied rubber bands tightly around it. He walked back to the bridge wing facing *Pequod* and lifted the package over his head. Julian waved his arms to let him know he saw it. Then Aviloff threw it as far out from the trawler as he could. It landed maybe thirty feet off. Maybe it would be sucked under. But at least he had tried.

He turned again and walked back into the wheelhouse. He saw the water coming over the bow now. The slant of the deck steepened. He picked up the detonator on the box with the red button on it. That would blow all of the classified communication and electronic gear to bits down in the lower deck. His last positive act for *Rodina*. He thought of Soya then . . . her warm breath on his cheek as she read to him from the Book every evening and morning.

He wished he could tell her about "the hound of heaven." Someday. When they both found that place the Book referred to as the "City of God." He felt peace then. And life larger than he had ever known.

Sebastian turned as he heard the splash over the port side. He heard Ryan shout. When he got up to look, he saw the Russian, Popov, swimming away from *Pequod* toward the trawler. Sebastian made a move toward the rail to go after him.

"Let him go, Mr. Sebastian!" Julian called out. "That's his right!"

Sebastian watched as the Russian paused close to the trawler, picked up the package the captain had thrown, and heaved it back another twenty feet or so. Then he proceeded. Sebastian made a move to go over for it, but Ryan had already slipped over the side of *Pequod* and swam out to it.

"Be careful!" Julian called. "You'll get sucked under with that trawler! She's ready to go!"

Ryan got to the package, turned, and swam back quickly, climbing over the side, handing the package to his father.

Then they watched Popov as he reached the cargo net on the side of the trawler. He climbed up onto the deck and ran to the bridge. Aviloff met him at the top. The captain seemed to be urging Popov to go back, but Popov did not move.

Finally the captain embraced his first officer and they went inside the wheelhouse. A moment later there was a flat, thumping sound that echoed across the water.

"He's blown his charges!" Julian called out. Now the trawler began its dive to the deep, bow down, stern rising. The captain and Popov came out and stood at the bridge rail, shoulder to shoulder facing *Pequod*. Aviloff had one arm around his first officer. He raised the other in salute. Julian lifted his cap and held it high as the trawler went down.

"He really saluted you, Mr. Sebastian," Julian said as the sea quieted. "He wanted to meet you."

Sebastian felt a strange sensation then, as though he had met the captain somewhere else, impossible as it seemed. He climbed up on the shattered dog house roof as if somehow he could yet see the man. But it was over.

Suddenly from the six or seven ships surrounding the scene came the long, mournful one-note sound from all of the bosuns' whistles. The last tribute to those who die at sea.

Only bubbles and a small wave boiled up from the sunken trawler. Then all was calm. A gentle breeze rippled the sea. The sun was warm and kissed the water with a benediction of kindness.

Julian would not board the American submarine to go home to Sydney. He went chin to chin with Lieutenant Commander Holland and another line officer from the cruiser *Simpson* as they stood on the broken stern of *Pequod* and had it out.

"I don't intend to return to Sydney in any vessel except *Pequod*!" Julian snorted.

"Sir, this boat is in a shambles," Holland argued. "You cannot make it back to Sydney sailing her!"

"May I remind you kindly, sir," the officer from *Simpson* added, "that you are still being hunted by the Russians. There are ships reported coming our way now, Russian ships. You will need protection—"

"Commander, my wife and I built this boat," Julian retaliated. "You have enough carpenter mates and machinist mates on board your ships to fix us up in a jiffy! Otherwise, I will sail her as she is! Let the Russians have me! You have no jurisdiction on how I sail home, gentlemen! And I would warn you not to alienate me further . . . Is that understood? If I need escort, I'll take that wounded Australian frigate over there!"

Then Holland laughed, and the very straight-laced protocol officer from *Simpson* looked at him with some irritation. "Excuse me, commander," Holland said, "but I think we are losing it here. Dr. Julian has earned his trip home his way!"

"I have!" Julian barked.

So it was.

Willard Banes found the president in his Oval Office. It was near 5:00 P.M. In three hours the president would go on the TV networks. He had been waiting for news of what had transpired in the Southern Ocean.

When Willard walked in, the president was sitting in his desk chair facing the window. Only one lamp was turned on in the far corner, keeping the room in shadow.

Willard stood politely in front of the desk, hesitant to break the president's meditation.

"What is it, Willard?" the president asked. Willard knew that his chief could tell his footsteps from a thousand others. "You want to sit down then, old friend, or are you going to stand forever?"

"Thank you, Mr. President," Willard said and sat down in the straight-back chair in front of the desk.

"Want to tell me about it then, Willard?"

"The situation is contained, Mr. President," Willard said with a sigh of relief. "I have it here in my report from Bill Connors. I gave a copy to Barney. He's with your speech-writers now preparing for tonight. No shoot-out. All of our people are safe. Julian as well. *Victor* is being towed in by one of our destroyers . . . Lost her engines after she did some kind of dipsy-do down there. But if they hit a big storm on the way back, they'll have to scuttle her. The captain of the trawler and his first officer were lost. Went down with the trawler after being sunk by their own submarine. They had the same thing in mind for Julian as we did I guess . . . Only they did it to their own people. . . ."

"Not much choice," the president said laconically.

"Something else, Mr. President," Willard went on. "The Russian ambassador delivered a message to me from Kamiloff for your response. I imagine the action down there got to him in a hurry. Anyway, he wants a Summit as soon as possible. To talk about peaceful uses of satellites in outer space. It's a ploy, of course, to give him more time to get OPAL up to speed . . . But it gives us time too for UNIVERSE ONE."

"He must have gotten stung out there in the Southern Ocean," the president commented with a wry note in his voice.

"They went for it but lost," Willard replied. "It was too close to call for a while."

There was a pause. The president still did not turn around in his chair. "What about that laser interference on our nuclear capability then?"

"Bill Connors said an hour ago that the signals are not consistent enough to knock out both us and NATO's missiles at the same time . . . But I think Kamiloff is ready to quit playing games considering his request for a Summit. . . ."

The president waited. "And that Russian squadron of ships steaming down toward the action? What of them?"

"Turned around . . . I don't think Kamiloff wants any more confrontations right now. . . ."

"Good for him." A long ten seconds of silence. Willard cleared his throat delicately, waiting. "And what about our clergyman, Sebastian, and his lady, Churchill?"

Willard hesitated, not sure what relevancy that had. "In what way?"

"Well, did they figure into it at all?"

Willard paused, feeling a loss for words. "Well, Mr. President, I guess all I can say is that they were there . . . They are okay, of course. . . ."

The president then slowly turned his chair around and faced his Secretary of State. His face in the dim light looked haggard, torn by the murderous pressures on him in the last days and hours. Purple pouches showed under both eyes. His skin was that same sickly pale, almost gray pallor.

"They were there, Willard?" he said, pushing his glasses up on his forehead, rubbing at his eyes with the heels of both hands, his voice carrying a note of incredulity. "All history, Willard, as you know, and the changes that have come about, the battles won, the medical and scientific discoveries . . . all are due to someone being there at the right time, the right place . . . But we never appreciate that until a hundred years later. . . ."

Willard felt uncomfortable. "I guess that's it, Mr. President."

The president sniffed, then lowered his glasses slowly over his eyes again, adjusting them carefully.

"You ever been to church, Willard?" he asked then. He got up slowly and walked deliberately over to the rack, reached for his topcoat, and put it on slowly.

"Beg your pardon, Mr. President?"

"Shocked your liver, hey, Willard?" The president chuckled.

"Come on, old friend, I'm going to introduce you to Someone who was there . . . back in history . . . a long time ago . . . in a little place called Bethlehem . . . Nobody knew then what was going on either . . . But mankind has never been the same since . . . Come on, you need to get another history lesson. . . ."

Willard stood up obediently, a bit confused. The president walked over and put his arm through Willard's and walked him out the door. "You know, Willard," the president continued as they walked down the long, carpeted hall, "I need to tell you the Christmas story one more time. . . ."

Epilogue

On January 19, 1987, in the little navy chapel high up on Watson's Bay above Sydney Harbour, they stood together and exchanged their vows. They faced the simple altar and stained-glass window that filled the full wall behind it three hundred feet above the sea. The chapel was small and austere but exuding the sweet breath of God.

The chaplain was young, but he spoke with authority and in tones of reverence, maybe the same awe that all presiding priests experience in the mystery of the unions over which they preside. But for some reason he seemed to be even more aware of his calling on this day as he touched the hands of the two people in front of him.

She wore light blue, his favorite. He wore camel tan, her favorite. The chapel could hold fifty, but there were only a dozen in the pews today.

But it did not matter to them. They were alone, oblivious of anyone else.

They made their promises facing each other, holding each other's hands. They had left behind all the twisted miles of pain and dying, so much of what they had endured and sought to heal or change in their journeys.

When they had finished exchanging their vows, he took her in his arms and kissed her. She said into his ear, "Now I do love you forever."

And so the record of Code Name Sebastian was put into the archives of the CIA in Langley, Virginia. Code Name Spartacus went into the "change of status" file in Tel Aviv and the "inactive list" at Interpol Headquarters in Paris.

The male choir sang "Amazing Grace" while Dr. David Julian hugged his son, Ryan, and his daughter, Elisa, tears streaming down his cheeks. He remembered his dead wife as he never had before . . . and a Russian captain named Aviloff who had found his "True North."

JUN 1 2 2023

Harry Jamison, his left arm in a sling, wrote copy on the lined yellow pad on his lap, the beginning of the greatest story the *Morning Herald* would ever print in his name. A story that would put Dr. David Julian back into the waiting arms of a hero-starved Australian population and vault the names of Sebastian and Churchill to the lips of storytellers worldwide who yearned for a new ending to Melville's *Moby Dick*.

And for this moment, the lion lay down with the lamb, the seas spawned gentle tides on a weary world, the leviathan played with the porpoise.

For this moment, frozen in time, the rage of man was forgotten. And true peace was seen and known and indulged one more time.

"And God saw everything that He had made, and, behold, it was very good."

And He was there.

JUN 12 2023